SACRIFICIO

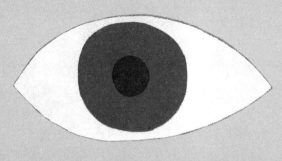

SACRIFICIO

ERNESTO MESTRE-REED

SOHO

Published by
Soho Press, Inc.
227 W 17th Street
New York, NY 10011

Library of Congress Cataloging-in-Publication Data
Mestre-Reed, Ernesto, author.
Sacrificio / Ernesto Mestre-Reed.

ISBN 978-1-64129-485-0
eISBN 978-1-64129-365-5

Subjects: LCGFT: Novels.
Classification: LCC PS3563.E8135 S23 2022
DDC 813'.54—dc23/eng/20211216
LC record available at https://lccn.loc.gov/2021061292
Illustrations by Dana Li
Interior design by Janine Agro

Printed in the United States of America

10 9 8 7 6 5 4 3 2 1

para mi madre, Marita Mestre
for Lorayne
to Andrew, Bella & Mateo

SACRIFICIO

PART ONE

I

We met in a rubbish dump, unlike any other, and yet they are all alike, rubbish dumps. I don't know what she was doing there. I was limply poking about in the garbage saying probably, for at that age I must still have been capable of general ideas. This is life. She had no time to lose, I had nothing to lose, I would have made love with a goat, to know what love was.

Samuel Beckett
Molloy

PARADE OF MONDAYS

In the early weeks of that long summer of 1997, before the bombs started going off in the capital, Cecilia came with me one last time on the Monday road trip to the village of Cojímar to help me mourn her oldest son.

As we strolled on the beach, she took my hand, and some time must have passed before I noticed, for I continued to look out to the sea and at first did not see our bodies merge in front of us as she leaned into me. It's a sign, she told me, pointing with her other hand to our single bulging shadow. The contorted passing of a one-winged bird, she said. A sign, también, that I did not notice these things, she added.

Shadows.

A useless solitary wing.

Every Monday morning, we drove the two dozen miles from the house on Calle Obispo in Old Havana to this barren fishing village that el pendejo Hemingway had made famous with his little fishing novel, and we sat, or strolled, or looked out to the sea—the place where her son, Nicolás, had picked me up a year and a half before. We ate the lunch that Cecilia had prepared perched on a sea wall outside La Terraza, a restaurant from where dishfaced Yuma—the tourists—stared out at the crystalline sea with etherized gazes.

I thought us as hapless and doomed as the poor old man of that novel. Other times, I wasn't that dramático. As Cecilia liked to point out: I was bored, dreaming about things that didn't exist in the Island. They never have. Did I know, she asked, that when the yanquis had made the film of the novel with *Meester* Spencer Tracy they had to go all the way down to the coast of South America because Cuban marlin rarely jump out of the water? And yanquis need that. Things jumping out. Why? I asked, playing along, not remembering if the marlin in the book jumped out. Why don't Cuban marlin jump out? Too passive, just like the rest of us, como cualquier cubano.

I snapped my hand free and waded into the sea, the water chattering on the crushed-shells shore so that I couldn't hear her sighs. She came there with me from the capital to appease me. Because I insisted, she reminded me. So many more productive things she could do with her Mondays. Vegetables and fruit to buy for the paladar. The earlier in the week the fresher the black-market produce, brought into the city on Sunday nights from nearby illicit farms, full crates of okra and plátanos and boniatos hidden under dusty blankets and peddled from darkened parlors—though the State had eased the restrictions on private enterprise, no one really was sure how much. Not even the inspectors from the Ministry of Agriculture knew, so they made up the rules as they went along. There were the crazy skeletal chickens to feed and their meager miniscule soft-shelled eggs to gather—flyers to get out to the hotels. Poor Juan couldn't do it all, Cecilia said. It's enough that he rents us a car for the day. Though it was, I knew, not rented at all, but one of the many máquinas privadas that comandante Juan owned and rented himself to taxistas in the capital to shuttle tourists around. Cecilia sacrificed her Mondays to come with me, to morbidly memorialize her dead older son, as she put it, and once here, coño, I ignored her.

I let her follow a few silent paces behind me as I trekked from one end of the rocky beach to the other, back and forth, back and forth, patrolling the shore as if not to let the endless parade of Mondays escape from us, mount a rickety balsa, and leave us forever. Soon, I feared, our weeks would be a day shorter—all the Mondays would have made their way out of the Island.

Nicolás had told me that he would leave the Island from this beach. On the day we met he told me, that he was scoping the territory, that he had stolen a formidable dinghy—those were his words, un botecito formidable—from the marina in the city where he worked as a pier scrubber and was in the process of refashioning the motor from a Russian Lada, its fan blades bent and bowed into double propellers. When I finally saw the thing, hidden in the shadows of his mother's henhouse, it was no more than a leaky rowboat.

Noah building the ark, hidden in the shitdusty shadows of his mother's henhouse as tourists ate their dinners a few paces away, and the starved chickens pecked at the dirt in his toenails. He was already dying the day I met him. Soon, las viejas of el Comité would notify the thugs from the Ministry of Health, who would grab him and take him in for a test and later deliver his mother a mimeographed letter on the seriousness of her son's condition and the precautions that she and the rest of her family should take, including sterilizing any silver or plates that he might use and boiling bedsheets after his supervised visits, or better yet, reserving these things for his use only. But on the day we first met, he still thought that he had time.

So I came to this puta beach with his mother on Mondays to commemorate him, to pilfer time back, as if it were being peddled from darkened rooms with okra and plátanos.

Cecilia darted into the waters in front of me, knocked my hands from my hips, caressed my face with a calloused palm, and kissed me on the cheek. Mi mulatico tan lindo, she said and walked back to the spot on the beach where I had dropped my shirt, picked it up, and continued following me. I sat on the shore and she joined me, watching a pair of amateur fishermen on an inner-tube raft returning for the day, at first sight, their balsa not so different from the ones used by the many that had left this beach never to be seen again. They wore nothing but frayed straw hats and thread-bare swim trunks that fell from their bony hips. They were young, no older than me, but they moved with the resigna-tion of the elderly, their sleek eel-like brown bodies bent at the middle with obeisance. They had caught nothing. They tossed their empty nets on the shore and sat by them, as if mourning some giant sea monster that had beached itself. The water rose slowly around them and caressed their long still legs and their bottoms, and then it ebbed just as slowly, as if it wanted to linger there.

I kept my eyes on the boys. How does the coast guard know who is leaving and who is just fishing? I asked.

They don't, Cecilia answered. They guess.

Maybe I'll become a fisherman.

You'll die of hunger, she said and added that if I stayed with her, I would never die of hunger. That she could promise. She picked up a handful of sand and smashed it on my belly.

I threw the sand back at her. Gran cosa. I'll die an old man serving tourists boliche and arroz con pollo.

She stood up. It's a good life, Rafa. She turned her back to the sea. Good enough.

I kept my eyes on the fishermen, intently enough for her to take it as an affront. After a while, she put the shirt back on my shoulder, careful not to brush my bare skin.

I'll be in the car when you're ready.

Later that night, I knew she would watch me sleep, as she had clandestinely watched us in the henhouse when I was with her son. She waited one or two hours till after I had gone to bed, after I had helped her and her Haitian-Dominican cook, Inocente St. Louis, with the prep work for the following day, snipping the dark skinny innards from shrimps, chopping vegetables, baking bread, then she sat in the shadows of the kitchen sipping spicy rum, hoping comandante Juan wouldn't come by, hoping she could just be by herself for a bit till I fell asleep.

Mondays were the only time she did this, she would admit to me much later that summer, when the bombs forced us to remain alone in the house. Every other night there was too much to do for such boberías, the last diner would often not leave the brick-paved patio until the early hours of the morning. She had heard once from comandante Juan that the best restaurants in Paris often close down on Monday nights, so she had decided to do the same. On those nights, she watched me, watched me as she could not watch me during the day, as she could not watch me after the bustling nights feeding the hungry Yuma, watched me on the tiny bed that had belonged to her younger son, my long body rolled up into it, like a serpent into a basket. When I stirred, stretching so that my legs lengthened off the bed, the toes open like fingers, she moved back, not wanting to get caught, till my body softened again and curled itself back into the tiny bed. I was like some boneless creature in my sleep, she confessed that summer.

On Monday nights, she didn't sleep. Sometimes on Tuesdays, while she and comandante Juan were readying for the lunch service, I said to her that she had wandered into my dreams. Comandante Juan teased me, told me boys shouldn't dream about real women, leave that to los hombres, and he reached for her with his fat fingers like a clumsy boy reaching for a plaza pigeon.

SIDATORIOCA

On the first Friday of each month, I went to the sidatorio, the new "AIDS sanitarium," to visit Cecilia's younger son, Renato.

Ese niño is your adoptive brother now, tu hermanito, Cecilia had told me on the morning we buried Nicolás in the mahogany coffin fashioned from the boards of the writer's empty bookcases, as if she could not bring herself to verbalize the corollary to this, that she was then my adoptive mother.

By that time, I had been working in the capital for a year and a half, and it was the only day that I ever requested off from waiting tables at Cecilia's paladar. Comandante Juan took over on those Friday nights, serving the Yuma in his tattered comandante's uniform, rusty gun in the leather holster that stank like week-old refuse, so that some of the weekend Yuma thought it was some kind of performance but that the more seasoned travelers saw as no more strange than the pediatrician that had bartended for them the night before or the literature professor that had been their cabdriver or the busty-chested chemical engineer that had offered her sexual services in the open-air market at the Plaza de Armas for twenty yanqui dollars.

I always returned with the tight curls in my hair newly colored, mostly in shades of red, because Bertila said it brought
out the fever in my tangerine eyes, and comandante Juan
made sure to ask me the following day as we prepared for
service, why it was, coño, that I worked so hard to endanger
our well-being, all of us, he emphasized, patting himself, the
martyr, on the green-stained cheap medals of his uniform.

Him, I told nothing of my Friday visits.

How is the putamamá? Renato asked, coming out of the
front gate of the sidatorio the first Friday of that summer.

She was fine. Why did he have to call her that?

Does she even ask about me?

No, I lied, because it was the answer he wanted, because
any other answer I had found would lead him to latch onto
the subject all day and night like a crab on a tightlipped
mollusk. Not once this past month, I said. Though Cecilia
never stopped asking. But I knew what Renato meant with
his question—oye, if she asks so much, why can't she just
come visit? Once. Maybe just once. After his brother died,
Renato had also tested positive for the virus and by government decree had to live at the sidatorio, what they called a
sanitarium for those that would develop AIDS, set up all over
the Island expressly for the purposes of keeping the virus contained. An experimental program that was the only one of its
kind in the world, and according to government reports, a
phenomenal success.

I didn't know why Cecilia did not visit. Only later would
I learn how much power comandante Juan exerted over
Cecilia, how costly the services and contacts he provided,
conveniences that kept her paladar thriving. How comandante Juan made it his mission to protect her from her own
children. O una barbaridad semejante.

By the time Renato had first tested positive, everyone knew

that life inside the sidatorios rose to a much higher standard than most other places in the capital, except a lo mejor for the residences of the Party insiders—though this contained only a smattering of the truth, as I would learn from Renato. Sure, they served three hearty meals a day, and there was a roof over your head, but you also had to consider lack of choice, the inability to control one's destiny, the eternal nature of the branding as a citizen of the sidatorio, a *sidatorioca*. Even if things had been changing lately with the furloughs. On Fridays, Renato could walk toward the front gates of the sanitarium near Cerro on the purlieus of the old city, straight down the gravelly path that led past the squat Soviet-built dwellings, and out the arches of the stone wall. This had been established as a new privilege because the government had taken a hit on its international image because of the strict quarantine of HIV positive patients. Before this, any visits had been confined to the sanitarium.

Getting your hair done, niñas? the guard taunted when he saw us leaving that Friday for our appointment with Bertila. He stood in the doorway of his little dark wooden shack— like a gray jutía rat peeking out of its limestone cave, his flinty eyes darting from under the shadows of the thick bougain-villea that covered the rotted roof of his hideout. The place had once been a school, a juvenile detention center before that, and there were small cinderblock houses at every exit, manned now not so much to keep people in but to keep non-patients out.

I shot my finger at the guard. Up yours, viejo. He became giddy, thrilled. He scratched his scruffy beard and giggled as he reached for a rifle that leaned against the shack. He mea-sured our passing through its crosshairs. Gunshots popped in his mouth as he pretended to dropdead us. We broke into a brief sprint until we were out of his rifle's sight, past the gate, beyond his taunts about our hair, about the peach-shaped smoothness of our asses, the meringue stiffness of our lips.

Renato stopped ahead of me and pulled off his shirt and turned to face me, his arms outspread like the monument in Baracoa of the Indian chief Hatuey at the stake. A large new tattoo covered most his belly up to the tip of the breastbone. It was a dark upside-down creature with wings extended and a body and neck twisted into a 6—its long beaked head buried in the shadows of its bosom, as if wanting to consume itself, and high above at the end of the tail, brushing up against Renato's prominent sternum, a pair of glowing sleepless eyes, like jewels. The creature, part heron, part reptile, hovered on Renato's pale skin, plunging below his belly button. A sloppy job, the ink embedded under the skin in jittery dashes—which made it seem fluttery and alive from a distance.

¿Qué cosa es eso? I asked, half-concerned that the thing was going to peel off from his belly.

It's us, coño, he said sotto voce, holding his arms up, staring at me as intently as the two red jewels stared.

Every new tattoo on his body was a version of his affliction or his apostasy, what we got together to celebrate on Fridays, the chain around his ankles, the winking eye in the webby strip between the base of his thumb and index finger, the skeletal hand rising up his shoulder blade as if to catch him by surprise, the yanqui flag torn at his thighs. You had to be liberal about interpretation. It was all us, our one day. I was still not sure who "us" was. I hardly knew him. Although a year later I could not ever think about him without thinking about us.

The creature on his torso was the largest and most out-landish yet. I reached out to touch it, but the thing flinched. Renato's skin bristled.

Don't be getting incestuous on me. Acuérdate, we're related

now. He came closer, taking hold of my shoulders from behind and blow-whispering on my nape. If you want, I can get you some when we get back. There are hundreds of sex-starved maricas inside, hopping from one encounter to the other like mad bunnies. Plenty. But not your brother, not your little brother, por favor. He walked ahead a bit, calmer now, with a purposeful hurried stride. I fell behind and he turned and waited for me to catch up, kissed me softly on the cheek, and disappeared sprinting around a corner.

Our appointment with Bertila wasn't until late in the afternoon, so we had plenty of time to do nothing, though we would soon have to abandon our spot, make sure we were moving around while doing nothing to avoid getting rounded up under the new laws against vagrancy, which the revolutionary police, la fiana, as we called them, *the snitches,* had the power to enforce at their own discretion. And like any law, new or old, they summoned them only when they saw fit.

Some in the park always seemed to be doing nothing, and la fiana didn't bother them. If your skin burned with the fire of the fields and your hands grew horny with callouses from the glory of labor, your shoes encrusted with the mud of production, the handkerchief wrapped around the brim of your hat the colors of the flag, then la fiana passed by close, their steps in unison, letting you know they were there, just in case, por si acasito your conversation wandered, your will weakened, but mostly they left you alone. But if you were young, pale-assed like Renato, or dark-skinned but unweathered like me, and there were piercings in your ears and your nose and your eyebrows and your lips and el maldito Dios knows where else, if your hair covered your ears and was bleached blond, or dyed a puta red, if your skin was tattooed like a savage, and your mind dizzy with the incomprehensible lyrics of corruption, then you were some roquero, some imperialized mutant version of a yanqui and prohibited from remaining still, from staying in one place; that was vagrancy, a great crime against production and therefore against la Revolución. Then the State asserted its right through the roving pairs of fiana—which marauded the parks and the streets like hungry stray tomcats—and you were sent off to cut sugarcane somewhere, to learn to behave like an efficient revolucionario. In this, Renato and I were fortunate during our Fridays. Anytime they had tried to grab us before, he pulled out his crumpled pass from the sanitarium. La fiana immediately knew what it was by its sickly yellow color, and they dared not touch it. Renato held it out to them at arm's length, his wrist overly limp, pinched between his index finger and thumb, a poisoned lace handkerchief.

When it happened on that first Friday of the summer, he actually warbled to the guards, We're from the sidatorio, señoritos.

That was it, then. Game over. Forfeit. We had been caught doing nothing, but the law didn't apply, not to us, not anymore.

They then asked for our papers, the carnet all of us were required to carry everywhere. But they would not even touch them, forced us to hold them in front of their faces while they scrutinized them. Maricones, they spit under their breaths as they backed away from us. Renato held his dainty pose until they could not stand to look at him anymore. That was his strength.

I reached out and rested my hands on Renato's bony hips and he jumped away from me in one motion: ¡Ay ay, por favor, hermanito! Estás de madre. Doesn't my mother get you laid? Besides, you're supposed to be in mourning. You're the raunchiest widow I've ever met. He put his hand over his mouth. Oh, I'm sorry, that wasn't very nice. He got down on one knee, made a sign of the cross, and murmured that he too mourned for Nicolás, the greatest brother a boy could hope for. He then dashed away like a spirit to a nearby wildflower field and waved for me to follow him.

Near the Christ-like statue of Lenin, he unlaced his scruffy black boots and threw them up in the air, pulled off his stained T-shirt and stepped out of his cutoff knee-length jeans, so that all his lower tattoos, the wisteria vines creeping up his calves, the spotted tarantula wedged between the veins of his left foot, the bloody arrow lodged in his right Achilles, and even the torn, fluttering yanqui flag high up on the inside of each of his thighs and the neat Gothic calligraphy on his toes—on one foot *S I D A,* on the other, *S A V E S* (in English)—all but one, were visible, as he did his daily regimen of pushups in the noonday sun. I sat down in the field and watched him.

The new combo of experimental medication had taken effect. The year before, a new department at Girón Medical College had been opened for the study of traditional and natural medicine. On the new pills, Renato had gained weight, though it was spread in odd pouches throughout his body, his face, his lower belly, his ass. His limbs were still emaciated and veiny, though on his torso, thin bands of muscle were now visible where there had only been the bare cage of the ribs. He had grown ill so quickly after he seroconverted that it seemed to me at first as if his body had been breaking down and preparing for the visiting virus beforehand, setting the stage for the quickest deterioration. But now the opportunistic illnesses were mostly in remission.

I clapped and egged him on, but he did not even glance my way. After each set, he sat on his knees and measured his breath and then continued. When he was done, he sauntered toward me, the creature on his belly swaying with exertion. His briefs were threadbare, torn at the band, barely a cover. He pushed his crotch in front of my face. I looked up. Renato's hair, parted in the middle, hung over his face, the shadows veiling his crooked smile. He was his mother's child. Although I had then seen only a few fuzzy photographs of his father, who seemed to have bequeathed all of his genes to his older son—the achingly elongated figure, the emphatic features, the penetrating dark eyes, the repressed fury that gave their pale skin a grayish cast—Renato had inherited almost no physical features from his father, except for the luxurious long curls that belonged to all of them. He had his mother's round expressive face, mellow translucent seaweed eyes, a sumptuous lower lip made for whistling or for kissing—the whole countenance a thing made for cheer, so that later when he grew morose and gaunt it was as if he were wearing a mask that he had mistaken for some other occasion.

Bueno, mi Rafa, this is it, he said. If it has come to this, if they are going to let you suck my pinga in the plain light of day, then it's no fun playing this game anymore. We can play this do-nothing game till kingdom come, till the yanquis litter our dirty little capital with bombs!

He turned half away and paused, then muttered, You came to wrong place with my brother. To that house. Whatever you were looking for. It's not there. Never was, huevón.

At least I met you, I countered in a weak voice.

Gran cosa, he said and lumbered away, putting pieces of clothing on one by one while still moving. A feat in his condition, I thought. There are a thousand of me, he continued, but none of them will save you, either.

You're wrong, I said without even thinking about it. I couldn't have survived on my own. I was on the verge of going back when Nicolás found me. He saved me.

He came toward me so that I could smell his stale medicated

breath. No one saves you in this city, huevón. You save your-self . . . if you can.

We left the park, not saying much for a while, walking along its northwestern edge until Renato came upon a man fretting over a large charcoal grill. There were splayed chickens and other meats spread out on the grill. Renato approached the man and asked him how much. The man glanced up briefly, examined him, and waved him off with his two-pronged carving fork.

¿Cuánto? Renato said, pushing his groin close enough to the grill top that it seemed a danger.

A young couple—clear-eyed, European, all stiff and well dressed in that casual manner that only Yuma can pull off, even when they wear rags and sandals—who had been standing near the grill, chattering in hushed tones, took a step toward us. The man put his arm around the woman's waist. He was tall and sinewy, and the ends of his long dark hair were bright orange, dipped in molten iron. The woman was lean and flat chested, and in her long T-shirt, hair tied high in a bun, and free of makeup, she could have been a comely effeminate boy. I had seen them in the park near us before but thought nothing of it, curious tourists interested in the natives. The tattoo on the man's right arm was half-covered by the sleeve of his T-shirt, the hindquarters of some feline creature that laggardly climbed up his arm. They had been to the beaches already—their skin as brown gold as the hide of the birds on the grill, and her cropped hair bright honey with the sun. They wore the Yuma uniform—long earth-tone shorts and leather sandals. The man had hair on the line of his chin and jaw that was lighter than the hair on his scalp, the rest of his face clean-shaven. His face angular and his features severe, his bony nose ran long and the shelf of the chin jutted upward at the tip.

They stared at Renato, but Renato did not notice them as he had surely not noticed them before. He scrutinized the birds on the grill, set in rows like schoolchildren, their legs spread open and their breasts flattened. Renato turned again to the man at the grill and pulled out of his pocket a wrinkly ball of crumpled green bills. He waved them under the man's face and over the grill as if sprinkling fresh spices on the meats.

I can pay, cabrón.

The man pulled his head back. He looked at the crumpled ball of bills, his eyes bleary from the smoke rising from the grill. Sweat gathered from both sides of his face and trickled measuredly off the end of his nose and chin like a pair of leaky faucets.

Any one you want, entonces, he said, dejected at having to make a sale to a local. He sunk his fork into one of the birds and turned it over. Except this one, this one is theirs—he raised his chin once toward the European couple and a dribble of sweat flew off him, did a somersault, and then hissed on the fire. Renato pointed to one of the other chickens, it was fatter than the bird for the Europeans.

¿Ése? the man said. Bien. He tapped it twice with the flat side of the prongs, then he pierced it just under the breast; a clear fluid flowed from the wound and a little fire sizzled beneath it.

It's almost ready. Son tres.

Renato flattened out three bills, knowing the man meant dollars and not pesos. Now that yanqui dollars had been made legal, it was all anyone took as currency.

Son tres para ustedes, también, the grill man said to the couple, and the woman kissed her man on the cheek. The man smiled and his face rounded out and for a moment lost all its severity. For whatever reason, I thought it was the round face that was his more common demeanor. He kept on glancing at Renato and then at me as he handed the money to the man at the grill, but the man told him that he had no use for European money, so the girl took some yanqui bills from her purse. The man grew upset, but then he did something odd, he asked the girl in three different languages—a combination of Spanish, English, and German—what the problem was with his deutsche marks. The girl waved him off.

The old man over the grill removed both chickens at once, plated them on doubled-up pieces of cardboard. When Renato was taking his chicken, his bare shoulder brushed against the European man. The man muttered something in his language, and Renato turned and looked at him for the first time. He seemed surprised and drawn in by the man's presence. He paused in mid-motion and acknowledged his presence for the first time, and then, just as whimsically, as if he were again a celestial body, did a half turn and orbited away. Renato looked over his shoulder as he walked toward me and said something in English I did not understand. The man smiled again and shook his head. Renato hunched his shoulders.

We ate the chicken seated on a curb across from the park. The couple wandered into the park and sat on a bench under a chestnut tree. The woman did most of the talking as they ate. Renato now kept his eyes on them. He ate most of the chicken as he scrutinized them. I just had a leg and a bite of a breast.

What did he say to you?

I don't know, it was German, but I thought he said he wanted us to come to the hotel with him. Where did he come from? I didn't even see him standing there.

What did you say?

I said fifty dollars.

He could be better with his clothes off.

Not if he's not paying.

Is this what you do with your weekends when I'm not with you?

Renato took a big bite of a chicken leg, his entire face smeared with grease. He spit out a little bone and swallowed, hunched his shoulders again, finished off the leg, and threw the bone on the cardboard platter. He stood up, wiped his face with the back of his hands. Ahora vengo, he said.

He walked across the street and sat next to the Europeans as if he knew them, his haunches grazing the man's. Renato did most of the talking, signaling once across the street toward me. The Europeans smiled cordially, the woman resting her head on the man's shoulder, her opposite arm draped across his belly. Renato stood up and pointed to their empty platter, and they all shook their heads. The man at the grill watched them and he raised his carving fork, toasting them. Renato shook the European's hand. The woman raised her left hand from the man's belly, and Renato took it and held it.

Watching him, as he walked back toward the curb, I thought of how much Renato was growing into his older brother's persona, not in the physical traits, but in the nearly imperceptible currents and movements of the body, the rhythm that the flesh exerted, not just in that gesture—the holding of the woman's hand, which he took with an open palm, pulling her toward him not with his arm, as some lesser seducer might have done, but with the gravity of his presence, with a look maybe, or a little turn of the hips, or an unnoticed raise of the chin.

That was the family's art: seduction.

I should have guessed it right away from how Nicolás, the older brother, had sure-footedly seduced me in a single afternoon, should have known that such talents don't rise from the ashes. Renato bore the ghost of his brother in all his bearing, in the way he walked back toward me now, his shoulders thrown back a little farther than before, his step lighter, a strut, a bouncing on the balls of his feet, the arms swinging from the elbows, the hands loose, his head bent a little lower, but his chin cocked slightly, as if surprised at how easy it all had been.

What? I said.

Nothing, they're just Yuma.

¿No me digas?

He says his name is Oliver. What the hell kind of name is that for a German?

What's her name?

Renato spit out a chicken bone—he couldn't care less. Come on, hermanito. We're going to be late for Bertila.

Bertila's place was on the second floor of a tenement house near the commercial wharves in Old Havana. Her job was her raison d'être. She had screwed an antique barber's chair, a gift from a Swiss lover, into the middle of her tiny living room. Except for a small cabinet for her tools and a floor-to-ceiling mahogany-framed mirror leaning up against the wall facing the barber's chair, there was nothing else in the room. Thin muslin curtains hung over the French doors that led to the balcony facing out to Calle Merced. If you leaned out from one corner of the balcony, you could see the bay and the ships coming into the wharves. There were two other rooms in the narrow apartment, a cluttered bedroom in the middle, with a twin-size bed over which hung a leviathan portrait of the Sacred Heart of Jesus, a wooden rosary draped on its frame, and a kitchen through which the customers entered and passed though the bedroom to the living room.

Nicolás had first introduced me to her a few weeks after we arrived in the capital from Cojímar. He told me that he had found her in La Iglesia de San Francisco de Paula many years before when he was still a boy. Nicolás had wandered in because he had never been inside a church and because

his father had run him out of his house—and because it
was dawn when he had reached the bay, and he knew of no
other place to go for shelter. Bertila knelt in one of the front
pews praying, the only person there. The walls in the church
were peeling and its many statues were blackened with dust
and smoke. Nicolás grew frightened by the haunted house
atmosphere of it all, so he walked up the center aisle and sat
beside her, the only living thing there, the only human form
among all those statues and reliefs that seemed to be free
from suffering. Her hands clasped together and pressed to her
lips—her eyes shut with an insomniac's empty determination.
She was a large woman but so gracefully proportioned, even
down to the flesh that seemed to wrap in diminishing folds
around her wrists and down her thick fingers, that it gave her
the appearance of youth, a toddler who had not yet shaken
off a formidable case of baby fat—a rosary entwined around
her fingers, and she whispered into her clasped hands. Nicolás
watched her silently for a long time, and when she got up off
her knees and sat back in the pew, she seemed startled to see
him there.

Ay, mi niño, what have you done? she said when she saw
him. Guessing what lay at the heart of the young man's troubles, she slid over and passed her hand through his brittle
hair. Nicolás nudged his head away, but she continued passing
her hand through his hair and digging through it till it felt,
Nicolás confessed, as if she were gathering his thoughts and
rearranging them. So he told her his story, how he had mixed
bleach with a dye he had bought from a school friend, just to
make his hair a little lighter, but how it had come to this pale
parrot shit.

Shh! Bertila had said, don't talk like that in here. But she
continued to listen, how once the boy's father had seen what
he had done to his hair, he chased him around the house with

one of his schoolbooks, screaming that he was going to beat him over the head until the lessons sank in, that no boy of his was going to grow up to be an embarrassment to the pioneros, to Fidel, to la Revolución, and how he had run, run as far as he could away from there.

Shh! Bertila had said again, don't you worry, niño. Nothing is unfixable in this world. That morning she took him back to her apartment and sat him on the antique barber's chair till, digging at the roots, she had unearthed the true color of his hair, and with organic dyes and natural conditioners had restored it to its natural hue.

Later, I was sure that Nicolás had invented this whole story. He had probably sought out Bertila, found her through his network of roqueros, who always knew who did the best hair the cheapest. Or that maybe he had found her inside a church, but not because he had been thrown out by the father, but because abandoned churches were the best places for the young to have sex, the only inner spaces in the whole Island always empty. Or maybe Bertila had found him, brought him into her fold because she gathered such malcontents for her own purposes. She had once been a promising chemistry graduate student at the School of Natural Sciences at the Universidad de la Habana. It was there that a boyfriend had lured her away from the proper revolutionary path. When I questioned Bertila once about the truth—Nicolás's story or the ones I had imagined or the snippets of confessions that she herself offered—she had smiled and put her hands to my cheeks and said: Ay sí, ese Nicolás, sí, así fué, that's exactly how I met him, not saying which version was right about the meeting or about her life.

Whenever I talked to her about Nicolás these days, she wrapped both her meaty hands around my face, pressing in as if to force some truth out of my pores. She held her look until I looked back. He didn't abandon you, she asserted. You know that, right? He was always going somewhere else, that boy. She slid her hands up and dug them into my head.

It was in his hair! she said. I knew.

Bertila had built a reputation with the roqueros that made up most of her clientele as a prophet of hair. In its strands she found God's fallen world—the hidden future, the forgotten past, the in-between—by its texture, its rootedness, its length, its thickness, she could push apart the miasma of memory and divine the days to come. She stood behind me and dug both hands into the base of my skull—she was also a skilled phrenologist, some said—her nails burrowing into the scalp, loosening dry soil, and when she pulled them out, the days of your life unknotted through her fingers. She kept her wisdom to herself, unless I asked her to share it.

Renato stood barefoot in the middle of her kitchen. She had made him take his boots off because she couldn't reach the back of his head.

I'm going to die, eh, vieja?

That's too easy, Bertila answered. So are we all.

She had the shape of a lollipop mango, plump in the middle but elongated, with a perfectly round head and a pair of stubby masculine legs that were her cross to bear. She seemed to be always barefoot and always on her tiptoes, so that her calf muscles were as thick as any muscle in Renato's pale body beside her.

¿Qué más entonces? he asked wearily, as if he felt he must. What's different today?

She led him by the hand and lowered his head into the sink. She didn't share today, for some reason. She turned on the faucet and tested its temperature with her elbow, and when it was just right, took a rusty white pail and poured water over Renato's head. She washed his hair with a big yellow bar of laundry soap. Renato took little steps on his tiptoes, his head sinking farther into the sink. I took notice of the spiny ridge of his back, exposed and barren, as if muscles no longer clung to it. Just a few hours ago he had seemed muscular and borderline healthy.

¿Qué mas, vieja? Renato mumbled, desperate from the water running into his mouth. I won't die from it—I can promise you that.

No, you won't die from it. She began washing his hair a second time, scrubbing harder and creating more foam than the first time. As if anyone chooses how they die, she said or some such thought escaped her that I heard—and she poured a pail full of water over his head so there would be no answer.

We walked into the living room. Renato stretched out on the barber's chair. He set it to the lowest position and kicked the footrest up so that it seemed a small narrow bed, a function that would serve useful at the end of that summer. He had opened the muslin curtains and the French doors. His hair hung back off the headrest, drying in the early dusk breeze. He hummed some lullaby to himself, his eyes closed. Bertila tapped him lightly on the shoulder. She moved hesitantly, afraid of disturbing him.

Vamos, we have to make you pretty and brave for another month.

I stood in the doorway, an intruder.

She bent down with fantastic effort and gathered his thick hair in both her hands as if it were a heavy bundle of wet cloth, and she kissed him on the forehead.

LITTLE LIES

Is it true? Oliver said.

There're lots of truths about him. Renato took a long sip of the cubalibre.

What a shitty name for a drink! El pendejo Hemingway again, wasn't it? Renato called it—the cubalibre—la mentirita. Make it a double—since this Island would sink to the bottom of the Caribbean without all the little lies keeping it drunk.

Renato had told me the last time I saw him that he no longer drank, and the previous month, for one whole Friday we went dry, but we were on our third drink now. The conversation proceeded mostly in English, and I could easily follow it. The German eagerly paid for each round of drinks and tipped the bartender generously. He had a wallet full of yanqui twenties now, which he made sure that we saw. Maybe to assure us he could pay for whatever he and the woman wanted. He wore a blue long-sleeve button-down shirt and tight blue jeans with the same sandals he had on that afternoon. Anna, his woman, as he had taken to calling her after a couple of drinks, wore a white summer dress with spaghetti straps that clung to her bony shoulders. She looked less like a boy now. Her silky dark hair loose and falling over her sunburnt shoulders, a dash of mascara and light lipstick to accentuate her tan, prettier than she had looked from far away. Her delicate features, accommodating smile, and seeming ignorance about the purpose of our dinner date lent her an air of insouciant virtue. She had barely touched any of her drinks, the ice melting from neglect—but Oliver kept ordering all of us fresh ones, and she never once objected.

A lot of truths, Renato said. His eyelids drooped, and when he put the glass to his mouth, he kept it there a long time, nibbling on the rim.

But they once tried to poison him, right at this bar, right? Oliver stood from the stool and slammed his hand on the bar. ¡El Líder! He tried to say the word in Spanish, but it sounded as if he had said *Herr Fuhrer,* or maybe the drinks were getting to me, because I laughed like an idiota, and the bartender stopped drying a glass and looked at all of us with the same contempt that he had looked at Renato and me when we had first walked in.

When we left Bertila's, night had fallen. Usually at the end of our Fridays together, we went to the Malecón and sat on the wall, staring out at the port, waiting for the city to light up behind us—or not to light up at all, depending on the apagones.

But that Friday, Renato did not turn toward the Malecón. He had never put his T-shirt back on after leaving Bertila's. On Calle Inquisidor by the piers, he walked in front of a slow-moving Oldsmobile. The headlights lit up the shiny steel buckles of his boots. He raised his arms and the lights scorched the shadows of his bones on his pale torso. The car stopped just as Renato lowered his arms and reached out with an open hand, which he closed around the polished hood ornament. The driver, an unshaven man with a greasy dome and sleepy eyes, stuck his head out the window, one eye opening widely as if peering through a scope. Renato walked around slowly to the driver's side, the very tip of his index finger gliding over the thick rusty hull of the car. He approached the driver, rested his forearms on the window frame, and leaned in, sticking his ass out. A group of young boys surrounded me and began cat-calling at the scene. One of them stepped up behind Renato and drew the perimeter of his ass with both his open hands, howling.

Renato and the driver ignored them. Their faces almost touched as they spoke. After a brief while, Renato opened the back door and hopped in. He waved me in.

Where are we going? I put my hand on Renato's leg. I had already, más o menos, guessed where we were going. He stared out his window.

Vedado then, the driver said, and after we were free of the boys, he turned around and looked at Renato and then at me and then at Renato, and he smiled—his teeth were the color of sunflower seeds.

He dropped us off in a park on Calle L and asked if he could pick us up later, but Renato just hurried out of the car. The man drove away without asking for payment, and I figured that Renato must have worked out something with him concerning some future assignation.

Oliver waited for us on the front steps of the Hotel Habana Libre across Calle L. He sat on the steps, his elbows on his knees, the hair on top of his head gelled and standing on end, each thick strand like a flare. His eyes were tawny yellow, and some of the color bled out from the pupils and cast shadows around them, as if they were bleeding some secret sorrow. Renato introduced me. Oliver smiled, and again he became some other person. His teeth were long and even, and against his tanned skin they seemed the color of pale sand struck by moonlight. He did not stand, but he shook both our hands.

By the time we had finished our third drink, Renato had worked up the courage to put his arm around Anna's bare shoulders. She let him. Oliver had his hand on her knee. He turned to me and put his other hand on my thigh: You're hungry, *ja*? You must eat now—

The more he drank, the more pointed his speech and the worse his English. At first, when we met up with him on the steps outside, he had sounded more like an Englishman, but now he was all German, and I was having trouble understanding him. His English was not as good as Renato's, who had studied English for six years at la Escuela Lenin, and who participated in the conversation with ease, egging me on to join, and when he could not find a word, not blurting it out in Spanish like I did but gesturing with his fingers, sculpting some new language in the air.

Sometimes Oliver and Anna spoke to each other in German, and she would become serious, her voice clipped, and he docile and complaisant, his head nodding. Then they switched horses and he would resume control of the conversation—though her English was as good if not better than his. Whatever Spanish they had learned, they did not see fit to practice it, which was strange, I thought, because most Europeans vacationing in Cuba, especially Germans, were proud of the many languages they spoke and were always eager to practice their clipped Spanish.

Oliver and Anna did not have any of this enchanting gall. To them life seemed no longer than this vacation. We drank and we ate together, but never once did either of them ask us about our lives before that morning, or the lives we might imagine for ourselves after that night. (Bueno, sin ton ni son, we ourselves, hardly asked or cared about theirs, already knowing the rules of this game.) They behaved as if the world was only half a day long.

Only the Yuma had the luxury of doing this for extended periods. I already knew this well from my short time in the capital. And for tourists in Cuba, it was not only a luxury but a necessity. Why *should* they dwell on the tragic past or the ominous future of this wounded crocodile of an Island, when its own sad laughing people had such a long history of not doing it? I had once heard fat comandante Juan tell Cecilia, in one of his poetic moods, that the great shame of the Cuban people was that they too often behaved as if a tempestuous tomorrow did not exist and the dreadful yesterday was only an occasion for a mournful bolero.

A bloated old Revolutionary Army crook, comandante Juan had little nuggets of the counterrevolutionary buried in his graylard brain. It was not the Virgin of Cobre that was our patron saint, he often announced to the Yuma when he had had too much to drink during the dinner service, but José Martí. Vamos coño, what other country has made a god of an inept poet-soldier who rides a white horse into war and is shot down before the first battle even begins—as if his tiny lyrics could protect him? Or to call it what it was plain and simple—suicide, the ultimate sacrifice to the godhead. Mierda, a Christ complex till his last breath, like so many cubanos.

The Yuma looked at him with befuddled smiles. Most of them had no idea who he was talking about.

At least Oliver had a passing interest in Cuban history, or at least revolutionary history, and he treated us right—we drank French wine now and feasted on suckling pig. Why should he be blamed? And he had mentioned the past, one time, when he asked about the attempted assassination of El Líder, right there at the bar. I had heard the story, how a young barman had once tried to slip cyanide into Fidel's whiskey one New Year's Eve. But it wasn't something you could really talk about in public, not something a Yuma would know about, either, which seemed odd. But I let it go then.

I had done this with Renato before, picked up tourists for a little cash outside some tourist club in Cerro. But those transactions were usually over before they got started, the foreigners so hungry for sex it was as if the act itself didn't exist anywhere else but on the Island.

This already had taken a different path.

Are you married? I asked in my halting English (though I could read it and write it without hesitation, the twisted, knotty pronunciations made me blush every time I tried to speak it, a language suited for a convocation of insects), rubbing the ring spot on my left-hand ring finger. Desserts had just arrived—flan and biscochos.

Oliver and Anna, across from me, both looked at their hands, searching for an answer there. Oliver wore a thick silver ring on his thumb, Anna a ruby on her pinky.

We don't believe in it, *ja*, Oliver finally said. You must know this. As in I *should* know it, he meant. *Must* was his favorite English word, and it served multitudinous functions for him. A command, a justification, a plea. They both turned their hands over, fingers extended, to prove they were not hiding anything. Renato mimicked them. The new herbal medications stained his teeth and made him self-conscious, but he was already so drunk that he had forgotten.

We had one last round of drinks. Oliver insisted that we try a shot of his favorite cognac, Hennessy XO, but none of us could do more than wet our lips with it; after he had emptied his snifter, Oliver emptied Anna's and then Renato's with two quick flips of his wrist. I got the feeling that he was numbing himself against some ignominy that had not yet befallen him.

You must finish yours, he said to me, his fingers laced under the hair of his chin. We must now go. He handed the waiter a pile of green bills without even looking at the check. The waiter bowed and tried to thank him in German. You're very welcome, Oliver said. Then they all looked at me, a hazy satisfaction on their faces—Oliver's features softened as easily with his drunkenness as with his smile—and sip by sip, swirled around the hollows of my mouth till my gums felt drugged, I finished my drink.

We came out of the restaurant and walked through the plant-filled patio of the glass-domed lobby. Oliver marveled at the flowers and trees and said their names in German, then in English, then in Spanish, though sometimes he was way off on the Spanish name. We laughed at this, then we took the elevator up to their room—the unspoken plan all along. Rules of the game. I forgot about Renato, watched the floors passing through the little glass window of the elevator door. I tried to count them, but between four and five I lost count.

Oliver led the way to the room, his keys in hand, taking such long-measured steps that the three of us fell far behind. When he reached the door, he seemed surprised that we were not right behind him. He held the door open, waiting for us. Renato reached behind Anna, who was stumbling between us, grabbed my wrist, and gave it a shake. Then he let go.

The room looked shabby, the lemon paint peeling from the corners where the walls met the ceiling. But spacious. A large bed with a thin mattress and bleached starchy sheets that had been turned down, a fresh papaya on the night table surrounded by flowers. The paneling on the headboard was cracked, the sliding doors to the balcony open. A gentle breeze passed through the room and out into the dank hallway. I could see the weightless lights of the city and beyond them the laden darkness of the sea.

Oliver turned on the radio already tuned to a jazz station. Monk, he sighed. A weight seemed to lift off him.

He took off his shirt and threw it on the bed, and I could guess right away that he was the kind of man who looked better with each article of clothes he cast off. He was more muscular, more defined than I had imagined—veins raced from his arms into his chest and sank from his stomach into his crotch. Tufts of soft hair grew around his dark nipples and his belly button.

You must close the door, *ja?* he said. Lock it. He went out to the balcony and leaned forward on the railing. There was another tattoo on his back, a wild-haired woman, reaching and touching the base of his neck. Anna threw herself on the bed, her arms over her head, her eyes shut. Renato sat on the bed by Anna and put his hand on her leg. I looked at him, and Renato must have read something in my eyes.

My friend's scared, he said in English, turning to the balcony. I grimaced and shook my head at him. I wanted to slap him.

Louis Armstrong came on next over the jazz station. *Didn't know how much I missed the home fire.*

Oliver pretended not to hear what Renato said and came back into the room. He mouthed the lyrics of the song, his arms in front of him as if holding a partner, and spinning on one foot. When he stopped, he removed his wallet from his jeans and set it on the beaten dresser, then went back out the sliding doors. He beckoned us to come out and join him on the balcony. You live in a great city, you must come out and look, *ja?* Leave her there; she's okay.

We stood on the balcony looking out at the old city. I had never seen the city from above like this, except in pictures, or in films, where the panning camera is ineluctably accompanied by the cáscara beat of tumbadoras and palitos or the rousing lyrics of a trova. But in reality, a pervasive silence hung over the shadowy skyline. Not that there wasn't sound—the incessant buffeting of the sea on the Malecón, the honking of máquinas, and the caterwauling of bicycle taxistas, trying to round up any Yuma going out for the night, and beyond the unlit dome of the Capitolio, which peered out of the darkness like a child's head from under the blanket, the drone of Habana Vieja, not with the busyness of production, but with a want of it, residents out on their doorsteps with opened old unread editions of *Granma* rolled up as fans, clothes hanging on the laundry lines above them that could never get dry enough, everyone searching for possibility even in the trumpet call of a hungry stray cur, the shimmy of necessity and the hiss of the ghosts of puerco asado, all like a busy wasp hive fallen from a branch and half-sunk into a muddy pit.

Oliver seemed to grow disappointed with the lack of a view—whole sections of the city already under apagones—and turned toward us.

When are you leaving? Renato asked.

The day after tomorrow. You must want to come with us? We also live in great city. Much changing now, *ja?*

He told us a little about his city, impersonal details about how the old communist side was where the young were congregating and transforming the place.

No, we . . . we . . . *must* stay here. Renato slid his hand on the railing and set it on Oliver's hand. He was smiling, looking down at the passersby below, his hair tucked behind his ears. We can be your Cuban boys, though, he said with an imbecilic smile, or girlfriends—la misma mierda—for when you come back.

I looked once back into the room—Anna had not moved. Oliver took his hand out from under Renato's and passed it over his bare chest, then he reached over and pulled Renato's ragged T-shirt off and dropped it gently on the balcony floor, tracing the outlines of the dark figure on Renato's belly with his index finger—a thin smile his only response, but obviously admiring the primitive artwork as much as he was admiring Renato—then he pulled himself closer and his hand plunged under Renato's waistband. His eyes sunk into their pools. His lips searched for Renato's, but Renato turned his face away, toward the darkness below, toward the sea. His arms hung lax at his sides. Oliver's mouth found Renato's neck and it clung there, a caterpillar on a leaf. Renato stretched his face farther away, otherwise remaining still. Oliver's hand went deeper down and with his other hand he reached around Renato and grabbed me by the arm and pulled me toward them. I wrapped my arms around Renato, my hands clamped over his waist, my cheek pressed to his back. Renato's skin was cold, and I felt the jostle of Oliver's hand, like some rodent seeking shelter on a blustery night.

Anna groaned from the bed and Renato spoke (his neck now fully stretched out) to the city and to the sea beneath the balcony, as if it had been them and not the girl who had cried out.

We can't leave her alone, I think he said.

He slipped out from between us, and Oliver's hand hung in the air, uncertain and turning in half-circles. I reached out and caught it and pressed it between my hands and slipped it under my shirt, up my belly, and to my chest. Renato scampered to the bed, on all fours, he spread over Anna, his hair fallen from his ears, his whispers incomprehensible. She groaned again, louder than she had the first time, and her ass lifted, hoisted by a pulley from some high point above them. Oliver touched my chin with two fingers, turned my eyes away from the bed.

You must let them alone, he said, and he kissed me, softly at first, so that the hair on his chin felt like a brush of wet green pine needles, and his breath smelled of leaves soaked in alcohol, and he spoke some more as he kissed me, now in simple Spanish, as if he suddenly could not understand whatever language was coming from the bed.

A pale moon had risen, and it was split in half and tilted forward, peering downward like a chaperone. Here, me enloquecí, maybe it was the booze, but I closed my eyes and imagined that in the darkness, the moon's hands were on her wide hips, and that she tapped her fat foot, stirring the dusty stars—and perhaps the matronly fat moon made me feel a little safe with the foreigner on the balcony, so that after I shut my eyes and craned my neck, I began to return the kisses, my mouth clammed shut at first but soon shucked open so that my body opened to another man for the first time since Nicolás. Oliver, who all night had cast no more than two or three glances my way, now explored my body with an archeological eagerness. His hands rubbed the surface of my skin in weighty circular motions, his mouth pecked at my flesh as if pulling threads through. My T-shirt came off, and he sat me on the rail of the balcony and pulled off my boots and my socks and my shorts and caressed my inner thighs gently, his hands moving as if through warm bathwater, and then he got on his knees and held my package with both hands and lifted it up, offering it to the old moon, to the black sea, to the stars and to their pale reflection in the city lights below. He put his mouth to it and wet my pinga and balls through the wafer-thin underwear.

On the bed, Renato had Anna's dress halfway up her belly, his head buried in her breasts, his hips grinding her legs open. Watching them made me hard. My pinga poked out from one side of my underwear, and Oliver sighed and put it in his mouth.

I kept shifting my eyes toward the bed. Renato had pulled down his shorts enough so that his cocowhite ass flashed.

His hips bounced sprightly now, a hare across an evening meadow. I told myself to just close my eyes, but I couldn't do it. I kept watching. My groin soaked with Oliver's spit. Since I couldn't close my eyes, I shifted, leaned backward from my toes till almost all my weight rested on the cold balcony railing. I wanted to come quickly so I pumped my hips, lifting my ass till I remained supported by only my arms grasping the railing. I looked over to the bed again—this time it took more of an effort, craning my neck, and tried to imagine myself not in Anna's place, but just there, by them. I thought of how Nicolás fucked, and the movement of my hips became more emphatic.

I wondered if the German had any condoms.

My feet abandoned the floor completely, and I now balanced myself with my hands on the railing and the backs of my legs on Oliver's shoulder, my briefs dangling off one ankle. Oliver moved underneath me, lifting my ass in the air, searching with his tongue, and I made a high-pitched noise so that I saw Renato look over at us from the bed, sweaty hair matted on his face, a grim smile. And that was the last thing I remember—before I went over and, but for a dangling pair of briefs, wholly naked over the railing.

Oliver was just able to grab the lower part of my right leg. He held on to it, locked by both arms and pressed against his chest. He muttered some harsh words in his language, his breath puddled. I dangled upside down screaming like a loca, cursing the German out of Oliver, my arms outstretched, my butthole peering up at the heavens. My other leg hung in the air like a beam, but Oliver dared not reach for it. The pair of briefs slid off and glided down to the city below. I went soft, but once Oliver had me in a tight grip, my pinga got semi-hard again. It leaked a watery precum. I reached up and played with my balls and stroked myself, now laughing

maniacally. I wanted to rain my cum on the pobrecita desolate city below. Oliver tightened his grip and finally jerked
me up.

You must come up, he said. What are you doing? *Jetzt* . . .
you must come up. Renato was there now, and he grabbed
my free leg. I looked up. Both of their faces rosy with desperation, as if I were already splattered on the street below. They
yanked on me again, harder this time, so that my butt almost
reached the top rail, though I was still dangling backward
over the balcony.

Renato worked his way up on my leg, never losing his grip,
till the backs of his fingers brushed my balls, and then he threw
himself at me and grabbed me by the waist and pulled me in
and held on to me tight, pressing firmly down, as if I had the
wherewithal or the desire to fly off that balcony. His shorts
and his underwear hung at his knees. His pinga was soft, but
still engorged, the thick Prince Albert shiny. I was all excited
now and pushed myself against Renato, but he pushed me
away and pulled up his pants. Oliver was on his knees, still
holding on to my other leg, his face pallid, his arms cold, his
pinga tinysoft. I wanted to cum quietly, but no one was going
to help me, so I just did it myself. I dribbled lukewarm on the
balcony. Renato dressed when I looked up, bleary-eyed. He
said vamos in a serious tone, all sober. Oliver kissed me on the
cheek and said something in German and walked over to
the bed and sat at the end eating a slice of the papaya quietly.
When he was finished, Anna reached out with a hand and put
it on his thigh. He crawled dutifully on top of her.

Renato gestured toward my bundle of clothes.

Póntela, he ordered. Let's go.

I couldn't pull my eyes away from the bed again, and
Renato slapped me on the arm, a disgusted look on his face.

Let's go, he told me again. He stood at the entrance to the

room, watching Oliver on top of his girl, and it was as if there was nobody else in that desolate room, as if they had spent the entire day alone and were now concluding it most naturally. Sweat trickled down the ridge in Oliver's back—he was all hot again—and Anna moaned softly with her lips pressed to his ear, deluded that only he could hear her.

After I dressed, Renato guided me out of the room with a hand on the small of my back as it had been on Anna's. He didn't even let me say goodbye to the Germans.

I never even saw him snatch the wallet full of yanqui dollars.

ASHES DON'T BURN

Cecilia tells me things when we are alone—before the first customer arrives and we huddle to smoke cigarettes inside the henhouse in the far corner of the patio, away from the taunting of Inocente St. Louis, who curses at us, waving his hands, so that we joke that he has been mounted by an orisha. Sometimes we know that he has drank too much with the mysterious novia that we never see but that controls his comings and goings by getting a randy rise from him from the other side of the old city. Sometimes he simply disappears in the middle of prep for the dinner shift to go see her and comes back just in time, sated, content, but enervated. When Cecilia and I smoke in the henhouse, he mutters that our cigarette smoke infects the aroma of his food, that it's going to give the chickens cancer. He says that one day he'll leave, he will make do on his own, just him and his jeva, and then we'll be ruined, serving tourists old picadillo and chicken shit.

That Friday night I spent with her son and the German couple had been an early one at the paladar. The last diners had left before midnight—a pair of French lovers who didn't seem too embarrassed to be the only ones in the place but were likely eager to get back to their hotel room or the nightclubs south of the city. Cecilia told me while we smoked that she thought of them as she rested face-up on the covers of her neatly made bed that night, of their brimming joy, their concupiscent feeding of each other with pinched fingers. The wet night air oozing in from the open window made her feel as if she were wearing nothing at all—her hands calmly at her side, half hypnotized by the blurry shadows of the ceiling fan, which at its highest setting moved its arms so sluggishly that it was useless against the soupy air. It had stopped once already as its motor coughed with disappointment, but soon, in less than a quarter hour, it kicked in again, lugging into motion with the gracelessness of a ponderous bird lumbering into flight as it always did. Cecilia wondered, often aloud apropos of nothing, in the middle of picking up a course from the kitchen, say, or on returning from a bathroom break, if the government thought it could fool the people by cutting off the power in such thin slices of time in the middle of the night, while all were ignorantly asleep.

At least we were lucky; we lived in a neighborhood well-traveled by tourists. She knew of neighborhoods where the power went out for days at a time. El período especial, that's the name that the government had given to the jejune times in which we lived, although nothing seemed special about it. Now is the time for sacrificio, we heard Fidel repeat and repeat on the television, on the radio, in the newspaper, vaya, any time he stood in front of a microphone or there was someone nearby to write it down.

Sacrificio. We saw that word graffitied everywhere, sometimes in puffy balloon-like letters, sometimes in baroque drippy crimson strokes, and sometimes in gray thorny dashes, which seemed to fit the essence of the word best. Cecilia wondered how much the government paid its graffiti artists, for certainly the people weren't doing it. Sacrifice was not something that had to be written out on the walls to be understood. She wondered if Fidel had gotten the inspiration for writing out the words that the citizens needed to most remember on the walls of the city from his socio's novel, where the characters forgot the names of things and had to tape them in a clean script on the door, the table, the cow, the chestnut.

It reminded her of the days when Inocente St. Louis had first arrived at the house on Calle Obispo and he had pretended as a joke to be a Haitian and speak only Creole. He had come to her some years after her husband had defected, appeared in the back patio one cloudy afternoon, soiled and muddy, making Cecilia imagine that he had burst free from a prison underneath the earth. He spoke in Creole, as comandante Juan had instructed him, so they both turned and went into the kitchen, presuming the stranger was hungry. Cecilia fumbled through the empty cupboards and the corroded refrigerator, and Inocente St. Louis watched them from the doorway, his arms folded in front of him. Cecilia found three moldy midget potatoes. Potato, she said with emphasis, and set it on the square kitchen table.

This is all, she said. Sorry, we have nothing else. I can boil them for you if you like.

Nothing else, comandante Juan repeated, and Cecilia was surprised at how broadly he was smiling when he spoke.

I can bake it for you also, Cecilia ventured, now chagrined.

Inocente St. Louis shook his head, but he stepped farther into the kitchen and remained there, his arms still folded in front of him, his head bowed, until comandante Juan led Cecilia out and left him there alone. They heard him pretending to rustle through the whole kitchen, slamming cabinet doors, shaking nearly empty containers in the pantry, clanging through the pots and pans. Sitting on the patio with Juan, Cecilia heard the clack of knives cutting on boards and tried to ignore the sharp perfume of bitter oranges that presented itself with the suddenness of ill tidings, and her breath quickened as the afternoon stuffiness and the aroma of the freshly wounded oranges wrapped itself around her. She put a hand on comandante Juan's arm and turned to him with a look of how could it be, we haven't had bitter oranges around here since the last coming of the locusts, who is this black devil in my kitchen, what magic is he working in there? But comandante Juan returned her look with a saintly expression, his bulldog cheeks only a dash rosy with the afternoon heat, his cloudy eyes half-closed, and his lips apart as if on the verge of a first kiss. He took her hand and pressed it between both of his. Tranquila, he said, I told you I would help you. He had snuck some treasure of ingredients into the kitchen for the chef to discover, she understood. Then, as he clenched Cecilia's hand and kissed it once, she heard the sizzle of the oil, and an unrepentant breeze of garlic made her jaw go soft. As an afternoon thunderstorm passed, the three of them sat at the kitchen table, enjoying heavy portions of yucca with garlic sauce and pork tenderloin sautéed with bitter oranges. It took only one or two other meals prepared by the criollo— the more exotic he seemed the more comandante Juan could pretend it had been some great Party connection that made the magical chef possible, though in fact Nicolás had introduced him to the comandante. The great chef no more than just another desvinculado, an undesirable, from the lower circles in which Nicolás more and more those days dwelt. A street vendor of black-market cuisine, though he rarely could display his talents for lack of ingredients.

Comandante Juan knew just the person that could get him all the ingredients needed. With Inocente St. Louis as chef and comandante Juan as chief investor, with the dollars that he now also had quick access to, he suggested they should open a paladar on the beautiful brick-paved patio of the house on Calle Obispo. Cecilia and her boys could become self-dependent. He would use his connections to obtain the government license, finagle the choice pick from the best suppliers.

It had all seemed so easy then, Cecilia would often tell me she thought while waiting for me to return from my trips to see her youngest son, listening for the groan of the mesquite door, calculating the time that had passed in her head, for she did not want to get up and turn on the light. Juan had made it all seem so easy, compared to everything that had happened afterward. With his first dollars, and later with the dollars they made from the diners, anything could be purchased on the black market. And Juan soon knew everybody in the bolsa, the black markets run out of back patios—the fishermen, the farmers, the market bosses with connections to the Party, and so many others whose profession and services were not so clearly defined. She could not have survived without Juan. She had given up plenty and was almost at peace with that, and all that she wanted back from all that she had in such a rush surrendered, was her youngest son. That's why she let me go see him on the first Friday of each month—in the hope that I could bring Renato back to her, if only for a brief stay. Ojalá pronto, she repeated, ojalá, ojalá, with the patient despair of those calling back a wayward god.

She had heard from Juan that the government had suddenly changed its policy a few months back, that now those sidatorio patients considered socially responsible were allowed to visit their families on weekends, or even, in time, move out of the sanitariums altogether and receive outpatient care. She smiled. What comunista bureaucrat would look at her naked young son, she would ask me later during our cigarette assignations—the tattoos all over his body, even on his toes, the painted fingernails, long on one hand, neatly trimmed on the other, the skull-shaped rings, the hair dyed god-knows-what-color now, cut and shaved into what pattern, the countless piercings on any dab of virgin skin, the gauntness of all those who too closely court death, and that haunting restlessness in his arborescent eyes flitting about like a winged insect trapped in an inverted glass—and consider such a child socially responsible? It had all happened in the space of a few years, a few handfuls of months even, as if someone had bought his body for some infernal art project. But there was hope. I had assured her that they did let him out one night a week and one weekend a month, all he had to do was carry with him at all times a yellow cardboard pass and report back before lights out on Sunday night.

Bring him to me then. Bring him to me next time.

Maldito, you know he won't come, Cecilia.

Then I'll go with you.

No. ¿Pa que? So he locks himself up in the sidatorio and then neither of us can see him?

He's my son, coño. She paused, looked down, reassessing her claim to such rights. He can't blame me. He's my son, coño; all I want to do is hold him until he's all right.

She'd had that conversation with me often in the past year, and I always went quiet and still when Cecilia mentioned holding her son, paralyzed by some fear that any slight sound or movement would shatter her delicate and outrageous fantasy. I had never seen such physical affection between mother and son in real life. I had never even seen her try—when Nicolás was still alive, when Renato was still home.

Sometimes she waited for me to return from my Friday visits the nightlong, she admitted to me, just to hear from me about Renato, even when she knew the waiting would be the greater torture.

That first Friday night of Renato's last summer, the power must have gone off and on, and the soft sudden light from the streetlamp made her think it had dawned abruptly. She was out of bed before she realized her error. She stood by one side of the window, her arms over her breasts, and peered at the street below. It was drizzling, and the broken cobblestones seemed freshly polished. A mangy orange stray slept on the front steps of the house across the way, its crusty body curled in on itself like a dried slug. Cecilia hadn't seen it before and she made a note in her mind to feed it if it was still around the following morning but made me do it as she told me about her vigil, insomniac with the waiting.

Often, without comandante Juan's knowledge, she would give out food to the neighbors from their inventory, sackfuls of rice and bread and potatoes and pots of whatever goat stew or quimbombó Inocente St. Louis had dreamed up for the week, all hoisted up over the patio's brick wall. She knew whom to prize with the meals. It kept her on the good side of the Comités. I would then slightly alter the numbers in comandante Juan's books, perfectly mimicking his precise girlish script. Comandante Juan hated the neighborhood Committees for the Defense of the Revolution, boasted that they were powerless against him, that no little group of gossipy old women would dare renounce him as a counterrevolutionary. But Cecilia knew how powerful the Comités were, how those little stooped ancianas with their thin, birdlike tongues could dethrone emperors, and like birds they were everywhere. Best to keep them well fed.

That night, Cecilia stepped out into the narrow balcony, leaned out, and looked up the hill to the top of the street, her arms still folded over her chest. A pair of shirtless men leaned with their backs on one of the houses, another shorter older man in a guayabera was speaking and signaling to them, but the two men seemed asleep on their feet, and Cecilia told me later she felt sorrier for these two men than she did for the stray across the street, who was at least in peace. She walked to the bathroom and sat in the dark on the toilet and urinated. Again, she tried to guess the time and realized she had taken off her watch when doing the dishes earlier that night. She had sent Inocente St. Louis—whose loins always ached for his lower circle hembra at that time of night—home right after he had plated the main course for the French lovers. Afterward, she had spent a long time cleaning the kitchen, scrubbing pots and countertops—somehow, she had known she would not be able to sleep before I returned.

She sat at the edge of the bed and lit a cigarette and smoked it slowly, cupping the ashes in her hand. Her husband, Pascual, had taught her that. She had told me once about the first time she did it, still a girl then, choosing to stay with an uncle in Pinar del Río instead of seeking exile with her parents on one of the last of the authorized flights to Madrid, a member of the Unión de Mujeres Obreras in the Great Harvest of 1970, terrified that the ashes would burn her palm, even though Pascual had proven to her, with his own palm, that ashes don't burn.

Ashes don't burn, he had said in a lullaby voice, hidden by the darkness near the naked black spears in some corner of a burnt cane field. Ashes are dead. And she trembled as he flicked his cigarette over her palm.

He was a leader. He had met the troop of women laborers outside their barracks the first morning dressed in the traditional guajiro garb, scuffed thick-skinned work boots, baggy sackcloth pants tied around the waist by a thin frayed rope and a heavy long-sleeve shirt (to protect against the blade-sharp leaves of the cane stalks, he explained), all of which hung on him like the borrowed clothes of a meatier man, and a straw hat that was a couple of sizes too small on him and sat precariously on the crown of his skull. From the first, he seemed a creature out of his habitat, constantly removing his thin gold-framed glasses to wipe the sweat from them and not knowing what to do with his canvas gloves, which he switched from hand to hand and from one back pocket to another. He spoke to them—a group of twenty or so young women from the union, all wearing the same traditional garb, with flag-colored pañuelos tied around their necks or over their heads underneath their straw hats—with a voice that Cecilia told me that she knew from just looking at him—his lanky poet's figure, long nicotined fingers, the exaggerated features, thick bushy eyebrows, a snout nose made more drastic by close-set eyes whose intense gaze seemed to cross at one point in the distance—was put on, a whole octave deeper than his real voice. He had let a three-day beard grow, but from the way he scratched it, under the chin and at the jaw muscle, Cecilia knew that this was also a pose.

He put on his gloves, picked up his machete, bent low at the waist, raised the machete high, and swung it at the ground, stirring up a cloud of dirt. That is how you cut caña, he said, at its base, pues eh, the best and thickest juice sits low on the stalk, as if the dead were sucking on it from beneath to remind themselves of the sweetness of this world. Some of the women giggled nervously as they took their gloves and machetes, but as they executed their first awkward practice swings, all their skittishness evaporated with the strenuous effort of the work. As they were carted out to an interminable, already-burned and prepared field, the stalks like an endless army of soldiers camouflaged in long spiny black feathers, the troop leader stood up from his perch next to the driver and turned and faced them, Oh, I am Pascual, pues eh, I almost forgot to tell you my name, I am Pascual Zúñiga, and I'll be by your side all day, working with you. Don't be afraid . . . Ten million tons! The great harvest for Fidel and la Revolución! He raised both his arms to the morning sky naked of clouds. By midmorning, Cecilia felt as if someone were pressing a red-hot brand to the small of her back, but it was less painful to stay bent low and continue swinging than to straighten up. They worked in a straight single file—Pascual moving from worker to worker, showing each how to perfect the machete swing. Looking back behind her, Cecilia told me of her dejected surprise that all their effort had taken them no more than ten steps into the infernal field. Cecilia remained in the camp in Pinar del Río, on the western tip of the Island, for over two months, growing accustomed to the long days in the field, the burning in her joints and muscles replaced by a more tepid sensation; still, she was so tired at night, her torso and limbs so rubbery with effort, that she slept soundly on the uncomfortable wooden bunks laid with rough canvas. Every third day, she washed her guajiro uniform in a nearby creek and set it on a boulder to dry, waiting beside it, wearing a colorful print dress that felt indecent and counterrevolutionary on her now, watching the moonlight enflame the mysterious blue volcanic mountains on the horizon.

Ay, sí, what relief after so much torture, like a long swig of dark rum, she said to me when she got to this part of the story. She only talked about Pascual to me when she had had a couple of drinks after a shift and after comandante Juan and Inocente St. Louis had gone home for the night.

Pascual was absent from them at nights, which he spent in the private quarters of the directors of the sugar mill. Sometimes music and riotous laughter came from within the spacious thatched roof bohíos. Crates of rum were often unloaded, and women from a nearby town arrived at dusk and left as the workers headed for the fields. One unusually breezeless night, while Cecilia's uniform was long in drying, an order came from the directors to set some of the fields afire. New fields needed to be prepared, denuding the stalks of their protective sharp leaves to speed up the cutting process. She undressed by the creek, leaving her printed dress atop the boulder, and put on her wet uniform. They rode carts out to the field under torchlight and Pascual instructed them on how to contain the fire, but he was so drunk that most of his speech was incomprehensible, and the field soon ablaze, the crackling of the leaves and the undergrowth overwhelmed by the agonizing cries and bustle of all the guiltless creatures chased from within. Cecilia looked to the smoky bristling sky, searching for the pair of storks that followed behind the macheteros daily, not really knowing what it was she was supposed to do to control the flames, waves of torrid heat slapping her far away from her set position.

She found Pascual. He ran from one end of the fire to the other, constantly pushing up his glasses with an index finger, bits of flying ash stuck to the sweat on his face and spit dribbled down his chin as he screamed orders to the men in charge of the mobile water tank—a wooden cart contraption with four men pushing and one riding, controlling the hose—whose wheels had become stuck in the mud. She helped to push it out, and somehow the fire that had spread to unripe stalks was split in two and then split again and then again till it was nothing more than a conflagration of small flames, like separate valley villages viewed from a mountaintop.

Pascual came to her and put an arm around her and thanked her for helping with the water tank. He had unbuttoned his shirt down to his navel, his long insectoid torso blackened with soot. White ashes clung to the soft sparse hair on his chest. He took a small silver flask from his pocket and offered it to her. When she refused, he took a long chug. He turned and ordered the workers back on the cart and thanked them for a job well done, but he held on to Cecilia by the cloth of her shirt and told her in a quiet voice to stay with him. They watched the torchlights disappear toward the sugar mill, and it was then that she noticed that some little flames survived in the field, shimmying on the embers or clinging to the naked blackened stalks like old regrets. Pascual walked into the smoldering field to survey their work, but she dared not follow him for it seemed from the implacable heat of the earth as if a greater fire were waiting to burst forth from beneath.

Ven, chica, he said, motioning for her with his hand, and then in English. It's just ashes. He lit a cigarette and cupped the ashes in his hand. See, he added, in English again. He returned to her and took her trembling hand and waved the cigarette over it, and all she could smell was the sour rum on his breath and the smoky sweat on his chest.

Ashes don't burn. Ashes are dead. In English, the tongue of his mother, he explained to her.

And short years later, she had learned it, she had used his words to create nonsense songs for her children, to teach them English, words she chanted to them as she breastfed them or put them to sleep.

> *Ashes don't burn,*
> *ashes are dead;*
> *now it's your turn*
> *to go to your bed.*
> *Ashes don't burn,*
> *ashes are dead;*
> *all you will learn,*
> *will stay in your head.*

Lonely songs that Cecilia would use in those first nights
of his absences, at meetings of the workers' union, or late-
night Party functions, or impromptu trips to the provinces,
as he quickly climbed the ranks of the Federation of Cuban
Workers and then later elected to the National Assembly,
till she became more used to her two sons sleeping on the
bed beside her than her husband. And now that side of
the bed remained neatly made when she slept, for not even
in her sleep did she wander past the threshold of all his
absences.

She had smoked three cigarettes, tossing the butts and the
ashes in her hand into the toilet, before she heard the groan
of the mesquite door below that Friday night. My arrival. She
pitched the final butt in the toilet and waved her arms about to
clear the smoke. I could always smell how many cigarettes she
had smoked. She heard me knock against the cabinet in the
living room, the china that we used for the paladar tinkling on
the glass shelves, and come up the narrow stone staircase and
pass by her door to her son's old room. She heard the thud of
each boot as I took them off. Then I came out of my room and
stood outside her doorway.

She said in a whisper that she could tell how much I had
been drinking by how much I failed to be quiet. She whispered that she could hear my heavy breath on the other side
of the door, as if I had run up and down the hills of the old
city on my way home, that she could see my eyes glowing in
the crack of the door. How's my son?—pulling up the sheets,
too obvious a motion to hide the breasts under her threadbare
nightgown.

I opened the door slowly, still trying to be quiet for no
reason. I poked my head in. In the morning shadows, her
body seemed hidden under a reluctant shroud. She said that
she could see the garishness of my newly dyed canary Afro

cut. It was buzzed on the sides and the top was manicured so that it looked like a rooster's comb, she said.

Are you awake already?

I haven't been to sleep, she said, not meaning to acuse me for her insomnia, but that's how it came out anyway. How's my son?

I stepped farther into the room, my hand still on the outside doorknob, shirtless, my gauntness more pronounced in the shadows than it had been in the light of the beach, she would tell me the following night as I cleared the last plates, my shorts low on my girlish hips, exposing the band of my underwear. Now she knew I was drunk. I was always careful not to expose myself to her inside the house, always going in and coming out of my baths fully dressed. She sat up in bed.

Pues, it's very late, she said. You have to work tomorrow. Out the window, the ruined city coming to gray. You have to work *today*, mejor dicho. She tapped the edge of the bed. Ven, entra. Sit here with me for a moment. Tell me what you did with my son all day.

I closed the door, but remained there, my back leaning against it. I hunched my shoulders again. What is there to do? We just hung out, vacilando. In the park. In the Malecón. I rubbed the sides of my skull. We went to see Bertila.

That's Inocente's woman, right? she asked. Everyone is somehow connected to my dead son.

I don't ask, I said.

She tapped the edge of the bed again, and I came to her like a rebuked child and sat by her, but kept my eyes cast downward. She put a hand on my bare shoulder and must have noticed something in me because she pulled it away too brusquely.

Did he ask about me?

I nodded. Sí, coño, ¿cómo no? He always asks about you.

And I instinctually bent over and kissed her on the cheek, knowing she was used to the familiar sourness of my rum-laced breath on these early Saturday mornings, my bumpy-skin grief when I gave in to her touch. She passed her hand over my upper back.

Do you tell him his home is waiting for him?

No, but he knows.

Claro, he knows, she responded. Then I got up and walked away. I stood with my back to the closed door again, now stupid with my arms wrapped around me, massaging the back of my neck. I was looking directly at her, and she took up the sheets with both hands again.

Why do you let me stay here? I said. Is it because you think I'll bring your one son back to you? Or is it because you want me to replace the one who died? I gestured to the empty side of the bed, aiming venom. Or your husband?

Stop it, Rafael. You're drunk.

I was—talking drunk, and I liked it. She seemed beautiful under her shroud. I had never seen her that way. The room smelled of her sleeplessness, her barefoot pacing, her bed-sweat, her twice-smoked cigarette butts, and I did not want to leave it, but did not know how else to stay, and she did not know how to throw me out.

This is how she waited for me, she always said later, not sparing details.

I stood there, my hand on my hips, seguramente looking girly again—which she did not like—as still as if I were the shadow of a tall lamp, face invisible to her in the morning but for the frightened glint of my unblinking eyes. Cecilia told me later that she could almost hear me counting before I made myself leave to pass out in my own bed.

BISNES

Ridiculous, she said to her husband. Didn't they tell you this was one of the best?

She poked at the open guidebook on the table. Her husband sealed his lips, adjusted his grimy bifocals, and leafed through the guidebook, as if to find proof that indeed this was one of the most highly recommended paladars in the old city. He passed his hand over his greasy bald head. Bah, the woman half-said. She had waved her hand in the air, and her heavy bracelets clanged like insect shells in a tin bucket. Before I had a chance to make it to the table, Cecilia passed by and swiped the plate from the couple's table, the woman left with her fork drawn. Cecilia handed the plate off to me and took over the table I had been attending, and now I was trying to coax Inocente St. Louis into replacing the piece of overcooked pork, but the chef, as always during the dinner rush when he had four pans on the fire at once, his cheeks charred mahogany, muttered to himself in a surly silent mood. He waved a spatula at me and then slammed it on the counter. Cecilia cocked her head toward the dining room patio.

There's a man out there. Says he knows you. I have this.

I walked back out to the patio. Comandante Juan was at

the Spanish couple's table, pouring them a glass of comple-
mentary wine. The woman smiled now, patting her cheeks and
her bosom as if she were coming down with a fever. The man
looked up from his bifocals, smiling also, more than pleased
to hand off his wife. Comandante Juan had easily won them
over with his effortless machote charm. The woman even
reached out and rested her hand on Juan's hairy forearm and
caressed it. They would return. That's why comandante Juan
was there, for the preposterous joy that emanated from his
being, that joy that all foreigners think is a natural attribute
of all Cubans, and when they see it in someone on the Island
it is like turning a narrow street corner and coming upon a
monument, or a bridge, or a façade that they had only seen
before in photographs, all the vicissitudes of travel momentarily forgotten.

I looked around for my visitor. Directly under the avocado
tree, a man sat alone at a small table. Someone had already
served him a glass of wine. He sipped it slowly and stared
directly back at me. I nodded. He raised a glass at me and
smiled. I pretended that it took me a while to recognize him.
He looked different enough, his hair all its natural color now,
a honey brown, dry and combed neatly to the side. He was
not as tan as he had been on the day we met him, but his skin
still kept the shade of the well-traveled foreigner. He wore a
pressed short-sleeve white linen shirt. He waited calmly for
me to approach him.

I'm sorry, he said, speaking in much more perfect Spanish
than he had used before. I had to go to the police. I had credit
cards and papers in the wallet. Which wasn't entirely true,
there had been a useless Canadian bank card, no legal papers.

The police? I asked too loudly, overdoing my feigned ignorance. He smiled with his eyes.

I nodded, looked around to make sure no one had heard.

I'm sorry, I said. You were very kind to us. We shouldn't have—

Oliver cut me off by placing a hand on my hip, Mira, it's over, right? I've replaced my cards, my papers. These things are not complicated.

Where is—

Anna? She left me. He switched back to English midsentence. Mira, long coming, is what they say? He gave a sibilant whistle of exasperation and took a long sip of his wine, then looked up at me and raised his glass toward me again. I'm here for longer now. Doing some business for a friend of my father in Varadero. Here now, so I must come to see you. This is where you work? Live, I mean.

It had been a couple of weeks since the night with him, but for some reason he made it seem as if it had been months, years even.

I nodded, gathered the sweat on my brow with the back of a hand, and wiped it on my apron. You look good, I said, and he did. I could see the shadows of the tattoos on his arm through the gauzy fabric of his shirt.

How's your friend?

Haven't seen him since . . . since our night. I lied—I had seen Renato twice since that night. A week after he had swiped the German's wallet, he tried to give me my share of the take. Hijo de la gran puta didn't pay us, was all he said. A couple of days after that the poli took him in for three nights then suddenly let him go. Who's going to entertain the tourists, huevón, Renato asked me, if they keep us all in jail for longer than that?

The police told me that he's in the sanitarium. They had seen both of you walk into the hotel with me. You should have told us, maybe. You must have.

He didn't do anything with—

Anna.

Sí, there wasn't time. I was watching them.

I wasn't. He sipped from his wine.

Other customers gesticulated for my attention, but I didn't want to move away from the table now. Sorry, I said. We were drunk. Sorry . . . for everything. By now I was, truly (though I hadn't given it much thought since I had refused my share of the loot from Renato), but was still suspicious of why he was back. And you've come to visit me?

Oliver looked away, considered something, then grabbed my forearm. Look, it's all right. Nobody's fault. I'm hungry. You tell me what you have? The concierge at the hotel says this is one of the finest places in the cities for an authentic meal.

He was going to make me wait to find out why he was back, so I played along. Pues coño, right, the best meal you've ever had.

I spaced Oliver's meal out slowly, bringing him little tidbits from the chef and wine from comandante Juan between courses of conch chowder and an avocado salad and ropa vieja with yucca in mojo and baked rum raisin pudding, so that by the time he had paid and tipped handsomely there was only one other table left in the patio.

I introduced him to Cecilia and comandante Juan as a friend—although Juan must have known exactly who he was—and brought him into the kitchen so that he could meet the talented chef. Inocente St. Louis dealt with us curtly, as he did with everyone—the only one I had ever seen welcomed into his kitchen with an effusive embrace was the profane and often fetid figure of Nicolás. Cecilia must have pieced the story of the comely foreigner together from the questions the police had asked her, from bits that I had told her, from the heartless gossip of the old ladies of the Comité.

On one of those mornings when she waited up for me to return from my visits to Renato, she ordered me outright not to fall in love with her other son, one was enough. I wouldn't, I promised. We all pulled chairs up to Oliver's table and finished the evening with a round of port.

So you have met my son? Cecilia said. Oliver glanced briefly at me. Sí, he said.

He took your wallet that night, she said, her voice too venomous for anyone to ignore. This one had nothing to do with it.

Oliver raised his hand, paused, and then thought of something else and shook his head. No, no, chica, doesn't matter now. That's not why I have come. We must pass over that. I'm going to be in the city for a time. He paused as everyone waited for him to explain why. No one stays a tourist extendedly for no reason. Doing business, he added offhandedly. I need friends. He raised his glass.

Comandante Juan joined him first. It was the perfect combination of words to catch his attention, *bisnes* and *friends*. Bueno, he said, clinking glasses, you've come to the right place. He waited perhaps ten or fifteen seconds, an eternity, before getting to the matter: Business, what sort, eh?

Nothing thrilling. Hotels and things. Scout—¿cómo se dice?—unfamiliar places for a friend of my father's company. Everyone waited for him to say more, but he dismissed the importance of whatever he was doing with a wave of his hand. Lonely job, *ja*.

Ah sí, I perhaps then can be of assistance, comandante Juan said, counting out with his fat fingers the European hoteliers that he knew intimately. Oliver nodded politely and said he might take him up the offer, which pleased comandante Juan so immensely that throughout the rest of the night, he interjected other names, until Cecilia begged him to stop. Juan, por favor, no one's here for your sales pitch.

Ah, but that's where you are wrong, mi niña, Juan said, gesturing toward Oliver, tapping on his temple but speaking of him as if he had paid and left. These Europeans, they're *always* thinking business. Bought up most of the Island. He nudged up to him. Soon, we'll be able to join the European Community. ¿No es así? At least before you let in all those barbarian former Soviet republics!

Ay, Juan, que pena, Cecilia sighed—but Oliver clearly enjoyed him, and he said that if he had anything to do with it, that's the way it must be. What better way to piss the yanquis off?

There won't be a postage stamp of land by the time the yanquis get here, coño! comandante Juan agreed, toasting again.

Oliver wisely veered the conversation away from the future of the Island by trying to get me involved. He asked how it was that fortune had smiled on me and I had ended up with such, and he struggled for the Cuban phrase, till comandante Juan supplied it for him. Gente tan maravillosa! Oliver nodded. Exactly, such wonderful people.

I muttered something about Nicolás, meeting him at the beach in Cojímar, and tried to explain who he was, but comandante Juan was far too interested in Oliver to let anyone else vie for his attention. So he told him the story at length, at several points checking in with Cecilia about a date or a detail, leaving out most of the harsh facts about Cecilia's two sons or the husband that had abandoned them, giving himself most of the credit for accepting me into their little family.

When he approached the time of Nicolás's quarantine in the sidatorio, Cecilia cut him off abruptly, using a tone of voice reserved for the middle of a busy service. Comandante Juan took the cue and emptied the bottle of port into our glasses, and as a way of atoning for his impertinence to Cecilia, explained that truly he was the outcast in this family, he who was the great beneficiary of Cecilia's hospitality. This seemed to turn the conversation over to Oliver who tried again to get me involved, but soon had to answer the comandante's questions about Berlin and other cities he had visited. When he mentioned Tangiers, Inocente St. Louis called out from the kitchen that it was the only city in the world that he would visit when his time had come, and he would be a phantom upon the face of this earth. Juan said that for him it would be Buenos Aires, Cecilia Paris. Oliver glanced at me, waiting for my choice, but I had become as silent as he had been at their dinner in the Hotel Habana Libre, watching only as the German wooed others with his ruffled sensuality.

Cecilia finally noticed how uneasy I had become and pulled Juan away from the table to help Inocente St. Louis finish closing up the kitchen. I apologized for comandante Juan's overbearing cheer.

But this must be very Cuban, no? Oliver said.

I said that maybe so, if you were receiving a prized gentleman caller for your only daughter. Oliver laughed. Maybe, he thinks he must be!

He asked me to walk him out but did not want me to accompany him past the side gate that led to Calle Obispo.

For the first time since I had arrived, the temptation to abandon the sheltered existence in the house on Calle Obispo became something physical, something that I could achieve with a few swift actions, denuding myself of apron, hanging it on the gate latch, and walking off with this foreigner, who if anything was offering a possibility, even if a dubious one, a passageway into some other world. It was a dance as common as the rumba then for us Cubans, with all its concomitant routines, styles, and traditions, the tilt of the hips, the swaying of the pañuelo, the bending and straightening of the knees, infinitesimally approaching the submissive position, all things cubanos use in a figurative way to snare the Yuma, if but for a few nights of freedom. Such a rite must be performed with a feline patience that I did not yet possess.

Stay with your friends tonight, Oliver said as if guessing my thoughts, a hand on my chest. I won't disappear again. He pecked me once on the cheek, and when I turned around, comandante Juan and Cecilia craned their necks from the kitchen counter where plates were put out. Inocente St. Louis had his back to them, still busy closing up the kitchen by himself, complaining about the late service for the German.

AFTERNOON PROJECT

About a year and a half before, I had met the first son and done what I had been tempted to do with the German: steal away, start anew.

After Nicolás had told me about the dinghy he had stolen and rigged with a Soviet car engine, he offered me a job. My mother needs a waiter, and, vaya, you seem to know what you're doing. As far as I can tell, anyway. He went on to stress that he would never work for his mother, but that it was a moneymaking venture.

He had been watching me from the rocky beach in Cojímar as I served drinks to tourists in a nearby bar shack. He lay facedown on a tiny beach towel all afternoon, alone, wearing only thin red trunks, sometimes napping, sometimes glancing at a book or sipping from a water bottle, but mostly resting his chin on his crossed arms and watching the sea, then turning when he got bored and scoping me come in and out of the bar. I had been at the place less than a week, one of a long string of jobs that I held when I first arrived in the province.

I finished my shift, collected my dollars, and went to sit by him. At first, he ignored me, lay his head in his arms again and pretended to nap. I had not seen him on his feet yet, but now up close I could see how long he was, the limbs, the hands, and feet, even the face, seemed to have all been pulled to match the narrow palm-trunk torso. He was perilously thin, seco y envuelto en paja, I later told him, but not, it seemed, from hunger but from a natural disposition, from some innate linearity.

You're a long way from home, guajirito, he said, his eyes still closed. After a silence, he raised his head and looked at me, the thick curly hair matted flat, as if some obstruction had suddenly checked the turbulent growth. A scrub of beard grew on the point of his chin, dark and prominent as an accent. He repeated his statement, this time slightly inflected as a question.

I told him that I lived with a grandaunt near the beach, a half sister of the woman who raised me, which didn't seem to interest him at all. And how did he know what long way I was from anything?

Ahí está, huevón, he said with a grunt of satisfaction. Once he had heard me speak, it was not hard to guess where I came from. Folks from Oriente, the easternmost province, are termed, by even the rattiest Habaneros, lengua de trapos, our tongues useless as wet dishrags. We eat syllables for breakfast, for dessert.

My admirer sat up, folded his legs in front of him, and held onto his ankles as if to keep the lower extremities from getting away from him. A patch of pubes poked out from the band of the thin trunks, and he caught me looking at it. Now half-vertical, his face was the only thing that seemed unsuited to his physique. Although oblong like the rest of him, with a prominent nose and ample forehead, its center was highlighted in womanly curves, round hazel muñequa eyes, surprisingly full cheeks, and a prominent lower lip shaped like a tiny bathtub.

¿Asere, qué bola? he said, as if I were some new person suddenly.

I told him I was done for the day, asked him why he was wasting his afternoon looking at tourists or at a guajirito. He turned around and faced the sea, watching the few fishing barks lined out in the calm waters, and then leaping up, directed my eyes beyond the fishermen, to a lonely coast guard vessel chugging near the horizon. There, that's what I am looking at, and over there. He saw the expression of surprise on my face and said that he didn't have to look out to the sea to know what was there, that he had been coming here for too many Mondays. Almost ready, he announced, confiding in me about the dinghy he had stolen, about his plans to equip it with a Lada engine.

Qué bobo, are you broadcasting it to the whole Island? Should we row out and tell the machotes on the coast guard vessel? I haven't even met you, cabrón. I extended my hand. I'm Rafael Puebla, from Baracoa.

He clasped my hand instead of shaking it, shook his head, my name and where I was exactly from not important. I've been watching you, but not like you think, ganso. And I may need you to do me a favor, un favorcito that will repay itself in a matter of weeks. He asked me how much money I made at the bar, and I took out the measly roll of single dollars, counted it out for him, half-expecting him to grab it and run. But I didn't want to lose him just yet, so I chanced it.

He looked at the roll and whistled. That's crumbs.

They're dollars, guanajo! Suddenly I got defensive about my five-day-old job.

Mira, let me take back what I said. It looks like I'll be doing you a favor. Maybe you can live on that in Baracoa, or whatever pueblecito you're from, but not here. ¡Qué va! He grinned again, waiting for me to take his bait.

My mother needs a waiter, and, vaya, you seem to know what you're doing.

Now that they were government approved, paladars were more popular than ever in the capital, the only way for the tourists to imagine they were having a true native experience, he explained. Claro, half the money goes up Fidel's ass, even though he hates dollars. But it was still worth it, the stranger explained, especially for the employees in the larger ones. The law stipulated that they could have no more than twelve seats, but his mother's had at least twice that, and when needed, even more.

He sold the paladar to me now, as I would later see touts do it in the corners of the old city, soulfully belting out the items on the menu as if they were the lyrics to a bolero. Diners tended to be much more generous, Nicolás added, money could be hidden from government auditors.

His pitch finished, he made a sack out of his beach towel, threw the water towel and the book in, slipped into his chancletas, and motioned for me to follow him.

I held my place against my instincts.

I'm offering you a life in the heart of the capital, pendejo! What do you have here besides your shitty ball of dólares?

I resisted, held still, looking out at the bobbing straw-covered heads of the hapless fishermen. I wanted him to say that he wanted me for him, not for his mother's lousy paladar. It was late. His shadow stretching out to the shore made him seem even ganglier, like some villain muñequito. He had his hands on his hips.

Do you even have time for yourself? ¿Sabes? He grabbed his crotch. My mother will give you your own room.

What do you think I am? I said.

The giant shadow dropped its arms, scratched its equine head. What?

Aren't there waiters in the capital? Why do you have to come out here to find one? Just leave me alone, go work your guayaba on somebody else.

He came and sat by me again, grabbed my chin, and turned my head toward him.

Look at me, asere.

I was glad he hadn't left, but my eyes wandered from spot to spot on his face, restless for a safe place to land. They finally settled on the prominent ridge of his upper lip.

Good. What do I think you are? I think that you're some pájarito guajiro who got tired of fucking chickens and you came to the capital to see what other passion the world had to offer. And now that you're almost there, al cantío de un gallo, you're too afraid to take the last step. That's what I think. Or maybe that last step is just not for people like you.

He wet his lips, so that my eyes momentarily flitted off.

When I first saw you, I decided to make you my afternoon project. Y vaya, here comes the truth—my mother doesn't need a waiter. That's what she has sons for, she always says. I have a little brother about your age. What? Seventeen . . . eighteen?

The truth was I didn't know my exact age.

So my mother doesn't need you, per se. He wiggled his long fingers. But the thing is, she will probably use you if I bring you home. I think she's getting a little tired of my brother's brooding over tables and me scaring off customers with my political diatribes. I saw how pleasantly servile you were with los Yuma. He kissed his fingers and blew the kiss into the air. Don't make a face. It's a great talent nowadays; their pockets keep whatever lights are still on in the capital. Once my mother sees that, your *talent,* my brother and I will finally be out of jobs. Which is what we want, for everybody's sake. But that's not why I decided to make you my afternoon project. He paused, chuckled. The truth, I was getting to that.

He stood up again and grabbed his towel sack. Vamos, I'll tell you on the way. And take off your shirt: it'll be easier to hitch a ride. This time, he walked away at an idle, not glancing back. I waited and waited and by the time I caught up to him he was already on the side of the road.

You got some cojones, maricón.

I'm glad you came; it'll just be a short ride. He looked both ways on the empty road. We have to walk a little bit to the plaza.

I know where I am.

Bien, then you know where to find the Yuma. Some of them'll be heading back for dinner in the city.

He remained two steps ahead of me, quickening his pace. I said that I had to get my belongings, tell my aunt where I was going, although the truth was that everything I owned, a couple of changes of clothes and some old sneakers would offend a beggar, and the old lady hardly kept track of my comings and goings. She didn't want to know, so that when they came asking questions she wouldn't have to lie.

The plaza was in fact a tiny square by the bay named after Hemingway, featuring a bust of the author, which had been cast with brass donated by local fishermen. Tourists usually began and ended their tour of the village there. In less than five minutes, we were squeezed into the back of a tourist taxi with a young Spanish couple that said that they were on their honeymoon. The driver glared at us and at first refused to let us in, but the groom handed him a bill and gestured for us to sit by them.

I am Nicolás, my companion introduced himself, extending a hand toward the couple, and this, this handsome mulatto is my boyfriend, Rafael.

He put one hand on the groom's knee, the other one on mine, and spoke all the way to his mother's house on Calle Obispo.

CARPENTER BIRD

The next time I went to see Renato, he wasn't there.
Your amiguito . . . he's gone, the foul-mouthed
guard said. Se fué. It's a free country, he said, all business now, none of the sexually charged taunts with which he
had ingratiated himself to us before. If I wanted to get in,
there either had to be someone to visit there, or . . . and he
looked directly at me for the first time. I knew the other way,
vaya. This was a serious business of the Ministry of Health,
not some country club. He stepped back into his bougainvillea-
covered shack, shut the door, and turned on a radio.

Even if he had let me in, I wouldn't have known the first
thing about where to find Renato. He always came to meet
me by the front gate, had never divulged any details about
the place and its other patients other than he slept in a very
uncomfortable cot in a makeshift *cell* that he shared with
another patient and that the meals were nothing compared to
the ones Inocente St. Louis could prepare from scraps.

There was a short limestone wall around the perimeter of
the facility, the yards neatly kept and dotted with bright poincianas and royal palms; flowering hibiscus bushes lined the
dirt road entrance. From what you could see of the two- or

three-story Soviet-era buildings from the entrance, it was a rather ordinary place that had not lost its groomed qualities as a school.

Renato had mentioned that it was much larger than it seemed, a cluster of other buildings beyond what you could see from the road that housed classrooms of the old school, which now had been converted into living quarters with shoulder-height wood-paneled walls, so that you could hear everybody's business at all hours of the day and night, a basketball court with no baskets, a dusty baseball diamond, and even a decent-sized swimming pool that went unused because it was so heavily chlorinated. A chemical bath, Renato had said, as if they wanted us to die like poisoned roaches. None of the staff lived there. Since strictures about patients coming and going had been relaxed the year before, only a handful of guards and nurses manned the facilities after dark. After night fell, I could easily hop the stone wall far away from one of the entrance gates and make my way to the living quarters, pretending I was a new patient with a bout of insomnia. By morning, I would know what had happened to Renato. But I needed to check on something else first.

Bertila pushed the door open for me, sneaking her head out into the hallway to see where Renato was.

¿Y mi niño? she said, shoving me out of the way playfully and peering down into the darkened stairway. Then she closed the door. What's happened now?

I told her what the guard had told me. She agreed that he would have come to see her if he had left on his own, but she didn't want me to go back. He wasn't there.

Mira, she said. He didn't want me to tell you . . . He had been coming to see her over the past few weeks, not just during the weekends, but during the middle of the week, often staying the night, insisting on sleeping in the fully reclined barber's chair in the living room, disappearing at dawn and returning days later. Sometimes he stayed the day through, assisting her with her clients. She was hesitant to make too many inquiries, but from a few curt replies she deduced that the Ministry of Health had been slowly implementing a major policy change, dismissing those who were not fully participating in the treatment, who refused to take their dosage of medication on the strict daily schedule. It seemed unbelievable to Bertila that the government would so casually give up on their decade-long struggle to contain the HIV virus just because of a few rebellious patients. The State did not give up on anything that easily. But these were difficult times—she also didn't think that Renato was lying. His brother had somehow been let go before he died. She didn't believe the government had its act together on this. It hadn't done anything right in forty years, why start now?

They were letting Renato slack, pushing him out by not forcing him to follow any of the regulations. Or, or, she reasoned, he had become useless to them as a subject, too expensive as a mere patient. Special times, indeed.

A subject? I asked.

Who knows what tests they're conducting on them while they're all caged in there like lab rats? she said. Nicolás had been convinced that what was killing him was the experimental pills they were giving him and not the disease.

What a boon if the doctors from the socialist paradise discovered the cure to the plague. Using human test subjects if they had to.

I wouldn't put anything past these monsters, she added.

Bertila had offered Renato her home as shelter whenever he needed it, just as she had done with Nicolás when he absconded from the sanitarium. The last time Renato had visited he had the smell of the streets on him, reeked of rum, she informed me, which I found strange, because I had never found Renato in a situation where he could not wheedle himself into a room to spend the night and get paid for it at the same time.

He goes to that somewhere his brother went to die, Bertila said, some encampment of desvinculados and roqueros on the rooftop aeries of abandoned buildings on the southern purlieus of Havana. She knew this by the condition in which Renato arrived that last time. Same condition his brother returned to her sometimes.

Bertila had made him strip right in the middle of the kitchen and crouch in her tin tub while she washed the grime off him. The skin of his back was engraved with dirt, she had to scrub it with a brush. She lent him a robe and washed his clothes in the kitchen sink, hanging them on the line out her window to dry. Those four hours were the last he spent with her, this time keeping a distance from the clients who passed him on the way to the barber's chair, as he huddled in one corner of Bertila's bed, a pillow over his head. When his clothes were dry and he had napped for a few hours, he left without getting his hair done. He had told her that he would return with me.

Do you know where this place is—the aerie encampment?

She shook her head and turned away.

We'll do something, she said, grabbing me by the arm and leading me to the barber's chair, I don't want you going to that place. It was the death of his brother. ¡Ahí no se te ha perdido nada!

I could feel her fingers thinking as they massaged my head, testing out any knotty conceits they found there for resiliency by pressing them into my skull, pausing to reconsider at the crown and tracing their steps back to the base before starting again on a different route. By the time she had finished massaging my skull, she was muttering to herself.

What?

She lifted her hands from my shoulders and stepped back. Renato knows that the German is back? He says there's something not right with that man.

That's what he's running from?

One of the things, she responded. Probably. Who knows? He's probably running toward something, as well—don't discount that.

Even as I approached the gate of the sanitarium that day, I hadn't decided what I was going to tell Renato about Oliver, if anything.

After his surprise dinner appearance, Oliver had returned once to the paladar, but only to have a quick cafecito in the lull of the siesta hour and to tell me that he would have to travel to Varadero for a few days. He promised to make some time to see me when he returned.

Are you asking me out? I responded.

I want friends, he said.

Comandante Juan hadn't yet arrived that afternoon, and Cecilia was out searching for fresh produce, so I could sit and talk to Oliver alone. He made only a passing mention of Renato and of his previous dinner at the paladar—although Cecilia had received a brief professional note in fancy linen paper, thanking her for receiving him and for the authentic experience.

His forced familiarity felt unnatural now, maybe because comandante Juan wasn't there as a foil, but Oliver continued talking, making vague references to wanting to get to know me better after he had taken care of some other matters, which he remained hazy about. It may even be that he would go into business with all of us, he said. I told him that I was just an employee at the paladar. A nobody.

Ja, but that must change when I am involved. Young people

like you, you're the only future of this country. The old man—
He flicked his fingers, trying to remember the name.

Comandante Juan?

Ja, sí, the old comandante and the mother, they are the last
phase of an era, of this—your Revolución. He whispered the
word, either in ridicule or awe, I couldn't tell. You must know
that it has been a very noble experiment, but— He sipped
his cafecito and leaned back. What can I say? Things have to
change. And that, *mein Freund*, is where we come in.

Who's we? I asked, hoping none of the listless viejas of
the neighborhood Comité had their ears trained on us from the
adjoining patios.

Who do you think brought down the wall in my country?
Do you think it was Mr. Gorbachev or the old senile Reagan
with his cowboy speeches? I mean, you must know who,
physically, literally brought down the wall? Have you seen
the pictures?

A stupid question if you knew anything about our country.
Of course, no one had seen the pictures, or at least we weren't
supposed to admit to it to some foreigner. Oliver had made
initial contact with the revolutionary poli after we stole his
wallet. For some things the State didn't need the gossip of the
viejas. In the kitchen, Inocente St. Louis was busy preparing
stuff for dinner and either unaware of my visitor or, more
likely, had long ago decided that anything beyond the serving
line where he put out his exquisite dishes was none of his
business. To this day I cannot guess how Renato eventually
convinced him to join his group.

Oliver went on, unaware now that I was only paying half
attention to him, my eye on the gate, waiting for comandante
Juan to saunter in and catch us in the middle of our counterrevolutionary chat.

They are misleading, the pictures. The hordes of young

people dancing on top of the Brandenburg Gate those brilliant chilly November nights, while others chipped away at the wall beneath with picks and axes and meat cleavers. I was one of them, drunk for days, dancing and . . . fucking complete strangers . . . singando, you say, no? But you must know, it was a sturdy wall. It had to be. It withstood that party as it had withstood the other Party for decades. It was not till later, till the following summer when they brought all the demolition equipment to start tearing it down earnestly, uprooting its towers, its stumps, and making a ghost of even its shadow. But way before the wrecking balls, it was the ones that came after the party, we called them . . . how do you say? *Der Specht?* He tapped hard at the wooden table with the ends of his fingers. I told him in Spanish. *Ja,* los pájaros carpinteros (what a poetic language you have!), the carpenter birds, all spring and winter long they went at the wall. Maybe just looking for a brick or two as souvenirs, tourists from all over the world, foreigners not rebels, not those that had suffered its consequences, outsiders, but they turned it into rubble in places before the official demolition began in the summer. All because they wanted a memento of the world's most famous death strip to put up on their shelves, a relic of human misery to add to their collection.

He finished his coffee and I offered another one, but he had to be on his way. We must talk more. I sound too unruly now, no? He stood up and pulled out his wallet, I thought to pay so I told him he didn't have to, it was only a cafecito, but instead of money he pulled out a small, laminated stamp issued in the winter of 1970. It was a Cuban green woodpecker poking a ghostly branch. He thanked me for the coffee and left the stamp sitting on the table as he took his leave.

Bertila said that the morning that Renato had appeared drunk on her doorstep he had been mumbling something about the German when she bathed him, had told her a little bit of the story of the day we met him, of my adventure on the balcony, proud of how he had saved me.

Who was this German? she asked.

I told her what I knew. That I thought he was one of those metíos, meddling and overly curious foreigners that have nothing better to do with their lives than thinking they can make a difference. I leaned back in the chair and asked her what she could read about this foreigner in the growth patterns of my hair and the bumps on my skull. Bertila remained silent for a long time as she pulled out my tight curls, trimming the ends before she set in the color, digging with her nails into the topography of my cranium, which she insisted changed with our experiences ever so slightly, the bumps and missteps of our lives marked there. I asked her again, and she responded that she could read nothing about the foreigner but that it didn't mean that there wasn't something there. She was preoccupied with thoughts of Renato, and it clouded over her prophetic receptors. This was no good. She would cancel the rest of her appointments that afternoon. She would go with me to look for Renato.

I let her finish. I had been living under the impression that Bertila rarely left her apartment, that others always came to her. I had known her only from our monthly appointments, from her profession. I did not know the person behind this façade. I did not yet know of her amorous exploits.

After hours of wandering, in which I discovered how wrong I had been about my assumptions, how well she knew not only every street of the city, but also the unnamed and unmapped blind alleys, narrow inlets between buildings, abandoned lots, and desolate untended gardens, we nevertheless failed at our task. At the end of the day, when I left her in the kitchen of her apartment, grumbling at all the notes that desperate customers had slipped under her door, we were no closer to finding out where Renato was hiding than we had been six hours earlier when she colored my hair. But I knew why Nicolás had latched onto her when he saw her quietly praying in the church that morning. Oliver was wrong, young people weren't the future of the Island, old Bertila was.

She was already living in it.

THE CAPACITY OF WANT

Fidel Castro does not exist.

For a Cuban to say that, wherever she was standing on the face of the earth in the summer of 1997, was like a fish saying water does not exist, or the moon saying the sun does not exist, or the Pope questioning the validity of the Holy Trinity, but that's the first thing that Bertila said when we stepped out of her apartment, and not in a whisper, either.

She had asked for a moment to change her clothes, while I waited for her in the kitchen, and when she came in a few minutes later I asked her if we were going to a wedding, for she was that transformed. Her dye-stained apron and house-dress gone. Now, she wore a loose long black silk top and a bright printed blouse, the colorful handkerchief on her head replaced with a shoulder-length red wig and her fleshy face so delicately made up, the paint inventing angles that weren't there before, that she seemed a decade younger. A dainty church lady's purse, her arm just barely squeezed through its straps up to the elbow, and a regal dark linen mantle, completed the ensemble. This is the way she appeared to Nicolás in his story, I thought. It surprised me that she remained barefoot, but she said that she had stopped destroying shoes with her plowman's feet long ago.

This is the way we must behave from here on, she continued, a way of getting ready for the inevitable. And she repeated it, just in case I had not heard her the first time. Fidel Castro does not exist. Or will not very soon. He's as good as dead.

But he will always exist, I said, possibly even more after he dies. Maybe it's better to do all we can to keep him alive, no?

The thing that we Cubans feared more than anything else was the death of El Líder, not because we loved him that much (although some of us certainly pretended), but that when he died we would have to create a living myth out of him or the Island would implode from lack of leadership.

He will not live past the Visit, Bertila asserted, and made a complicated sign of the cross that worked its way down from her forehead to her solar plexus in miniature crosses with a larger cross superimposed over them afterward. Why do you think he has accepted? She stopped walking and turned to look at me. At first, I didn't even know what the question referred to. Penance, she said. Ah sí, why Fidel had allowed the Visit.

The Visit was the one-word catchphrase for the expected arrival of Pope John Paul II the following year. Many still said that it was a rumor, that something would happen at the last minute to allow Fidel to cancel it, that he was using the possibility of it to lull traitors out of their nests with their signatures and addresses on petitions for a more open rule. Then he would do one of his roundups-slash-purges, the list in hand.

More than once, these people had come to the paladar, posing as tourists, ordering from the menu and chatting in English about the sights of the capital. They would wait until the restaurant reached full capacity, then they would leap from their tables and announce to the entire clientele their objectives for a free and democratic Cuba, asserting that they had come here for the signatures of the proprietor and her workers, a petition of the demands to present to the Party Congress in October, that the Island would never be free until the people presented their case to the State. The tourists enjoyed it all very much, to some of them, I thought—as we stood back and watched the show, all of us except Inocente St. Louis, who grumbled from the kitchen that his plates didn't care about revolutions or counterrevolutions or any other political mierda—it was some kind of entertainment dramatized exclusively for them. These protestors never got any signatures from us. Comandante Juan politely led them out, one hand on his useless rusty pistol.

But there were hundreds of signatures and addresses on the lists that they pulled out from their shopping bags. Many had signed, exposing themselves in the worst way imaginable, as comandante Juan, the grandmaster of political camouflage, would put it. The old senile Pope used as a pawn just like a bucketful of American senators and representatives had always been used. Even if by some miracle the Pope did set foot in Cuba, somehow Fidel would turn it to his benefit before his Revolución suffered even a lost eyelash. But there were others who were beginning to envision a turning point with the Visit—it had happened in Poland. Who remembered the name of the last communist ruler of Poland now, a mere decade later? Bertila said. He didn't exist. The Pope and the millions who gathered at his Masses existed, in farms and little villages, people appeared as if they hadn't seen the light of day in years, in their potato-colored outfits, creating the impression that they had been living under the earth and had been summoned forth.

The sad truth would become evident that brilliant January morning when the hunched-over Pope stepped out of his plane at José Martí International Airport, Fidel waiting for him in the dark suit that he had begun to wear for State occasions, erect and virile, and though they were about the same age, one could have been the other's father. No government newspaper mentioned this physical disparity.

That was in the future, when my search for Renato had become part of what turned into the kind of national spectacle that no government journalist dared whisper about. By then, the only way the State could know for sure that Renato himself existed was by the signs he and his cohorts left behind, dead pigeons and miniature graffiti art on the walls and sidewalks of the capital.

But there was as little basis to question Renato's existence that afternoon with Bertila as there was to question Fidel's.

Where're we going? I said as we wandered down byways and streets wholly foreign to me even though I had the audacity to consider myself as much a habanero as any native.

She walked at a clipped pace for a person who lumbered, leaning on walls, from one end to the other of her apartment, now one hand clutching tight to her miniature purse, the other gesturing ahead, down the block, so that she was always around a corner ahead of me no matter how fast I walked. More than once we ran into folks from the neighborhood that wanted to set up appointments. They grasped the necks of their children and bowed their unwashed heads toward her so that she could offer a reading on the spot, then I caught up with her. But just as soon, she traipsed off again.

The path from her apartment on Calle Inquisidor to La Catedral de San Cristóbal could be traveled in the space of fifteen or twenty minutes, but it was over an hour before we arrived at the square, crossed to Calle San Ignacio on its west end and entered a dimly lit chapel on one side of the church. Penance, Bertila repeated the word, now in a whisper, pulling out a hanky from her tiny purse, wiping her brow and covering her mouth with it. Why else?

We sat in one of the pews. Or I sat, Bertila knelt and dug a wooden rosary out of her purse, stuffing the dampened handkerchief back inside. I stared at the sooty statues, at the rows of small metal enclosures lit up with votive candles, like miniature dollhouses ablaze. I have never understood the concept of faith, of lighting fire to gods, of praying, particularly, though I had seen my abuela Puebla, the woman who raised me, and the handful of devout in my town do it before in the abandoned Church of Nazarene in my hometown, just as Bertila was now doing.

Pero vaya, I've always associated prayer with a sort of weakness, of woundedness, of servility. A fire that humans give away to the gods for nothing in return. Though Abuela Puebla had always been quick to point out that it was the archbishop of Santiago who had saved Fidel when he had been captured on the failed attack on a government armory. Without the archbishop, no pardon, no Fidel in Mexico, no Che, no leaky *Granma* boat sneaking the rebels home, no Revolución.

I had never seen Bertila this way; in prayer, she seemed to close herself off, create a seal that seemed irreverent to break. It made her willfully alone. I sat by her and started thinking again about how to break into the sanitarium, forgetting about Bertila's fantastic pronouncements and thinking of more realistic strategies for finding Renato. But she wasn't going to let go of me so easily. She soon stood with a theatrical effort, leaning so hard on the pew in front of us that it tilted forward.

We made our way out of the chapel, circling streets again. It was as if Bertila metamorphosed into someone else through her wanderings, shedding the layers of her prophetess persona in mad circles farther and farther from her neighborhood. At the chapel, the two or three other ladies had briefly glanced up at us and nodded but none of them approached her as strangers had in her immediate neighborhood. Here she had become an unknown. As we headed toward the government buildings near the Capitolio, the more famous parts of the city, no one even looked at us. We veered back toward the Prado and began heading for the sea. After a few blocks, Bertila put a hand on me, breathing heavily, and said she had to rest. She set her prim purse on her lap and told me to keep an eye on the people passing by us—I thought because she was afraid that we would be cited for loitering or miss Renato.

What do you see?

People. Walking? Not Renato.

I'm not here, she said, her eyes closed. You are not here. She emphasized each word, an almost trancelike cadence.

What?

And neither is Renato.

She let me stew in my confusion for a while.

What did I see? Or whom? People walking. Mostly tourists, easily spotted by the hang of the clothes on their bodies, not necessarily the quality, just the position, the wearer's relation to them. If you take the exact same yanqui jeans or fine linen shirts or Bermuda shorts and see them on a Yuma and then on a cubano you would know what I mean.

The first wears it almost forgetfully, something that he grabbed out of a drawer or pulled from a hanger where there were perhaps a dozen more like them, a whole fraternity, and will no more be missed in its place than a bucket of sand scooped from Varadero beach; it hangs on the wearer almost as if it is not there, because in a sense it's not. The wearer has no awareness of it; if you asked him to close his eyes and tell you exactly what he wore, the color, the fabric, the number of pockets and so forth, he wouldn't be able to do it, not even close.

This is the ignorance of plenty.

On the second person, on the cubano, the same piece of clothing leaves a void from where it was pulled, and this energy transfers to the wearer with a magnetic force—the thing clings to him unnaturally, partly because he can feel almost every fiber of it with the nerve endings on his skin; and he knows it—this specific article of clothing—almost as if it were a living thing, as if it were an old lover, or a patch of grafted skin that were it to be ripped from him, would cause intense and deep-rooted agony; if you were to ask this hexed soul what he wore you would get not only an exact description down to its most recent wrinkle, its most faded stain, but also a convoluted story of what cousin or pariente sent it or left it for him, and a day-by-day accounting of its worn life.

This is the capacity of want.

Y vaya, though I am not really thinking this as I separate the tourists from the natives, to a cubano, noticing such distinctions comes almost as effortlessly as reading.

What do I see?

Tourists. Mostly tourists, the most famous boulevard in Cuba is full of tourists. ¿Pero y qué? Hasn't that always been the case?

Not always, but make sure you know what you're seeing. She made me count aloud, keeping score on either hand five by five, and I was surprised that the Yuma did not outnumber the natives by all that much. In fact, somewhere in the middle of my counting, as a group of six women passed by, the two old grandmothers with canes ahead and the middle-aged daughters following behind, scrutinizing, on the lookout for something, their own daughters in their brown school minifaldas right behind them, oblivious to their elders, holding tight to their books and chattering with each other, the cubanos took the lead, and a little nationalistic pride swelled in me as if it were a maldito beisbol game or something. As I continued to count, the natives took a commanding lead.

Bertila wore a ready smile. The mottled sunlight airily falling on her lifted little patches of paint from her face so that they hovered just above the surface of her pockmarked skin. She looked like a painting, a ghostly mask, beatific.

I told her that I was wrong, mostly cubanos. So what? She told me to look again without counting, but to pay attention to what was happening this time, and sure enough, the cubanos seemed to disappear, fade into the background, and I only saw Yuma, my eyes hardwired for this, my compatriots fading into the background as if they existed on another plane, a hazier film strip on which the prominent Yuma were superimposed.

I waited quietly for an explanation—sensing that Bertila knew what had just happened, that she could see more with her eyes closed than most people could see with them wide open.

Así es, she finally said, we are existing less and less. One day not too far into the future, she went on, you'll be able to sit on this exact bench and not see the cubanos at all, no matter by how many they outnumber the visitors. We're becoming a nation of ghosts. She picked out a young woman chatting with a pair of foreign college students, a vampiric smile in her face, the two boys at once repelled—shifting their upper bodies away, their faces slightly turned, maybe her very breath offending them—and captivated, their feet glued in place, their groins thrust forward, their eyes nailed on the low cut of her blouse.

Why did I think that Fidel hated tourists so much? Because

it is the only way that his people can survive. Now it's all he has to offer, and he was slowly becoming the biggest ghost of all.

Ghosts exist, I ventured, watching her phantom face that now seemed to have lifted even higher above her flesh, every detail shadowed into miniature chasms. She straightened, and the illusion of the broken light quickly settled into the sad mask that she had painted on, now seeming an inch thick.

We weren't going to find him, she announced, bolting up so fast she lost hold of her purse. I picked it up and handed it to her. It felt empty. This wasn't a good sign, she said. He had made his way far from the city. Horrible things must be afoot, and he was either trying to escape responsibility for them by seeking refuge in this village in the air where his brother had died, or he went to plot those things from there.

What things?

His head becomes infected with his brother's delusions, always has. We're not going to find him, not until he wants to be found.

Right then, it dawned on me that she was keeping things from me, that she had been doing so all afternoon, that this whole excursion, her little counting game had been a ruse to distract me. Or maybe not a ruse, maybe to teach me a hard lesson that she could not get across any other way. I would never really find the Renato I had known for the last eighteen months again no matter how hard I looked. He had crossed some threshold. Become a ghost not as we were imagining in the eyes of his own countryfolk but a ghost as in the eyes of the State. And the State did not tolerate such hobgoblins.

The only way I would ever find him would be by doing the same.

II

What is the malaise? you ask. The malaise is the pain of loss. The world is lost to you, the world and the people in it, and there remains only you and the world and you no more able to be in the world than Banquo's ghost.

Walker Percy
The Moviegoer

TWO FILMS

In the summers of 1994 and 1995, two films by the renowned director and proclaimed defender of la Revolución, Alejandro Tomás Gutierrez, were shown in my hometown of Baracoa and convinced me to leave it forever. The first one, *La rebelión y la paz,* I had to sneak into because Abuela Puebla, who knows how—by then she was on her deathbed, inanimate the daylong, had two of her older sons twice prevent me from entering the theater.

It was a rather ordinary película about a young well-bred pato, a photographer who falls in love with a hardline communist, a soldado (the *rebelión* of the title) who just happens to be monitoring him for counterrevolutionary activities, and through various travails, they come to an understanding of each other and establish what can be finally accepted as a devoted, if still tenuous, friendship (the *paz*). There is the requisite santera also, as there has to be in any Cuban story—one of the divas of Cuban cinema, who also happened to be married to the director, though I can't remember her name.

Most of the tension in the film comes from the way the camera lingers on the body of the tall dark communist, catching him from almost every angle, even in the quotidian minutiae of folding his undershirts.

The second movie is perhaps more memorable. *La última aria* features a main character, a true diva, who drops dead during an aria, center stage in el Gran Teatro de la Habana, minutes into the film. We never see her again. The entire movie is the corpse's trip back to her hometown east in Oriente, to a plot beside the boy she had loved as a girl and who had died of dysentery as a teen—all this as expressed in her last will and testament—through the labyrinth of the communist bureaucracy and in spite of the insatiable sexual appetite of the young stud, who is a civil servant by day and black-market fruit-truck driver by night, put in charge of the mission. The role played by the same actor that played the pato photographer, now almost unrecognizable as the prototype of raw Cuban machismo.

The truth is—and I was only able to put this together later, after watching both movies more than three times with Nicolás in the capital—it was the only thing playing those days. This was after I had begun to feel at home with Cecilia and the Zúñiga brothers, long after the films had touched some primal nerve in me to abandon the grooved life that my schoolmasters and my dying abuela Puebla had set me on, to become something, something not necessarily better but other than that. Both of these films are broad and ballsy swipes at the troubles the Island faced during the special period after the collapse of the Soviet Union and the disappearance of subsidies. But in the end, they settle for a bland, if hilarious, sentimentality about the hardy good-heartedness of cubanos; both the committed revolutionaries and the counterrevolutionaries have the best intentions at heart, and everyone is just making do, trying to be happy, even the dead. Nicolás hated that, but he was obsessed with hating it, and kept returning to see the first movie only to denigrate it.

He was right to be indignant, even if at the time I told him it was no use to get so worked up over a movie. In the real world, things were much more tedious and demoralizing than in the comic world of the films, as our daily coveted life serving tourists taught me, which Nicolás and Renato from the first saw clearly for the denigration that it was, and the rest of us—their mother, comandante Juan, Inocente St. Louis, and me—saw as a blessing—a way to make a living unavailable to thousands of others, certainly not where I had come from. Yet, the brothers mocked my prized skills with the Yuma mercilessly, their derision in barely veiled questions. Was this really why I had absconded to the capital? Wouldn't I have just been better off as a good little revolutionary back in my pueblo?

There is a scene in *La rebelión y la paz* where the photographer and the santera invite the handsome communist to one of their shared dinners. He agrees to go only because of his sense of duty. It's rumored that many in the capital are now feasting on stray cats, which have in their migratory nocturnal lives sharpened their vision to an extent that those who consume their flesh are said to acquire the power of momentary clairvoyance, long enough perhaps to foretell the numbers in the illegal juegos de númeritos, the black market lottery. The communist, claro, sees it as his duty to uproot this sort of counterrevolutionary activity, for la Revolución cares about its stray cats, too, but only if they are complicit in any counterrevolutionary mierda. So we are treated to a scene rife with confusion about the served meats that ends up with the communist's gorgeous head in a toilet bowl, with the photographer and the santera gleefully at his side, patting his neck and cheeks with a damp cloth. Their chatter about the quality of the chicken meat they bought through la bolsa only serves to induce more violent retching from the helplessly gorgeous macho, who looks like an exquisite headless condemned soul from the camera that watches the scene kneeling behind them, both the photographer's and the santera's free hands inching down his sweaty back to his perfectly round nalgas. It is a critique of the economic and political system any way you look at it, but it's also a comic celebration of the cubano's ability to be human above anything else, to cast away politics for more pertinent needs, the visceral revulsion of certain types of food, the allure of a perfect set of nalgas. In *La última aria* the diva gets her wish after all and lies in eternity with her first love, those left alive in the devastated Island the butt of the comedy after all.

What all this misses (o vaya, likely leaves out on purpose) is the flip side of the mask, the unfilmable desolation that is the better part of day-to-day survival on the Island and that with its infernal trickle carves away at our stalwart souls, a tedium that begins from a day before you even learn how to read, to make sense of reality, and don your first pionero's hanky. The farce of some of the outrageous things that we have to do to *resolver*, to live on, is nothing compared to this, a mere sideshow, an afternoon's entertainment that stringed one after the other can make for a tolerable comedy. But let the camera linger for a moment on that hilarious santera with her stale breath as she kisses her first Yuma that night, on the photographer's toilet when he sits down later that evening to masturbate thinking about the man who is his oppressor, on the petrified eyes of the civil servant's wife, whose husband has surrendered the best of his nature to a fleshless cause. Not much of an international sensation there for the critics, not much of a story at all. So it hasn't been filmed, it won't be written. We survive though, and the valor of our survival is pulverized into folly for the world to see and marvel at and label our great humanity.

But in mid-summer of 1997, a year and a half after I had arrived with Nicolás at Cecilia's house on Calle Obispo, it seemed for a moment as if his tame comical vision of our quotidian world might vanish forever—in the early hours of a breezy July day, a bomb went off at one of the inner patios of one of the busiest tourist hotels in the Vedado district, killing, the government newspaper *Granma* said, an Italian tourist.

THE LONG SUMMER
OF THE BOMBS

This became the first of over a dozen bombs that went off in the capital during the late summer and into the end of the rainy season in November. The explosions occurred mostly in tourist areas, hotel lobbies, across the streets from nightclubs, beach cabanas, all of them in the hours before dawn, to ensure, it seemed, the least number of casualties. After the first round of bombings, the Italian tourist remained the only casualty, although a pair of unlucky, early-riser fishermen catapulted into the sea by an explosive between the Malecón and another hotel suffered critical injuries. A body count could not have been the objective. In fact, it seemed as if almost the opposite were the purpose. The only bodies were those of the more languid pigeons. This meant to sound an alarm by only suggesting the danger, the locations and times chosen specifically with two things in mind: usually crowded Yuma areas but during their only tranquil moments of the day. Someone wanted to change the tone of the national conversation, away from the collective sacrifice required in the special period to a more dangerous possibility, that the sacrifice and the hypocrisy of getting our souls besmirched with the influx of foreign imperialists would not be worth it.

But no one knew at first who that someone that wanted a new conversation could be. In fact, no one ever took responsibility for any of the bombs. Even long after. Yet a mere five months before the world would train its curious eyes on the Island for the Visit of the stooping drooling pontiff, trips from the outside world were suddenly canceled or rescheduled, departments of state across the American hemisphere and Europe issued travel warnings, and revenue from the golden tourism faucet that had meant to replace Soviet subsidies dwindled to a trickle. The Party immediately assumed the bombings to be a covert attack devised by the yanquis in cahoots with the Miami Mafia or vice versa. These terrorist acts had been encouraged, organized, and supplied—both in terms of material and personnel—from within United States territory, the Interior Ministry proclaimed in an official statement.

In protest, dozens of student marches through the first three bomb sites arose spontaneously from the people, according to *Granma,* although schools had been officially closed and students mandated to generate such spontaneity. A memorial service, equally spontaneous, took place in front of the Hotel Nacional where the Italian tourist, a Canadian resident who had been going out for an early morning jog and stretching in the inner courtyard, according to his traveling-companion father, had been killed. The two injured local fishermen, according to some official reports second cousins, and to el chisme in the street homosexual lovers, became national heroes and appeared on television stations denouncing the foreign terrorists. But the bombs continued, every other week or every third week and, one Friday in September, twice on the same day, devastating prospects for the beginning of the busy tourist season in November.

At home, comandante Juan put a padlock on the entrance gate to the paladar, which he locked from the outside every night when leaving, so that anyone who came in and out during the off hours had to pass through the house. He might as well have kept the padlock on at all times because our business all but disappeared. One or two parties straggled in every night and were treated like royalty. A bad late summer to be in the Yuma *bisnes* and a horrible sign for the coming season.

Inocente St. Louis grew increasingly impatient with nothing to do in the kitchen but play with eating the fires under the empty cast iron pans that comandante Juan had procured in the black market. The giant chef disappeared at first for hours at a time, returning as if he had just been outside having a smoke, Cecilia on the grill, cooking for whatever brave stragglers had come in. He shoved her over with a hip and took over, enlivened. But soon he began to disappear for days at a time, returning only for an hour or two and not even going near the grill. It was as if when he didn't have three fires going on in front of him at one time, other more dangerous fires began to sizzle inside him.

Perhaps we should have read something not in his disappearance, but before that, in his unwillingness to socialize with the rest of us, an unwillingness that was matched in the house on Calle Obispo only by the two brothers. Comandante Juan said he would go looking for him but soon realized that none of us knew where he lived, and we knew very little about him except for his talent with the fires and the identity of his novia. Because he could eat and spit fires in the kitchen— comandante Juan called this a counterrevolutionary talent before we could guess how much that might matter later. The chef would perform his fire-eating rituals for the amusement of the clientele even as he prepared their dishes. When the chef vanished, Cecilia took over the kitchen duties, not that there was really anything for her to do. At first, most of our produce was used to prepare lavish after-hour dinners for the ladies of the Comité. But soon, there was not enough cash in hand to supply the paladar, and we had to shut down for over a month right in the beginning of the busy season.

Agents from the Dirección General de la Inteligencia, the Directorate, the most feared branch of the Ministry of the Interior, raided the homes of suspected subversives. The protest signatures collected to present to the Party Congress in October had been sought out and confiscated, put to good use after all: hundreds of signatories taken in for questioning as suspects in the bombings. Some never returned to whatever domestic tedium they had left behind to accompany the compañeros from the Ministry, or so comandante Juan recounted. In their slippers and pajamas and camisetas, all these foolish signatories disappeared.

By October, a week before the Party Congress, three months before the Visit, the inscrutable flint-hearted agents from the Directorate began to grow anxious. They needed to make an arrest and stop the bombings or there would be no Visit, and without the Yuma, the battered economy would plunge the country into chaos. The Visitor would be coming to a war zone.

Throughout the long, listless days of the end of that rainy season as one bomb went off after another, I began to suffer from the sensation that no one could understand what I was saying. The few people I saw, the diners at the paladar that wanted to avoid hotel restaurants or in my increasingly long investigative peregrinations through the old city, either constantly asked me to repeat myself or simply continued whatever they were doing, making me feel like a bird, my incomprehensible cawing like a yearning that could not be expressed.

Maybe it was, I thought, because I had no one to talk to that summer aside from Cecilia, and by that time—working together in close tandem five days a week and rarely outside of each other's proximity, except when we slept or on the Friday nights I went to see Renato—we communicated mostly in the cropped language, coded gestures, and allusive grunts of long-married couples. With the disappearance of Renato, I feared that I would forget how to relate to anyone other than the only person left in the house on Calle Obispo.

Twice I went to Bertila's apartment to see if Renato had returned to her, but for the first time since Nicolás had brought me there to meet her, Bertila was not home or would not answer. Could she have been rounded up in the massive purge of subversives and signatories? Had they taken Inocente St. Louis, too, caught in the middle of one of his amorous marathons with the hairdresser?

The fourth time I went to Bertila's and got no answer, I sought out some of her roquero clients who loitered in the neighborhood or by the Malecón and Parque Lenin at nights. I explained that I was looking for the prophet of hair, that she hadn't been answering her door for weeks now. Could she have been rounded up? Could she be dead and rotting in her barber's chair? I asked if they knew her novio, the tall Haitian.

The roqueros worked their jaws back and forth, rubbing their bearded chins, then said they had no idea what I was talking about, socio, though many times I had passed them going up and down the crumbling stone stairway to Bertila's apartment. They knew me.

With the roundups this was the natural survival adaptation of this group: talk to no one, know nothing, admit less. After Nicolás's death I had become a stranger to them, an outsider—or worse, they might have thought that I had become a chivato, reporting to the ladies of the Comité or to the Directorate. I tried with others in the neighborhood— shop owners, housewives, even the local Comité—but no one knew anything about Bertila or her giant novio. Most pretended that I was some houseless beggar asking for food and made as if they could not understand me at all. After days of this, I stopped searching. There were more important things to worry about than whether others could decipher my frenzied chatter. Days to make it through. At first, no one knew if and when the bombings would intensify, begin to proliferate past the predawn hours, target others than the Yuma. For the moment though, there seemed a way to avoid it.

So even natives took their time getting out of bed, exercised a monkish patience at the breakfast table, even Cecilia, whom I rarely saw previously in the mornings, too busy making the rounds with her group of black-market merchants. Comandante Juan insisted on doing this on his own now, even as he tried to keep up the façade that everything would soon return to normal. Cecilia consented and put off going out, waiting instead for me to awake, seated under the avocado tree with the reheated leftovers from the night-before's impromptu dinner for the ladies of the Comité. She was the only who had no trouble understanding me. So that when I began speaking loud and obnoxiously, underlining each syllable with a harsh tone, as I had done in my fruitless search for Bertila, she rebuked me.

Why are you yelling again?

I couldn't respond, couldn't tell her what I had been doing all those days wandering around the old city for fear that she, like the others, would pretend not to know me, for fear that she would begin to grill me about the whereabouts of her son. So she came up with all sorts of answers for her own question. There must have been explosions in my dreams. But then why spend all day out there where real bombs are going off? she chastised. Why go chasing your nightmares when wide awake? Or maybe I was angry, convinced that she was going to fire me and put me out in the danger zone due to the lack of customers—my peregrinations preempting her unmerited cruelty. Or I was going morningdeaf to not have to hear the real explosions—till one morning I finally explained my predicament. No one could understand me. At times, my thoughts even felt like gibberish. My intentions like a broken convocation of fireworks (which is what many hoped at first the bombs were), misdirected all over the place, buried in the ground before taking flight.

I had forgotten why I had come to the capital.

The whole city is going purposefully deaf, Cecilia explained. It's not just you.

Eventually, there was no reason for her to go out in the morning at all. There was no one to buy food for except us. So our mornings were spent under the avocado tree, sipping bottomless cups of her sugar-whipped cafecitos.

Since she had decided that she couldn't stand going to the rocky beach in Cójimar on Mondays anymore, and there were no customers to tend to, Cecilia challenged me to be with her in a different way. We could invent our own family.

Your idea of family is not some cause like it has always been for the Zúñiga men. Right? And look what that has gotten them. There are other ways to live.

It's not just the Zúñigas, I corrected her, it's all men in this country. You have Juan, pues. You don't really need me for your family.

When she promised me in a hundred indirect ways that I would always have a bed and a meal in her house—as if that had to be enough—or our house, as she took to calling it the rest of the summer of the bombs after this conversation, I realized that perhaps I had not fully understood the terms of our relationship. We didn't have to sneak around anymore, she said, whispering to each other like schoolgirls so that comandante Juan and Inocente St. Louis couldn't hear us. In truth, it felt as if the whole summer had become a parade of our barren Mondays banded together.

Resigned to this, in essence, trapped in the house in Calle Obispo after a second wave of bombings, we did what any two people who are forced to spend time with each other, who are supposed to be intimate—close in all ways but sexual, although even that seemed to be pushed to the precipice at times—but have little or no basis for it, do: we spent hours reinventing our parceled history with each other.

Did I know, for example, Cecilia said one morning, that she was genuinely frightened on the early evening that I appeared on her doorstep with Nicolás, hand in hand. Imagínate her astonishment. For one, that her son found it necessary to announce his arrival by knocking. And two, that he had brought one of his little putas with him. Perdóname, Cecilia said, laughing as she got up to pour me another cup of cafe-cito. Bueno, Nicolás had never done that! Brought *someone.* Cecilia had not seen him in weeks. Those days, he disappeared for weeks, and came in and out of that house—or the henhouse to be more precise, where he had transferred all his belongings, stuffed into burlap sacks that he hung from hooks in the tin ceiling so the chickens couldn't get at them, and slept inside an old rowboat that he must have stolen from the marina where he sometimes worked—like some phantom.

Nicolás introduced me as her new waiter and left me there alone in the parlor with her. Freed of his grip, I immediately made a move as if to go. Maybe I could run and catch up to the Spanish couple, and they would take mercy on me for the night. But Cecilia closed the mesquite door and apologized for her son's rudeness.

What was I to do? she said. Turn you out into the street? She thought about doing just that, claro, letting me disappear into the shadows of Calle Obispo, but some vestige of courtesy, or maybe pity, at the look of a fur-knotted tomcat that I presented, let her deduce, rightly, that I hadn't eaten a good meal in months.

The first customers were just arriving in the paladar, and she sat me at one of the tables, brought me a moist cloth to wash my hands. She brought me a Coca-Cola, or what we called Coca-Cola, dangerously sweetened carbonated water colored with something. She still had not said a word. As I ate whatever was set in front of me without much bothering to taste it or figure out what it was, Cecilia knocked patiently on the wobbly door of the henhouse, another plate in hand, only to be rebuffed by a dismissive grunt from inside. She then set the plate down on my table and informed me that she had another son, and that perhaps he would deign to join me.

She had no time to sit and chitchat with me, for the paladar was soon bustling with customers, and she shuffled back and forth between tables and the kitchen with such agility I thought there might be a twin sister. At some point, the man who was in charge of seating the guests, greasy-faced, potbellied, in an old Revolutionary Army uniform and as leaden in his movements as Cecilia was swift, came over to my table and picked up the plate of cold food that belonged to Cecilia's other son and solemnly set it in front of me, announcing that neither of her sons had eaten a morsel of food in years, that they subsisted on air like some malignant breed of orchids. After I was finished, I could decide whether I wanted my new job or not, he announced.

No te creas, Cecilia confessed at our breakfast table the late summer of the bombings, comandante Juan liked you right away. He saw that streak of the laborer in you, she said, something that was blissfully absent in Cecilia's two sons, who would rather starve on principle than put in a good day's work, who had become obsessed with perfecting the dangerous art of la nada, their little charade against revolutionary society. Hire him, he whispered to Cecilia on one of her passes through the dining patio. He's hungry. Cecilia said that she had planned to feed me and send me on my way. She couldn't afford another mouth to feed, another boyheadache, particularly not one that belonged to Nicolás's band of grifters.

So what convinced her? She had never told me any of this. I had always thought that it had been her choice, that I had been left sitting there at the table, long after I had sipped far too much sweetened soda water, and they had retreated to one corner of the patio, partly blocked from my sight by the back wall of the henhouse, because *she* had to convince *him*.

She came to me in the end, with what I thought to have been the exhaustion of a night's work, but was more likely I now realized the vexation of having to negotiate who can and cannot stay in her own house. She announced she would show me where I could wash and sleep, and then guided me to an upstairs bedroom with an adjoining bath, where she filled the bathtub with a puddle's worth of cold water, and then reaffixed the faucet handles with a bar that locked them shut. She left the room and returned with a clean set of clothes, a pair of jeans and a T-shirt that she unfolded and hung alongside me to make sure they fit. Tomorrow I would be trained as a waiter for the paladar, she said as she handed me a pebble of small soap in a hotel wrapper from a basket overflowing with them, if that's still what I wanted.

Like I had a choice, I said. There you left me, knowing the mad boy in the attic wouldn't be able to resist investigating who the hell his mother had stolen his clothes for.

I undressed, not really knowing what else to do, planning

to scrub myself, put on the new clothes, stuff my pockets with some of the pieces of soap, and get the hell out of there.

Claro, Cecilia said, I guess in some way I did know. Maybe down deep I fantasized that Juan was right: you would help with the boys, lead them by example.

She paused. Forced a woeful smile. Not hasten their departure.

She walked away from the table, disappeared into the house. We did not as much as talk to each other the rest of the day, except when I peeked into her room and asked her if she wanted to prepare something for dinner. She seemed startled, went down to the kitchen, prepared a meal for both of us, and left mine on one of the three tables still set up in the paladar in case any brave Yuma strolled in. If that was the case, she said, tonight they were all mine to care for. She took her dish up to her room, and I did not see here until the following morning.

When I awoke, she had already prepared our breakfast and cafecito.

She apologized for what she had said at the end of our conversation the morning before.

You shouldn't listen to my locuras. It's . . . I just don't know what we're going to do if this continues. I shouldn't take it out on you.

She caressed my cheek, added that we should talk about happier times.

What, she wanted to know, now as talkative as she had been the morning before, did I think of her younger son when I first saw him?

Renato had knocked lightly on the bathroom door after Cecilia had left me alone but had not waited for a response. This was the first time I had told Cecilia about that part of the night. He came in, closed the door, pulled down his pants, and sat down on the toilet before he looked at me. A loud gush of urine and a fart caused him to smile obscenely—his two front teeth jutted out slightly, like a set of jammed doors, but otherwise he remained expressionless. I was a cockroach drowned on the surface of the bathwater he watched peripherally. He stood up, pulled up his pants languidly, sat back down on the toilet before he reached back and flushed, but thought better of it and continued his side-glance scrutiny of the dead insect in the tub. He told me, unprompted, that he always sat down to take a piss—it was one of his mother's rules. His dick was pierced and urine splattered all over the place. He pulled it out and showed me.

Was I the new boyfriend? he asked. I could wear his clothes, sin problema, he was just asking.

He spoke like he had just met me at some bar and not burst in on me in the middle of my bath. At first, I was too taken aback by his intrusion. But now I looked at him, probed back. He was wearing the same kind of jeans that his mother had brought for me, the kind Yuma wear, rather new but beaten up a little bit at the factory so that they seemed weathered, a camiseta that was two sizes too big for him and that he had rolled up and tied at the belly button when he sat down to take a piss, and leather-soled chancletas.

He was shorter than his brother, and more filled out, a lamina of baby fat softening the features on his face but not quite masking his budding athlete's build. The battalion of tattoos that in less than a year and a half would stake claim to most of his torso had already begun to make its appearance on his upper arms and in thorny bracelets around his wrists, but they were meek heralds. His high-pitched voice, the greasy baseball cap that he wore over the back of his skull with the brim pointed heavenward, and patches of acne around his temples and under the rim of the jaw made him look younger than I knew he was, around my age. He pulled back, looked away, and smiled again, a demure smile, but not from modesty, I thought. My nakedness seemed to cause no more discomfort in him than the nakedness of an animal. I wanted him to stay.

Why? Cecilia asked. You wanted to fuck him, too? Both my babies lusted after in one day, coño?

No, it wasn't that. I lusted plenty after her older son, even when every part of me wanted not to. Not Renato. He was too much, something, too much a kid, a little rebellious boy. But Renato convinced himself that I had stayed that first night because I had been lightning-struck, pierced right through the guts by the sight of him. He could smell it on me, he said, the musty, faintly offensive smell of unrequited desire. I could refute it; for one because the cold clinical way that he showed me his dick, the way he would always do it, holding it cupped in one hand like a comatose rodent, registered as a gesture that precluded desire, turned off my sensors. I wanted him to stay because he seemed to be the first one in the family who seemed interested in me for no apparent reason.

He was awfully lonely, you know, Cecilia interrupted me. After his father left, and his brother started disappearing for weeks. Renato's friends had always been his older brother's friends. Though three years younger, he had pushed himself and excelled just for that, to be nearer his brother, moving up one grade and then another one, enrolling in the prestigious Lenin High School, until eventually, before they both decided to run afoul of State truancy laws and stopped attending school altogether, they were in the same grade.

Renato, though, was different than his brother and his compadres, most blatantly in that he had been an ideal student of la Revolución, a model pionero and leader in his Communist Youth League, something that for all his efforts to be among his brother's gang, he paid for dearly by being the butt of all their barely disguised rage at the system. He realized that if there were ever a chance that he would be treated as one of them, he would have to abandon the system just as they had. He would have been better off if he had stayed a proper revolucionario, moved up through the labyrinthine bureaucracy just like his father had done, Cecilia admitted, no matter that in all the years of growing up she saw how his heart was not in it, how he was just doing it to impress his father, and then, after Pascual disappeared, because so many of his days past had already been committed to it.

One evening, Renato's mealtime socialist lectures and parroted speeches had just gone dry. He came down from his room, not in the crisp khaki uniform of the Communist Youth League, but naked as a jinetera at an orgy, and sat down at one of the three dinner tables that then surrounded the avocado tree.

Like now, Cecilia explained, there were almost no customers. Back then, paladars were not yet legal, but many houses served dinners to la Yuma clandestinely, for a small charge.

He took his usual place at the table, next to his brother's empty spot, and did not look up till after he had taken three bites from the avocado with mojo salad that I served nightly. Juan told our guests that the fruit grew from the very tree under which they were eating, the thing producing just ripe fruit all year long in the Yuma imagination, vaya.

Cecilia let out a chortle. Who knew back then it would come to serve them so well, the three little tables, multiplying, spreading out from under the avocado tree and toward the henhouse and the fern-covered back walls? Back then all the guests sat together, Cecilia and her younger son and often Juan with them. When Renato looked up, ay mijo, you would have paid to watch that scene. The Europeans, who had been staring at him, their forks suspended in midair, their mouths parted open, the culinary experience suddenly deposed, every one of them looked away at once, tried to go back to the meal, to their casual conversation with Juan and Cecilia, while Renato helped himself to a second serving of tangy avocado.

I think I need some new clothes, mamá, he said, before he introduced himself to the guests as he did every night, except that night there was no discussion of the Party, no wide-eyed admiration from the Europeans as comandante Juan recited the lists of Renato's accomplishments. An un-Cuban silence descended upon the table, the only sound the clinking of flatware and the announcement of each new dish brought in by Juan from Inocente St. Louis's kitchen. Before he left the table, Renato secured a promise from Juan for a whole new set of clothes, grabbed the napkin from his lap, which Cecilia had casually placed there as Juan served him the first course, and set it on the table, excused himself a second time, and went back up to his room, his mother the only one who dared to look at his pale Castilian butt (his paternal grandfather had the same milky skin, Cecilia noted).

Cecilia offered the guests a dinner on the house, but none of them accepted, all of them leaving three times the previously agreed upon amount, begging her to get the boy some clothes. That was it, Renato's days as a communist were over, but if its objective was to be accepted by his brother's group, it failed. He was ostracized more than ever, and until the day I arrived spent the greater part of his day locked in the upstairs room, sometimes coming down for dinner, sometimes making trips to the market at the Plaza de Armas, but more often waiting until all the guests had left and raiding the kitchen for his only meal of the day. Cecilia had not been allowed inside his room since the evening of his naked dinner. The morning after, she found the six pairs of uniforms and the six pionero hankies, the same kind that she had devotedly washed and ironed every Sunday morning since the boy was six neatly folded on top of her bed.

So that smug smile that he greeted me with might have been nothing but the leer of solitude, Cecilia ventured. She was too busy with the paladar, too content with the knowledge that at least he was in his room.

He adopted you right away, didn't he? You became a brother he could love. Or, mejor dicho, one that could love him back.

He adopted me by waiting on the toilet, jimmying the bar that locked the faucet with the palm of his hand until a slow warm trickle slowly filled up the bathtub. He took the soap from my hands and washed my back and scrubbed till it had worked up a thick lather. He then went to throw my dirty tattered clothes into the water but thought better of it, told me he would tell Juan to get me some real clothes. My old ones we should throw in the grilling pit, might add an indigenous aroma to the slop his mother served up for the tourists, he suggested.

You'll want to resist her subtle attempts at exerting control every opportunity you get, he pronounced, as he led me to his own room down the hall. I talked, I must have talked because he continued to say nothing, as he offered me his bed with a sweep of his hand—a stained bare pillowless mattress on a steel cot—which was the only piece of furniture in the room, aside from the makeshift desk and chair, pieces of thick plywood stacked on top of thick columns of books as legs, which looking at their spines I guessed were remnants from his days in the Communist Youth League, all dealing with some version or other of the creation of Che's New Man, or the Newer Man version that the Ministry of Culture came up with every year, bible-thick tomes that we had all been force-fed and that I had never seen put to better use. Later I would notice how other columns of books shifted within the tiny space his room, by his bed, leaning against the wall, rising from the desk, the ever-changing skyline of a futuristic city, growing taller or shorter with each transformation—and had I taken the time to read some of the spines on the volumes, I would have realized that an entire library was making its way in and out of his room, one that if confiscated could land him in prison for a thousand years. When I finally did start reading the spines and eventually opening up the books, it took me a while to recognize the expanse and range of the library, mostly in Spanish, but up to a quarter of the volumes in English or French, ranging from Plato, Aristotle, Homer, Lucretius, and Herodotus to the latest American and British fiction, including a first British edition of Graham Greene's comic classic of the inventive vacuum-cleaner spy in Havana. But although these were the prized editions in the collection, there were others by outlawed Cuban writers such as Arenas and Piñera and Padilla, as well as an extensive collection of homosexual erotica from the early French decadents to American physique magazines from the fifties, which I would find out later Renato would openly hawk in the Plaza de Armas nearby. On that first night though, all I did was talk to Renato—and he was the first I told about the life I had abandoned, maybe because I sensed that he would one day do the same with his own life.

ABANDONED DESTINY

One morning late that summer, on top of the table where we usually had our breakfast, Cecilia had set out something that I recognized well—the crisp white shirt, red shorts, and hanky of la Organización de Pioneros José Martí—a uniform every school-age child wears until they graduate from the eighth grade. This was one of Renato's old uniforms. Cecilia had saved them all. At first she thought that his counterrevolutionary bender would just be a phase, that as soon as Renato realized that there was nothing he could do—not even abandoning the Revolución—to ingratiate himself with his wayward brother, he would relent, he would come back to the life that his father had set him on. Later, she kept the old pionero uniform for sentimental reasons, just as she had saved in an old pine trunk every piece of clothing that the infant Renato had inherited from his older brother, so that at times she said she would get the sensation in caring for her younger son that she had been granted a second opportunity at motherhood.

She wanted me to try on the last uniform Renato had worn before high school. She asked as plainly as if she were asking me to read to her from the newspaper. I obeyed as simply, too—I stripped down to my underwear under the shade of the avocado tree and put on the same type of uniform I had put on for ten years of my own life, my fingers not having forgotten one of the seven movements that it takes to tie the perfect knot of the handkerchief and fold the starched collar under it at the proper angle.

I stood there, barefoot, my chin pressed to the knot of the handkerchief but not taking my eyes from Cecilia—feeling more naked now than when I had been in my underwear—her face cupped in one hand, her eyes glistening.

Happy? I asked.

Oh, don't be such a gruñón, she said dismissively. Why couldn't I just placate an old grieving mother? I clicked my heels and gave her the pionero's salute, the heaven-facing palm to the forehead. I was hers, I announced in a bullhorn voice, hers for the day, for the summer, for—

Wait, wait, she laughed. You can't be mine, you can't be mine until you keep your promise, until you tell me as many secrets as we have told you, o mejor digo, as you have been forced to live with us.

Isn't that what these useless mornings were for, I thought, now that the capital had gone so quiet and desolate with the bombings, everybody walking around as if inside a church planted with mines, waiting for the drum blast of the next bomb?

Your . . . what did you call it once when you came home drunk? Your . . . abandoned destiny.

She was not trying to mock me. I *had* called it that. I went into our abandoned kitchen, searched the lower shelves where we kept the bottles of Havana Club and poured myself an early morning drink. I must have been a sight—groggy, bare-foot, in Renato's starched schoolboy comunista uniform, sipping rum at eight in the morning, staring at Cecilia, afraid that if I took my eyes off her for one moment she would have me transformed into some misshapen offspring to whom she had never given birth. I served myself some eggs with picadillo, still simmering in the cast iron pan, offered her a glass of rum, which she refused with a polite lift of her coffee cup.

I had never told her anything about my life, because there was nothing that she could not have heard from any child of la Revolución, nothing that was different from her own upbringing, from the upbringing of eight out of ten Cubans still living on the Island, all of us who had come of age after 1959.

Pre-revolutionary history was a period of capitulation and servitude, of ignorance and subjugation. It was the Dark Ages that we lived through until one sunny January morning in 1959. In that world, someone like me—orphaned, poor, dark-skinned, from the countryside—would have disappeared from the notebooks of history. Disappeared, no, not even as much as that, perhaps never as much as have been a scribble in a long-lost chronicle. La Revolución changed that, it offered, and I took another sip of my morning rum before I said it . . . a destiny.

Cecilia got up and rummaged the lower shelves for the bottle of rum and a glass. She filled mine and poured herself one this time. Bien, she said, then tell me about it, coño. If it was such a grand gesture, this . . . this abandonment, then why can't you even talk about it?

I had talked about it—with Renato that first night. But this morning she wanted to hear the stories directly from me, costumed in her son's schoolboy uniform. So I spoke, knowing that none of it mattered, that my old life, the grooved life of the boy in the pionero uniform that I once had been meant nothing now.

I was an orphan before I had any memory, abandoned on

the front gate of Abuela Puebla's house wearing only a soiled cloth diaper and a frayed campesino hat that had belonged to my father, and for seventeen years hung on a rusty nail in my room like some saint's relic. Abuela Puebla said that she wasn't sure why they had put the diaper on me—for once she removed it, the first thing I did was signal to her that I had to go, and I stood in her airy bathroom peeing for hours. I was two or three, she wasn't sure, because though I was tall and long limbed, un hombrecito parecía, I could barely speak and only signaled at things. Abue Puebla wasn't truly my grandmother, of course.

Since 1959, after she descended from the mountains with the rebels, one of the few women who actually fought in the skirmishes that they later called a war (though there were many others who tended to the men, both domestically and sexually), she had served as a mother to a battalion of abandoned children of whom I would be the last one, el nené. By the time she took me into her house she was in her sixties and my long line of brothers and sisters had already grown into la Revolución, an impressive list of government ministers and Party honchos whose pictures covered every inch of wall inside her small seaside bungalow.

If I knew that she were still alive, I would send her one of me, of this morning, me in my pionero uniform, this uniform, to finally fill up that little corner of the wall that she was saving for my picture.

Cecilia said that she would get her camera, but I stopped her. She was probably dead, the house a museum by now.

Everyone in Baracoa called her Abue, because she tended to shorten her children's names, making them earn their last syllables on their way to adulthood. So I became Rafa, named after the archangel, not the painter, because that's what her mother had wanted to name her after seeing a vision of the angel during a troubled delivery. It was only when she became ill, vomiting sulfurous watery bile that I realized that I did not know her real name—no one in our pueblo did. This began a few years before I left. For an entire week she lay unconscious in the town's only clinic, fed through tubes and breathing with machines, her life story and the fruitless search for her legal name the subject of lead articles in the town newspaper.

It was how I learned of her life before Baracoa, of her heroic feats in the jungle mountains that bordered our town against Batista's Rural Guard. She was the commander of the small battalion in the Mariana Grajales Women's Platoon that descended on Baracoa on the same morning Fidel entered Santiago de Cuba and Che secured his control over Santa Clara, splitting the Island in two and forcing the dictator Batista to flee to Miami.

The articles rehashing those days in search for Abue's real identity stated that there was great ignorance among the populace then, such the price of isolation, and no one really cared which side won the war, for it was sure not to affect them in any significant manner. At one point, it was considered a failure, in an economic sense for her family, if a young woman did not establish herself as a prostitute by her quinceañera feast. And the tradition continued well into the twentieth century, the articles revealed. So when the rebel forces staggered down from the mountains, a women's battalion at the head of the phalanx of barbudos, it was as if a group of Martians and not Marianas had landed. No one quite knew what to do. The mayor hastily prepared a delegation to receive the visitors. But the first thing that la comandante did was to appropriate his seaside home for the establishment of the provisional revolutionary government. Her first batch of children, it was rumored, and this was not generally known until those articles many years later, were orphans of those who had been tried and executed as agents of the Batista regime, though in truth the city leaders had had no more contact with the thugs in the capital than they had with any foreign government. But that was the mood of the time, cleansing and rebirth.

Abue never left Baracoa again until her stretcher was flown in an Air Force helicopter to a hospital in Santiago de Cuba for her chemotherapy treatments three years before I left for the capital. When she returned, it was only to the hospital bed that they set up in her room and to the care of round-the-clock nurses. During her unending death throes, all of her sons and daughters returned to visit her.

She hardly recognized any of them, complaining that there were too many people inside her little room and she could not watch the sea through her small bay window. When they turned to me, returned from school, in my crisp pionero uniform, with my back pressed to one of the corners of the room, she screamed at them to leave me alone, that she had raised me to care for her in her old age and not for any maldita Revolución.

Soon, the visits stopped. And though she was bedridden and in diapers, her sense seemed to return. During the afternoons when I would sit with her after school, she confessed to me that she had driven them away on purpose, that they were a bunch of termites feeding on the totem pole of la Revolución, and that they would end up toppling it over with their insatiable hunger. She had wasted her life on raising a generation of pests.

I sipped the rest of my rum and stopped, though Cecilia hadn't interrupted, hardly moving since I started to speak, not touching her own rum at all.

She waited out my silence. It was as if she were behind a pane of glass watching me, smoking now and burying her butts on the remains of her huevos con picadillo.

It wasn't she who had abandoned me though, I finally began again. In the days after she told me that, I only saw her when I went into her room in between the nurses' shifts to take coins from her purse. Her eyes were closed but she watched me, raising her hand from her side and extending it toward me, but only half-heartedly, knowing that I was already on my way out. It took me a while to leave for real, going to school and doing all my revolutionary duties, but basically living on my own, eating the nurses' leftover meals and often sleeping in the silent rooms of the schoolhouse. Then I saw those two movies—I had talked to Cecilia before about that, though she was probably one of the few people on the Island who hadn't seen either of them.

So you abandoned your destiny (and the kind woman who raised you) because you didn't want to have some bit part in the sentimental comedy that is la Revolución? If there is anything revolutionary about those movies from what I heard, it is that they bring down all the grandiosity to the farcical level it deserves.

I didn't know who I was, but I knew I wasn't one of those photographs on the wall. I was already taking off Renato's uniform, folding it as neatly as I had found it.

And my son, that first night in our house, he solved that for you.

No, but I knew then that I would never go back. Until then it had always been a possibility.

Renato, my viciously antisocial son, did that?

He's not really all that antisocial, not out there. I signaled in the general direction beyond the wooden door of the patio to the city of the bombs. And yes, he welcomed me into your crazy family. Did it for no reason. He might have been the only reason I stayed, at least those first few days. I was fascinated with your older son, but he frightened me.

Cecilia finally took a long sip of her rum. But you haven't told me anything, she protested.

It was as much as I had told Renato on the first night and I thought that I had opened my soul to him, so I grew defensive. What else is there in such a preordained life?—little room for adventure or the stuff of stories. Cecilia said that for her it had been different. There had been no Abue Puebla as an anchor in her young life. It was all adventures, or misadventures—mejor digo—for her, traded from one foster family to another, sometimes simply a ward of the State, cared for by well-meaning wet nurses who always had three or four babies to feed and little energy for the older children. Eventually taken in and traded monthly by distant kin who called themselves uncles and aunts. I grew up on my own, she said, probably much like you did, except you had some revolutionary saint hovering over you. It wasn't until she joined the Federation of Women Laborers that she found a purpose. Then she met Pascual, then became a mother. She said it as if listing the secret failings of a close friend.

Somehow it got back to talking about me, she protested. You, you, I want to talk about you, mi vida, shifting into a pleading tone. Invent something if you have to. Make these days pass without us noticing.

I don't know how to invent. Maybe that's my problem in this hive of inventors.

Well then, what was it like growing up with this Mother Teresa of socialism? You act as if you have no feelings for her, your own mother. And weren't you ever curious about who your biological family was if they only lived a few villages away?

If I had not been curious, it was not because Abue Puebla had forbade it. In fact, at a certain point, she began to show me a weathered photograph of a pregnant elfish dark-skinned woman, with a kind face, bovine eyes, translucent black hair, and a neat white worker's smock standing by a shabby bohío, telling me who it was, three months before she had given birth. She stressed that she was my mother, that she had loved me and that the proof was the navel on my belly. That's where she had touched me last. As a child, it made me fear this woman who with a touch could put holes in your body—that's what had made her unfit for motherhood, I thought.

She was a good woman, I said. She had told me stories of sneaking up on sleeping soldiers of Batista's Rural Guard and slashing their throats, those hands that I saw finger the rosaries every morning had once been covered in the calid blood of the executed.

Ven, siéntate conmigo—Cecilia said as she refilled the rum glasses. I had never been so drunk so early in the morning. I stumbled trying to pull out the chair next to her. And she stood up and grabbed me, laughing now, drunker than I was.

What were we going to do if someone showed up for lunch? Comandante Juan had stopped coming early, so we would be on our own. Cecilia downed her rum, and I put my glass to my lips.

Se jodió la cosa if someone shows up. We are closed in mourning for the bombing victims, past, present, and future victims. That's what we'll say. She made a move for the bottle, but it was empty. She searched for more in the cabinets and cursed comandante Juan for not having had the sense to replenish our personal supply, so she opened a bottle of rioja from the paladar's supply. We drank in the same cups. To the Italian and to all the other dead in the atrocities of our history, Cecilia toasted, sounding like her older son and unconcerned with the big ears of the ladies of el Comité.

It would not surprise her if all the tourists that ever had stepped into the paladar had fallen too under the curse of the house on Calle Obispo, she leaned in and whispered in my ear, like when we wanted to keep secrets from comandante Juan and the paladar was full of tables.

We stole this house from a widow. Pascual and his thugs at the Ministry of the Interior. It *is* cursed.

I had heard different versions of the story from Nicolás and Renato. The husband's gay lover consoling the widow, the dead husband, the cursed library. But it was the first time that I had heard Cecilia say her husband's name aloud or admit to the ill-gotten nature of her prized house, the only thing in the world that she would be left with years later. She hugged me. Aside from the clamorous and grueling sexual encounters with her older son, this was as hearty a physical welcome as I had yet received into the family.

Her lips wet my neck. A hand patted me gently on the shoulder. You have a mother here, sabes. Esta misma—she beat her chest. If you want her. All this is yours. No one is going to throw you out. We could be eating the pigeon crumbs or the bony chickens and there will be as much for you as there will be for me, for Juan. It will be our own rationing system, carajo. Here you will always have what that poor vieja could not give you. A home. Her one hand fell from her chest to my knee.

When Nicolás was at his drunkest or more outrageous, he used to say that both his father and his mother had sexually abased him. And though it was clearly one of his many egregious gestures for attention, Nico at his martyr best, it was the first image that flashed through my mind when I felt Cecilia's hand on my knee, a drunken rageful Nicolás, shirtless, grimy from living on the streets, or in the makeshift shacks of the azoteas on the outskirts of the city, as he often did before he was taken away, screaming at the heavens of all the sins that had befallen him because of his family, because of his country.

The same kind of shame, pena del alma, held me in place with Cecilia's hand on my leg, the stink of our imprisonment coming from both of us, not a scent of the skin—which we dutifully washed in our rationed bathtub puddles every day—but deeper within, as if from a rotted molar. ¿Pero qué? She had hugged me, slobbering on my neck, her hand was on my leg, and we were drunker than anyone should be at ten in the morning, strangers who thought that they had grown to know each other through sheer proximity during the past year and a half, through chitchat inlayed in the hectic chatter of serving tourists, through late-night pauses at open doors, through silent grieving, through one lonely burial. It might have served others, but that morning we were still two strangers, disoriented by how each other's secret stench momentarily became one hard vapor, infrangible.

I wanted to pull away, and she did not want the shame of her hand on me for so long—but the mesmeric force that had been building up that summer held us there, until I finally broke it and threw an arm over her back and she collapsed, but not from weeping, but from the mortification of how much we had come to depend on each other. If I was ever going to tell her the secret I had been keeping from her, what I had witnessed and where I had failed her most—it was then, there. And she sensed it, she straightened up, wiped her face with a dishcloth. What? ¿Qué, mi cielo? What? Tell me.

I told myself that it was that, how she smoothed her T-shirt and tamed her wild curls and prepared for what I was about to tell her. I felt the silence indurate around me like mud troweled on a hot hard sidewalk.

I reached for the glassful of wine and knocked it on its side, the sound of glass shattering on the brick patio freeing me from the moment.

CRICKET'S NEST

In the evenings, I couldn't tolerate her. After our third meal of the day, all those hours spent orbiting the tables under the avocado tree like a couple of mayflies, she would go up to her room to read, telling me I should come get her should any customers show up, so that she could explain the situation to them herself. Mostly though, she just stayed in her room and smoked and read by candlelight, not even bothering with the lights so that her reading wouldn't be interrupted by the blackouts, which since the bombs had become even less predictable.

The door remained open and when she heard me coming up the stone stairway, even when I did it barefoot, she would sigh, and I could almost see the calm languid movement as she lifted her eyes from the book, waiting for me to come in to continue whatever conversation we had cut off after dinner, but I passed by the open door without even looking in, gathering whatever I needed to get in my room before heading out for the night. There was no goodbye, but I knew that she would wait for me, that if she had to, she would spend the length of the night reading and smoking until I returned, and she could cook me breakfast.

During those nights, roaming the streets of the old city, I realized that I would soon have been in the capital for two years and I didn't have a single friend or acquaintance outside of my adopted family, Bertila, and Inocente St. Louis. I had never wanted one until that summer. Unfortunately, it was not the best time to make new friends. Native Cubans were kept from tourist spots more strictly than ever by groups of five or six fiana patrolling on foot. And they had become more suspicious of us and even of each other than at any time since I had arrived in the capital.

It was a tricky proposition for the government, Cecilia said when I told her about it one night on my return, for the more the natives were kept from the tourists or the tourist areas, the more the city would feel like any other crumbling Caribbean metropolis by the sea. Tourists came to mingle with Cubans, at least during the evening hours, to get some sun on their private beaches during the day and then to experience the real capital at night. The longer the natives were kept out of the tourist spots, the more serious the crisis would become. The government was too easily letting the terroristas win. By the time the eighth or ninth bomb—we were losing count—went off in the cathedral plaza, the counterrevolutionaries had perfected their methods. Only the palomas were hurt—that night, I saw the charred feathers still floating around the area bounded by a perimeter of guards passing cigarettes and flasks from one to the other, drunkenly aiming their rifles at anyone who approached—but the points of contact between the two worlds (between the foreigners and the natives, the ones with dollars and those without) were being methodically singled out for disconnection by the very same State agencies whose long-term survival depended on their illicit union.

In that sense, as far as Cecilia was concerned, her little

paladar and others like it were the truest patriotic and revolutionary institutions on the Island, and thus she would not be surprised if soon, very soon, one of them were to be targeted by the terroristas. She used this as a strategy to try to make me stay home at night, por si acaso. Some early mornings that summer, I arrived to find her pupils so dilated from watching shadows that it looked as if a surgeon had lathed holes into the jelly of her eyes.

I wanted to disappear completely from the house on Calle Obispo, if only for a few days. I meant to go searching for Renato but I also wanted to get away from those bullfrog eyes that greeted me on my return. Soon, there came a perfect excuse for my departure—on returning one morning from my wanderings, there was a tourist postcard of a hotel in Varadero, no mailing address, no text, with a postage stamp of a red-bellied woodpecker, a new release, not like the collectible Oliver had given me, but I got the message.

I put a hole in the postcard, looped a string through it, and wore it as a necklace, donning the best Yuma clothes I could find in the stash in Renato's room.

What will you do if you find him? Cecilia asked when I told her I wanted to make sure Renato was safe.

I'll bring him back, I said.

Lie! ¡Mentiroso! she said, grabbing me, burying her hair in my chest. She smelled of cigarettes and chispa de tren, the kerosene flavored black-market aguardiente, and the sweat of the silent summer.

I opened my arms wide and promised that I would return when she needed me.

It took me almost two weeks to make it to the sidatorio, where I knew Renato would not be. First, I looked for Oliver, hitchhiked to Varadero where the problems in the capital seemed to be taking place in a neighboring country. The tourist hotels were packed with South Americans and Europeans and, most conspicuous, the new capitalists, the freshly minted Russian plutocrats, with their gilded hair, sun-scalded backs, and puffy vodka faces.

These Russians were the rebellious sons and daughters of a generation of Soviet parents whose visits to the Island were of an entirely different order—as teachers, factory foremen, military advisers, and scientific collaborators, even truant officers. As opposed to their elders, these descendants had no concerns but pleasure and sunning, their own young families now in tow. It was difficult not to be distracted as I looked for Oliver, always careful not to linger too long at any specific spot on the perimeter of the beaches and the hotel lobbies. I thought that if maybe I could befriend one of them, I could more easily make my way into the hotels and search for Oliver in earnest, in the restaurants, pools, and hallways. Maybe they could even tell me which hotel was pictured on the postcard. But my skin, my mangy appearance, and perhaps most obvious, some silent desperation in my every gesture, gave me away as a native to the core in spite of my Yuma gear.

Like I had told Cecilia, that summer I was already under the impression that no one could understand what I was saying, I would speak to my own people and they would either ignore me or look at me as if I had spoken in Flemish, so it was a relief one day to lure in a Russian boy who seemed to have wandered away from his parents without having to use any words. Desperate for any type of carnal companionship, I forgot about the postcard hanging around my neck for the moment. He was a few years younger than me, round of face with blunt Slavic features, a resplendent head of silky sable hair, and a fuzzy dark mustache that seemed part of an ill-conceived disguise. I guessed that he was looking for someone like me, slowly making it the task of his morning to increase the distance between him and his parents by going into the sea and letting the current drift him eastward before he body-surfed back onto shore—repeating this again and again until he was free of them.

I caught his attention by taking off my shirt and from the very edge of the beach, pretending I was bringing towels to one of the tourist areas, which was dotted with colorful parasols and basted bodies. About halfway up the peninsula, a good mile from where the young Russian had begun, it became easier to sneak onto the beach areas unnoticed.

I walked on the beach to the pace of my swimmer. It was something to do. Someone. Por fin. And he had definitely noticed me now, for he stopped the game of returning to the shore and simply treaded water in place every thousand meters or so to make sure that I was still there.

When the Russian finally came out of the water, he shook my hand—then realized the ridiculousness of the gesture and walked quietly alongside me. I calculated that he must have swum a couple of miles but he looked unscathed by the effort, as if he had just gone in for a dip. It was remarkable, the endurance and strength so well hidden in the narrow-tapered space of his torso—the bony shoulders, the slightly concave chest with a smattering of pubescent hair, the long skinny arms, the waif's waist. With my rudimentary Russian, which I had once spoken fluently and had now mostly forgotten, and his workable Spanish, which he spoke syllable by syllable, I learned that he was not like the others that summer. He understood me, my broken Russian, my Spanish, and was not only looking for a little afternoon sport, but had long-range plans that included a full-fledged escape from his parents.

He planned to defect and stay in Cuba. I told him (I felt I had to warn him) that not the entire Island looked like Varadero. There were problems, serious problems, for instance, now in the capital, silent subversives setting off pigeon-killing bombs. Had he heard of the bombs? Yes, he had, and that was one of the reasons he was staying. Mother Russia has abandoned your people, he said. That was the source of all our troubles; we had no one to support us in our struggles against the cancerous imperialists.

He wore brand-name yanqui swim trunks, the kind that Olympians wear, his hairy thick-muscled thighs betrayed some of his power as a swimmer (some of his peasant stock, I later kidded him), but no one on first looking at him would have guessed that he was anything more than another well-heeled European. But the more he talked—half of which now I could not understand, the Russian or the Spanish, but whose sense was clear by the orator's body language, by the outmoded zeal in his voice—the more I could picture him in an officer's coat, huddled with others in the Senate Square, a chilly Russian December scene that had been branded in every tropical pionero's schoolboy's mind, the spark that gave birth to a century-long struggle for freedom and equality, where now, half a world away, almost two hundred years later, we were the only true heirs, for even the Chinese had begun to abandon the principle of that holy sacrificial band of officers. All this, and as we walked side by side on the beach, I still did not know his name. Names were not important, he said. Action was. When he finished pontificating, we were well past the golf course connected to Xanadu, the old DuPont residence.

He was trying to convince me of something—but I was not sure what—as if I had missed some important primal lesson in my revolutionary upbringing.

The shore thickened with sea grapes, coconut palm, and monumental umbrella-shaped cacti. A pair of tourist diving boats bobbed not far off, anchored and joined by a rope, empty but for an ancient bald shirtless captain reading on the gunwale. He glanced over at us, and then looked down into the water as if to ascertain if perhaps we were a pair of tourists that had been left behind, but then went back to his reading without ever looking our way again. The Russian insisted that he had no money, or (I couldn't quite understand) that even if he had money there would be none offered, for such transactions were the quintessence of everything he did not believe in. The only member of his family who had ever been to Cuba before he had come with his parents was his great-grandfather, or his grandfather's uncle. He had worked as an engineer for—

Before he could begin detailing the whole saga of his family back to Lenin and Trotsky, I grabbed his hand and pulled him toward me. I had not kissed anyone since the night I almost toppled off Oliver's balcony and before that since the afternoon I gave a final kiss to a demented, raging, frail Nicolás that last time I saw him. The Russian meant to pull away, but I had an arm wrapped around his lower back and a hand cupped under his scruffy chin. He continued speaking into my mouth, slapping his wagging tongue against my lips, grating his teeth into mine, but soon the whole history of his great-grandfather's or his grandfather's uncle's service in two revolutions dissolved in the marshes of our mouths.

We moved inland into the nature preserve at the end of the peninsula, full of caverns and other hideaways, and when we were finished, he put on his trunks, held my hand on the way back to the shore, let go and waded back into the water, vanishing as nonchalantly as he had appeared. I could easily make six or seven such friends if I couldn't find Oliver, to rid me of the claustrophobic stench of the house on Calle Obispo. The Russian had said goodbye and wished me a good time during my stay in a more perfect Spanish than he had used in the whole time we had spent together. I could have spent days in this new paradise with him, staying off the tour paths, hiding from the passing tourist groups in the limestone formations that opened into the sandy church-like gateways to some netherworld.

I had completely shed all of my clothes and left them in one of the limestone caves while I fucked the Russian on a flattened boulder overlooking the sea, then accompanied him to the shore semi-naked. Unconcerned with my nakedness, even as the Russian was in the very act of vanishing, I was thinking that this was it, this was why I had run away from Abue. I had found my new country with a descendant of a Decembrist colonel. I had never thought of the house on Calle Obispo once in such terms.

The only possession I had on besides a pair of Renato's Yuma briefs was Oliver's postcard tied around my neck. Now, in my natural state, I had forgotten what it was and would have discarded it perhaps if in that barren shore by the virginal nature preserve, I did not hear his voice as if it were a phenomenon happening inside my own head.

You must not be afraid, I heard from somewhere and turned around but then heard from somewhere else. I turned again. He wore an expensive linen guayabera, the color of green tangerines, unbuttoned halfway down and way too neatly pressed not to appear incongruous in this wilderness. He signaled to my postcard necklace. You've found me! And he opened his arms in welcome, then added, gesturing to the empty sea, With a little help. I'm sorry, I must do it. Your government, it is very nosy, in everybody's business. I awkwardly stood my place, dying to know how much he had paid the Russian. He signaled toward the place I had christened with the Russian. Had he watched? I need your help, he announced cryptically as I followed him inland.

I submissively made my way into the cavern, too quickly

got dressed (Oliver had basically ignored my nakedness), sat cross-legged on the rocky ground, and waited. The German seemed so pleased that it annoyed me, and it made me want to get up and head back to the capital. But something held me there, something that I did not know and that he did, I sensed. Now with a pleased half grin that made it obvious that he enjoyed what he was recounting, Oliver told me how he had convinced the Russian to lure me away from the heavily patrolled main tourist areas. It was a long tale that involved his own morning swims and dalliances in the jungle with the Russian.

I thought you had gone back, I said to the German, to break his gleeful mood. Like all the other Yuma that have scattered from the Island.

He buttoned up his guayabera and collected himself. Ah sí, I have to admit, it was in my thoughts. But then something arose that I could not pass up. And, in truth, I think you may be of help. His Spanish was the same, fluent, but hesitant and with a marked accent.

How?

I stood, but he ignored my question.

Unfortunate for that Italian, the wrong place at the right time. He laughed too self-consciously at his clumsy humor. But it will all be over soon. Things will return to normal.

What do you want with me? It came out as if I had been forced here under some duress. He raised a finger counseling patience, then he looked around as if the viejas of the Comités were omnipresent enough to infiltrate even the State's nature preserves. Apparently he hadn't been too far during my encounter with the Russian, because he went to some cranny far away into the cavern and pulled out a handbag containing fancy guayaberas, brand-name pullovers, linen shorts, and leather sandals, nicer Yuma stuff by far than Renato could ever get his hands on. He opened the handbag and spread the goods (including underwear, I saw) on top, signaling that I should pick something to wear. We didn't want to stand out, he explained. We should match. I got naked again and picked out an outfit similar to what Oliver wore. This time I felt his eyes on my nakedness.

We headed back, first stopping at the hotel where Oliver had been staying to pick up his suitcase. He went to the safe and pulled out a hefty billfold full of American dollars. We stopped at the bar for a drink but on the way Oliver told me not to use his name. He leaned into me and whispered in my ear something about the need for namelessness, and then licked my earlobe once, there in the middle of the day, among a throng of tourists. We must be European lovers or something, he muttered. The leering bartender somehow sensed a weightlessness within my fancy Yuma disguise and knew that I was one of the ghosts.

We hired a taxi to return to the capital, paid up front, and I slept, my head dropping into Oliver's shoulder most of the way. The driver chattered in my dreams up front. Knowing that I couldn't take the German back to Cecilia, that she would somehow see it as a betrayal, I wanted to keep him with me, not as much for whatever possible sex, I told myself, or for his billfold of yanqui dollars, or for the illusion of togetherness with someone—with anyone—since Nico's death, but because I wanted to find out why he needed me now. Me and not any other local he could have picked up while hiding from the bombs in Varadero.

Approaching the city, Oliver asked the driver to veer south toward the district of Santiago de Las Vegas, and I knew where we were headed. I looked at him, feigning confusion. The nearby Parque Lenin is where Renato and I had first laid eyes on him.

I need to see him also, he said. But it will be no good without you.

He's not there, I said, telling the driver to turn back toward the old city, but he clearly wasn't going to listen to me. We arrived at the gate of the sidatorio near midnight and walked straight through the unmanned gate. I wondered if our tormentor was taking a midnight nap, and would come out shooting when aroused, or if Bertila was right and these places had been abandoned by all the patients and anyone watching over them.

Once inside, I became curious. Not once in all my visits to Renato had I been able to cross the threshold of the gate. I began to hope that I had been wrong, that somehow he was still inside, insulating himself from the world as he had been doing in his room in Calle Obispo when I met him.

The main building, the Soviet-style box, was dark, except for a few meager bulbs glowing in two of the top floors, and the grounds mostly deserted. Renato had told me about the old classrooms in the back where most of the patients lived. Easy to walk right in, we found. Shoulder-high plywood panels divided each room into separate spaces, each mini-room equipped with two cots, a night table, and a small reading lamp; a lone incandescent bulb in the center of the classroom cast shadows over all.

Most of the tiny apartments looked unoccupied, though they all appeared very lived in, as if whatever life there had been there was abandoned in haste. On each cot still a tangle of bedsheets, which in the darkness made it sometimes seem as if they were occupied, and Oliver tugged at the nonexistent legs. Photographs or pictures from yanqui sex magazines covered the walls, sometimes covering up the bits of counterrevolutionary poetry scrawled with dark markers. When we did find someone, and Oliver tugged at the legs, the patient looked up hazily and waved us away. We went through three classrooms before we found a lamplight on.

An old hairless half-naked man sat cross-legged on a cot reading, a hand-rolled cigarette dangling from his lips and trickling ashes onto his lap. He had called out when he heard us enter the room, but it took us a few minutes to find him through the labyrinth of plywood panels, so he had gone back to reading serenely. We stood in the opening of the cubicle for a long while before he looked up, finally lifting his eyes when Oliver dropped his heavy tourist bag from his shoulders. The old man took hold of his cigarette and smiled, his lower teeth almost all capped in gold, his upper row almost all rotted and so long that they tapered precipitously from the gums. But a happy smile.

Coño, this weed must be good! he said. I've begun to hallucinate. He closed his book, a new translation that was all the rage in Spain, some garbage written by a Miami exile about la Revolución, in English, imagínate, los pobres, a waste of time for those of us who have time to waste (los gusanos writing about us, what do they know?)—all this said as he motioned for us to sit on the empty cot across from him. He offered us some cafecito from a hot plate sitting on the night table and rummaged around in the drawers for clean cups.

Don't refuse a kindness from such a viejito pelao, he said, handing us each a cafecito in chipped dainty porcelain cups decorated with hummingbirds. They are a treasure, no? he said, before offering to sell it to us for a fraction of the price of what they were truly worth. They were not stolen, he assured, not strictly. As a younger man, he had worked in the Ministry of the Interior, a whole department in charge of repossessing not just the homes but the millions of valuable items left behind by the first wave of gusanos gone to Spain. Claro, the government did not pay enough, so many of the fine goods disappeared into homes of ordinary Cubans like his mother. China and jewelry and silver and leather-bound books that remained wrapped in newspapers, stored under the bed, and then over the years sold off piece by piece.

My mother is a hundred and two, imagínate, the old man said, and down to the maldito coffee cups. She would outlive their treasure yet, though thankfully, he wouldn't. He straightened the sheets on his bed and tapped his pillow. This is my grave.

He crossed himself.

I noticed a profusion of other books, stacked under his bed and in descending piles making their way out the partition door, many of them the type with thick leather covers. These covers had been visibly ripped out leaving the sepia innards exposed, the spines coated with torn threading. This was a last resort, the old man explained when he caught me looking, the selling of the leather for purses, belts, shoes, and sandals. The insides didn't matter. Would we be interested in buying the teacups? Chinese porcelain exported to the Netherlands by the Dutch East India Company.

Oliver pulled out his billfold and paid him, counted out bills till the old man seemed satisfied. I drank the bitter coffee in a gulp and handed the artifact to Oliver, who wrapped it in a pillowcase and put it in his bag. Bueno, for *all* this money, what else do you want, my beautiful apparitions?

We're looking for someone, I said.

The old man laughed, his quivery Jolly Roger grin now almost mocking. He counted out the dollars Oliver had given him, all in twenties, thinking he told us, how much he would have to return, because with that, with finding one of the missing, he was certain that he could be of no help at all.

Renato Zúñiga, I said.

Ay, ay, the old man said, frantically waving his hand in front of him, a duel it seemed against some invisible swarm of malaria-carrying mosquitos. ¡Ése! El Grillo.

With a convulsive effort, he bent over and reached under the bed to grab a knotty cane. He placed the bills in a plastic purse that he kept under his mattress, unfolded his legs from underneath him, and stood, signaling for us to follow him. His toes were so bent from arthritis that his nails tapped on the wooden floor like a dog's paws. At a spot diagonally opposite from his cubicle, he stopped and waved us in.

This is where he slept. The Cricket's nest. Or where they slept—the Cricket never slept alone, from one to the other, así asao. The cubicle was the same size as the others, but arranged differently, the two cots pushed together and centered in the small room, a makeshift marriage bed, the night tables on each side, the lamps with their bulbs in locked cages neatly centered in the middle, the walls bare, free of any photographs, mementos, or graffiti, except for a neatly torn piece of brown paper bag taped just above the bed with a list of neatly written names, the writing so small it was almost illegible, but I could tell it was Renato's script. It was the same microscopic script that lined the margins of the books that he had taken from the writer's library. After a moment's hesitation, I went in and turned on the night-light, searched the drawers, under the tousled sheets, beneath the bed. Nothing. I handed the list to the old man, he set it under the lamp, and with the meat of his index finger followed it down till he came upon a name, David, el Alacrán Prehistórico, and tapped it joyfully with his long curved fingernail (which was perhaps one of the reasons why they called him the Prehistoric Scorpion), celebrating his name on the Cricket's list, his ecstasy in the Cricket's nest.

The rest, he said, all gone, everyone on this list, either dead or gone with the Cricket, good as dead. Los sacrificios, they called themselves. They were going after the Visitor. They had started already, frightening all the other visitors. Things would get uglier. Uglier how? Oliver said, taking the list. What have they said?

David proffered his happy tenebrous smile again. Could be, could be . . . anything. Read the news. ¡Qué será será!

I accused David of inventing stuff, Renato had plainly told me that he did not associate with anyone at the sidatorio, that he hated it there. Looking at the place, no great surprise.

Fine, what do I know? David asked, click-clacking back to his cubicle. I'm just a sick old queen. What do we know?

Oliver scrutinized the list, counting out the names in a whisper until I could no longer follow him. We both watched him for a long while, till he quit, there must have been over three hundred names on the list. Were there that many patients in here?

Where is he from? David asked politely, and then broke into a staccato hurried Russian that I had no idea at first Oliver could understand, but after a few moments, after having shown off enough and noting that Oliver's East Berlin Russian didn't exactly qualify as fluency, David turned to me, Ay niño, he said. Don't be so surprised at my expertise. When I was in the business of redistributing the wealth, I eventually had to deal with the Soviets. Everyone had to, once that hijo de puta sold out la Revolución. Este guapo, he is just like they all were, coming here with their Old World pessimism about the human race.

Gracias, Oliver said, apparently taking everything the Scorpion spit out as a compliment.

Just then, I remembered my last conversation with Bertila. *Horrible things must be afoot.* Were they going after the Visitor? They're going to assassinate the Pope? This is crazy. But taking the list back from Oliver, looking closely at Renato's fastidious script, all in capitals, the first letters just a little taller than all the others, it did look like a recruiting roster, and somewhere on that list I knew that I would find my name. It took me awhile, because often the letters were so close together, the names teetering one on top of the other like badly balanced children's blocks so that they were impossible to read. But there, surrounded on all sides by a sea of letters, bobbing like a lifeless body on the black sea was clearly my name, in small stubby letters, *Rafa la Jirafa Mulata*, which meant that I was one of the army, and there must have been others from outside of the sanitarium. I did not think to look for Oliver's name, but later I thought that was the reason he had been going over all the names so closely. Though if the baptism was in the turbid waters of Renato's bed, I had no idea how I had made it on the list, unless he was counting the night with Oliver.

Oliver grabbed his bag, took me by the arm, and led me out of the maze of cubicles. David hobbled behind us, brandishing his cane in the air, begging us not to abandon him, shouting that this time he wanted to go out and join the feral and final revolution. His tremulous voice waned before the click-clack of his toenails and cane as we hurried from the classroom.

We hopped on the back bumper of a crowded city bus taking hotel workers into the old city. The fumes nearly knocked us out as they whirled up from under us. I was surprised when Oliver hopped off in a familiar section near the piers. Perhaps sensing some of the danger to follow, I held on for half a block till the bus stopped. Oliver ran up behind me and pulled me off, kissed me on the cheek and told me not to be afraid, now back to the more perfect Spanish he had used the night we had met him.

He oriented himself, looking up at street signs and signaled for me to follow. I could have told him exactly where we were, but I pretended otherwise. When we made it to the spot on Calle Inquisidor where I had guessed we were going, I thought for the first time that Oliver must have known Nicolás, that our run-in with him and Anna in Parque Lenin must not have been the chance occurrence he had pretended it to be. I don't know why that popped into my head and not the more logical question of how he knew Bertila. But my sleeping brain must have connected the two. Noting my hesitancy to follow him, he turned to face me with a stern expression. You need me, he said, but there was no mistaking in the tone that he meant that he was not going to let me walk away from him.

As we walked up the dark creaky stairs to Bertila's apartment, I became for a moment hopeful that he had found Renato and had somehow kept him prisoner there with Bertila as warden. He refused to tell me anything else after he had given me the look on the street. To my surprise, he did not knock at Bertila's door, but let himself in with a single key he pulled out of a sleeve in his wallet.

Before I could raise a single question, he said, I must explain, don't worry. In the kitchen, he went to one of the cupboards and pulled out a bottle of Bertila's homemade moonshine and poured us each a shot.

There's not a lot left, he explained. I waited here for . . . for three days. There was barely any food. I don't know what the gorda subsisted on. He grabbed the bottle and poured us each another round of the throat-peeling liqueur. Nothing else to do but drink this and sleep it off.

I wanted to ask a thousand questions, including the obvious one of how he got access to someone else's apartment. But only two questions came out. What did you do to her? Where's Renato?

Oliver went to the small refrigerator, pulled out a tub of leftover frijoles negros, and ate scoopfuls with two fingers.

Look, he said, looking at his fingers and the frijole mush in mock disgust. Don't be angry, no. You must know, I didn't want to deceive you. But I needed to get you here, so you could see for yourself. I figured Varadero was far enough of a side trip so you would come. Mira, your amiguito, Renato, your friend the hairdresser, the cook at the paladar, and now we think the bombastic comandante also, what was his name, they've all disappeared.

I didn't think of it, or miss him, but I hadn't seen comandante Juan much since the closing of the paladar. He had not disappeared at all but gone into reclusion during the long summer of the bombs, resurfacing much later after the Directorate had arrested a Salvadoran national in cahoots with the Miami Mafia for the bombings.

This apartment is now under the jurisdiction of the Ministry of the Interior, Oliver said. Someone reported Bertila missing a few weeks ago; people need housing. A family of six'll be moving in here as soon as we clear out. Very simple . . . and just, that's the way our Revolución works.

That's not the way it works, I said. She owns this place. It's hers. She just can't sell it at a profit in the open market or leave it to anyone outside her family when she passes. That law is as old as the days the rebels marched down from the mountains. Such a law made sure there was no such thing as profiteering slumlords in our country or anyone without a roof over his head that wants it. But a Yuma wouldn't know this. That's how *our* revolución works.

Where's Bertila? How did you get in here?

She's not here. She really is gone, amigo. He seemed unfazed that I had caught him in a lie. He wouldn't deny that he knew her whereabouts but instead returned to his claim to la Revolución.

You must understand, esta cosa, this grand experiment, your Revolución, it is *not* just yours, not just for the Island, it's the world's, and it can't be understood any other way. El

Che knew this. He was desperate to export it. For the benefit of all mankind.

El Che had been dead for thirty years. By the time I had reached indoctrination age, teachers treated el Che with the same begrudging if distant regard as the Virgin of Cobre, another icon of a bygone era that nevertheless had been spared desecration.

Right, right, he said, juice from the frijoles dribbling from one side of his mouth. Very dead. Well, we must not dwell too obsessively in the past.

I had my back to the sink counter where Bertila washed hair. A sudden fatigue hit my legs and my lower torso, as if something washed through me. I sunk down to the worn linoleum. The German kneeled by me, his face as close to mine as it had been that evening that seemed so long ago in the hotel room. I thought that he was going to kiss me, but a dolorous look washed over his face. His breath smelled stale, his BO almost intolerable, like a real European now. He was not in the same mood as the Oliver of our passing encounters. He took my chin in his hand, and he pressed tight so that I would not mistake the intention.

Listen to me, beautiful pendejito.

His eyes were so intensely focused on mine, I had to fight the urge to look away, because for the first time with this foreigner, I felt helpless, doomed in a way I had never felt doomed in my relations with Nicolás or Renato, fucked in a way that I had not even felt fucked dangling bare ass off a tourist hotel balcony.

I'm listening, I said.

We're going to find him. You must help me. For the good of both of you. You're in deeper mierda than you can imagine.

He let go of me, walked out of the room to the front of the apartment. I heard the creak of the barber's chair as he settled into it, and when I walked into the room I realized he had reclined it all the way back so that it seemed he was taking a siesta. His hands were folded on his chest.

When he spoke, he seemed like his old self again, ingratiating and pleading. Bueno, we must start over, go look for the kid, find the movement, join it if it's what we must do. It's what you truly wanted, isn't it?—to join him in whatever way. It's what I want.

Why? You want some little adventure.

No, it's much more complicated than that, although that might have been how it started. Here's what you're probably thinking about me, he explained as he continued in a rude impersonation of my mannerisms. This fucking bastard, Oliver, or whatever his name is (because it is surely not that, you must have guessed by now), must have been setting us up all along, from the moment we ran into him along the edges of Parque Lenin, the moment he lured Renato over, perhaps even faking his passion on the balcony, perhaps even, sí sí como no, now it's all clear, even giving me that little tap on the back of the thighs that threw off my balance and almost set me reeling over the balcony, all an elaborate setup to make himself look distracted, so that Renato would feel it easy to grab the nakedly displayed wallet amidst the ensuing commotion, a fat roll of bills coming out of it like the melted cheese from some overstuffed pastelito, and he would have a way to stay in touch with us, just in case, just in case, we were to run into him as he tagged us. Is this about right so far? You must know, you're not wrong in thinking all this. Perhaps we were a little clumsy.

Although not half as clumsy, I thought, as this confession played out, though I figured that it was best to remain quiet and let him go on.

We put one of our own in great danger. Your sick friend,

he was already in her. She had to "retire" after that. He signaled the quotation marks with one hand, his eyes still closed.
Sent her back to school in Germany. But she was fine, fine, no
harm done.

I waited, knowing that asking questions might stanch the
flow of his slapdash, oblique revelations. And that he would
eventually have questions for me, of things that I didn't really
want to talk about, which after the drunken mornings with
Cecilia, I had promised myself I would never reveal to anyone
if I could not reveal them to her. Soon enough, the German
continued with his speculations on what I must be thinking
about him, up to the point of how he had lured me to Varadero
and reassigned me to one of his foreign cohorts. Dinnya, he
told me his name was.

You needed a little relief, and he was up to it. I wanted to
make sure you were happy when you returned to the capital. He smiled, and still in the reclining position, extended a
hand toward me, revealing his real name, Steffen Seafarer, or
Seifert, or his new fictional name for all I knew, but it seemed
as if he was in a mood for truth-telling.

He went into one of the cabinets and pulled a hidden bottle
of chispa de tren. I told him that Bertila made it in her own
bathtub, and he said he could tell, he'd hallucinated the three
nights he spent in the apartment. He poured out two more
glasses and waited for me to take a chug. He lent me a hand
and led me to the barber's chair, which he straightened up
with a kick from underneath.

The time had come for the truth, he said.

What is neither the truth nor a lie, man perceives as the truth.

José Lezama Lima

A PARTING GIFT

I had disappeared without warning—just left like the rest of them. I was no different from either of her sons, from Inocente St. Louis, from comandante Juan. He too had disappeared, at least momentarily. I had left her all alone, left the capital for much longer than I had intended. Although by the time I was back in the neighborhood, to the barber's chair, eager to drink shot after shot of Bertila's chispa de tren as truth serum (which Steffen kept finding hidden in cubbyholes all over the apartment), I had embarked on what I had promised to myself.

I had begun to look for Renato in earnest. I had begun to run toward him as if he had taken a part of me with him that I wanted back. That Steffen had some connection to others who also needed to find Renato did not tempt me to go on my own. They would be watching me anyway, whether I did this alone or with the German. What he wanted, I feared—what all Yuma want—was an experience, a revolutionary adventure that he could recount to a lover in his middle age. This thought, though, made me question more seriously the nature of my endgame if we were to find Renato and the others. Would he still be the tattooed wild boy that met me at the gate

of the sidatorio with such childish glee? Or had he metamorphosed again—from dutiful pionero to wild boy to whatever
the next incarnation that had possessed him? Had the recluse
of Calle Obispo become the thing he had always wanted to
be, a subversive that would make his brother proud?

Who are they? Steffen asked. What is it about that house?

I wasn't really sure that mattered or would help us find
Renato.

What is it about that house?

I leaned back in the barber's chair and closed my eyes.

I'm on your side, the German said.

That's good, that you've figured out which side I'm on.

Why did you leave her?

Cecilia couldn't have expected anything else out of me. Her
whole life had been a series of abandonments. With Pascual,
her husband, it had been as if he had never been there after
the birth of Renato. He had become more and more involved
in the National Assembly, which required him to travel all
over the Island, implementing revolutionary programs in the
countryside, along the way becoming a master electrician,
which surprised Cecilia, she told me during the mornings
of the summer quarantine, because he was so inept with his
hands otherwise, so unsuited for physical labor. As a lover, he
was surprisingly different, his hands nimble as Soviet gym-
nasts, so spry she could never keep track of where they had
been, where they were heading, so often she felt as if more
than one of him was there. Over time they became spotted
with calluses, along the base of the fingers and the meat of the
thumbs, la Revolución giving him the hands of a field worker;
during the early days of their marriage, when he returned to
the city, when he snuck back into their marriage bed late at
night, unshowered, smelling of the dirty business of la Revolución, the cigar-smoke-filled meeting halls, the sweaty workers'

trucks, the shit-tilled land that stuck to his boots and left little trails from the living room, up the stone stairways to their bed, when he reached around and put his hand on her belly, on her breast, on the small of her back, on her temple, all at once, they felt as soft as on the morning when he had grabbed her wrist and taught her how to swing a machete, when he was as untutored a revolutionary as she had been.

Not that he hadn't cared for his sons. This I knew from Nicolás and Renato as well as from her, who made it a point never to say an ill word about him, and to announce they would never do such a thing. This house, my business, she would say after a busy night at the paladar, sipping rum and smoking cigarettes, none of it would have been possible without Pascual. I had to be a mother, and he was a provider, a good one. But this was just talk, because except for the house, which was never really theirs except to live in till they died, as it is not mine now, Pascual had left them with no means of sustenance. It was comandante Juan who had stepped in and stole Inocente St. Louis from Nicolás's band of misfits, offering him the kind of salary a chef would make in the embassies in Vedado, who found channels to buy choice produce sometimes unavailable even to the tourist restaurants.

Pascual had also left her at the worst possible age for the brothers. She would never admit to me how lost she had been as a mother, how unnatural it felt. But I knew from the way she talked about motherhood, and her sons sensed it also. They went from calling her mamá, to Cecilia, to even the formal *usted* sometimes when they wanted to be real sarcastic shits. She became a stranger, one they wanted nothing to do with, or worse, a collaborator with a system they wanted to destroy.

At first, it had been the other way around, at least with

Renato, as she tried to seduce him away from the flunky life of his father.

When Renato was eight, she remembered one of these opportunities. He had seen a violin in a music shop in the old city, the body scratched, a sorrowful sight to see, the strings hanging loose down its neck. Small dents on its rib and its pegbox made it clear that more than once it had been dropped, or someone had used it as a beating implement. He had told his mamá he wanted it for Three Kings' Day, much too old to believe in such fantasies anymore, magi bearing gifts for children, but still.

Nicolás never talked to me about those days in the entire year we spent fucking. ¿Para qué? he said. What have I lost back there, pendejo? Nicolás too often pretended that he had been born on the day in which he was living, but when in a certain mood, Renato could talk about little else but the past. Their mamá had told them that Fidel had passed a law that forbade the three Arabian kings from entering the Island. Whatever little toys they got, piled up under a corner of the giant branches of brush pine that served as their Christmas tree, they should be grateful, because Melchior, Balthazar, and Gaspar had to sneak into the country without their camels and carry everything on their backs.

¡Huevona! Renato said when he retold the story, during one of our Fridays traipsing up and down the Malecón. And we believed all of it. Me, already having memorized Engels and Sandino and I still believed in magical Arabian kings.

The only reason that they could be allowed to believe, that they even knew about the three Arabian kings, that a nativity scene was allowed in the house, that the birth of the baby whom his mother only mentioned about this time of year, was because Pascual was usually gone into the countryside at the beginning of the year, one of the busiest times of the sugar harvest.

Nicolás played with the statuettes of the nativity scene, laying the kings' faces down and hiding them behind hillocks of hay that belonged in the manger, imagining the crab-like guerrilla warriors greater than Fidel and his barbudos, stealthily making their journey from one end of the Island to the other, on elbows and knees, in one magical night, the baby Jesus and the resplendent fire over Bethlehem far from their minds. The three Arabian kings as bearded counterrevolutionaries.

Nicolás wrote long impassioned letters to the kings, addressed to their castles in the heart of the African deserts, promising the freedom fighters would soon liberate the Island from the tyrant. He thanked them for all the great risks they took, pledged to them his loyalty as subject. Their mother sealed the letters and secretly burned them before their father could read them, for those were the days before he had been cast out of the Federation of Cuban Workers, before he himself took the voyage out and grew to pretend his life in Cuba had been a life lived by some distant brother.

Although his mamá knew that Renato would not soon get his violin, she told the brothers that she had mailed the letters, but that Castro too was in control of that, that there were workers employed in the basement of the Palace of the Revolution whose only duty was to open letters and read them, discarding the objectionable ones by submerging them in buckets of water till the ink ran before they put them back into the envelopes. Todo, we believed it all, Renato guffawed. But his mamá made sure that they did not forget what they longed for, because it kept them perturbed and tenacious, she told me once, so that they would not become the docile mule their father had turned into. At night, when she put Renato to bed, she caressed his hands, pressing them between her moist palms so that he could feel the thousand little bones shift this way and that accommodating to her pressure.

Week after week and month after month, his mamá took him to the old music shop on Calle Colón and made him watch the leaning violin, knowing she would not be able to buy it, but letting Renato pine for it. Afterward, she took him to the National Library and listened to scratchy recordings of the great violin concertos, sonatas, chamber pieces, Renato sitting on her lap, already too heavy—when I repeat this story back to Renato to ferret out the truths, as we switch the telling of each other's childhoods, it is almost a satire, a giant boy, his legs dangling to the side, sharing one bulky headset with his mother, her eyes closed, her cheek pressed to his, her arms tight around his belly, as if she were afraid that he would get up and flee. They did this so often that Renato became convinced that his mother was beginning to gather admirers, pale skinny men who sat at other record players on the opposite side of the room and stared at them. Who knows if they were not staring at him? On the hours after the siesta when other kids were playing béisbol on the cobblestone streets or watching muñequitos in cool shadowy rooms, Renato began to regret the object of his longing, the leaning violin, grew to hate the stubborn optimism of the lonely young men sitting across from them, the drawn haggard look on their faces giving them the appearance of starving grasshoppers.

Then, just before Renato's tenth birthday, fate broke the routine. His father came home early one evening and announced that they were moving, finally leaving their cramped two-room apartment on Calle Amargura.

The spacious home that had belonged to an infamous disgraced writer had just become available. He showed them the writer's brief mimeographed obituary that he had taken from the Ministry of the Interior. Only his wife, whom he had married at the behest of his dying mother a few years before his death, survived him. A sepia photograph, no larger than the little piece of paper that contained the whole man's life was paper-clipped to the back of the mimeograph. The Ministry had annulled the sham marriage and taken possession of the man's house, and in a lottery awarded it to them.

A house, carajo, their father said, a house, por fin. Cecilia tried to smile, but the brothers already knew that a hundred houses or a thousand kisses could never make up to her all the days that Pascual had been absent. That night, with the writer's obituary carefully folded into his pocket, he took the three of them to Calle Obispo so they could see their new house.

We won't be able to go inside, he explained to Nicolás and Renato, one on each side of him, Cecilia trailing behind. The ersatz widow was still in there. But she had orders to leave by the end of the month. The government has revoked her marriage to the old writer, he repeated. ¡El viejo era un maricón! Their father checked the number on the houses and consulted the obituary repeatedly, as if he were following the trail of a treasure map, Renato thought. By the time they approached the site of their future home, night had just begun to fall. The heavy mesquite door lay half-open. A pair of old unshaven men in dark rumpled suits stood outside and conversed quietly, their heads downcast, staring out at the cobblestone street. They looked at the visitors once and must have assumed they were there for the wake, for they stepped out of the way and one of them informed the father in a whisper that the widow took mourners out on the patio. He took a step out toward the street and the family walked into the house, blinded by the more pronounced darkness.

Renato said that he remembered holding onto the hem of his mamá's dress till he could see again. An old iron chandelier hung from a wooden beam high above the living room. Its little bulbs, most burned out, gave off a meager light.

There were two closed doors on each side of the living room and Renato sensed that the body lay in rest behind one of them. The family stepped carefully around the books and papers that littered much of the floor. The mourners looked them over and glanced at the widow, whom they could now see through an archway, seated out in the stone patio with her back to them, under a withered midget tree. One of the mourners, a young man, whispered something in her ear, and she turned and looked at the young family, her face floating on a bundle of black mantles wrapped around her shoulders, her hair frizzy and uncombed and gathered around her neck, a pallid ruff. Looking more closely, she shook her head slowly this time, hunching her shoulders and turning away.

The young man came into the living room; he shook their father's hand and said that María was glad that they had come to pay their respects, but she was with friends at the moment.

Cecilia turned to leave.

Pascual resisted for a moment, insisting that it was their right to have a look at the house that was for all purposes theirs, but he followed his family out.

Me cago, this is what it's come to, Cecilia said, loud enough for Pascual and the loitering mourners to hear. We must steal houses from old widows. What a glorious thing, your Revolución.

Pascual made a move to shush her, but she dashed away.

Yet, a month later, when the father came home with a set of ancient jangly keys, they set off again for the house on Calle Obispo, this time a lot less enthusiastic than before, the father leading the way, the boys and the mother following dutifully. The father kept the keys buried in his pocket, and every few steps he would reach in there and check for them, their whole future something that could slip out through a hole in his pocket.

Ya casi llegamos, he said, and raised his free arm over his head and swung it forward, a mounted general leading a charge—un puro Máximo Gómez, Renato remembered—and then he stopped, awed in front of the tall mesquite door, which from its charred splintery surface seemed to have withstood against the force of invaders much greater than their father. He stood there in front of 175 Calle Obispo looking up at the door, dwarfed by it, the fiber of all his previous enthusiasm frayed.

The keys, their mamá said as they approached him—and she grabbed the arm with the hand still buried in his pocket. Pascual remained motionless, his shoulders hunched. He squeezed his eyes and looked at Cecilia, a shrill birdsong drowning her words and the garish noonlight effacing her figure. Renato listened closely for a voice coming from within the house, for he guessed that that was what Pascual was listening to—the condemning ramblings of the enraged ghost of the writer that Nicolás had told him he had heard on the first visit. Although Renato heard nothing that day or ever again, he soon grew to believe that the ghost had cursed the house with his death. Before their father came back to this world, before he somnambulistically took his hand out of his pocket and reached out the large key ring to Cecilia, his fingers held fast around it, Cecilia took over. ¿Qué te pasa? she said to him, this is our house, our house now, remember—it was she who had to put the keys to the rusty lock and thrown open the door to their new life, but before all of this, before the father could join them in their new life, before their mamá grabbed him by the arm and led him, dragged Renato past the threshold, while he still listened to a frenzied voice from the beyond, Pascual looked at Renato (at this point in my retelling of the story, Renato always took it back from me, he did not want me to get the look wrong), a gentle indulgent look directly into his son's own eyes, something of fear, but also of awe, of the surprise of a man on a bolting horse, which he held as long as he could, so that for a moment it was as if his mamá and brother did not exist, and this, this, that he too might have heard, the phantasmagorical jeremiad from the one whose house they were stealing (porque their mamá was wrong in this—as they would find out as soon as they stepped through the mesquite door—it was not from the widow they were stealing the house, but from him, the corpulent old sodomite writer, as Pascual had begun to refer to him, for every room on the first floor of his old house still reeked of his presence, of his pungent dark cigars, of his moldy manuscripts and musty collection of photographs from American physique magazines, and of his rank unquenchable lust, and of the old woman they had seen wrapped in blankets under the avocado tree, nothing—no scent, no photograph, no token of any existence), his, the discomfited ghost in their new house.

In the living room, Pascual tried to regain his composure. He put his hand out, and Cecilia readily returned the key ring. With a severe gesture, he threw open the heavy drapes of the front window, which had apparently not been drawn since the death. A cloud of dust and light engulfed him. They had cleared the room of furniture, but there were still sundry books and papers in the bookshelves of the living room, bowed like the hull of a boat, and the terra-cotta floors were littered with hundreds of pieces of yellowed brittle paper. There were termite trails threading up the frame of the doorway and wriggling on the wall and behind the bookshelves. A thin layer of termite dust covered the floor of the first room. Pascual walked in circles. His heavy worker boots left stark ghostly footprints on the dusty terra-cotta. He shook the bookshelves to see if they had been bolted to the wall. Little puffs of dust emanated from them. Their father would have little use for any books, whatever he had learned about la Revolución he had done so from the mouths of others, from their actions, not from books, and that's what he intended to do with his sons.

Pascual dug with his fingernails into one of the termite trails and hummed dramatically as he inspected the damage to the wood. Cecilia, Nicolás, and Renato stood near the entrance and watched him. Renato felt as if they should all be holding hands. They each stood there alone with their hands at their sides. The father walked to the far-left corner of the room; there was a narrow askew doorway there, crudely boarded up with thin pieces of plywood, which he punched through with the base of his palm and with his boot.

The eye of the needle, he said, then he snuck under and his whole body disappeared through the little doorway as if through a hole in the ground. They stared for a moment, and then Cecilia grabbed them. Come on, she said, there are other rooms to see. She turned to her right and tried the door in the inset doorway, to the room from where Nicolás said he had heard the voice, but it was either stuck or locked. It would be months before they would find the many books in there Renato would later sell at the open-air market. She didn't call out to Pascual for the keys but pressed her knee to the lower part of the door and gave it a hard push—but it did not budge.

She went outside to try to look through the window, but it had been boarded up from the inside. When she returned to inform her sons of this, the father was back in the room, his blue work pants and white T-shirt, his face, and his arms stained with an orange silvery powder, the dust of a sunrise. He pointed to the ceiling, smiling.

There are rooms up there. Three, coño, three, you can see the roofs of the city. They must not have used them.

Cecilia examined the narrow doorway. He could not have fit, she said simply. The father looked back at the doorway.

He laughed loudly. She was right, they would soon find the other wider catera stone stairway that had been built for the writer, although there must have come a day when he could no longer ascend them.

The stairs are worn out, broken. Even if el pobre maricón could have fit. He threw up his arms in the air and did a half-circle so that he faced the archway to the patio. We'll fix everything!

I want to go with you, papá, Nicolás said. It was the first time he had spoken that morning. I want to see the roofs. In those days, he was the only one who asked things of the father freely. The father turned and looked at Nicolás as if the whole purpose of their morning expedition to the new house had been this, for his elder son to speak up, to ask him to see the roofs of the old city. He crouched beside Nicolás, put his arm around him, and asked him softly if he was sure he wanted to go up. It was dark, musty, spiderwebby. Nicolás nodded vigorously, lips in a tight pout of courage. They went through the eye of the needle, the father with his hands wrapped around Nicolás's waist, lifting him up the first steps. He had not asked Renato if he wanted to see the roofs of the old city, and Cecilia must have sensed the younger son's disappointment. She stood behind Renato and put her hands, one over the other, on his chest.

He can't take both of you at the same time. It would be too dangerous, she said. Renato nodded half-heartedly. There are other things to see. Look at all the books they left behind. Maybe some of them are worth something. He nodded unconvincingly again, and she made him walk, pushing the back of his legs with her knees—and with her hands still crossed over his chest, tapping lightly, she led him out to the patio.

When they had crossed the archway that led outside, she let go of him and with a little shove pushed him away from her.

Look at all the room you'll have to play, she said.

He looked around, turning his whole body in a circle, and quickly realized that there was not that much room. But since they had never had an outside area that was quite their own, even in its neglected state the patio seemed paradise enough. A pair of crumbling brick walls that met at a wide angle in the deep end enclosed the area; a determined fern crept along the craggy surface of the walls and along the cracks of the broken stones that made the floor.

Maidenhair, Cecilia said, and Renato thought of them sitting in the library, listening to violins, her hair brushing his cheek and falling on his neck. Maidenhair, she repeated, it's everywhere. It's the only thing that survived. And the widow, the widow too, she survived.

She went under the withered avocado tree potted in a rusty pail, half-sunk into a hole in the center of the patio. The sharp edges of the pail folded over and chips of white paint clung to its sides like hungry insects. The tree's trunk was brittle, its bark peeling to reveal a sallow flesh. Its leaves few and limp and wan, its branches thin and crooked—all this I imagine not from Renato's retelling of it, but from Cecilia's, who always bragged of how she had saved that tree and gave graphic descriptions of the state she had found it in. In one low branch that grew out toward the brick wall, almost against their will, there hung a pair of wine-dark fruit. Their weight seemed a dire threat to the whole equilibrium of the old tree. Cecilia gently pulled the fruit off and held the pair of avocados close to her chest.

We'll have these for dinner tonight, she said. She looked around the patio. There was some life left in this old house, after all, she added. But to Renato it seemed as if all life that grew there was trying to escape the withered brown patio—everything was verdant just beyond its perimeters. A thick canopy of branches from neighboring trees, níspero and mango and guava, shaded the patio from any direct light. Their overripe fruit fell and stained the cracked stones of their patio, leaving misshapen black marks. Other fruit hung in the air with much more dignity than the cumbersome avocados.

On one side of the patio stood a wide low archway into the kitchen, a big square room—with its own red tile roof and chimney—that seemed joined to the patio more than to the rest of the house. A long oak table, lonely without its surrounding chairs, sat in the middle of the room. And though only a little light from a far window fell on them, the white appliances and the tile countertops gleamed. Cecilia explored the kitchen, the avocados still pressed to her chest like newborn birds, a placid satisfied expression on her face that her son had not seen in a long while, not since she used to tuck him into bed and massage his hands. He knew that day that the freestanding kitchen would become Cecilia's favorite room, a little house all to her own, and only while in the kitchen or sitting under her born-again avocado would any of them see that expression on her face again.

At the other end of the patio stood a narrower rectangular structure with a half-shut sliding door that hung from a rail. It featured a makeshift corrugated tin roof, its walls shoddily made, the stucco falling off in chunks to reveal its rusty and precarious skeleton of thin slats and chicken wire. It seemed no more than a lean-to. Renato looked at the darkness through the cracks in the hanging door. He peeked in through the slats and wondered if the ghost of the old writer snoozed in there, as well. It seemed a proper place for a ghost.

Anything? Cecilia called.

She had moved from under the avocado tree. He was surprised that she was still watching him. He shook his head and moved away from the shack toward the back of the patio.

To impress his mamá, he tried to scale the brick wall and peer over into their new neighbor's yard, but just as he was about to jut his chin over the crest, his foot slipped and he went sliding down. He sat on the stone ground, staring at the ripped skin on the heel of his right palm, waiting for it to start to bleed. Cecilia ran over and crouched by him. She tucked the avocados in the folds of her dress and took both his hands in hers. She kissed the wounds. A droplet of blood, viscous and brilliant as a pomegranate seed, stuck to her lower lip.

Ay niño, she said, how are you ever going to be able to play the violin if you don't take care of your beautiful big hands? He looked up into her burnt-sugar eyes. She hadn't mentioned the violin since the day Pascual arrived at the apartment with news about their new house. She stared back at him and offered a secret smile, signaling to him that if they had a house of their own anything was possible. As if having heard this, Pascual caught their attention. He stood on the second-floor gallery, with Nicolás in front of him, by a section where the railing had cracked and jutted outward, leaving a wide gap.

Nicolás told me that he did not remember any of what happened next. During one of our last conversations, I asked him about it, and he laughed, said his little brother had been hallucinating since he was a child, that perhaps it was a wish-fulfillment vision. He had wanted to see the father endanger the life of his older son. This happened a few months before he left forever, anyway, endangering all their lives—so a prophetic vision, perhaps.

But this is what Renato remembered, as he told me the story of their first two visits to the house on Calle Obispo the night I met him.

Pascual's hand slowly slid behind Nicolás. A moment later, Nicolás appeared to take a few tiptoe steps toward the edge of the cracked railing, and as he put his hands out (to protect himself, Renato said, why else would he put his hands out like that, to stop whatever force was pushing him from behind?), a sliver of the railing came loose and tumbled down to the tin roof of the henhouse below. It was a short drop; Renato knew there would be no great harm in a fall, so when he looked back up, he did not feel the panic of his mamá, who dropped his hand and ran toward them. Pebbles and dust from the unswept floor of the gallery hit the tin roof first, and Renato kept his eyes on his brother, who was looking back directly at him, laughing maniacally, his arms waving in the air. Just as he became air bound, his forearms now crossed in front of him, his hands shielding his face from the fall, Cecilia halfway toward the henhouse, the avocados smashing wayside, her arms outstretched absurdly to catch him, all silent except for the echo of pebbles on tin and a timpani giggle that Renato at first thought was the ghost's breath bouncing off the inside of the rusted roof, Nicolás was drawn back up from his waist and hung suspended in the air for a moment, before he floated back up to the edge of the cracked railing. The snigger grew now to a full-blown guffaw—Pascual's—with both his arms around his son's waist.

Cecilia ran up, it was then that she found the other stairway in one corner of the patio, shaking her head, muttering their father's name under her breath. Renato watched her pull his brother away from Pascual in one tug, which was no easy task, since by thirteen Nicolás had almost reached the height he would be by the time of his death at twenty, skinny as a lizard, the ends of bones poking out all over the place as on the day I met him, but still significantly over six feet tall. Cecilia grabbed her husband by the shoulder, turned him around and slapped him once, composed, but seriously enough so that Nicolás saw the need to pull her away. Pascual still laughed, screaming that it was nothing, that he was a boy, that he enjoyed such pranks. ¡No jodas, mi amor! How do you know, Renato heard his mamá say, how do you know what they enjoy?

Pascual turned from them. He went to the edge of the gallery, spread open his arms and nodded once at Renato, seeking his approval. He was as wiry and tall as his eldest, his arms coursing with thick veins, always flushed, bristling with an energy that flowed just underneath the surface of his skin. Renato had no memory of his father ever holding him, but he always imagined that papá would be feverish, dangerous to hold too long.

Standing on the edge of the gallery, cleaving open a wider space so that more pebbles clanged on the shed's tin roof below, Renato told me that he knew he would soon disappear from their lives, that this house was a parting gift to Cecilia, a consolation prize for how he had failed them all as a husband and a father. But at that moment, at that moment exactly, as Cecilia and Nicolás disappeared from behind him, it seemed as if he was going to fly, as if he were going to leave them, right then and there. He screamed and leapt, and like Nicolás, it seemed he remained suspended in the air for a second. But there was no going back for him. He plummeted to the tin roof with an astonishing crash because of all the pebbles that had gathered there. Cecilia appeared below holding onto Nicolás by the hand, sensing perhaps that he was still somehow in danger.

This part Nicolás remembered, their father jumping and crushing the roof of the shed, a ball of dust rising in the air like a bomb had just gone off, Pascual bursting through the leaning door, a smirk still on his face, his face and shirt smudged with chicken shit.

All they had ever known of their father was the diligent Party man, shuffling in and out of their small apartment with

reams of papers and documents that needed his attention, disappearing for weeks at a time, and returning as if he had just
left that morning, patting the boys on the head at the dinner
table, kissing their mamá on the cheek, later at night, coming
to their room and quizzing them on what they were learning
at school, lessons from their books that he could recite from
memory, arcane facts to the exact kilogram of a certain sugar
harvest or a turn of phrase in an early Fidel speech, before the
rebels had even arrived in the capital, grooming them for the day
when they would begin to make their way up the labyrinthine
ranks of the Party. And here he was, maddened with this new
acquisition, a home for his family, so maddened that he had
tried to push his son off a ledge and then leapt off himself.
Here he was, shit encrusted, full of the devil's joy, a raving
lunatic in another man's asylum.

After that day, they only saw their father again a handful of
times, after they had moved into the refurbished house—the
plaster walls around the narrow eye of the needle stairway
torn down, a gallery with mosaic tile floors and a new wooden
balustrade built all along the second floor bedrooms, new, or
only relatively used, white appliances in the open-air kitchen,
a profusion of bromeliads, gardenias, and other garish orna-
mentals scattered throughout the patio in ceramic pots and
hanging from the eaves gigantic coconut heads sprouting
forked leathery leaves, and a fresh coat of paint in various
earth tone hues for every room in the house, even the sealed
room where Renato had thought the corpse lay, which even
after they had dusted it and scrubbed the tile floors clean still
felt cramped as a crypt due to the profusion of books there.
When Pascual reappeared from his last trip to the countryside, all the renovations finished by workers he had hired,
he announced that he would be traveling to Madrid, on the
way to what would soon become the former Soviet Republics,

where the State was trying to hold on to its crumbling alliances.

Pascual never returned from that journey. The next time that Cecilia heard from him was about three years before I appeared on her doorstep with Nicolás. He wrote from one of his mother's cousins' house in Tampa, Florida. He asked about his sons, about the house, and about the city, neglecting to inquire about her well-being at all, but making a note of concluding that he was enclosing some money and presents for the children inside the fancy-colored sleeve of the envelope, forty crisp twenty-dollar bills, punctiliously folded into sharp-edged rectangles and a pair of gum sticks in their silver sleeves. Cecilia gave the dollars to comandante Juan to use for funds for the paladar, in those days when they were establishing enough stock and inventory. When I asked her what she had done with the gum, she told me that she had dispassionately ground each of them in her mouth until there was not a mite of flavor left.

During the summer of the bombs, Cecilia stopped me every time I tried to get a more detailed version of these days, daring to broach the topic only after the third or fourth shot of afternoon rum. But no matter how much rum she had drunk she always insisted that the story was inconsequential. The family had won the house in a lottery, it no more belonged to Pascual now that he had abandoned the family than it belonged to the dead writer or his widowed bride.

LOS INJECTED ONES

Renato never got that violin.

After a while, he said, he even stopped yearning for it, though seven years later, a few days after I arrived, he took me to the store where it still rested in the display window. The place had stopped selling musical instruments and the violin stood among a congregation of cheap tourist trinkets and T-shirts. I pledged to myself that I would steal it for Renato, that I would give him what his parents had failed to provide for him in all the years of their cold ineffectiveness, or so Nicolás put it and laughed when I told him of my plan, said that only a guajiro from the boonies in Oriente could be so sentimental, that I should write a bolero about the violin. Then a few days later, I saw the thing resting in a corner of the henhouse, in the same docile pose it had been leaning in the store window for seven years.

I asked Nicolás if he was going to give it to Renato himself.

It's now mine. Boy doesn't need his delusions.

It was enough that his brother had dropped out of school and now trailed him day and night like a motherless lemur. He would do the same thing with me one day, Nicolás threatened, so I should beware. Although in the end, it was I who went chasing him, as if I wanted to be possessed by him as he had been possessed by his older brother.

Nicolás once emphasized that he had brought me here to work for his mother, not to be his little brother's caretaker. This was a week or so after I had arrived at the house on Calle Obispo. I had seen him no more than a handful of times for bouts of frenzied half-sex in the henhouse, Nicolás barely acknowledging me otherwise on his comings and goings, although I remained the only one who dared enter the henhouse for something other than collecting the rare eggs or feeding the chickens pulverized clam shells that were supposed to make their eggshells harder. It was difficult to be in there for more than a few minutes without your eyes watering from the fetid air, but I withstood it because of the way he made me feel when he pulled my face close to his bare skin, and he smelled of all the things that I could never smell on my own flesh, of the secret places in the city, of strangers I would never meet, of a liberty I would never dare. When Nicolás came by, he played the hermit of the henhouse, tinkling with his dinghy and the Lada engine, only taking a break for me. The morning after the Ministry of Health took him, his ark and its motor disappeared overnight.

I had asked him what he planned to do with the violin.

Burn it.

When I made a move to grab it, Nicolás leapt on me from behind and pressed me to the floor. He had stood a few paces away but moved so fast that I barely made a gesture toward the violin before he pinned me to the ground, his forearm to the side of my head, my cheek smeared with shit mud. Don't become too interested in my little brother, he said.

It was early in the night, and from the patio I could hear the chatter of the first few patrons of the evening, the click-clatter of pans and dishes from behind the line, Inocente St. Louis wailing that appetizers were ready to be picked up. I had, by that time, already worked four straight shifts in the paladar as a waiter, stumbling my way through the complexity of the menu, which I had to recite to each dining party from memory. Cecilia probably wondered by now where I had gone. As Nicolás lay on top of me, beginning to grind, unbelievably heavy for such a skeletal creature, I protested that my waiter's uniform was going to smell like hen shit, that he could do what he wanted with the maldito violin. She won't fire you, he said, she has fallen half in love with you already. La puta.

Which was a surprise to me, because aside from Renato, no one had taken the slightest interest in my life or where I had come from, perhaps because they sensed that I did not have much of an interest in it myself, that what I wanted was a new life I did not know where to find. Nicolás lifted his hips from me, a great relief, but somehow, I still felt pinned and shit-smeared to the ground by his presence over me. He reached down, flipped me over with one hand, and then effortlessly lifted me, carrying me as if I were a fainted bride to the dinghy where he sometimes slept, layered in blankets that had not been washed in ages and were permeated with the briny stink of the place. My feet were hanging off the sides of the tiny dinghy and Nicolás assiduously began to undo the laces of the shiny mocasines that Cecilia had sold to me as part of my uniform, two sizes too big. He explained to me that these had been his own shoes once, that by the time he was ten his feet had grown so large that when they had gone on a snorkeling field trip once off Cayo Coco, their father had joked that he did not need flippers. He took off my shoes, my socks, my pants, and my button-down shirt, carefully folding each with a care that I could not imagine he ever took with his own clothes now, ratty jeans and T-shirts splattered with paint from his part-time job at the marina. He expounded on the history of each article of clothing I wore, all part of the extensive uniform that would take me more than a few shifts to pay off, down to the camiseta and briefs that had belonged to his father.

He added that he could see my hard-on peeking through his father's spotty underwear. I made one attempt to resist, partly because I didn't want to lose my job, but also because I was sure that we could easily be seen through the wooden slats of the henhouse, that if we started anything we would be providing dinnertime depravity for the stream of guests now filling up the tables. As I heard Cecilia drumroll through the long Apostles' Creed of the menu, I got up on my elbows and tried to throw one leg over the side of the rowboat, but all Nicolás had to do was put his hand on my chest, and then gently pull off his father's old undershirt.

And so you made love to him, real love, not like the other times, Steffen said to me, excited at the prospect. I sat on Bertila's barber chair and he was now in front of me, in an old rattan chair that was the only other piece of furniture that Bertila kept in the living room, for clients to wait for their appointment in case they came early.

We fucked for the first time, I said. Once, twice, three times, we fucked in the leaky rowboat until we could hear the last guests leaving the paladar. Fucked. I wasn't in love with him.

But a few days later you must be?

Sí, a few days later I must have been. Or with his brother, who knows what I was thinking. I rubbed the sides of my temple. What are we doing? I asked.

We had been sipping Bertila's chispa de tren for a few hours. There seemed to be an endless supply of it.

Did you know anything yet? Steffen went back to the story.

No, not yet.

And this, this I must know, when you made love to him.

We fucked!

Yes, did you—

¿Qué?

Steffen shot up his index finger and with his other hand made as if to wrap it in a sausage casing. I shook my head, took another sip of chispa de tren.

So, he was initiating you?

No, we were fucking, I repeated. The initiation to the group dealt with blood and needles, at least from the way it had been described to me. It seemed a ritual, weirdly Catholic in a way, the needle with the infected blood raised to the air like the priest raises the chalice.

But you never saw it? He never tried to recruit you?

No, I said. I never saw it. I don't even know if any of it is true.

As for the nights in the henhouse, it wasn't that at all. It was just two horny kids having sex, making love, fucking, whatever you want to call it.

By the time I came out of the henhouse, my uniform crisp as when I had gone in, dinner service was over. Cecilia and comandante Juan sat by themselves at the table underneath the avocado, Inocente St. Louis gone. I couldn't look at them and went directly up the stairs to my room. Comandante Juan cat-whistled at me. I heard Cecilia chastise him. The next day, Nicolás had left. Everyone pretended that nothing had happened. I went back to my new job, my skills at reciting the menu, knowing just which ingredients to stress, which items to accentuate (in both cases, whatever comandante Juan had bought in bulk through his bolsa connections), soon becoming as refined as Cecilia's, whom I often heard reciting the menu at some other table simultaneously, a few phrases ahead, a few phrases behind, a culinary harmonizing that lent authenticity to the place. This went on for a few months, Nicolás appeared, and in the henhouse by the excited cackling of the hens, our rooster had come for a visit. On those nights, Cecilia tacitly accepted that she would have to take the extra burden of tables, that comandante Juan would even condescend to step down from his position as maître d' and wait on a few tables.

It was during one of those nights that he began taking me out with him and I began to learn about their group, about the new revolución, this one stealthier and deadlier than the old one, with its apocalyptic visions and Operation Pink Plague. The irony was that it had begun a few years too late, that soon their strategy for conquest and devastation would be overcome by science, that cursed as they were, they were the last to suffer a death sentence from the disease they meant to spread all over the Island. Not that it was ever serious anyway, schoolboy comic book fantasies.

When did you know? Steffen asked.

We were just lovers, coño. There, I said it. We were lovers, once a week, or every ten days, or every two weeks, or so. Who kept count? So it was during one of those nights, after a few months of this that he told me about the group, introduced me to some of them who slept in trees in Parque Lenin.

It had been happening on the Island almost from the day that the first sanitarium opened, he said, so many of the young men, almost never women, injecting themselves with infected blood, because it was an act of rebellion, because they wanted to get some of the conveniences offered in the sidatorio that were so lacking on the rest of the Island. Acuérdate, this was the beginning of the special period. Steffen nodded vigorously. He had been around enough he had heard about the special period, not that we were out of it.

The economy collapsed after the Soviet subsidies dried out. The opposite of what happened in your capital. Complete economic collapse. There wasn't shit anywhere. There was gravelly rice for dinner every night, with a watery touch of frijoles-colored water. There was washing your cojones and under your armpits with your own slippery drool, just to mimic the sensation of soap. We were living like plaza tomcats. And they still expected us to go to school, Nicolás told me, in our crisp pionero uniforms, moving up the ranks, to join el partido. Many opted out, and with just a little bit of infected blood was the easiest way. They did it because of rebellion, but mostly, he said, they did it because they were desperate for something else. All this Nicolás told me in the most casual way, his arms wrapped around me as I lay on top of him half-covered by the fetid blankets on his lifeboat. It became a cult, almost, los injected ones, they called themselves, the yanquis even got into it.

Nicolás knew a boy at the first sidatorio he escaped from, a bugarrón named Puchito Canals, who was interviewed by a yanqui reporter from Nueva York, followed around for days as he told her his woeful tale of injecting himself with tainted blood, having to leave his wife and young daughter with his mother, whom he visited on weekends, and how he now at once regretted and took pride in his decision, how he came to condemn the foolishness of his rebellious act as well as finally feeling a sense of destiny that he had never felt before, or so it was eventually written. Carajo, who knows what Puchito Canals really told her, Nicolás said.

For days, he carried around the copy of the magazine that the reporter had sent him from her newspaper, the piece written with the melancholic air and politely condescending tone that only a yanqui writer could muster. How paradoxical a system that drives its young to do this then offers them such care! There were pictures of Puchito Canals in the sidatorio cafeteria speaking seriously with other patients, as if they were discussing the most pertinent theological or political questions, pictures of the sorrowful mother and the betrayed wife, a tight close-up picture of the innocent face of his daughter, and finally near the end of the endless article, a picture of Puchito Canals in a bathing suit, under a waterfall, his face lifted up, his arms outspread, either angelically embracing death or begging you to come and fuck him. The perfect Cuban San Sebastián.

It was all based on a simple lie, on a story that Puchito Canals had told his family, and himself, and his friends at the sidatorio, and then told to the yanqui writer, long enough and with enough conviction that he probably came to believe it himself. And once it was in print in a yanqui magazine, it might as well have been in the government newspaper. The truth, however, was that Puchito Canals never injected himself, that he was one of the biggest bugarrones in the capital.

What? Steffen stopped me, saying that I must explain to him what this means, this word. Ah, though he had yet to reveal to me his own mysterious involvement in all of this, it was clear that whomever he was working for had not briefed him completely. But I knew that he could help me get to Renato with whatever information he was willing to barter, so I had to humor him. I explained to him what a bugarrón was. Of all the different distinctions of homosexuals on the Island, the bugarrón sits at the top of the food chain. He is usually married, with children, a family, often a solid member-in-standing of the Party. Like most Cuban men, he can't stand the sexual confines of the family structure, so he finds a way out, sometimes with other women, but usually with other men or transsexuals, always taking the active role in the act. Pero bueno, we all know how messy sex can be, how unpredictable, how a thing of some other galaxy. In the blackout that is the bedrooms of the city, who needs to know what's what, no?

The way Nicolás put it, and this was from his own experience, Puchito Canals had long been a committed bugarrón, a famous one at that—the boys yearned for his talent, for his expertise with his mouth, his fingers, his cosa, which was shaped like an obelisk, growing fatter and fatter toward its base, ay mami, who could resist the temptation—but after his daughter was born, something did a flip flop in the horned chamber of his brain, and Puchito Canals himself did a flip flop on the mattresses thrown in the bedrooms of the tiny houses that he rented for two dollars a day. Whereas before, it was a monthly or bimonthly adventure, often with the same boys, something to just get him through the days until their next meeting, after his daughter's birth, he rented the houses for weeks at a time, a parade of men filing through, the price of admission a little bit of rum to keep the party going and a little bit of youth to keep it exciting. It was during one of these orgies that Nicolás had met him. Puchito Canals had become infected with the virus the old-fashioned way, because after a day or two of rum-chugging he was throwing his ass higher up in the air than any of the other boys there, a bugarrón no more.

It had grown dark in Bertila's dining room. Steffen had thrown himself back in the rocking chair and closed his eyes, for a moment I thought that he had passed out from the chispa de tren, but when he spoke it was in an even and sober tone.

Did he ever explain to you . . . Nicolás . . . how this new revolución of his would work? Aside from this absurd scheme of mass infection.

Mira, I said, if you're asking what I think you're asking. It was just among the people they knew. The counterrevolution thing was some dystopic fantasy. These people are neither killers nor rebels. They don't have an unflinching belief in a cause like true rebels do. The whole ceremony thing, in truth, I only saw it once. I wasn't—

How? When? Steffen sat up. You said you had never seen it.

It doesn't matter, I said. It's not going to help us find anybody.

I stood from the barber's chair. Maybe I should just go home.

Is that house a home to you? Of course, I was free to go, he smiled. No one was holding me here.

What's your interest in all this? Why do you even care?

I'll tell you. But you have just begun your story about your involvement with the brothers, *ja*?

He stood up beside me, throwing his arms over my shoulders, schoolyard socios suddenly. We could go out and get some dinner, I could continue, and he would answer any questions I had. When I protested about the curfew, he told me to let him worry about that. No one was going to bother one of the few Yuma left on the Island willing to spend money. We would find a place at one of the hotels.

We chugged one last shot of chispa de tren and went out. There was barely anyone out in the darkening streets except la fiana, who patrolled the streets in double pairs since the bombings had started but never once approached us or asked any questions.

FURLOUGH

I had seen it once.

The series of events that led up to it had begun the afternoon in which Nicolás began his first furlough from the sanitarium. He appeared at the house on Calle Obispo as if coming down from a possessing orisha that had dropped him from the peak of the dome of heaven. For the first three months straight, he had not been allowed to leave the sidatorio, and we only heard from him sparingly.

The previous rainy season, la fiana had stopped him on his way to work and thrown him in a van with a group of other young men, part of a major roundup of those suspected of flaunting the regulations of the Ministry of Health. He was taken to a revolutionary hospital, had blood drawn by a military doctor while still in handcuffs, and kept in the municipal jail for days awaiting results. He tested positive for HIV, as did many of the others (some of whom he knew well from Puchito Canals's monthly orgies).

They held them in a military hospital for five days, while further tests were performed. Perhaps Bertila had been right, perhaps there was more than just thoughts of the common welfare when the government hatched up its sanitarium schemes.

Upon their release from the hospital, all of them were herded onto a bus like prisoners—except for the chains—and taken to the sidatorio in Cerro. The only thing that was missing were the cuffs, Nicolás said, and most of the rest of us in his gang still allowed to roam free in the capital kept waiting for them to be slapped on us at any minute. We walked with our wrists pressed together in front of us, waiting.

At the sanitarium, with these young men and the ones already there, they had begun to think up the plans for their new revolution, their summoning of the apocalyptic infectious flood. They offered the names of others as if to bring them into the fold.

Because Nicolás had probably given them my name, or because the ladies of el Comité knew everything, and I had been included in their report to the Ministry of Health, a few days after they had taken Nicolás, as we were setting up for dinner, a pair of doctors in military uniforms came to inform Cecilia of the news about her son and to follow up with me.

They spoke in a declarative monotone. Her son had been infected with the virus. He would have to be quarantined. There was some hope with new medicines. But for the collective good the quarantine was open-ended. They paused for a moment, waiting for the mother to break down and start sobbing, as they had probably witnessed hundreds of times before, but Cecilia held her own. That was her. She would rather have been disemboweled than shown them tears. Her chin did begin to tremble, as I watched askance, setting up the tables around them, listening. I could tell that she was thinking as much about me as about her own son, and she could not stop herself and cast a quick glance my way. The doctors did not need such signals. They knew.

This then is Rafael Puebla? one of them asked. He's going to need to come with us. Cecilia glanced upstairs to the gallery leading to Renato's room, but the military doctors missed that, their attention now focused on me. After they drew the blood for my own test, they let me leave—as they had not allowed Nicolás and his street buddies—given an appointment to return in a week, but not before being warned by an old nurse of the serious nature of the situation.

I did not have to go in, the military doctors returned before my appointment date and took me outside on Calle Obispo. They handed me a sheet of paper that showed the negative results of my test, warned me I was to carry it with me at all times, along with my health ID card, which they took from me and stamped with a red *H* on the right-hand corner. From here on, I was required to take the test every six months. If I remained negative, no problem. There was a pause, then one of them handed me a fistful of condoms without looking at me, like giving alms to a dirty beggar, and a mimeograph sheet documenting safe sex practices.

The truth was that none of us used condoms because it was too much of a hassle to get them once you strayed too far from the revolutionary core, even in the Yuma stores. Sure, by the time I was ten, they had become a staple in our school, and being schoolboys and not sure how these monumental sausage skins would one day really fit over our tiny flautines, as we had been taught in health class, we tore them from their casements, washed them off at the beach, and used them as giant balloons, as water bombs, as wind catchers, and with a circle of them tied together as life preservers. We heard stories about how some of the older boys used them with goats and chickens.

Once I left the school, I never saw them again. They certainly weren't for sale at the local bodega or pharmacy. Outside the system, it was hard enough to find toilet paper, much less condoms. Good luck finding even cotton balls if you had a tooth pulled, Cecilia once told me.

When Nicolás returned, on the furlough, I wanted to tell
him all this, everything that had happened since he had been
gone, but he did not seem interested and had never responded
to the many letters and goods I had sent him.

He came back to see his brother. Although during all the
months that I had previously spent there, I hardly ever saw
them together. Renato knew when his brother appeared, and
he made sure to let me know that he was in the henhouse,
but he would never go in there himself. They avoided each
other like a long unhappily married couple, communicating
in grunts whenever they passed each other, or more often,
simply ignoring each other even on the rare nights when they
sat down at the same table to eat.

When they took Nicolás the first time and came to confiscate the boat and Lada engine, they left the violin behind. Its
face had been pecked to bits by the hungry chickens, splattered with shit, but its peg and strings remained intact. It
looked like a corpse that had been half-flayed. The bow had
disappeared.

One morning, I took the damaged instrument from the
henhouse, carefully cleaned it with vinegar water, tightened
the strings as best as I could and brought it up to Renato's
room. He smiled when he saw it. He was doing what he
always did alone in his room, smoking one yanqui cigarette
after the other, the butts piled up in a deep ceramic bowl, the
ashes scattered on the floor, reading while lying faceup in bed,
the book hooked up to a medieval contraption that he had
screwed to the wall and made it possible for the open book to
float suspended above him. He did not help in the paladar, so
whatever money he had, it came from the sale of the writer's
abandoned collection and the benefactions the tourists gave
him on the nights he disappeared.

I think that Cecilia remained happy as long as her younger

son did not disappear as her older one had. She was happy as long as her younger son, also, did not become some slavish hero to a cause like her husband. This, she expressed to me outright during one of our rum mornings during the long summer of the bombs. Because in the end, Renato was the one most like his sententious, mock hero papi, no matter how much he wanted to be like his nihilistic brother.

After that first night that I spent in Renato's room, dozing off on his mattress after the bath, in and out of the stories that Renato recounted nightlong about his childhood, about the longed-for violin, about how they first came to live in that house, I had moved into Nicolás's old room on the other side of the wall, and my interactions with the younger brother consisted of small talk at the dinner table, whenever he deigned to join us. Sometimes, I would wander into his room, but it would be a while before he learned to trust me with as much abandon as he had that first night.

When they took Nicolás away, Renato became interested in me again. Whenever he was home, he kept the door to his room open, so that the smoke wafted into my room and seemed to somehow beckon me. I decided then to give him the violin. Smoke swirled from his nostrils and mouth, a spasmodic fit of coughing and hacking overtaking him. He appreciated the thought, he said, plucking at the strings gently, as if afraid that they might disintegrate into dust. He then placed it under his chin and with an invisible bow suspended above the strings, cigarette ashes snowing through the henpecked roof of the perforated box, pretended to play, his face taking on an ecstatic mask of an adolescent achieving his first memorable orgasm. His performance over, he threw it atop a pile of books. I never saw him pick up the thing again. But it was my ticket into the ashy cavern of his room.

I began to follow him like he had told me he had once

followed Nicolás and his socios, lagging a few steps behind, never intruding into the long conversations with the yanqui santero at his book stall in the Plaza de Armas or with the female tourists who would pause at first from their sightseeing the moment their eyes crossed his path and hesitantly approached him as they might prey, as if he might at the slightest provocation dash off. He was probably the only young Cuban man who hadn't even bothered to notice their existence, so they would have to initiate the conversation, but not until they were so near that they could see the unusual color of his eyes, a heart of palm milky green, and smell his tangy body odor through the coating of cigarette smoke.

Renato chatted with anyone who approached. Watching him on the streets, keeping my distance—because he had insisted, he did not want people to get the wrong idea about us—it proved difficult to believe that this was the same taciturn and reclusive boy who spent hours alone in his room, cocooned in smoke and ashes. He wore the same tattered jeans and sandals every day, switching his white camisetas every third day or so. When his hair grew too greasy, he donned a frayed straw hat that he had stolen from his father's closet, the one that I liked to imagine Pascual wore on the night he first spoke to Cecilia. I never once saw him use the bathtub of the house on Calle Obispo. Though when he disappeared with a group of tourists—after a while, the women realizing that it would take three or four of them to capture him, so that by the time they began to lurk away from the yanqui santero's stall, Renato, completely encircled, waved over the top of his head to his santero friend, shouting at me to tell Cecilia not to expect him for dinner. He resurfaced freshly bathed and neatly shaven, days later, the comb furrows still holding in his hairdo, wearing new linen guayaberas, jeans with ironed creases and leather-soled loafers, a bagful of other presents in tow, all which he refolded neatly, reboxed, and had the yanqui santero sell to other Yuma or to the black marketeers from his stall.

I often imagined these women going through the ritual of bathing Renato, each slipping off a particular item of clothing and assigned to a specific portion of his body, scrubbing and rinsing and perfuming him. More than once, he went away with older men, too, and from these excursions he returned with even more extravagant gifts, clothes, but also watches and brushed-gold bracelets, and boxes upon boxes of fine Cuban cigars, the kind reserved for the Party honchos and not sold anywhere, Renato bragged. He didn't smoke these but pre-ferred the cheap American black-market cigarettes.

I sometimes like to think that had Nicolás not returned, I imagine that Renato would have gradually torn himself away from his mother's house, soon established his own life among the Yuma and the santero. But that wasn't him, Cecilia was right. He was a dutiful-hero type like his father. His truer nature. He would only discover the unruliness of his last days later, after the burial of his brother in Cemeterio Colón.

After that day, on which his brother returned home during his first furlough, Renato regressed to the ways that he had adopted after he had quit the pioneros and dropped out of school. He left his room less and less, only to buy cigarettes. Sometimes, he ventured out of the house to go visit the santero, but now, he rejected the tourists' advances in an aggressive way, screaming at them to go to some other butcher shop. He let his beard grow, which made him seem older, more ragged, more heroic, like the pictures in our schoolbooks of the half-naked rebels descending from the mountains one sunny New Year's Day, long ago. It fit him, as if he could now inhabit the heroic New Man if only by looks.

Ironically, barbudos were now deemed suspicious, so every

time he went out, he was harassed more often by la fiana, stopping him and carefully reviewing his carnet, peppering him about where he lived, worked, what he was doing out in the street looking like a degenerate. For some reason, he was never carted to the hospital to be tested, not yet, as any other young man looking like him would certainly have been— comandante Juan, for sure, had something to do with this, spending all his favors for Cecilia's sake. Eventually, he had me go out and collect his share of the profit from the santero, take bags full of books from the writer's library, pack whatever goodies he still had left over from his conquests with the Yuma, and run his cigarette errands.

When his brother first reappeared, Renato came down to the paladar during the middle of dinner service to warn me. Rush hour, right after eight o'clock, and Cecilia had forbidden him from coming down during service lest he frighten the clients with his barefoot, deranged, prophet-come-back-from-the-desert look. He stood behind me and whispered in my ear while I was taking an order from a French group. El huevón has come back. Standing on the street casting pebbles at your window like some demented Montague. Renato waited for me by the front door as I set some entrée plates down on another table and told Cecilia to cover me for a second. Fine, she hissed, just keep them both out of the dining room.

Nicolás crouched in the shadows of the narrow sidewalk across Calle Obispo, shirtless, barefoot, the soles of his feet black as cattle hooves, holding a stray cat on his lap. He smiled and motioned for both of us to come over.

She doesn't want you in the house till after dinner service, I said, as if making this the purpose for coming out of the house. I had not seen him since the afternoon he had disappeared. I had written him several times at the sidatorio, asking to visit, and he had sent a cable back, saying that he was too humiliated to see anyone and asking for sweets and cigarettes and dollars, the only form of currency accepted in the colony. When I tried to bring him the package that Cecilia and I had prepared, I got no farther than the gate. The lecherous guard told me that the patient was not accepting visitors, and he tore open the box and pulled out the most valuable items, cologne and soap and razor blades and the dollars and cigarettes, and set them aside, assuring me with a leer that . . . the patient . . . would get everything.

When Nicolás appeared that early evening, though, he looked plump and fleshy as a fatted calf (from the lard in which everything was cooked in at the sidatorio, he explained later), a little potbelly even protruding over the waistband of his shorts. I repeated what Cecilia had told me.

Nicolás said, Si, claro. Nothing to disturb her thriving negocio, not even a dying son. God forbid.

Renato giggled, and his brother grabbed him and pulled him down on his lap. The cat hissed and jumped off. Tell this one that sometimes he's better off than any of us. He wrapped his arms around his brother. Renato looked up at me, surprised and elated at the same time, it seemed, his chin lowered, his eyebrows raised, and his pupils dancing on the roof of his eyes. Nicolás must have caught a contrasting look on *my* face. ¿Qué? A brother can't show a little affection? He kissed his brother on the pit of his neck, under the scruffy beard, and Renato leaned into him, his cheek resting on Nicolás's shoulder. Then—so much affection, too lavish a display—Nicolás threw his brother toward me and crossed the street moving toward the mesquite door. He banged on it, calling out his mother's name, shouting that the prodigal son had returned.

The door opened a crack, and comandante Juan squeezed through the opening. He looked at me first, clearly laying the blame for the ruckus on me. He took hold of Nicolás by the arm and walked him across the street.

You're needed inside, he said. I'll deal with these anormales!

Nicolás pulled away from him, but comandante Juan grabbed him by the waist, easily lifted him in the air, and threw him on the sidewalk. Nicolás landed on his forearm and curled his body around it, grunting obscenities at the comandante. Comandante Juan waited for him to finish, one hand on his rusty pistol. He signaled impatiently for me to go back inside, but I stood my ground. Renato crouched by his brother, keeping his distance, sensing that Nicolás would lash out at anyone who tried to console him.

Why didn't you tell anyone you were coming? comandante Juan said in an even tone. We would have prepared.

Prepared? Nicolás began to stand, and when he noticed that his arm was scuffed and bleeding, he made a fist, wielded it like a weapon, and charged the comandante. Rotund as he was, the comandante was also very nimble—he had to be to keep up with us in the paladar, so he scooted out of Nicolás's way with a quick two-step, shoving him out on the street, but not before some blood had rubbed off on the lower part of his military jacket.

Nicolás was about to charge him again when his mother appeared at the side gate, greeting some new customers. She dexterously diverted them from the scuffle on the street through a maneuver of hands on shoulders and lower backs, nudging them inside. She reappeared a few moments later, crossing to us.

Renato had lit a cigarette, and she pulled it from his lips and crushed it on the sidewalk. She did not even look at Nicolás—who was holding up his wounded forearm to show her—as she hooked arms with me and forced me back into the busy paladar.

You should be careful before you end up like him, she said.

Inside, the diners had begun to grow restless, even the ones who had been served their meals glanced around. The couple that Cecilia had led in waited by the entrance, whispering to themselves. Cecilia pointed to an open table where I led them.

I worked the rest of the night, toiling to ease the unsettled spirits of the Yuma, responding to their every request with a string of sí, señores and claro, señoritas, but with one ear cocked to Calle Obispo, although it had gone silent.

After a handful of hours, when only a few patrons lingered in the paladar, comandante Juan finally reappeared, rosy-cheeked and stinking of rum. He sat down so that Cecilia could serve him his dinner and announced that the boys would be returning soon. They were in the market in the Plaza de Armas, haggling with a vendor over a hammock. He said that if it hadn't been for me, the situation might have gotten out of control. But that once Cecilia grabbed me and led me back inside, she might as well have pinched me by the ear and dragged me, for such was the effect on the brothers. Nicolás's rage instantly transformed into a fit of guffaws that soon infected his younger brother. Cecilia, half-listening to all of this, refused to even sit down with us like she usually did. It was almost as if she did not have the strength to play mother that night.

Inocente St. Louis ate his meal in the kitchen, standing up by the hot stove, as he did every night, but always attentive to what we were saying, as if part of his job was to watch for our failings. I always felt he judged the whole family for its abandonment of the eldest son. He uttered something in his mother's native patois, and Cecilia countered whatever he had said by condemning the ungratefulness of one's own flesh.

Comandante Juan continued with his story, reminding Cecilia first how lucky she was to have had him, the comandante, during the most dire of times, how much worse those two delincuentes would have turned out if not for him, not just with a roof over their heads (for surely once Pascual had disappeared, the Ministry of the Interior had set their sights on the house), but who else could have for so long averted the attention of the Comités and the revolutionary police from those two.

After the brothers tired of laughing at me and bemoaning my yoke—Is this why he escaped the mountains? they laughed and high-fived each other, to be some servant—the Zúñiga brothers embraced like two soldiers that have found each other on a battlefield as the only survivors of an apocalyptic struggle. Sensing an opportunity in the sudden burst of brotherly cheer, comandante Juan convinced them they should take their reunion to the nearest bar, around the corner on Calle O'Reilly. Comandante Juan offered to buy drinks if Nicolás told them about the sidatorio. After drinks, they walked the Malecón, and comandante Juan felt like something had passed—some storm had skirted but mostly averted the house on Calle Obispo—hoping the visit could proceed without trouble now. He looked over at Cecilia who ignored him. That's the way Nicolás had always been since his father disappeared, comandante Juan explained to me. Anytime that Cecilia showed any interest in his life, he did all he could to distance himself from her.

No greater torture than one's own flesh.

As he was saying this, Nicolás and Renato entered the patio through the side gate, dragging the sisal hammock they had bought at the plaza. It was a humid night, and both were shirtless now, shuffling in their sandals, in that taxing confounded state when the alcohol has begun to wear off and the weight of the night settles into the pockets of the joints and the soft spot of the bones. I had never had the chance to watch them together like this, at ease with each other, loving almost. Their hands constantly reaching for the other.

Nicolás briefly glanced at comandante Juan and at me and then settled on his mother. He kept his eyes fixed on her. Cecilia fiddled with plates of food that she had kept warm for them in the oven. She carried them out, three full plates, lined up on her forearm, a dishcloth draped underneath them. She set them at our table and motioned for her sons to sit. Nicolás asked for rum and Cecilia said that she would get him some if he ate something first.

Me too, Renato said, emboldened, rosy. Some for me, too.

Cecilia went to fetch her bottle of spicy rum and five glasses. She waited for the boys to sit down and start eating before she poured all around. She lifted her glass and waited for everybody to do the same, but did not offer a toast, so we all sat there waiting for her to say something, anything to break the staring match with her oldest son, who downed the shot, and poured himself another.

Welcome home, muchacho, comandante Juan finally said, and all of us sipped uncomfortably. This is good. Tonight we eat like a family.

Nicolás chortled. Rum dripped out of his nose. I'm only allowed a couple of days with you. He pulled out the yellow card. He looked back at his mother who had not taken her eyes from him. They're the ones who're going to be there, watching me when I die.

Cecilia dropped her fork and knife on the plate, threw her napkin on top, and removed herself from the table, busying herself in the kitchen by scrubbing the last pots and pans that she had instructed Inocente St. Louis to leave for her.

Why do you have to be so refunfuñosa? Nicolás shouted at her, gulping more of his mother's rum. I am only telling you the truth. No? He slapped Renato in the arm, seeking his support, and then gazed at comandante Juan, who pursed his lips and seemed to be assessing which promise to him Nicolás had just broken. But Nicolás would not relent. He continued with his invectives aimed at his mother's back, his chin raised, biting his lower lip, arching his back, more than ready to spit toxin at her from across the patio.

At least, I'm happy now. I know my end. He paused, poured himself more rum. I really don't remember the last time you were happy, not even when we were kids, not even when that bastard was still here.

Cecilia continued with her chores, leaning forward into the sink now, the scrubbing of the pots like the dull rasp of a cracked güiro. Nicolás raised his chin higher, adjusted his aim. And look, look at all the things that you have to be joyful about in this little patio, your thriving business, your beloved comandante, your . . . your new son . . . and your two old ones. He tapped Renato on the belly with the back of his hand. You would think a woman would be grateful for such things. Not everyone is so fortunate in this fucking prison of a country.

Something had hit the mark. Cecilia stopped scrubbing. She let her soaked hands dangle on each side of her, dripping sudsy water. All Nicolás had to do was fire a couple of more well-aimed missiles, and she would have to mount a counter-attack, or . . . or accept everything he was saying. The new alcohol had revived Nicolás, creating a surge from what had been nothing more than a ripple on the surface of his disgust.

If you had your way, you would let your son die in the hands of government doctors, just so you would have something else to complain about. Isn't that right, mamacita? Wouldn't that be the easiest way to lose me? If you could at least blame part of it on Fidel? There was a ballet of butt shifting in our chairs, comandante Juan even readying if called upon to protect the vituperative son from the physical onslaught of the mother. Renato stopped giggling. His face adopted a constricted look that I had only seen on him before when he returned from his lost weekends with tourists.

Cecilia slowly dried her hands, her back still to us, finished hanging the pots and pans on the hooks above the serving line, and when she came back to sit at the table, she poured herself a glass of rum and drank it slowly, not engaging anyone with her eyes, as if she were alone at that table.

We all waited, even Nicolás knew by this point that the next thing she said would mark their relationship for the remainder of his brief life. She relished the corpulence of the silence, sipping her rum with the patient gusto of someone who is suddenly free for an unexpected expanse of time.

Bueno, two days, she finally said, looking directly at Nicolás, who after his previous bravado, could barely look back at her, his chin pressed to his chest, that is all they give you to spend with your family. I didn't think you would last this long there. I've been waiting for two months for someone from the Ministry of Health to knock at the door to inform us that you had gone missing again. I'm surprised that you even thought to come to us with your free time.

Nicolás regained his resolve. He slapped a hand on my thigh. I came to see my boyfriend, not you. I *had* forgotten about you. But then who would care?—since the sight of me in your house seems to disgust your clientele so much. Maybe like we all disgusted Pascual before he left. I get it, no digas más.

Suddenly, it was as if no one else was at that table but them. Comandante Juan, Renato, and I had dissolved from the frame. Phantoms. A precious vase was sitting at the precipice of a high table, and underneath there was a fitful child shaking the table's rachitic legs. We waited. When Cecilia got up and walked away from the table, again surprising us, we knew that she had begun the process of mourning for her son, who despite his newfound plumpness, would be dead with the coming of the rainy season.

Coward, Nicolás muttered dejectedly after Cecilia had mounted the stone stairs to her room, and the three of us suddenly took shape again beside him. The rage would be turned on his brother not too long after this scene, and on me as he bewitched me to serve as witness, but now only the mother mattered.

Don't let her weep beside my casket, he ordered. Don't you dare let her!

Soon after this, comandante Juan excused himself, but he knew better than to go upstairs and try to console her. He bid us good night and made us promise to avoid any ruckus that would force her down to the patio again.

Why don't you go up there and protect her and stop with all the silly pretense? Nicolás said. My boyfriend's sleeping in the henhouse with me. He slapped Renato on his bare chest. Maybe I'll even let the little brother join in if he behaves.

Renato downed more rum. But Juan, perhaps sensing some danger, put a hand under his armpit and lifted him, telling him to walk with him a few blocks, that he had an important bisnes deal to discuss that could be lucrative for both of them. I don't know why he let Renato return but he was not close to as good at guessing the motivations of the oldest son as he imagined, and he could not have foretold the rest of the night.

They went for a long walk. Comandante Juan correctly guessed that before Renato returned, Nicolás and I would be too ensnared in each other to notice his return.

Nicolás asked me to sleep in the sisal hammock with him. To lighten the mood, I joked that I would miss the chicken shit on the ground where we usually slept. He turned away without as much as a chuckle. He walked to the entrance of the henhouse and held the rickety door open for me. I sensed Cecilia watching us from the second-floor gallery but I glanced up and could not see her.

There were days after what happened that night as I went over the series of small moments of those mere minutes, memories that accumulated in the flow of my daily activities like toxic silt, when I imagined that by just making one move, I might have changed the entire current of events. I should have given in fully to Nicolás's sexual advances, I admonished myself, perhaps prevented everything that happened after. Had Renato walked into the shed and seen us desperately entangled with each other, he might have simply slid the door closed and let us be. But drunk as he was, infatuated with the brother who had finally returned all of his affections—poisonously distilled into a matter of hours—it may not have mattered.

For hours, it seemed, I held Nicolás in that sisal hammock as it swung precariously on two corner beams of the shanty. He twisted and turned like a sacked animal, at times, I think, truly having dozed off but suddenly electrocuted by some catastrophe in his dreams. It must have been almost morning, after a marathon of aborted fucks, both of us soaked in sweat, the hammock slung low, almost to the dirt floor, when I heard the tin door drag open.

Nicolás, naked, tumbled off the hammock and let out a sigh. He composed himself, smiled, and reached a hand to the visitor. In a moment, I knew that it was not for me that he had been desperate all night. I suddenly became a minor player in the scene, my ripped T-shirt, the torn zipper of my work pants, the grogginess from the sleepless night, the only things that connected me to Nicolás now.

Renato slid the door closed, somehow locking the light of

the slate predawn hours in the shed, and came and sat by his brother. They began to talk in whispers, giggling like they had at the dinner table a few hours before. Renato had found some liquor (ripped the lock from the cabinet in the kitchen), and they sipped the spicy rum straight from the bottle. I curled up and imagined myself dozing off, when the hammock turned over and flipped me to the shit-speckled ground. Both brothers cackled violently.

Carajo, Nicolás said, not even a nibble tonight from this puta that I saved once! He's afraid to catch something. They laughed some more, shaking their heads in ersatz admonition. I crawled over to a corner where the chickens roosted. Dirt splattered on me. Nicolás continued with his verbal abuses, relating to his brother how he had picked up this transient at the beach in Cojímar, given him a life in the capital, and now, in his time of need, the ingrate had abandoned him. I ignored him. Finally, I got up and walked toward the door. But he was not going to let me escape like he had let his mother escape at dinner. As I turned to say something to Renato, to offer him a way out with me, Nicolás put an arm around his brother and held him in place.

Didn't I want to know about the sanitarium? he asked. When we had first settled into the hammock that night, I had held him, asked him to tell me what it was like, when they would let him go. He grunted and responded that he didn't feel like talking about it. Now, I didn't feel like listening to it. I said nothing and reached for the door.

My boyfriend is leaving me, he said to his brother in an overly theatrical sotto voce. I guess it's just you and me like old times. He grabbed his crotch.

I should have walked out, but I turned around and looked. Nicolás had stood, and bent over, in adulation, had taken his kneeling brother's face in both hands and was kissing him on the forehead, on the bridge of his nose, on the cheeks, on the bearded chin, circling over the lips like a hummingbird. Renato, too drunk to be disturbed, tried hard instead not to break into laughter. Stop it, I said.

They both turned their faces toward me. Nicolás grinned. Renato put a hand on the back of Nicolas's thigh, and then slid it to the front of his leg and pushed him away. When they had been out drinking, Renato now spoke, his brother had told him all about the sidatorio. He said it hesitantly, looking up at his brother for approval. Nicolás nodded and Renato continued: without knowing it, the State was creating its own worst enemy inside its treatment facilities. A movement had already begun, some of the caretakers counted among the plotters.

Had I heard of los inyectados? he asked me. I told him I hadn't. By now, I had made my way back and sat on the unsteady hammock beside them. Nicolás then took over, in a more peaceful tone than he had adopted so far this visit, but also enlivened somewhat, like a child that has noticed something gone long undetected by the dull-witted adults. Half the patients in the sidatorio had placed themselves there willingly, either by contracting the virus through repeated sexual exposures, or . . . or by injecting themselves with infected blood.

Nicolás saw the expression on my face, which likely seemed to him as much horror, as utter contempt, a hatred he had not even seen in his mother's face that day, he would tell me later, the last time I saw him, when he delivered his convoluted jeremiad about the significance of the movement he had founded. Was that what all the groping had been about? An attempt to recruit me into this new counterrevolution? And he might have said something then, because he was likely not only reading my mind, thought by thought, but tenaciously moving forward one or two thoughts ahead, deciphering some consistent pattern, culminating in his threat to have his way with his brother, by intimating things about the past that I should have known were ridiculous (since, by all accounts, before this night, Nicolás barely acknowledged his brother's existence).

So he had me. I would be there as his witness, his accomplice, my days as his erstwhile boyfriend over, and all the groping on the hammock had simply been a way to pass the time until his brother arrived.

They continued drinking. Nicolás recounted the prison-like tedium of the sidatorio, which was only alleviated after lights out in their parceled three-walled cubicles—the same abandoned rooms that I would roam through almost a year later with Steffen. In the air above these partitions, the future of the Island crackled, on the cusp of setting ablaze, like invisible particles of hay in a hayloft. At night, from their beds, each patient shouted out the names of each and every person they had infected, at times unwittingly, but often with intent. Each night, a single person was in charge of compiling the names that were shouted, sung, and blubbered over the low walls to turn in to the medical supervisor, who would in turn hand over the list for the Ministry of Health's roundups.

It was no foolproof system, more a typical Cuban bachata than anything else, with the person writing the names in the darkness trying to conduct the mad symphony of names and surnames, often shouting for silence so that he could discern the quieter strains of the melody, or simply to ask for a spelling. Many on the list did appear at El Cerro and then widened the net to include many others. There was no doubt, this would be the final transformation of the Island, a crocodile-shaped sidatorio in the Caribbean which no foreigner would ever want to visit and could finally shape its own destiny.

You could say that in the following moment I may have

been acting of my own volition, that I had read a few moments ahead in the script of the scene and knew exactly what Nicolás planned to do from the moment he appeared, and that I decided to go off-script, to disrupt his perfectly calibrated drama.

I grabbed Renato under the armpit, with one strong pull got him to his feet, and began to lead him out of the shed. Scene canceled; drama derailed. I was almost on the verge of congratulating myself, when Renato snapped his whole body and shook free from me. He was so drunk that the force of the gesture sent him reeling back toward the hammock, over which he tumbled to land facedown on the spot beside his brother from where I had taken him.

Nicolás tried hard to seem undisturbed by my gesture, convincing me even more so that I had somehow upset the delicate dramatic balance that he had been carefully calibrating since the moment when he appeared in a barrage of shouts on Calle Obispo. He threw up his hands, faux grimaced in disgust with me, curling his lips in a gesture that in any other situation I would have seen as playful. He gathered the bundle of his brother, pushed him back up into the hammock, and then violently flipped it, so that Renato landed resolutely on his side, right underneath him.

Go, he said, both of you. Neither of you belong with me. Renato was too out of it to catch the suddenly sober tone in his brother's voice. He giggled, his arms wrapped around his head, as if he were about to get struck. But Nicolás did not move. He waited for his brother to get up, wipe the mud and shit from his ragged T-shirt and jeans and remain still beside his brother, suddenly sober, a resolute expression on his face.

I should have left. My part done. Only later I would realize that I had played it exactly to Nicolás's specifications. Renato was now willingly by Nicolás's side because of me, because

I had returned to the paladar when Cecilia took me by the arm, because I had failed to side with Nicolás at the dinner table, because I had conceded to sleep with him on the hammock, because I had fought off his advances all night, because I thought I could save them, both of them.

You still think that, Steffen chided me, with the living one.

I might be the one who needs saving, I protested.

By the time I had made the decision to sit down, my back leaning against the corrugated tin of the far end of the henhouse, Nicolás had already reached his bag and was pulling out the simple instruments that he would need for the ceremony, two latex bands and a syringe absurdly sheathed in its sterile package, items that he must have pilfered from the sidatorio. As if in preemptive penance, I replicated every single motion that Renato performed for his brother, although I was not aware of it until later. I turned the palm of my right hand upward and reached out my arm. The fingers curled into a soft fist when Nicolás tightened the latex band around a strip of flesh just above the elbow. Soon, the fingers relaxed again, on their own, though not quite at rest, a quarter curled, the veins in the forearm rising, casting the translucent skin with a fetal glow. Renato turned his head, at first, I thought to avoid the sight of blood, but he looked at me and I stared back at him. What were we to each other now? Nothing. No one was anything in the presence of his brother.

He remained still for a long while, his arms extended, tumescent, arched upward, while Nicolás performed the serene task in the unfocused shadows behind him, wrapping the bandage around his own arm, sacramental as a priest with the Host behind the altar. But no prayers. Everything proceeded in a lulling silence that made it seem much more dangerous than any other ritual.

At one point, Nicolás glanced at me. I felt his familiar

lover's eyes circle around the perimeter of my crouched figure, almost an endearing look but also domineering. It gave me the sensation that I was in the process of disintegrating and only the silhouette of what I had been remained.

Nicolás fumbled with the needle as he tried to get it into the right position to insert into his vein, looking at it first in his hand and trying a few different approaches before he sunk it into the twine-thick vein in the crook of his elbow. His body tensed, the stab of the needle causing a momentary jolt that straightened his spine and made him take an almost imperceptible step back away from his brother. When no blood oozed into the receptacle of the syringe, he let go of it for a moment and it flopped down on the flat underside of his forearm. He winced and I noticed that his hand trembled. He looked down at the bottle of spicy rum trying to communicate a silent message to Renato, to reach it up and empty it into his mouth. But he did not let the moment deter him or make obvious to his brother what he had just made obvious to me, that this was the first time he had done this. When he had his hand back on the syringe, he quickly gained control of himself.

Renato, still snickering but not from amusement, had indeed reached up and poured a gush of rum down his brother's throat. Nicolás pushed the needle in and then slightly back out and adjusted its position in half-circles until the barrel began to fill with more blood than I would have thought necessary. When Nicolás pulled the needle out, he reached for the bottle of rum himself and splashed the puncture wound, using the hem of his camiseta as a bandage and bending his arm to hold it in place. He held the syringe by his side in his other hand, not like a weapon but like something innocuous but essential to him, a pair of reading glasses, a handkerchief. He let the pressure on the puncture do its work before he continued, looking off into the cramped distance of the far wall of the henhouse.

When Nicolás uncrooked his arm and let the bloody hem of his camiseta fall, I saw Renato rise as he came into my field of vision. I must have stood also, my hand outstretched as his. Nicolás raised the syringe, the needle facing upward, and flicked it before turning it over and forcing a squirt of blood out. He paused, taking up the bottle and offering Renato a drink, which he refused. The rest was almost anticlimactic. Nicolás waved the needle over his brother's arm but could not decide on a vein, so he asked his brother to clench his fist by doing the motion himself with his free hand, and blood began squirting from the puncture in his vein. Both of them began to laugh so hard, and at the same time trying to stifle their sudden mirth, that to a stranger bursting in on this scene, it might have seemed that the brothers had been discovered at a small, easily forgivable transgression.

Renato took off his own shirt, balled it up, and pressed it to his brother's forearm. Nicolás put a hand on his brother's shoulder, and they waited without saying a word or laughing anymore, a patience they had perfected at the interminable bus wait at the nearest esquina, like all Cubans, a patience taught at every hour of the day, every day of the years.

When the puncture clotted, Renato gently lifted the blood-soaked shirt and peering under to make sure, they continued. They now seemed completely in sync. Renato gave his brother the arm—the left or the right? I wasn't sure, disoriented, witnessing the scene as if through the reflection of a convocation of mirrors—and Nicolás quickly found a vein and inserted the needle and the blood disappeared into his brother's arm.

Then it was done. And I stood there and merely watched.

Had Nicolás walked into the house in Calle Obispo that previous afternoon and slashed the throat of everyone who lived there and all the Yuma who were lunching there, he could not have been more victorious. But there was no celebration on his part. When he removed the needle from his brother's arm, he pressed two fingers to the puncture and held them there until it clotted; then he took the syringe, wrapped it in the two bloody shirts, and put the bundle in his sack. He stretched out in the hammock, reached out a hand to his brother, and pulled him down beside him. They embraced on the hammock with an intimacy that Nicolás and I had not found all night or in all the days that I had known him.

I curled up into a ball, thinking that I would only pretend to sleep, as if I had witnessed nothing. It must have been no longer than a few seconds, and I know I did not sleep, but when I opened my eyes again, the brothers were gone, an intrusive late-morning light was making its way through the pinholes and slats of the roof and walls. It seemed impossible that I had fallen asleep, but when I went out into the courtyard, there were already lunch customers and Cecilia looked at me with relief in her eyes, glad that I had had the courage to stand up to Nicolás. He had left in a huff, she said. I was afraid to ask for Renato, but when I went up to bathe, I saw the bottoms of his feet poking out from under the covers of his mattress.

He was splayed facedown on his bed softly snoring, untroubled as he had been in his brother's presence for the length of the short visit.

PART TWO

IV

And to put an end to sin, you must be hard and merciless.

Juan Rulfo
Pedro Páramo

OPERATION MARIPOSA

The graffiti started appearing a few months before the Pope arrived at José Martí International Airport, colorful circus-like script that Steffen assured me had been done by the same group responsible for the bombings, which had come to a sudden stop. Then the little signs began to appear, as if ghostly shards left behind by the explosions. At first, the graffiti appeared in exactly the type of places in which the bombs had been detonated, mostly in the tourist hotels in and around the Vedado district, where most of the foreign press had begun to warily set up camp in wait for the famous film festival and then the Pope.

Steffen and I began sleeping during the day and prowling such areas at night, hoping to catch someone in the act of creating these little masterpieces. But soon the street canvas began to widen. We began to find the same graffiti near the more boutique hotels in the old city, and even across the bay, near the Church of Our Lady of Regla.

It took the authorities a few weeks to figure out that there was a pattern to the scattering of neat festive script all over the capital, which Steffen found hilarious, because after he noticed the first two, the same individual word, carefully

drawn on the door frame of a bar in Calle O'Reilly and on
the trunk of a chestnut tree in el Prado—in the fauve palette
of late Matisse, and with the delicate hand of what must have
been a fine horsehair watercolor brush—he knew we were on
to something.

The Ministry, however, had no interest in connecting these
innocuous acts of street vandalism to the bombings, knowing
it would mean that they had not only failed to catch the real
culprits but that they were being openly mocked for their
failure.

By then, Steffen and I had made Bertila's apartment our
headquarters, where we fucked because there was nothing else
to do, no one else to do it with, and slept—Steffen stretched
out on the barber's chair in the living room and I on a bed of
blankets on the floor beside him, for without saying it aloud,
we did not want to desecrate Bertila's bed with our drunken
groping and intermittent bouts of fucking. It was secondary
anyway, something that we saved for the early morning hours
as we finished our bottle of rum, after we had come back from
our nocturnal searches, which is what truly began to bond
us. That, and Steffen finally opening up to me about his true
interest in Renato and me.

After the last bombing, a few weeks passed, then a month.
Thinking it a safe political bet that whoever had committed
the acts had either been killed making one of the bombs or
gone back underground, *Granma* reported that the Directorate had captured the Salvadoran nationals responsible,
financed by the Miami Mafia to unsettle the city before the
Party Congress and the Pope's visit. Within weeks, the Yuma
returned to the capital as if they were being summoned back
to the bed of a childhood sweetheart, desperate to make up
for lost time.

Cecilia and comandante Juan reopened the paladar, which

on my visits back I heard quickly grew as busy as it had been before the silent long summer of the bombs. Cecilia asked me to help them on the three busiest nights: Thursday through Saturday, even if I didn't stay the night in my old room. I needed the money to support us as Steffen's stash ran dry. Other questions, about what I was doing with my time and if I had seen Renato, she asked only obliquely, and I answered likewise.

Steffen waited for me to get out a few blocks away, on the corner of Calles Obispo and Compostela, and we would begin the search for Renato and his group, which usually proved fruitless and lasted till we saw the first rays of the sun over the dome of the capitol. As December neared, with the International Havana Film Festival early in the month and the first ever openly celebrated Christmas holiday since the triumph of the Revolución, we discovered that more and more often that wherever there happened to be a concentration of tourists, the miniature colorful graffiti sprouted on walls, on the bark of trees, and through the cracks on sidewalks, one single word in a kaleidoscope of colors, created with such condensed grace that it was as if we were seeing the word and understanding its meaning for the first time, a word that the State had long ago made its property, one of its main instruments of instruction in revolutionary society, now transformed into a thing of rare beauty, by its palette, its proportion, its placement.

Every night, I questioned Steffen more confrontationally about his stake in all of this. How I could be sure that he could not just go off and disappear one day, exposing me to dangers with the State he didn't have to fear as a foreigner? Were we being watched? Was he the watcher?

Perhaps afraid that one night I might be the one that abandoned him, Steffen began to confess how he had been drafted into the fold of our lives, the reason that he had even associated with Renato and me that afternoon near Parque Lenin.

I knew from stories Renato had told me about his ministrations to tourists that the Directorate liked recruiting foreign students for many different things, especially young ones who had come to the Island as much for their educational possibilities as for their revolutionary romanticism. It was easy to recruit them into the cause, any cause, offer them further educational advantages and a few extra spending dollars, always dollars. All executed with one purpose in mind, the idea that they could more easily infiltrate the Island's restless youth culture and monitor it for the Directorate, from within. The young foreigners could remain on the Island after their visas had expired telling family back home that they had come upon a diplomatic opportunity, which was the story recommended by the Directorate when it hired them.

Steffen had met the Russian way before he used him as bait for me in Varadero, just like he had met his girlfriend, Anna, through this network of foreign students under the hire of the State. So the narrative of his past stitched from a mosaic of seemingly spontaneous reminiscences perhaps wasn't really his life, or perhaps parts of it were and parts weren't. To some degree, I figured his past, what I learned from it, had to be a professionally crafted fairy tale co-authored by him and the many magical-realist-wannabes at the Directorate, whose ultimate purpose entailed creating a foolproof believable fictional world for the citizens, a place where the Revolución never falters and all the Yuma are its ardent admirers.

These young foreigners served as the legion of informants to the Directorate's fictionalizers. The foreign students reported their observations in detailed daily entries in journals that they turned in at the end of every month. The Ministry of the Interior exploited these from-the-trenches data of citizenry to quell counterrevolutionary activity and to reinvent the source of such rebellion, the intolerable reality of the hours and the weeks, and flip it inside out, turn it on its head, or dye it with fresher colors to concoct a more palatable world that did not exist.

So you worked for the Party? I asked after Steffen had confessed enough of it, which made me want to go back to my room at Calle Obispo and forget I had ever considered him anything more than a john. Still, he would not be confessing anything if he was still committed to whatever he had been doing for the Directorate.

Steffen responded that perhaps it could be interpreted as work he did for the Party, but he never took it very seriously, not till the end, and because he was not a Cuban national, the State had no hold on him, it could not require anything of him—except the monthly delivery of his journal, which he had to admit contained mostly fiction to keep things interesting. Dearth, boredom, apprehension, grievance, and banality existed in much greater proportion than counterrevolution among the masses. He imagined that most of the foreign chroniclers must have been fictionalizers (so what the Director's chroniclers composed as their version of reality for the people was then twice-fiction, if such a thing could be).

It had been a fantastic way to subsist during the three years that he had been living on the Island, even if he had to manufacture his own adventures more often than not. As a diarist on the State's payroll dutifully turning in his observations, he could stay in perpetuum in fine tourist hotels and truly get to know our beautiful Island. A proposition most young foreigners fleeing from some conflict at home wouldn't turn down. It wasn't until a few weeks before he *ran into* Renato and me on the southern edges of Parque Lenin that he had been given a direct assignment. I guess they did that a lot, he told me, they wait until they know they can trust you before they give you any information that might prove harmful if used against them.

Can I trust you now? I asked him.

Steffen chuckled, did not look away. *They* never had my trust if that's what you're worried about.

I kept my eyes fixed on him, and the long silence that passed made it seem as if I had repeated the question aloud.

Why they had learned to trust him, he could never figure out, he explained, considering he was turning in surrealist fiction instead of investigational reports—but maybe things had gotten to a point where the agents at the Directorate could no longer tell the real from the fantastic. Maybe there was a shortage of student spies who were willing to infiltrate this one world that they had yet to crack, maybe they saw something in him that tipped them off.

During the perfunctory meeting in the basement of the capitol one month, the ancient State official who was usually there had been replaced by a young, well-groomed man in his twenties, the ghost of a smirk on his face, the demeanor of someone who refuses to share some profane gossip. He leafed through the entries in Steffen's monthly notebook, labeled it with a red sticker (where Steffen's code name and the zone for the month were typewritten) and cavalierly threw it on top of a slush pile of other similar notebooks.

This was normally the moment when Steffen would be handed an envelope of American dollars and told to keep up the excellent work. But this time the young official held back, clasping his hands over his taut belly, leaning back in his chair, and ceremoniously plopping his boots up on the desk.

Are you a homosexual? he asked, as nonchalantly as if he were asking the young German if he liked mangos. The undercoat of a smile appeared on his face again.

Steffen looked away, guided by some perverse instinct of self-preservation. He felt the heat rise to his face, certainly not prepared for this. The young officer noticed. That is not what he meant at all, compadre, he explained. It was the business of the State and not his own personal curiosity that led him to ask. Guapo as he would admit that Steffen was, in the way of pampered Europeans, he was not interested, macho, he had a wife and three daughters. He leaned forward across his note-book-cluttered desk and put a purposefully manly hand on Steffen's shoulder. It was simply a question as business of the State, he repeated more forcefully. He threw back his shoulders suddenly as if the burden of authority had caused a crick in the middle of his back.

Are you a homosexual? ¿Sí o no? If you are, then the State has an interest in furthering our association and increasing your financial remuneration from a fistful of dollars to a more substantial sum.

Fearing a trap, Steffen apologized, said that he wasn't, and as if to prove it, he pulled out his billfold and showed the official a picture in his wallet of his girlfriend back in Cologne, who was in fact his sister in Hamburg, he told me. The official looked at it closely and then for an almost indiscernible second at Steffen's face, unable to suppress a grunt, pulled out his billfold and in turn showed off a small black-and-white photo of his wife with his three daughters, the oldest of whom had inherited his fine delicate features and facility with a smile. They shared a congratulatory slap on the back and said farewell until their meeting the following month.

For the next few months, Steffen was incredibly careful about any of the stories that he made up for his monthly journal. Before, he had mostly based the entries on characters that he picked up on the streets, those he talked to in passing, and then invented a sordid counterrevolutionary life for them, which in all probability they never had the courage to pursue. He invented names also, claro; so it probably would not be long before the authorities caught up with him and shipped him back to his father's candy factory in Hamburg.

The next three meetings in the basement of the capitol were uneventful (making him suspect that the notebooks went mostly unread), the old, nose-hair-sprouting viejita in the comandante's uniform had reassumed her position behind the wide desk, and cordially apologized for having missed the meeting the previous month. She expressed hope that Steffen had been treated well in her absence.

Steffen thought it best not to reveal the offer of the young official, although his mind had started to ponder the financial benefits of doing whatever they had wanted him to do, if only he could be asked the question again. He told the old woman that the young officer had been very cordial and to say hello, which he hoped would be taken as a sign of his willingness to comply. During his following two visits, he dutifully presented his carefully tendered notes of the Cubans he had met, growing increasingly frustrated with the tediousness of their lives, but unwilling to reveal himself carelessly to anyone but the young officer who had made the offer originally.

Two more months passed before Steffen abandoned hope of seeing the young official again and had begun thinking of ending his long *vacaciones* on the Island. The adventure had become tedious and he suspected might become dangerous if he got more involved. Approaching the basement offices of the Ministry of the Interior, ready to turn in his resignation and return to Hamburg to take over the management of his father's candy factory from his overwhelmed sister, as had been the plan for two years before, Steffen was surprised to see the young official again, busy behind the wide desk, going over the notebooks with a red pen he used to underline potentially useful intelligence, marking passages that might be of interest and tearing out useless pages.

It's very good to see you again, the officer grinned as Steffen reached out and handed him the monthly notebook, his note of resignation paper-clipped to the front cover. The young official pushed aside the work he was doing and made a clean space on the desk for Steffen's notebook. He read the resignation note slowly without removing the paper clip, at times even using his fingers to go over certain passages, trying to make out Steffen's hurried handwriting. The note was more or less an explanation of his duties back in Germany, a brief expression of regret at not being able to further serve the cause of the honorable Revolución, and a few phrases of gratitude to the State for his education both at the university and at the hands of people of such great honor and bravery.

I scoffed, but Steffen shushed me and went on. He had been scared, he explained. He wanted out, even more now that he had seen the young official back at the desk. He had decided it was time to return maybe precisely because he knew that such a choice might have suddenly become compromised. Who knew what the government had on him or what they could invent?

The young official did not even look up after he had finished reading the resignation letter. He threw the notebook and note into the pile behind him. He stood up, handed Steffen his envelope of dollars, and motioned for him to follow him, as if he was a doctor guiding him into an examining room, further diagnostic tests necessary.

They came out of the side exit of the Capitolio and took the Prado to the Malecón, the young official casually chatting about some problems he was having with his youngest daughter, as if Steffen were an old school chum he had happened to bump into. The daughter, it turned out, had told her mother that she wanted to be a Christian, that a janitor in school had told her the story of the Christ child, and it was the best story she had ever heard.

Steffen remained silent, trying to listen for some meaning in this story of a child's longing for conversion, feeling for the first time suffocated by a commitment that he had made almost half-heartedly a little less than three years before, after he had been approached by another student at the university in an offhanded manner. A simple journal, documenting his experience in dealing with the cubanos that he encountered on a daily basis, something that surprised him in how arduously he took to the task, for even when he was inventing a good deal of his narratives, it was always sparked by a chance meeting with some stranger in the gritty world of the capital.

Steffen had briefly found a lover in this world and moved in with him in his rooftop aerie, a shack made of cinderblocks and discarded tin sheets. He abandoned the university and with it, he thought, any chance of returning home to his father's business to become a proper Western capitalist with an education on the humanitarian aspects of socialism, as was the requirement for most high-minded German businessmen. But now that he had had enough of it, he was beginning to find out that it couldn't be abandoned with the simple nonchalance that you might get up and walk away from a card game after you had lost a few hands, although he had lost nothing. Not yet.

The young official continued to talk about his daughter, and his dismay at her devolved into naked contempt. He chastised his daughter for ingratitude toward her family, y peor, her country, not just for believing this preposterous story about impregnating angels, and virgin births, and three magical kings from the East, but also for refusing to identify the janitor that had told her the story. Then, as if he had committed some grave faux pas, he apologized profusely, reached out his hand to Steffen, and introduced himself as Arcadio.

When he returned to the tirade about his daughter, Steffen was sure he was meant to understand it as a threat. It wasn't someone at the school he was sure, Arcadio said, it was one of the many Catholic missionaries beginning to invade the Island in preparation for the Pope's visit the following year. They converged in the purlieus of school zones, dressed as civilians, their colorful counterrevolutionary literature concealed in plain-looking bags.

Arcadio stopped, he turned his gaze back out to the bay. Steffen waited in silence, curious to see how all this was related to his resignation.

I want you to come with me, Arcadio suggested with a forceful gesture of his hand.

He stood and walked east atop the Malecón wall, his arms spread like an acrobat, his military uniform now seeming more a disguise than a mantle of authority. Yet, with a leap down from the wall and a subtle stiffening of his posture, the cloth reasserted its command as Arcadio hailed down a private máquina, a storm-cloud gray Ford Crown Victoria, and ordered the driver to close the fare of the current riders and take them to an address in Vedado. The Yuma whined as they climbed out of the cab. State business, Arcadio asserted.

You will see my family, he said at some point during the ride, nothing else otherwise. As they veered south away from the water into the leafy streets of Vedado, he put his hand on Steffen's thigh and kept it there until he had to reach for his wallet to pay the fare.

His wife greeted them warmly, a visit that she had seemingly been expecting. The daughters were still in school, she announced, a rehearsal for the May Day festivities. Steffen had

been to the parade the year before. Amidst the bravado of tanks
and fighter planes and marching soldiers, bands of pioneros and
pioneras from every province in the country marched solemnly,
their young faces stern, turned three-quarters to the dais where
El Líder, his brother, the president of the National Assembly,
and a whole battalion of other ancients looked on.

Have you ever done it? Steffen asked me. Of course, of
course you have. You must have been a sight in your crisp
uniform.

Arcadio's wife briefly stepped out and, in a moment,
brought back hot cafecitos and brown sugar galleticas with
coconut sprinkles. Arcadio reached over and grabbed her, his
whole arm around her ass, and then put his face to her crotch.
She pushed his head away and asked Steffen to excuse her
husband's vulgarities. She tapped him on the head and walked
out. The following week, he attended the May Day festivities, sitting on the Party dais, and he thought he recognized
Arcadio's daughters from the photographs, marching by with
the same pinched look in their eyes, mingled with the fiendish
smirk.

What happened that afternoon was simple, methodical,
official, vaya. After they had finished eating their afternoon
merienda—which Arcadio did silently, smoking a cigarette in
between bites and sips of his cafecito—Arcadio stood up and
signaled for Steffen to follow him. By the time he had made it
to a dark screened-in back porch, he already had unbuttoned
his shirt and was undoing his belt. There was nothing else to
do, Steffen said, he wasn't sure he could refuse neither what
was being asked of him now nor what would be asked of him
in the future, not if he wanted to leave the Island without
problems.

You could have just gone to your embassy, I said, not
without a tinge of envy.

And have to deal with my father and this story? Steffen responded. That wasn't much of an option.

He gave Arcadio the best blow job of his life, or so was the intent, though they both remained almost fully clothed, as Steffen was told all the details of his new assignment, what Arcadio called Operation Mariposa. At one point, during the middle of the thing, stifling moans so the wife might not overhear, Arcadio took out a notepad to write down some numbers, including the number of the medical director of the sanitarium in El Cerro, where Steffen was to check in the following week. He pushed Steffen's head away when he was done with his directions, threw the pad and pen on the floor, and finished himself off. They walked back to the office in the capitol building in silence, a pact sealed between them, and Arcadio became his contact within the Directorate. When Steffen made his reports afterward, he had to take two buses to Arcadio's home, where the wife would always receive him with the same cafecito and merienda, and the two men would convene to discuss business in the screened-in back porch. The wife knew better than to bother them there.

For some reason, the order to check into the sanitarium changed. It would risk exposure, too many variables, Arcadio explained. Instead, some weeks later, Renato received instructions to approach one of the young men of el sidatorio during one of his weekend furloughs, a young man who engaged with tourists for sexual favors, an infected jinetero with suspicious connections to a group of counterrevolutionary terrorists that had been led by his brother, now himself one of the commanders of a burgeoning movement spreading through the Island's sidatorios, a mantle that he had inherited from his dead brother.

This was the day I met you, you must know, Steffen said.

I nodded, annoyed that he would think I wasn't following closely.

Anna, the girl he was with, was another student agent, not really German, but an Italian who was fluent in most of the Western European languages.

Steffen recounted his relief at seeing us appear that day at the Hotel Habana Libre, how Anna had instantly morphed into character when we walked into the bar. Not that Steffen had not also been playing his part. The whole thing had been choreographed, their passion, the wallet left on the table, all so that he could have an excuse to stay in touch with Renato at first, and then when Renato refused to meet with him (perhaps sensing some ruse), Steffen came to me.

After that afternoon chat, Steffen grew disheartened. He saw that I was no traitor, just a boy from the provinces trying to get along. The plan had been to try to get to Renato through me, but even that he saw as absurd after our conversation. He gave me the stamp with the woodpecker because that was about the best tradecraft he had learned from his English spy novels. After the first few bombs that summer, he had simply stopped going to see Arcadio, by then already sickened by his participation in what he feared had become a much more dangerous tango than what he had imagined. For all he knew, the Directorate might now have listed him as persona non grata. Arcadio did not seem like the type to dismiss indifference.

Steffen stopped talking. It was already dawning and I had to report to the paladar that afternoon. He wanted me to get some sleep. He sensed that we were on the trail of Renato. That night, we had found six more miniscule graffiti scattered around the old city, in an area no larger than twelve perimeter blocks encircling the cathedral plaza. Steffen had been examining the locations, marked on his tourist map with tiny, penciled x's, as he told me the story that night, at times stopping to ask me what hotels were on which street and what kind of Yuma stayed there. The following night, he promised as he tightened the circle of his calculations, we would catch one of them doing it. They would lead us to Renato.

How would that make things right for you? I asked. Why not just go back to where you came from now? Adventure over.

I must ask the same thing of you, but it's too late for that, isn't it? Steffen said. If Renato's group got scapegoated for the bombings when the time comes to find other culprits, then both of us would be part of that purge, he assured me. I was too close to the fire and he had outlasted his value.

Or you could still be working for Arcadio, I responded.

CEREMONY OF SMALL ACTIONS

We had each confessed things to the other we hadn't confessed to anyone else—or so I thought at the time. Maybe because of that, I gave Steffen's secret as much credence and weight as I gave to my own for the first time, as if by giving it voice I could begin the process of exculpating Renato for what I feared would be crimes greater than his brother ever had the focus or gall to commit. Neither of us told the other that whatever Renato was planning was something that we had to stop. Neither of us, either, had the courage to admit to the other, at first, that such a rebellion against the barbaric government might be an act of the highest virtue.

Although from this moment on, I believed both, if only as a way to forgive Nicolás for what I had seen him do and to forgive myself for allowing it.

There was no proof of any of our surmises about Renato yet, anyway. All we had were rumors about the source of the bombs and little miniature pieces of artwork that had begun to crop up with more regularity through the cracks of the crumbling old city, on the fresh stucco of all the recent renovations—the Visit a mere month away. Steffen mused that with the manner and preponderance by which the diminutive graffiti spread, it was hard to imagine how we had not caught a single person in the act.

A few times, we had come upon samples so recently painted that Steffen smudged the colors together. The variety of them, at least five or six different brilliant hues each, the intricacy of their miniscule designs, each letter encased into leafy or seascape backgrounds, made evident that they weren't executed in haste or with stamps, but were meticulously crafted, maybe not with brushes but with fine-tipped markers (the kind his father's candy inventors would use when illustrating new designs, he explained), in what must have taken even the most experienced draftsman more than a few minutes. But in these gorgeous miniatures, Steffen read a kind of cataclysm that belied both their beauty and their almost imperceptible presence.

By the time I told him the story of the night Nicolás infected his brother, Steffen had already calibrated, in correlation to our discoveries at night and the proximity of the pontiff's visit, how scary things might get. The State had not been so wise; its strategy so far, as with most protests that it can't figure out how to quell or decimate, had been absolute silence and befogging.

It could be ignorance, Steffen claimed. Each insular ministry might be thinking it the work of some other ministry. He seemed proud of this inside-game jargon he had learned from Arcadio.

The word itself, I explained, was almost a property of the government since the late eighties when it became evident that Soviet subsidies would vanish, but even before that from the speeches and manifestos after the rebels descended from the mountains, from the savage early tribunals, from the defeat of the yanqui-backed traitors at Playa Girón, from the rallies for the Million Ton Harvest in the early seventies. *Sacrificio* had almost acted as the loyal earthly servant to the more exalted *Revolución,* without the panache and plumes of *Hasta la victoria para siempre,* but more consistently present, more unflinchingly true.

One night, we began to see evidence contrary to this supposed State ignorance of what this micro-vandalism might signify: pairs of la fiana, their rifles slung over their shoulders, a bucket in one hand, a scrub brush in the other, suspicious eyes fixed not on undesirables as usual, but on brick walls, on the edges of sidewalks, on rusty lampposts, on the trunks of trees. We followed them until they found a target. They worked quickly and carefully not to attract attention, one scrubbing, the other standing cover, spreading his legs shoulder-width apart and crossing his rifle over his chest, the finger on the trigger, the other hand grasping the barrel—which had perhaps the opposite effect than intended, attracting curious onlookers. By the time the Pope arrived in Havana a month later, there would be specially trained cleanup units, with power hoses loaded with bleaching fluids, following the Bishop of Rome's caravan to each of his stops on the Island.

Only by luck, it seemed, did we make any headway into our search. Lingering at the cathedral plaza one early morning, a few weeks before Christmas Eve, too fatigued to go back to the apartment and negotiate our sexual arrangements, I watched the congregation coming out of early Mass and was about to comment on its scarcity, when I saw the shadow of a towering dark man, his imposing body language and brusque gestures unmistakable, crouching and supporting a much shorter, rotund figure, wrapped in flowing mantles from the crown of her head to her bare twisted feet.

Bertila, I said.

Steffen tried to convince me that it could not be her, but only half-heartedly. How would you know? I asked him. He had never even met her.

I ran toward them and easily caught up, Steffen following, still trying to dissuade me from causing a scene that would bring unwanted attention to us.

At first, the giant man wrapped a long arm around the woman's shoulders, ready to protect her from falling boulders if he had to, to do battle with any adversary, but when he recognized me, a zombie smile spread over his face. My mere presence seemed to have the effect of completely untangling him from the woman. They stood there, the woman folding back the mantles on her head as if to be known, the man now erect and useless as her protector.

Bertila spoke. But first, she turned her head with a theatrical indignance away from me, scrutinizing Steffen as if he were the one she knew. Then she turned to me and seemed to make it a point not to glance at Steffen again.

Mi niño, she said, her features softening, but the doting tone sounded forced, rehearsed even. She tapped Inocente St. Louis to get him to acknowledge me also. The giant nodded politely.

Ven, ven, she beckoned me toward them. My instincts told me to embrace both of them, hold them tightly so that they would not wander off pretending to be others again, but I had never been so demonstrative with either of them. I shook the Creole's hand and lightly hugged Bertila with a graze of a kiss on the cheek.

Qué cosa, shouldn't you be at the paladar?

I'm not staying at Calle Obispo anymore.

Sí, sí, I know where you are. I'm sorry I couldn't leave enough food. Caramba, left in a hurry. I'm sorry it has to be this way.

What way? I asked. Then the meaning of her words sunk in, and I saw Bertila steal a quick look at Steffen again, not as if she were trying to figure out who he was but as if trying to communicate something wordless to him.

Will you be coming back? I said to distract myself from what I had just noticed.

Soon, soon, she said.

You told me you didn't trust him, I said, finally admitting there was more to their looks than I knew. Didn't trust Renato with him.

I could see that Steffen made a conspicuous effort to remain in the wings of this scene, as he perhaps had been instructed to do.

I want to see Renato, I said amidst my confusion, turning back to Bertila. Take us to him. If he can tell me to my face that he meant to abandon me, I'll return to Calle Obispo and forget about him. But I want to hear it directly from him. Where is he?

Bertila grabbed me by the arm. She could see how upset I had grown. She shuffled me away from the other two.

He will say no such thing when you do come to him, she said in a hushed tone, although there was hardly anyone else in the deserted cathedral plaza. Had it not been for the recent bombings, it would have been packed with Yuma, even at this hour of the morning.

Bertila continued. When you do see him, he will say the opposite of all that mierda. He has been asking about you since the day I found him.

Take me to him then, I said.

She pulled me farther away from Steffen and Inocente St. Louis to under the archways of one of the shuttered restaurants on one side of the plaza. The bombs had made it so that it seemed, now in the middle of the busy tourist season, as if the city remained under a perennial hurricane alert or an extended quarantine. They had arrested the perpetrators. Why weren't things back to normal?

It's too dangerous now, niño, Bertila protested. Who knows if the Directorate is not going to round us up any minute like they wanted to do in the first place?

Does Renato have anything to do with the bombs? I said. It killed someone. As if this last part would surely exonerate him. He was not a killer. She waved a dismissive hand, a teacher tired of teaching the same lesson repeatedly to an obdurate pupil.

Nobody has to be guilty of anything to get condemned. A sigh. You know that, coño. Bueno, we can only see.

Our conversation ended, she led me back to the other two. I saw Steffen and Inocente St. Louis apparently engaged in a weighty conversation of their own by the manner in which they tried to out-gesticulate each other even though they spoke in such whispered tones I could not make out the content. As we got closer, they noticed me, both their hands stopped moving, and they slowly lowered them. I got a closer look at the Creole. He had grown a gray beard and wore a baseball cap with the tip of the brim pulled almost to the base of his broad Nubian nose, but the gruff voice with the shadow of a Creole accent was impossible to disguise once he greeted me a second time.

In the year and some months that we had worked together, we had never once had a complete conversation. It wasn't that I disliked him or that I thought he disliked me. He purposefully made himself unapproachable, unknowable, camouflaged by the dozens of stories about his past, narratives at crosscurrents with each other. He was a Creole, a sometime fire eater who had made a good living from tourist tips before coming to work with Cecilia, maybe not even hailing from the eastern province as comandante Juan had first announced to lend him an air of otherworldliness, but making an honest Yuma living a few blocks away from Calle Obispo before getting entangled with Nicolás's crew and later becoming the paladar's chef. The history with Nicolás told me that his arrival at the paladar was some kind of debt paid to comandante Juan by the itinerant son. Who knows how long Inocente St. Louis had been Bertila's lover? Neither had ever talked in any detail about the other. Ever. Not directly. The paramours they referred to always remained nameless. Nicolás was the crucial link, as in most things I had discovered recently.

I now saw Inocente St. Louis removed from his hideaway at the stove line as if for the first time. He was almost two meters tall, sinewy and vascular, as if his veiny skin concealed the secret wiring of a superintelligent and dangerous machine, with a crown of serpentine dreadlocks, half of which were coiled into a bun at the apex of his cranium, which made it seem he looked down at you from its very zenith and not from his gentle round mahogany eyes. But it was something else that had made having more than a few words with him impossible (I had seen Cecilia and comandante Juan try). He gave the impression—through his over-aroused voice, smoldering still from the fires he had once eaten as a Yuma attraction and which seemed to have as little variance as the snorting of a bull, through the way that he ate his dinner alone behind the line after having cooked for everyone else, not because he considered himself a servant (we were all servants to the Yuma, weren't we?) or because he wanted to have nothing to do with our paltry lives, he listened to us and interpreted our conversations for some invisible audience, one more sophisticated than us who could make sense of his proverbs and flagrant pronouncements—that whatever it was that he lived through in the far eastern province, or wherever he had come from, the cataclysm that had made him leave and the faith that had made him seek refuge in the capital both made an ineluctable part of who he was now. Tragedy and hope. Cecilia could not have expected him to stay forever. No fire just sits in place without seeking more tinder.

When he had disappeared a few weeks after the first bombings, we all missed him, but there had never been a plan to go and find him, or to report his status to the authorities. We didn't have standing to investigate his absence, as Cecilia put it. He was not family, not really a friend. But here he was. Our solitary Inocente St. Louis, with Bertila, and with Renato and the others from the sanitarium I suspected strongly.

Now unmasked, he would not engage with me further than his initial greetings, perhaps afraid that I might read in his eyes an entire history that had been previously unavailable to me. But he had been talking to Steffen as if they shared a long history. I realized that no matter what bond I had formed with Steffen in the recent weeks, what unsaid vows we had made to each other about our destinies, I knew him as little as I knew the mysterious Inocente St. Louis.

I made to go off on my own—I would hide nearby and follow all of them to Renato, whatever truth I needed to hear had to come from him, but Bertila let out a plaintive, No! She signaled for me to come back to her, and when I got close enough, she reached out and clasped me with both hands. She hooked one arm with mine.

He saved Renato, she said. Had the boy not fled, they would have rounded him up. He told us they were coming after him.

Where is he? Bring us, I begged, not caring to hear of Steffen's heroics, though I imagined it was information he had gathered in his meetings with Arcadio about Operation Mariposa that had saved Renato.

I now knew that when I had seen her last, she had already begun planning her escape, and that my talk about the German must have hastened her plans. Maybe because she thought I would insist on coming with her to Renato or would convince Steffen to help me do it on my own. I also realized the risk that Steffen had taken by crossing Arcadio and passing any information about undesirables. I didn't think he had either such cunning or cojones in him.

So when Bertila turned to me and in a pleading tone told me that I had to return with Steffen to her place and that they would take us to Renato when comandante Juan had made sure the threat from the Directorate had passed, when the news of the arrest of the Salvadorans and whatever show trial they cooked up had calmed the populace and the foreigners, I rebelled.

If comandante Juan knows where he is, I said, the Directorate does also. That man never works for just one side if he can work for two or three.

Then I realized something drastic that might forever keep me separate from Renato.

There'll be no more bombs, right? That will be the dumbest thing to do.

Bertila looked down, as if for the moment she didn't have an answer, but when she raised her eyes to me, I saw how committed she had become to a struggle that I never thought was really hers.

No one said the Salvadorans weren't the ones who really did it, she said in a hushed tone. Let the courts figure that out.

I wasn't sure if she meant that she was fine with letting a few innocent foreigners suffer the humiliation and draconian penal retribution of el Líder's tribunals or if she knew they were guilty because they had been willing accomplices.

As she grabbed me again and almost shoved me toward

Steffen, I noticed the smattering of paint colors on the tips of her fingers and almost wanted to shout out to Steffen. It's her, it's her, we found the artist of the miniature graffiti. But then realized he must have already known and had been leading me on our little detective-novel outings to kill time while we waited for word from her.

Bertila must have noticed the change in me, because for the first time since I had spotted her coming out of the cathedral, she dropped the charade about our chance meeting and confessed that she had needed to see me to make sure I would not endanger Renato or myself. I needed to do as told for now. They were likely watching her apartment and even watching us right now, but they would not do anything in front of a Yuma, not unless they became desperate. Satisfied that her message had been delivered, that the only way I would be safe right now was with Steffen, she moved back toward Inocente St. Louis and did not even turn back when the chef approached and shook my hand.

Nos vemos pronto, pendejo, he said. Soon enough.

I held onto his hand longer than he expected, long enough to scrutinize the rainbow of paint in the webbing between his thumb and index finger, a sloppier artist than his teacher.

I followed behind them as they lumbered out of the plaza heading south toward the Bay Area. They moved with the insouciance of those that have nothing to do, two aimless characters in search of a story that would deign to have them, but not in a hurry to commit to any particular type of narrative. I knew this was not true, that such purposelessness was as much a charade as our chance meeting at the cathedral plaza.

It kept eyes off them.

They crossed Calle Obispo and out of habit, I almost turned and followed my old path, like a rivulet down a groove in the pavement. They continued south. I felt Steffen following a healthy distance behind me, but I did not look back just like no one looked back in search of me.

When they reached Calle Muralla, the site of the old fortress wall that had once circled the city as a bulwark against invaders, their pace quickened. I was close enough behind them that I could hear the strain of the new step through Bertila's pronounced huffs. After heading west toward the Capitolio, Inocente St. Louis hailed a rickshaw at an intersection, and I waited as he helped Bertila mount.

Rickshaws did not move any faster than foot traffic in the old city, particularly when bearing such a heft as Bertila and the giant, so I knew that I could keep up with them. But I also knew that they rarely traveled farther than the tourist areas, so it would not be taking these two to their final destination, which had to be south, very south in the outskirts.

Past the Capitolio, I lost them. They turned into a narrow alleyway between buildings and when I turned into it less than thirty seconds afterward, nothing there, as if the thing had flown into the air like Apollo's chariot. I raced down to the street where the alleyway connected to a main thoroughfare leading to the Capitolio esplanade and saw nothing but bureaucrats on their way to work. No rickshaw in sight.

I retraced my steps back through the alleyway and two blocks the other way in search of Steffen, convinced they had coordinated to lose me somehow, and now he too had vanished.

I sat on the curb to have a drag of a cigarette, before I repeated the path through the alleyway both ways a few times, sure that at least one of them would turn up. Then I began to widen the circle of my search block by block, cursing the German for lying to me and cursing Renato for putting me through this, for not trusting me any more than he trusted his mother or comandante Juan. I wanted to believe that Bertila was right, that the German and I were under watch, better to remain on the outside—visible—to keep them confused about the nature of Steffen's betrayal.

Up until that moment, neither of us had talked about what we would do when we found Renato, perhaps because it had seemed so impossible to imagine how we might drag him away from the hell that had swallowed his brother whole. If that indeed had been our intent all along. Maybe we never talked openly about it because it was the other way around: we were desperate to find a portal into his world.

I finished the cigarette and continued searching fecklessly, stumbling into bars and restaurants, trudging through side streets where atypical local Christmas celebrations that had been legalized in honor of the Visit were already in full swing, sans the Yuma, spilling from homes out into the sidewalks. Things that had always been done in secret now giving the celebrants a false sense of liberation. I knocked on any half-opened doors and inquired about the giant and the mantled woman, about a German, and from the drunken befuddled looks I received in return, I began to sense how futile my every inquiry was, how I might have well been asking if they had seen the Pope yet. Eventually, I stopped at a local cafeteria that served morning rum to tourists, but that took dollars from anyone—particularly now in these jejune days after the bombings. I sat down and had a brandy from a dusty bottle sitting on one of the top shelves, slapped a bundle of dollars on the counter, told the bar woman to keep refilling me until the pile ran out. The drunker I got, the more I imagined that the few all-nighter foreigners that trudged in had come there for me. I wasn't wrong, even in their state of crapulence, they wanted to plan, to hook up with a local to complete their past-dawn excursions.

Eventually they approached me.

I had never been a native in this city this way, had never wanted the facile disappearance into the brief other-life of tourists. It wasn't hard, with all the drinking, the drugs that would surely follow while in private, to adopt a certain role and keep to it until you served your purpose, a ceremony of small actions that should be insignificant to someone our age, natural and thoughtless as breathing, like breaking into a sudden sprint, or so Renato put it once.

But I was not thinking about him when I gave in to these young drunk yanquis, what might have been the only preying Yuma in the city that morning. They took me back to their hotel room just off the Prado, near the old Bacardi building, and as the sun came up full force through the opened windows facing the water, we all passed out in the same bed in a state of semi-undress, not really getting to anything, although I imagined that we must have done something because when I awoke having missed the entire day we were all completely naked, limbs braided into impossible alliances, so that my dark callused feet appeared at the end of a ginger milky white wrist, my right thigh pressed against an ass, and my cock curled in on itself like a dozing cat under a stranger's pimply cheekbone, the sun beginning to set in one corner of the window, our distorted, elongated reflections visible in the opposite corner.

If I could tell them the story that I had told Steffen over the past few nights or the stories that he had told me, they would have all untangled from me with great alacrity.

But on we slumbered and pressed together into the new night.

Had I asked, I could have stayed with them for the remainder of their little adventures on the Island that time forgot.

Hooked up with those that came next and next and next, because surely even the mollycoddled Yuma would soon forget about the bombs.

THE DIZZINESS OF FREEDOM

After the night in the henhouse, I only saw Nicolás once again. He never returned to the house on Calle Obispo. He would not allow himself, he wrote in a scribbled note, handed to me as I took a cigarette break out on Calle Obispo. From this, I constructed an entire ethos for a new Nicolás. That he could not bring himself to see his mother or even his brother—it would be two months still before they would come to pick Renato up with an appointment for an HIV test—let me create a fictional character that was not Nicolás at all (as I would quickly find out the last night I saw him), but someone who had committed an error in judgment, a political error a consequence of political oppression, someone that had zealously overstepped the very broad boundaries that he had set up for moral behavior by wanting to include his brother in that something greater than all of us, something that both his brother and their father had always been chasing.

Even as impending death chased Nicolás, I imagined it admired him as a worthy opponent. Sleepless, feverish, noosed in musty sheets, haunted by hallucinations where incarnations of his brother marched past him, each one more physically ravaged than the last, jabbing its bony fingers on him, lifting his upper lip, and scraping his teeth when Nicolás dared to close his eyes and pretend to sleep. For a moment, before he arrived at our assigned rendezvous spot, I imagined that such torture could redeem what he had done, or at least put a human value on it, and perhaps redeem me as well, my inaction. My cowardice. I wanted to see this new man, redeemed and purged by guilt. Or maybe I just wanted to see some such version of myself. It was the only reason that I agreed to meet him in the bar he had chosen on Calle O'Reilly, a local haunt listed in all the guidebooks and therefore crowded with Yuma.

As I sipped my third whiskey, he arrived, an hour late. It was still early in the afternoon and most of the Yuma in the bar huddled at tables, scheming for the coming night. Nicolás paused at the threshold, making some evaluation in his head that had become second nature. He wasn't much thinner, but things had shifted, and his every movement seemed to be pulled down with considerable tension to some spot beneath the soles of his feet. Dark blotches glowered on his chest, which he displayed proudly and I thought at first to be the sign of the skin cancer that was one of the most opportunistic infections, but up close they seemed nothing more than botched tattoos. His long-sleeved dress shirt was open to the belly button, his old jeans rolled up to the knees, and something dark and sinister, winding its way to his right shin from his calf, another tattoo only of a smidgen greater quality than the stains. He had not been suffering sleepless nights or entangled in sweaty visions. His madness was of another sort. A bright pasted smile, a resplendence in the eyes of those that have crossed over, something of the formless in his demeanor.

I quickly downed my whiskey and turned away from him,

letting him approach to have his say, even if I just had to sit there and not say a word, listen to his ravings.

In his note, he had purposefully not said why he wanted to see me. I was curious, just like I had been curious about the life he had once offered me in the capital. I wanted to know what it was like to be tracked down by the hound of this disease.

He sat close beside me. A shoulder rubbed mine. He slapped some money on the bar, loudly ordered two more whiskeys, and leaned over to kiss me on the cheek, but I turned away at the last second so that the kiss landed on my ear. He smelled not ill, not the urine and ordure of unchanged sheets, but the squamous unwashed stink of the days crusting on him. For a moment, I imagined that he was living in Lenin Park, that he had escaped the sanitarium and disappeared further into the realm of the desvinculados. But one of the first things he said to me was that they had him on a new round of medications. He had finally decided to stop rebelling against the treatments. He was going to survive this.

He remained silent for a long time after that, barely sipping on his whiskey, the thick petals of his lips just grazing the rim of the glass. He waited for me to start. I couldn't, though for the moment at least, it consoled me that he had chosen to survive, or to try. He scratched at his right leg and I couldn't help but look down, expecting still to see those sores that they say spread on the skin first.

It gave him an opening. Macho, my ex, like the yanquis say, if you're not going to talk to me, I can't tell you about them, all the tattoos. He stood up, gave his back to me and lifted his right leg onto my lap for me to see the tattoo that ran from his ankle to the back of his knee. He half-turned to explain it to me, pointing to the dark coils, a charred Medusa's head, that wound around his lower leg, emanating from a point in his Achilles where there was a great flash of orange light and in an inkless square of skin, the first time that I saw the word written outside of government-sponsored graffiti: SACRIFICIO, in precise block letters (the only thing with any precision in the tattoos) down the inside of the tendon. He said that the smoke plumes of the new revolution would be visible from the moon.

Sí, now you see it, he said, touching it with his dirty fingernail, a gash of the moon here, another there, as if the coils had reached up and cut it into pieces.

There was a series of stories behind each of the images, but nothing about the one signal that perhaps needed no introduction, the word, the government's word, which here was so different in style and presentation. It had either been done by a separate hand or purposefully shielded from the ink-hemorrhaging chaos. I asked him where he'd had it done, and he quickly removed his leg from my lap and sat back on the stool, inching closer to me.

The señorito speaks! he said.

Is this why you asked to see me, to show me your tattoos? The word was to remain harbored in some slip of my memory—in the unassuming and dangerous way that it presented itself, without need for elaboration, almost like a brand.

Did he want to reconnect, to involve me in his final days? I asked him. Is that it? Because if it is, I'm not willing. Not after how—

Who are you? he interrupted, turning lively, the jitteriness animated by a joyful tune in the antechamber of his voice box, sitting up on his stool. Who's inside that orphaned little head? How are you going to die and who's going to be involved in *your* final days? I tried to save you, huevón.

I had decided before I arrived that if he needed to cast rage

at someone—better that he did it with me and not some other
Renato. By then, I had deliberately blinded myself to the possibilities of the larger mission of which he might be but an
infantryman, and to which what I had witnessed was nothing
more than an inconsequential aside. Did he at least want to
know how Renato was doing? Had he mentioned his name
to any of the medical staff at the sanitarium? They had not
come for him yet, I informed him. He seemed unconcerned
with such news.

They will.

He ripped open his shirt in a violent motion that sent the
lower buttons flying. It was not the dark patches on his sternum
and splotched over the half-dome of his ribs that caught my
attention (and now I thought that perhaps they were the skin
cancer after all), but the absence of muscle tissue in his chest
and even on the surface of his gelatinous belly that gave the
pallid skin the semblance of transparency, as if he were something artificial, a waxen figure.

Around that time, at the beginning of the rainy season of
1996, there was still something medieval about those who
succumbed to la SIDA, as if the instincts of the government in
setting up the sidatorios had been merited, a biblical scourge
that had no place, required no more rational response.

Dime, cabrón, I'm not afraid of the truth anymore.

Tell you what? I said. You're dying. Is that what you want
me to tell you? And soon your brother. And maybe even me,
I don't even want to know. And that will begin your glorious
overthrow of the State?

He had lost his fine-tuned ear for sarcasm, I saw. His
eyes widened and he clutched my hand. Sí, that's it, así, así
mismísimo.

I snapped my hand away and ordered two more whiskeys. The bartender served us and waited for me to pay him,

ignoring Nicolás's pile of singles. He glanced over, guessing that I was some Yuma fending off a desperate local. I signaled that I was fine. He took my bill and I told him to keep the change, which he must have mistakenly taken as a sign to keep watch, because for the rest of our time there, whenever Nicolás became impassioned, he stepped over to meticulously wipe a spot on the bar top right next to us.

You don't understand, do you, pingú? I might as well have left you in that little playita, offered you nothing. Coño, I'm even sorry I let you touch me all those times. He spit on the floor. A waste of my time. He waited for the insult to strike, stolidly, like an archer that imperceptibly lowers the bow to peer at the target. Ay, no te hagas el sueco, do you think I did it because I desired you? Because you had something that the thousands, the tens of thousands of others did not? For love? He waved his fingers as if releasing pixie dust. I expected him to break into a snickering that would match the demonic quiver of his pupils, that would let me define the twisted purpose of our impromptu meeting, and confront it quickly and directly, then leave until he called on me again, which I was sure he would. I was convinced that I would hold his hand as he took his last breath. But Nicolás gazed at me, suppressing a smile, the look of a man on the verge of confessing a sin so silly it could only be told to a despised ex-lover.

I loved you, cabrón, he said when he turned back to me, his voice official, assessing. I loved you just like I loved him.

Who?

My brother.

You love . . . love . . . present tense . . . everyone is still alive! I said.

Ay sí, yes. Love. Everyone alive, one big happy family.

But as soon as we were on the same page, I couldn't stand it. I wanted to hit him. Is this why he had asked to meet with

me? I reached over and patted his pockets, felt under the seat
of the stool to see where he had it hidden, his little death
packet. He submitted passively to my search, even getting up
and raising his arms. If I had been blind and deaf, I would
have never guessed it was him, not simply because the absence
of flesh on his bones made it feel as if I were handling one of
the starving stray cats that sun on the rocks under the fortress
of El Morro, but because something else was missing, some
give and pull that had always been there—some band had
snapped inside him.

I felt foolish after my search. But then I recalled that in
spite of his height, it had never been Nicolás's physical presence that made him imposing. It had never been his voice, that
like his brother's and his mother's (even comandante Juan's)
had that feminine capital lilt that made even the basest denizens of Havana seem like prim aristocrats when compared
to brassy Orientales like me. It had never been his demeanor,
indifferent-seeming, turtle-calm even at its most pining. It
hadn't even been his toothy, disarming smile, which was irre-
pressible (even in moments of great distress it could be read
in some feature of his face), full of undefined promises. What
had made him imposing, even after dealing with him for only
a handful of minutes, was his ability to avoid the sticky silk
of consequence, the talent to exist just above the surface of
the deadly instruments of self-torture we all create from the
infinite regrettable small actions of our days.

So when he said that he loved me and Renato, it didn't
startle me, something that he might have said to me before,
but I would have never thought to hold him to it. He was no
more fettered to such declarations than a spider to its web.

What an intricate design he chose to spin that night. He
was just getting started. Minutes after his declaration, the
reproachful focus to which I had subjected him since he

walked in shifted. His eyes widened and grew empathetic for a moment, a look I had not seen since the day he picked me up on the beach in Cojímar, and that soon I forgot had once existed, had allowed me to trust him, to want to be in his presence.

You've never been in love have you, papi? he said, now adopting his own prosecutorial contempt. You can't even lie about it. In all the months we fucked, I never heard it once, not even in the throes of passion. For the thousand times I said it you—

I *had* forgotten.

And now, now you think you love my brother because of what you saw that night. But you'll never say it. To him or to anyone else. The little orphan boy grown into a machine, trained to serve la Revolución, but ends up serving tourists. Ya, colorín colorado, this tale is done. Now I'll die, and Renato will follow me, and you and Cecilia will mourn. You'll live on like her with the rest of the ghosts in this crypt of an Island . . . you won't even notice how alike you are.

That's why he chose me on the beach that day, he continued. Like comandante Juan, Cecilia and I were both dutiful Fidelistas at heart, which meant not that we idolized Fidel but that we would suffer any indignity at the hands of the State, submit to any humiliation. Not like Pascual, he added, at least Pascual had once truly believed.

There's something heroic in that sort of faith, no? But what would you know? Why am I asking a weasel about the surface of the moon?

Nicolás had heard that in Barcelona his father had published books with gory details of how he had been tortured and raped at El Morro prison, live electric wires to his balls, kitchen utensils up his culo, cigarettes put out on the hairless spots in his inner thighs, all fiction. Pascual the victim instead of the perpetrator, the martyred hero instead of the silent accomplice. Cecilia had hated him for that, for having the gall to save his own life, even if it meant drastically reinventing his past. But at least he always believed in something, for or against.

More than I can say for any of the rest of you, Nicolás said. Did she try anything with you? He grabbed my crotch and squeezed. Huh? Lecherous old whore. Or were you afraid that comandante Juan would put a bullet in your brain?

This was then at least part of the purpose of our meeting, what would later become the subtext of many of my get-togethers with his brother, Cecilia's semi-incestuous obsession with me and her groveling acceptance of the State's status quo, as long as the Party kept its long-fingered pilfering hands off her paladar. I let Nicolás tire himself cursing his mother because I knew that he was prattling toward a point.

It took him a couple more whiskeys to get there; and when he did, his demeanor changed—his chest inflated, his finger wagging at the heavens, as he had surely seen any Party speaker worth his salt do.

Throughout our brief independence, our country has been populated by two types of men, revolutionaries and counter-revolutionaries, and although they take turns at the helm, if you tuned out the volume of their rhetoric and watched the movements of bone, flesh, and armies, you could not tell them apart, the same offending gestures at the gods above, the same principled tilt of the chin (bearded or not), the same tautness of limbs (as if they were warring against a puppet master), the same mock erectness, an unintended parody of the famous cubano pinga, the same lyrical tempests brewing in the pools of the eyes. I had watched Nicolás even fuck with similar gestures, as if still at our most vulnerable, our most anti-public, we have to borrow the pageant of the politico's dais to be men. I had probably done it myself. When it came down to it you couldn't tell them apart, the revolutionary and the counterrevolutionary, from Martí to Fidel, they were all one and its opposite, switching places like twins trying to dupe a straying lover.

Vaya, but in the end, that was us, the cubanos, a hapless band of disgruntled lovers.

There had been so many versions of the New Man and the New Society that it was difficult to take seriously the version concocted in sidatorios all over the Island by the undesirables like Nicolás, a haunted land from where the money-laden visitors had been frightened away, an incestuous place where the curse of the blood would be passed from generation to generation until nature itself took its course, an oasis, an Eden from the madness of the modern world. In Nicolás's mind back then, it had only been some inchoate fantasy. Renato, Steffen had surmised, would have been the one who molded his brother's bad dreams and given them infinite space in the concrete world.

Beginning with the harmless bombs. That was just prologue.

But back then, before the long summer of the bombs, it all seemed like the ravings of madmen.

What are you talking about? I said, not quite following the verses in Nicolás's as-yet-unformed apocalyptic vision.

The only path to freedom, he said—his voice scientific, suffused with a purposeful logic—was to disconnect ourselves from the world at large, to cut off the lines of the State's alliances through something that would at first seem like a bloodless rebellion, but whose effect would last for generations, a purging, a cleansing through the disease. It would not be impossible, not if there were a conscious revolutionary zeal to undo the State's work in the sidatorios wholeheartedly, to spread the plague so persistently and comprehensively that any outsider would be committing suicide by stepping onto the Island.

The ghosts in charge of a haunted dilapidated mansion.

He didn't want me to join them, he said, that's not why he'd asked to see me. I didn't have the mettle, anyway, he explained. I was not of the right stock. Our servile class: me, Cecilia, comandante Juan.

I didn't respond, this was part of the reason I was beckoned as well, to be derided. But sex is how the new world would both be established and kept alive, he promised. There is going to have to be a whole lot of fucking.

Our country would be the first where the disease is passed on to the coming generations, not as a curse, but as a blessing. He must have noticed the look in my eyes, not ire or indignation, but sincere concern, thinking the disease or the whiskey had begun to eat away at the front lobes of his brain, because he paused, but then picked right up again, detailing how it would be us, the serfs who would be put in colonies, where we would be forced to work the fields and join the army, serve, since that's all we knew how to do anyway.

I'd had enough. I dropped some extra bills for the bartender, who seemed concerned that Nicolás would snatch them and quickly came over, thanking me as I made to walk out. When Nicolás realized that I really did intend to cut our meeting short, he bolted up and wrapped both arms around me, resting his head on my shoulder.

No, no, hermano, ¿pero qué? ¿Qué? Perdona, he said.

I didn't want a scene or to attract any kind of official attention that would make Nicolás even more frenzied. The truth was that I hardly knew who he was, and I had never seen this side of him. I patted him on the shoulder, pushed him back at arm's length but he would not raise his eyes to look at me.

It's alright, I'm fine. Todo bien, I said loud enough for the rest of the customers to hear and sat back on the stool. The bartender refreshed my drink but ignored Nicolás, who remained standing now beside me, an arm draped over my shoulder. He continued to apologize, his voice growing maudlin, sniffling. Then he grew aggressively playful, grabbing my upper arm tightly, pawing at my chest and head.

Once I took a long sip of my fresh drink, and he grew certain that I would not threaten to leave again, I could see that he had been merely distracting himself with this put-on madness from the contempt that swelled from somewhere deep in his guts.

What did I ever want from you? he said in a flat neutral tone.

Not sex—plenty of that elsewhere.

Not friendship. I'd never sought that from anyone.

Not pity, he continued.

Not judgment—I got plenty of that from others, too.

He paused, waited until I caught his eye. When I cast my eyes downward, he lowered his head clumsily to remain in my sightline.

You're never going to ask me, pendejo, are you? Are you, eh?

I feigned ignorance, brusquely shoved his arm off me. But he wasn't deterred.

It's the only reason you came. I knew you would come. Just to ask me. I knew you would need to know, and this might well be your last chance. But once it came to it, I also knew you wouldn't have the cojones. You'd rather remain in ignorance.

He sat back down on his stool and leaned back. He spoke to my profile.

You don't really want to know. You're too much of a coward to admit that what you saw thrilled you. It made you

free in ways you had never been before. Too much of a coward
to admit that you would have been even more thrilled if it had
been you instead of him. Think about what he felt submitting
finally to the unimaginable. You didn't stop it because you
were imagining that it was you. Right? But it wasn't you.

Spittle slipped down one side of his chin.

I really don't know what I ever wanted from you—but it
wasn't cowardice. I'd had to live with plenty of that all my
life.

I took hold of Nicolás's shirt, tightened it around his neck,
picked him off his stool with surprising ease, threw him on
the floor, and had thrown a fist back, ready to strike him,
when the bartender leaped over the bar and landed on top of
me. He must have reserved this show of force and speed just
for this type of situation, because up to this moment, he had
been laconic at his quickest, but he fell on me like a bundle of
sugar sacks, pinning me to Nicolás, our cheeks pressed to each
other's—almost tenderly. Before we knew it, he had dragged
us by the shirt collars out onto the cobblestones of Calle
O'Reilly. Nicolás's bundle of dollars rained down on us. A
few shirtless boys, who were playing marbles on the sidewalk
across the street, made off with most of them, their colorful
game pieces scattering everywhere. Nicolás made a half-assed
attempt to follow them crawling on his knees in their direction, then gathering some of the marbles and putting them in
his jeans pocket as consolation. He said he was going to stick
them all up his ass and shit them out on the doorstep for when
they returned, but he continued to simply gather the marbles
until his pocket bulged with them. He crouched across the
street and buried his head in his arms.

When I sat beside him, he cringed, the whiskey perhaps
causing a bad reaction with whatever medication he was on. I
tried to pick him up, but he tensed into a ball.

Leave me alone, maricón. What good . . . can you do me . . . now?

He struggled to get out even a few words. I opened his arms and checked his belly, his groin, afraid that the bartender had underhandedly stabbed him or something. But whatever was happening to Nicolás was not on the outside, something rather ripped open in the entrails, and it had caught him by surprise, because he became enraged again but not from the pain. He scuttled away from me like an injured crab, and we sat at opposite sides of the front door of the boys' house.

Come home, I said, a place that was not mine to offer.

¿Qué?

Come home. Comandante Juan can fix it so they let you out of that place.

This amused him, lent him a new strength. He straightened up a little bit. He said I was right, comandante Juan probably could have fixed it from the first day he was there.

But he hadn't. That should tell you where I stand, no? Where I have always stood since Pascual left.

Did you love him? Your father? I paused, offered some context to ameliorate the blow of the non sequitur. More than you do your mother.

Nicolás remained silent for a long while, pretending to nurse his injuries. I respected him, he finally whispered. Although he had nothing to offer.

I have no home, either, I told him. Nothing to offer you. Whatever it was you wanted from me.

I asked him if the bartender had punched him. He shook his head, said it was his intestines. They were riddled with ulcers. Maybe I have just been living with them all along and was numb to it . . . the pain, quiero decir. I shouldn't have drank so much, but I wanted to see you. And that's all we ever did, right, fuck and drink and smoke.

Well, *he* smoked; I had found after two days with him
how allergic I was to marijuana, my stomach clenching like
a salted gastropod with every inhale. He had thought it was
amusing that I hadn't done a lot of things. Sometimes living
a few hours in freedom is worth a whole lifetime of this, he
had said once, standing at the entrance to the henhouse, signaling with a disregarding hand at the neatly set tables of the
paladar, ready for the tourists.

I reminded him.

That wasn't the only time I told you that, huevón, he said.
You forget a lot of things.

Look at me now, he added after a long silence, then sibi-
lating with a grimace, he wrapped his arms tight around his
belly, as if he were protecting something precious in there
from some new onslaught. A few of the marbles slipped out
of his pocket and rolled down a groove in the sidewalk.

Had Nicolás gained all the hours of his freedom now, and
this was the price? Is that what he had wanted for his brother?
Could it have been that simply misguided? That well-inten-
tioned?

I didn't have the gall to ask him, although he was right.
That was the real reason he had wanted to see me. So that I
would ask even if he couldn't tell me. Why?

La libertad, that evasive perra. Cubans had been teased for
a whole century and never as much as held hands with it.
The brothers had seen how the State had robbed their father
from his mother and then from them. For what? So that Pascual would abandon it himself in what must have been the
simplest decision in his life? In the argument of Pascual's life,
some place might have been reserved for them in the prelimi-
nary notes, when he had first courted Cecilia, when there was
still talk of the glory of la Revolución and the grand role to
be played by those who performed their duty, which of course

included creating future revolutionaries. ¿La jodió bien ahí, eh? Nicolás had once said, no future revolutionaries here.

Nicolás became el hombre de la casa by default when his father disappeared into the entrails of the Party, methodically, almost imperceptibly, as if set up beforehand in a carefully calibrated schedule by some ink-faced bureaucrat, Pascual's absences overtaking his presences, and according to Renato, Nicolás's hold tightening around his mother. At first, he harassed her for what he called her failure as a wife, never mind that she had never been much of a mother, that she had forsaken her role as her children's protector to her grief over her failed romance with her husband, and his failed romance with a cannibalistic political pipe dream.

To be fair to Cecilia, when Renato repeated such things to me after Nicolás's death, he seemed to be doing it more out of honor to his brother than anything else, or so I felt, sometimes even trying to mimic his brother's rage, but mostly with the comic despair of an actor caught in the wrong play.

That was Renato. He found it somewhat absurd that he had inherited his brother's role. A few months after my last meeting with Nicolás, when Renato arrived in the sidatorio, contrary to what I had thought at first, he must have been like some young prince anointed without ever having seen a minute of battle, or ever even visited court. He became their ragged king, perhaps a truer leader than his brother, because he had been brought into the fold unwillingly, passively, without a doctrine of his own, and a much bigger threat to the legacy of their parents' revolutionary romance than either one could have imagined on the night that he submitted to his brother's crime.

It was certainly part of the reason why my offer for Nicolás to return home proved absurd. He had already abdicated, and it was just a matter of time until he became inconsequential to both of his families, the one in Calle Obispo and his new family at the sidatorio in El Cerro.

Nicolás stood up, his body bent at the middle, obeisant, and turned his pockets inside out in front of the door, the marbles clattering on the stone steps and spilling back onto the street, creating the sensation that his figure was shattering into pieces before me. He bent down his head to let me kiss it and walked past me down the middle of the cobblestone street, his hands fisted up against his belly, nauseated with his freedom, the tail of his shirt fluttering in the breeze, his steps so heavy that he seemed to lack all human buoyancy, that if he kept on walking directly into the sea, his feet would never lose touch with the sea floor, the waves would wash cleanly over him.

In the distance, the ping of a last few marbles falling out of his pocket, and the sight of the boys returning, making a wide turn around him and reaching with their hands for the spilled booty.

I would never see Nicolás again.

CITY IN AIR

I returned to Bertila's place after spending a bevy of insomniac days fueled by rum and cocaine with the Yuma trio, whose names I must have known well at the time but slipped my mind the moment I parted from them, the moment I fled from them, mejor dicho. I could have never parted with formal goodbyes because they had grown so attached to me that anytime I made any gesture or voiced any word that would suggest my decampment, they lavished me with clothes and colognes and wristwatches and jewelry from their suitcases. Because none of their shoes fit me, the girl washed my feet and trimmed and polished my toenails one morning after we had returned from the clubs. They napped during the days with their limbs draped over me, as if I were the hostage of a giant octopus. They wanted to me to stay with them for the duration of their trip, to show them the *real* Cuba. These were the brave kind of Yuma that ventured onto the Island these days.

When they were sober enough, they never tired of talking politics, like Yuma tend to do on the Island. As well-informed as they seemed to be, they never succeeded in luring me into their arguments. They all want us to be as free as they pretend to be, but such pretense is a harsh luxury for us. Drunk one early morning, I must have mentioned the paladar and told them the nights I still worked there, so when I fled, I could not return to the house on Calle Obispo. I felt as if I had done it on purpose, as if part of me knew that if I mentioned that part of my life to them, I would be purposefully cutting off myself from Cecilia, from any past in the capital except for Renato.

Fleeing was as easy as it had ever been for me since the moment I had decided to leave my childhood and my abuela behind in Baracoa. Maybe that had been Cecilia's fear. She had picked out that itinerancy in me early on—since she knew it so well from how it manifested in others—the maudlin trips to Cojímar I forced on her, the nights of disappearing into the city, first with Nicolás and then with Renato. She must have known I would not return from one of those excursions, that I wasn't as loyal as I pretended to be.

I wanted to feel guilty, but I felt the opposite, weightless, defiant, rid of Cecilia as I would soon be rid of the Yuma trio. I gathered all the goods I had been gifted in one of their suitcases and absconded from the room during their afternoon nap before going out for the night. They slept so little that those few hours in the middle of the day they lay as rigid and impassive as cadavers.

Steffen had been playing house while I was gone. I arrived at Bertila's place that early evening to a freshly cooked pot of arroz con pollo, dinner for two set on a little marble table in the living room on which Bertila kept her supplies. We sat in upturned old milk crates that had held her backup supplies and ate, neither wanting to look at the other for more than a glance. As if expecting this, Steffen had bought an old phonograph and played loud, aggressive piano concertos by some Russian in the background. We didn't have to speak. With this elaborate setup, I wondered if this wasn't the first night in which he had been expecting me, if there had been an empty plate setting and the cannonading piano in the background all the nights I had been gone.

When we were finished and I helped him clear the table, I noted that he had cleaned up the place too, the bed neatly made, the floors swept and mopped, the counters dusted, the shelves in the kitchen stocked with food, the fridge with fresh vegetables and fruit. He had run out of Bertila's moonshine, but he went to one of the cabinets and pulled out a bottle of the fancy rum they sold at hotels and the Yuma shops.

He poured a couple of shots and I downed mine quickly and signaled for a refill. I had a thousand questions but I wasn't sure that I wanted the answers to any of them. I satisfied myself with emptying a third glass and moving to the bed, throwing myself on top of the covers that Steffen had tucked in military style with hardly a crease. It was the last thing that I remember noticing before I passed out.

I dreamt of the cathedral plaza, although it wasn't in the right place, it was somewhere on a beach much like the rocky one in Cojímar, and the waves washed in balseros on their makeshift rafts, one which carried Nicolás, looking not like the day he met me but crazed and disturbed and claiming to be free like the last day I saw him. He greeted me and introduced himself. I awoke and lay with my eyes open for minutes or hours or mere seconds, not knowing where I was, not caring. Then I just as easily drifted off to sleep again. I could not be sure if the presence that I felt hovering nearby, always just out of the reach of my vision, was part of my dreams or if Steffen kept vigilance over my sleep right next to the bed. I was in both places at once, but it felt right, and I did not want to leave either place.

Days must have passed, for each time I woke, it was day, it was night. Day and night.

Once, when I awoke, I shifted and turned on the bed, thinking the cycle would continue forever. But by then whatever drugs I had inhaled or snorted with the Yuma had transformed in my system, and I felt a million tiny vacuous spaces right underneath my skin and in the lining of my thoughts. They kept me awake.

I asked Steffen the day of the week. He told me, but it made as little sense as if he had mentioned a primary color. I had lost hold of the string of time, and it would take me a few days to grasp it again. I remained in bed, and Steffen brought me a plate to eat, knowing I must be ravished though I could hardly take in more than three miniscule bites.

I asked for water and gulped it when he brought me a glass, asking for two more this way, and then just taking the glass and standing by the running kitchen faucet and drinking until my belly distended. When Steffen fell asleep in the barber's chair that night, I thought about leaving, but my thirst kept me in place. Since my stomach now ached from chugging by the sink, I filled the bathtub to the rim from the cold tap, opened the small bathroom window facing a patio to let in the cool bay breeze, and soaked in the tub the entire night.

When dawn broke, Steffen found me shivering, wrinkled, and as disoriented as I had been when I arrived. Now, he decided to take control of me, to bring me back to our world by telling me the truth. He began to offer answers to the questions I had not had the wherewithal to ask yet. I sat in the barber's chair, wrapped in a multicolored coat of a dozen towels, sipping the hot cafecito that Steffen had brewed.

You must know now that the truth is dangerous, he started. Not just about Renato, but for us. That's why Bertila wanted to keep it from you. At least until she was sure that you wanted to hear it. You must make a choice now. That's what comes with the truth.

Have you made it?

My choice is not the same. I could walk into an embassy tonight if I had to. They couldn't touch me there.

But still, it had been a choice.

He had warned Bertila that the Directorate had set its sights on arresting Renato and others in the sanitarium as a preventive action. There had been chatter and threats even before the first bomb, many picked up by chivatos inside the sanitarium. Arcadio had expanded Operation Mariposa and sent Steffen to confirm some of this intelligence by befriending Renato again during his furloughs. The intelligence directly implicated Renato and many others in the sidatorio of plotting bloody and widespread violence against the State.

Bertila had enlisted Inocente St. Louis to get Renato away, because he had resisted at first when she offered him the information, insisting that he had things to finish and that the German couldn't be trusted.

The intelligence from the Directorate wasn't wrong, Steffen asserted. That's the big news, really. You must know. Things could have been a lot worse.

It sounded too much as if he were congratulating himself. Yuma have major savior complexes. Every single one of them. Even the good ones.

Steffen went on. Not only had the removal of Renato and his cohorts from the sanitarium disarmed one of the more radical elements of the web of insurgents involved in the bombing campaign but it also had allowed Bertila and Inocente St. Louis to infiltrate the higher echelons of the counterrevolutionary agitators south of the city, which had a further quelling effect. Although they couldn't stop everything, not right away. But the worst was prevented.

He meant to kill? I asked.

He was stopped, that's what's important. The Italian tourist
. . . is . . . como se dice. Wrong place. Wrong time.

He wasn't stopped, entonces. Why did you save him?

Arcadio didn't give a shit about saving anybody. All he
cared about was his operation and pleasing his superiors. I
couldn't help him anymore. It had become too serious. But he
wasn't wrong about Renato. I don't think.

They must be out looking for you right now.

He went to the window, peered down to the street through
a crack in the drawn wooden shutters. They're not looking
for me. They know exactly where I am. And exactly everywhere you went with your Yuma. Exactly almost everything.

He latched the shutters, but in truth, it wouldn't have mattered if he stuck his head out the window and waved at them.
He was right. No matter what he had done. They couldn't
touch him. Not now. Not a European. Not with the city
empty of Yuma. Not with the Visit just a month away. That's
why Bertila had him ensnare me in all of this.

Protection.

Still, now I became more hesitant about our excursions.
I told him about following Bertila and Inocente St. Louis
in the rickshaw and their disappearance into thin air in the
alleyway. He laughed and said that by the time they mounted
the rickshaw, it likely had not been them anymore but dou-
bles, kids from the hideouts dressed to throw off the tail from
the Directorate. The rickshaw had probably been driven to
some abandoned horse stable in the alleyway, and the decoys
scampered up the balconies like rhesus macaques.

Poof, Steffen said.

I was lucky the Directorate had not picked me up right
there, Steffen explained, lucky that I found my trio after all.

For the next couple of weeks, we only went out a few
times, and had no trouble finding the signs that I now

imagined had been left specifically for us and others who wanted to join the insurgents. The little *sacrificios* mostly decorated in either festive red and verdant Christmas colors or the white and yellow-gold colors of the home of the Visitor. I kept on peering around trying to discern which of the late-night stragglers and vagrants nearby were the eyes of the Directorate on us, but Steffen seemed wholly unconcerned with this. He had bought a map of the city at one of the hotel shops and had begun to mark each sighting on the map. At dawn, he opened the map out on the marble dining table and tried to spot any pattern, any message, any prophecy in our discoveries.

You're giving them more credit than I think they deserve, I said from a supine position on the barber's chair. Those things are random. They're not that smart.

Those bombs, they could have killed hundreds, he responded, but they didn't. That takes a lot of planning. They weren't random.

I humored him, pretended his map mattered. I followed him everywhere. Got better at spotting the tiny graffiti than him, could tell him if it was a fresh one before he looked in his map by the sheen of the colors, by the particular palette and style of the artist—there were at least a dozen of them, I figured.

The false days that had led up to the meeting with Bertila meant I couldn't fully trust him anymore, no matter what explanations he came up with and what he had done that had proven his mettle with the insurgents. But as far as getting to Renato, he was the only one I could rely on.

We continued to sleep in separate rooms. Neither of us tried to revive the peremptory sexual entanglements we had engaged in before. I made Bertila's bed mine, partly because now I understood that Steffen had not been lying about one thing. Bertila would never return to live here. She had given up that privilege as far as the Directorate was concerned.

In mid-December, the city marked its first full month free of bombs. At Mass in St. Peter's Square, the Vatican confirmed the Visitor's arrival in January to the troubled citizenry of the capital and to the rest of the world. Then, as if some edict had been lifted, the Yuma began to return in droves—first for the famous yearly film festival and then for the end-of-year celebrations.

It was an awful thing to think, but with the return of the Yuma, the city felt like a real place again. The natives all came out of their self-imposed quarantine to join the prodigals. Soon, it was as if the summer had never happened, or as if it had been some violent storm thundering just offshore that veered back into the deep. No one mentioned the bombs, the dead Italian jogger, the captured foreign nationals.

The only reminders of what had happened were the tiny graffiti now sprouting farther outside the perimeter of the old city and the coastline. Steffen taped blank pages to the edges of his map and drew new maps with new x's on them.

The festive nature in the streets near Bertila's apartment soon began to make me anxious. I began to see it as some sort of grand performance put on by the Directorate, which had now employed the entire Yuma population and not just a handful as Steffen had described. Although I wasn't sure why. To believe Steffen, the real perpetrators of the terror that summer had not been apprehended, and a new wave of bombings could erupt at any time, only now during the busy season—with the eager Yuma taking advantage of the slashed prices to lure them back and inspired by the historical momentousness of the coming Visit. Not to mention the truly faithful from all over Latin America, who began arriving right before Christmas Day.

There would be carnage this time.

One night, the potential for such a scenario played out right before us as we ventured farther and farther south from the old city in search of x's for Steffen's map. The engine of one of the gargantuan tanker trucks that bring potable water to neighborhoods with dilapidated pipe systems overheated and caught on fire. The engine exploded just as the drivers and ministry workers dashed from it. Had it not been for the cistern cracking and flooding the cabin and the engine, the fire might have spread through the huddled shacks of the ramshackle barrio because no emergency services existed in that forgotten part of the outer capital.

For a few days afterward, the whole city panicked that the summer had returned with its bombs. The Party daily, *Granma,* ran front-page stories about the fire every day with headlines that stressed the lack of connection between this event and any recent violence or to counterrevolutionary malcontents. The Ministry of Tourism posted flyers in every hotel and on street posts and kiosks in the old city, explaining in detail that the fire and the consequent explosion had been an accident, an old engine overheating, as common an experience with a motor vehicle in the capital as any. The newspaper articles and informative flyers made no direct mention of the bombings that summer, but everyone got the point. The explosion had not been a bomb—but also, the government was nervous about something still.

I understood. But even after Steffen had confessed to me everything he had lied about, even after he had laid out the proof of Renato's involvement as if he were the head of one of Che's merciless tribunals, and even as he tried to convince me that he had undergone some sort of epiphany about his role and purpose in our country, one that would involve taming Renato's most destructive and anarchic instincts, I still did not believe that this new version of Renato even existed. The younger brother had surely been mistaken as the heir of a brutality and moral recklessness that wasn't his and would never be his to carry.

Another part of me feared what I would do when I finally found that version of Renato. Would I just run back to Calle Obispo, knowing that Cecilia would take me back for the busy New Year season no matter how many shifts I had missed? If so, I should just do that now, before she hired someone else. Or would I want to be taken in by Renato and his group, no matter what their purpose, their history, their intentions? Whatever penance I sought by searching for Renato, I didn't know if I could live up to what he asked of me in return.

As Christmas Day approached, Steffen's map looked like the work of a cartographer that has just discovered three new worlds, extended and expanded with so many taped sheets that the original disappeared once it had been folded up. But in the end, the effort paid off. Unfolded, the map extended beyond the edges of Bertila's marble table like a makeshift tablecloth in a kid's make-believe party. Steffen had to hold one end up to show me. There was a method to the randomness of the graffiti, he announced. It was crowded with x's at the center, in the heart of the original map, and at first, I could discern no pattern. But the longer I looked at it, a kind of geometric fractal of concentric circles emerged as if floating above the names of streets until the whole thing unraveled in the new parts that Steffen held up, and the string of a path disappeared off the edges.

It's a way out, Steffen said. He placed the tip of his index finger almost in the exact center of the fractal. It starts here, he said. I squinted and looked at where his finger rested. The cathedral plaza.

They'll lead us from there.

Who? When? I asked.

The hour when it's most crowded, and the agents from the Directorate are at home drunk and stuffed with lechón. Midnight Mass of Christmas Eve, what Cubans call the Mass of the Rooster.

Originally, back in colonial times, or when they had been allowed to grow old in the city and not been sacrificed in cockfights, roosters must have crowed early on Christmas Day during the celebration of the midnight Mass. And for this occasion, in honor of the Pope's coming visit the following month, they had rounded up a handful of brightly colored ones and set them in cages near the entrance of the cathedral, stacked in columns so that roosters in the higher ones were shitting all over the ones in the lower cages, and clearly not crowing as they had been brought there to do.

Steffen looked at the cages and said that there were sugar-drunk mice that lived in his father's candy factory who were probably saner than any Cuban.

Steffen was right in predicting that when we found Renato and his group it would not just be composed of Cubans who had disappeared, but foreigners, young foreigners that the State had invited into the game and then forgotten about when they had lost their value. Of course, the Directorate had not forgotten about Steffen, and we would also conveniently forget about that.

Had it not been clear where we needed to go from Steffen's map, as I moved closer to the cathedral, I noticed something that might have escaped others. Made of coral blocks, the cathedral surface is speckled with tiny and colorful marine plant and animal fossils that disguised the miniscule graffiti in the pale colors, details of secret murals that could pass for the remnants of prehistoric sea horses or mutilated starfish. Hundreds or thousands of graffiti high up both bell towers.

But no one seemed to notice. Steffen had to scrutinize a few up close in the entrance archway to make sure, but I knew from thirty meters away.

By the time we had made it inside the church, there was nowhere to sit, so we stood on the far right-hand aisle, blocked from moving forward by a group of old nuns. It was odd to me that not one person offered any of these viejas a spot in one of the crowded pews, even though some were clearly so decrepit that they had to huddle together for support. Steffen stood on his tiptoes and peered over them, scanning the heads in the pews ahead. He saw something on the other side of the church. We shuffled to the left-hand aisle. In the third pew from the altar, sat the round figure of Bertila, her shoulders again draped in dark mantles, a mantilla over her face. Inocente St. Louis sat beside her, towering over the other parishioners, though he was kneeling, and all around them, to the sides, in the pews in front and back, the unruly, unwashed mops of muchachitos, young men conspicuous by their ragged, unwashed clothes in this sea of primly dressed nuns and priests and seminarians from all over the hemisphere, all arrived a month early to begin preparations for the Visit.

When I saw the back of Renato's figure, as we were pushing through the dark-vested folks on the left side of the church, the unwashed black curls, which became tighter the dirtier and oilier they got, the thrown-back shoulders in the brazen imitation of his older brother, my first instinct was to go and grab him and take him back to wherever he had come from. Why were they all here? Were they planning some atrocity tonight? I tried to ask Steffen, but he shushed me and got a few of the old nuns to turn and do the same.

But whatever I felt like doing about Renato didn't matter. The moment didn't belong to me. Steffen held me tightly by the hand, leading me to the front pews, maneuvering our way

past the disapproving looks of all the frocks. We wedged ourselves into the end of a pew a few rows back from Bertila and
Inocente St. Louis, buffered by the ragged boys. At one point,
as the priest made his way down the center aisle swinging
an incense burner, the mountain of Bertila's mantles shifted
and she slowly turned her head to look at us. From behind
the mantilla, I saw a shadow of a smile. I was glad it was her
and not some disguised boy impostor. Renato never turned.
Throughout the entire service he stood and knelt and sat as
the service demanded, as if he had been a lifelong altar boy,
although I would bet that this was the first time that he had
been inside a church.

Qué carajo are we doing? I ventured to ask during one of
the bustling shifts from standing to kneeling. We're going with
them tonight, Steffen informed me. Pick one in the group and
don't lose them.

Where? What about your map?

Wherever. He tapped the folded map in his blazer pocket. If
we get separated, we'll meet there. I looked at the heads of the
young men, trying to pick one who looked as if he couldn't
climb up the sides of buildings.

Steffen took the map out and handed it to me. I've become
an expert at following people in the city. If you get lost, follow
the path.

I continued to follow cues in the endless ceremony,
kneeling, standing, sitting. I wouldn't have been surprised
if at one point, the whole mass of people, including all the
decrepit viejas in the left aisle, lay flat on their backs and
started speaking in tongues and levitating. I expected it at
any time—I imagined Renato would love such a scene, laugh,
revel, and join in—and I would have done it with them. With
him. I kept pace, except when everyone filed to the front,
including Bertila, Inocente St. Louis, and all the boys. Steffen

grabbed my wrist, made me sit at an empty spot in a pew with him. This was only for the pure of heart. He explained about confession, about the eating of Christ's flesh, the drinking of his blood. These people were nuts. Everyone went up to the priests at the front.

They got their flesh. Their blood. On their way back, they chewed hesitantly, discreetly, their expressions pursed. The flesh must have been soft, the blood bitter.

Renato looked up, saw me, saw Steffen. A brief flash in the eyes. Then he looked away. He knelt at his spot, and I kept my eyes fixed on the back of his head, hoping he would turn. But he didn't. When the Mass ended, the priest and his celebrants marched out the center aisle to a song of praise to the Holy Virgin to the tune of Beethoven's Ninth, the "Ode to Joy." The Savior has been born, Steffen whispered to me, alleluia, carajo—don't lose them.

But by the time we had made it out of the entrance, we had already lost most of them. The bevy of old nuns had somehow crossed in front of us, clustered even closer together, moving as one, even the weakest members on the inside contributing whatever miniscule droplet of dispelling power to the force field around them. We dashed to the alleyway once past them, looked around quickly, followed the first few blocks toward el Prado that Bertila and Inocente St. Louis had taken the last time, then doubled back and sprinted to the cathedral square, thinking that perhaps we had missed them, that they too were gathered around the priest with the old nuns, or gawking at the roosters, not out of curiosity as we had, but rodent-eyed, fingers nibbling at the cages. A giant black man; a rotund, almost lame, mantle-clad vieja; and more than thirty boys had vanished into the night air.

We'll wait, Steffen said. Sweat built up in a neat row at his hairline. He passed his hand through it, making his hair stand up in spikes like when Renato and I had first met him. He knew something that he wasn't telling me. That was my life in the capital, on the fringes of revolutionary society; everybody always knew a little more than I did, as if I stammered through the lines of a play a few pages behind everybody, their dialogue at times both baffling and intriguing, though not foreign.

Wait for what?

There, Steffen said. The message.

He gestured toward the opposite corner of the plaza. At first, I saw nothing, just some jineteras loitering at the entry arch of a building. Christmas day was high season for jineteras, gifts that Yuma offered to each other. This was a long tradition, dating back to long before the prospect of the Visit had made the day a national holiday.

There, Steffen said again. And now, I saw a boy that I had not noticed inside the church, darker than all the others, his face and naked torso almost invisible in the shadows of the alleyway where he loitered, leaning against the corner of a building. When he noticed that I had seen him, he shifted his stance, turned, and disappeared into the adumbral light of the narrow passageway.

Off we went, chasing some other vision. But this time our guide looked back every so often, making sure that we did not lose him. Who is he? I think I asked, but, claro, there was no response from Steffen, so intent on both not losing the boy and not getting too far ahead of me that he kept a hand wrapped around my wrist and his eyes peeled directly ahead on the alleys and dark streets that we crossed.

More than once though, we did lose him, and Steffen patiently unfolded his map and kept us on the path delineated by his x's, until we saw the vision of the boy ahead of us again, still moving but as if he had never lost us.

At one point, the city went completely black. We entered

the realm of eternal brownouts, where inhabitants were lucky if they had electricity for an hour or two a day. I had heard about barrios like this from Nicolás, places where he and his friends slept the daylong in windowless makeshift rooms, where the only light that ever graced the walls were from candle flames, where orgies were scheduled by three or four a day. It was where he had gone to die when he abandoned the sidatorio forever, his bloated remains found wrapped under a series of sheets in the shack of a rooftop aerie. Is this what Renato had come looking for, the realm where his brother's ghost would be roaming?

After a meandering journey, the boy stopped in front of what looked like an abandoned tenement building that must have once housed government clerks and bureaucrats. The framework of the missing front doors had been ripped off its bolts, and there was the shadow of a grand staircase beyond the threshold.

We went up the wide staircase, the steps almost nonexistent beneath us, crumbled and narrow. I had to climb it on my tiptoes. We turned down a narrow hallway and when I went to put my hand on the wall for support almost fell over—no walls, just a twisted network of wet, rotted wooden beams. Down a few more hallways and then we were outside, climbing a series of wrought-iron stairs and tapered balconies. Then inside again, and out, up and up as if we were climbing the circles of some inverted hell.

I was drenched in sweat when we came to what must have been the top of the building and a short rope ladder leading to the roof. The boy continued on the way up.

Steffen climbed first, and he hesitated on the top rung so that his ass bumped down against my head and for a second pressed down. What? Nothing, he whispered. You'll see. He reached a hand down once he was securely on top. He pulled me up beside him, and when I looked up, I felt that the ground beneath my feet had shifted, that instead of climbing we had been falling this whole time and had finally landed in a foreign outpost underneath the earth. The city had been razed—all the ancient colonial buildings, the churches, the Soviet cinderblock buildings, the alamedas, the plazas—and another more primitive pueblo, of doll-size houses, with clumsily nailed wooden board walls and tin roofs and sackcloth doors, had risen in its stead. We were in some corner of that crowded pueblo, the hovels sharing walls and leaning on each other, and toward each other across the narrow streets, where a few inhabitants mingled.

We walked, guided by the light of oil lamps that hung precariously off the eaves of the tin roofs. All one had to do, I imagined, was tip one over and the whole makeshift town would burn to the ground in a matter of minutes. Later, we would find out that there were spots in the city where exactly such a thing had accidentally happened before, but this city we saw extended far beyond the top of one building, and chasms with crossways over the neighborhood streets below prevented such fires from spreading.

It was not long before we came to one and began to make out the entire layout of the commune. First, the crossways between the tops of the varying crumbling buildings themselves were the flimsiest things imaginable, long wooden planks, paired or tripled, extending from each side of the rooftops of adjoining buildings, buttressed by canvas bags full of rotted bricks or sometimes extending from the windows of an upper floor, nailed to the very framework. The makeshift bridges lacked handrails, and they undulated in the air with the slightest breeze. It seemed impossible that they could sustain any human creature that weighed more than a six-year-old.

We didn't dare attempt crossing, though it was not long

before we saw how others did it. The crosser crouched, leaning forward like a racer and embraced the sides of the planks, his legs bent behind him like a grasshopper's, his bare feet on tiptoes for better propulsion. Then it became a matter of scurrying across faster than the time that it took the bridge to recognize the burden upon it.

Steffen would have none of it. We wandered around the perimeter of the one roof where we were stuck for a while, and he decided that we should split up if we were to find Renato. He was going to check the streets below, although they had looked wholly deserted when we arrived. Make a friend, he said. Have someone show you how to cross. Heights get you all excited from what I remember. He winked. Meet back here in a few hours.

There were plenty of people out and about in the pueblo in the air. I saw the first crossers traipse from one section of the city to the other, even a line forming at one particularly busy corner that led to a more raucous and peopled open space of the camp. I approached someone in the line, a ragged-looking teenage boy, wearing a vest and what looked like cloth diapers, though it might have been a towel. I had only seen males so far, not just the darker-skinned folk that I imagined lived in the poverty-stricken neighborhood below, but lighter-skinned kids and even some that looked Cuban only by the attitude they seemed to have taken on from the others, a sort of laissez-faire pessimism that was the only thing the State seemed unable to control. Renato Zúñiga, I asked, Bertila Paredes, Inocente St. Louis. I tried to pronounce the last name with a Creole accent, like he had taught me. I tried with others, describing physical features instead of using the names, the agglomeration of tattoos on Renato, Bertila's Siberian layering of scarves, Inocente the fire eater's height and his operatic voice.

Soon enough I grew tired of asking and walked closer to

SACRIFICIO | 271 |

the plank to see if I could divine the physical orchestration necessary for the crossing. A constant file of crossers skittered to the open area in the adjacent building, but some returned to ours. It seemed odd that they were all muchachitos, boys all about my age or a few years younger, but then I realized that I would not have been able to distinguish one gender from the other anyway, because they all wore the same outfit, baggy threadbare shorts, camisetas, and chancletas (which they held in their mouths when they crossed), some were shirtless, bone thin.

Finally, a taller potbellied man approached carrying a young child; both were semi-naked. He wore an incongruous pair of gold-rimmed spectacles that gave him the startled air of a weary magistrate in some fantastical court. But he was the first one to acknowledge my clear interest in the acrobatics needed to cross from one roof to the other. I expressed surprise that the plank would hold up someone of his own stature.

Me and the kid, he bragged, throwing the boy on his back and dashing across. Before I knew it, he was back, standing in front of me. I mentioned Renato's full name and he whistled and looked up at the stars. The Cricket has visitors, he said. Cubano, even. From the East. He tapped his shoulder, and I jumped up on him, wrapping my arms around his neck, my legs around his waist. The feeling of crossing on the precarious plank, the inside feeling, because I kept my eyes shut tightly, was the sensation that a parachutist must feel before his contraption opens, that Satan's angels must have known as they hurled past the purlieus of paradise, a tickling in the solar plexus that intensifies until the moment that you are tugged up.

We had reached the plaza area. My companion guffawing because I would not let go of my tight grip on him, his child mewling with jealousy at his calf. The man carried me and sat me atop an old rum barrel, among many others, which made a sort of parapet around the perimeter of the otherwise open space, with a pair of claw-footed bathtubs at the center covered by plastic tarps, where often the people went to lift the tarp and fill tin cups to drink. There were plants here too, I noticed, dwarf palms and thin blooming poincianas and bougainvillea potted in old rusty garbage pails, a mini park of sorts. On one of the rum barrels, I thought I noticed one of the boys who had been at the church, because he stood out here, the only one wearing long jeans and a T-shirt. He fiddled with a tres guitar, and when he sang, his voice had a high-pitched melancholy sweetness that immediately had a salutary effect on my mood. He sang three or four songs, before he approached me.

Vamos, he said.

He wasn't asking, I was being told that I needed to move on. And this time, as I found out, I would have to figure out how to cross the plank bridges on my own. I looked around for my friend with the professor's glasses, but he had moved on, passed me off.

It took me about ten crossings before I got the hang of it, the proper feline angle of the crouch, the grip of the splintery sides of the plank with the fingers loose enough to glide, but soon I darted from one roof to the other as if I had lived there since before the Revolution. I thought that the troubadour was taking me around in circles just so that I could practice, but with each go-around, the revolutions around some inner sanctum became tighter and tighter, the spread of the city around us more magnificent, until we arrived at the center of the town, where no unguided outsider could dream of penetrating, the building on which it sat, a mere series of naked rust-infested iron skeletons, the ghosts of the outer walls with pockmarked cannon ball–size holes. Another nameless guide disappeared, leaving me alone. This part of the city had been designed differently than the others, the wooden hovels arranged in a circle, a large metal cistern, split in half and turned over, the home to a robust fire that lit up the faces surrounding it and distorted them with its vapors.

Leaning against the wall of one of the hovels, his arms around Steffen and passing a bottle back and forth sat Renato Zúñiga, shirtless, the winged tattoo on his belly now a host to other grotesque shapes that encircled his torso, a mad tea party. He glanced once my way. Steffen, not at all flustered about having been found in such a compromising position again, stood up and waved me over, gleeful that I had found them.

I was just about to send a search party for you, you must know, he laughed.

He made a spot between them, and I sat down, waiting for Renato to say something. But he didn't. He passed the bottle to me, and I took a long gulp of something foul and familiar, the purging tranquility of Bertila's famous concoction.

We've been waiting for you, Rafa la Jirafa, Renato said, his hand clasping mine as I handed him back the bottle.

How's the putamamá? he added. Does she ask about me?

ASCENSION

Comandante Juan had found him.

Nicolás's body had been rotting in one of these very hovels for over ten days, his disciples wrapping him in rags and keeping vigil. Although it might not actually have been here, Renato said to me passing the bottle again, it might have been in a nearby pueblaire, which is what they called these lofty encampments—towns in the air.

Renato said that he had heard about the discovery of his brother's body from some of the santeros at the sidatorio who saw it in their trances—one day a giant bird appeared in the air and hovered over the pueblaire and down dropped the military man from its gut, in full fatigues, wearing a gas mask, a pistol strapped to his holster. He took the bloated corpse up with him, carrying it in his arms like the Magdalene holding the Christ, or was it Mary the Mother, he forgot how the santeros put it, except that Nicolás's body was so bloated that it looked more like the size of half a pregnant cow. After that, there began the deification of his brother, the idea being that he had, of course, ascended to the heavens and was still keeping watch over them.

By the time Renato had arrived at this nearby pueblaire,

his own group from the sidatorio following him (along with others, including lovers, and some mothers, grandmothers, wives, and children of the condemned), the myths of his brother's life and death had grown enough that he did not recognize the Nicolás in their stories.

Renato said that he himself had never heard his brother talk about any of these things (although I had), that when he arrived, the people presumed that he had come armed with a mandate. But he and his group were merely fleeing, seeking a little more freedom.

I reminded him that his brother had injected him with infected blood right before my eyes.

Sí, true, but I wasn't a saint before that, asere. Who knows if I had already been infected? Probably. Somehow, nobody ever bothered to check me. I remember you said that the day they brought his body home from the morgue la putamamá wouldn't even let it in the house. Didn't they bury him that very day, without a funeral or any other ceremony? Or did Juan have the body burned? I forget.

I don't remember telling Renato either way what Cecilia had done with his brother's body. I remembered that conversation as one of the most straightforward that we had during those stolen first Fridays of the month when Renato was first at the sidatorio. Yes, the body had been brought back. Yes, Cecilia had taken care of it, I had told Renato then, although he had not inquired, not about his mother's reaction, not about the fact that he had not been summoned from the sidatorio for the burial. But in fact, it had been from him that I had first learned the rumors of Nicolás's death during one of our visits to Bertila. He was sitting under the hot lamp in Bertila's living room, strands of his hair wrapped in aluminum foil, swirling different colored polishes on his toenails as if they were a series of canvases. I was in the chair, Bertila doing her thing to my hair.

They say Nicolás is dead, Renato muttered as if he meant
for us to dismiss his statement as the hissing of the heat lamp.
Bertila and I both stopped. I craned my neck back to get
a look at his face, to read any malice or revanchism in his
announcement.

Who says?

People, he responded.

You don't know, I said. You can't.

Not me. People.

It would be another two weeks before the news reached
comandante Juan, informing me but keeping it from Cecilia
until he was sure. One night, in the middle of our rush hour
at the paladar, he appeared, putting on such a false cheer and
narrating such an outlandish story to cover for his absence as
maître d'—important mission for the Ministry of the Interior,
rooting out a ring of pigeon thieves who later sold their produce to paladars and tourist restaurants as quail, that I knew
that he had found Nicolás's body.

How do you think, Renato asked me on that early Christmas
morning, that comandante Juan knew exactly where to look
for my brother's body?

He has his connections, you know. ¿Qué se yo?

Renato nodded. Sí, verdad, he has his connections. But
who would have cared to keep track about some desgraciado
in the last throes of the illness, hiding in one of the most ramshackle sectors of the city?

Was he saying Juan was responsible for Nicolás's death?

I'm saying someone was.

You didn't see him. You didn't know him during those last
days. He was doing a pretty good job of killing himself.

Mira, Renato said, now huddling closer to me, almost
nudging his head up under my armpit. It was like one of our
lost Fridays. Mira, huevón, I'm the one who told you he was

dead. Remember? He let out a yawn of one just about to nod
off. But why are we dredging up these old memories anyway?
You finally found me. It's Christmas morning. He didn't want
to talk about it or plant any other suspicions in my mind
about his brother's death, he said.

He closed his eyes and pretended to fall asleep with his
head on my chest. I'm glad you came, he sighed. That's the
way the conversation always ended. In the brief months after
he had first predicted Nicolás's death, he never questioned
much about the nature of his brother's death, or about our
crazed meeting at the bar, or about comandante Juan's version of how he was led to the decomposing corpse. I talked
about it incessantly, to him, to Bertila, even at times when
Cecilia wasn't around to Inocente St. Louis—who seemed
to mourn Nicolás's death the longest with the willingness to
listen without cutting the conversation off.

And where was the truth?

What did it matter in the end?

Whether Nicolás had died as a crazed loner, which was
comandante Juan's version, what he himself surmised after he
had found the body, because after I had told him about Renato's offhanded comment that he had heard others say Nicolás
was dead it became a single-minded obsession for him, to find
this boy, or the body, the corpse, to bring back to the mother,
not because he cared for the boy—though he did, claro—but
because it would finally, sin duda ninguna, offer proof of his
uncompromising devotion to her, to the mother, proof to trump
all other things he had done for her—his condoling presence
after Pascual had disappeared to Barcelona, his stewardship of
the boys when they began to stray from the fold of la Revolución, his financial backing for the paladar, all these beneficent
gestures powerless to accomplish anything more than a fleeting
sexual flurry—certainly nothing on the scale of this final act, to

carry the son so that the mother could grieve with him in her arms, to give her, finally, an opportunity for sorrow.

Only it didn't quite happen like that.

Comandante Juan did not descend from the flying helicopter as some of the stories that he repeated had it, but a young soldier with the strength to hold onto the bloated shrouded body. Comandante Juan was above in the helicopter. In the middle of the previous night, another one of his soldiers had climbed up to the top of the pueblaire and reported on the condition of the body. He carried with him a small photograph of Nicolás, but when he found the body, lit a silver cigar lighter, and peeled some of the strips of shroud, the face that emerged was so bloated that it no more resembled the handsome face in the picture than a goat does a prince. Then how could comandante Juan have known it was him? Renato asked at first when I told him the story that Christmas morning. How unless his brother had been followed or taken there weeks before, sent to his death?

More likely, Renato surmised, he had been hunted down as a counterrevolutionary and summarily executed, clearly the only way comandante Juan could have known about his whereabouts, trapped him in his airy cage and there either forced him to swallow poison or had their infiltrators commit the act. Or perhaps right in the middle of another of his grand orgies, where some bodiless limb reached tenderly for him and administered a choke hold that was not released until the body went limp. The morning after, his very disciples, perhaps even the one who committed the act, must have wrapped the body in the funerary strips, and left it there hoping for a resurrection, quien sabe, but Renato thought it possible that he might have heard about Nicolás's death even before it happened, that someone had planted the information that he received from the santero in Plaza de Armas.

I have the body, comandante Juan said to me a few weeks after he had first set out on his mission, and waited. It has always befuddled me why he needed my approval before he took the next step. He had taken it to the morgue, where it had been cleansed and prepared for burial, though there was nothing they could do about the skin distended by the bloating, it gathered in the pockets of his body like loose pig hide.

Did I want to see it? he asked. Shouldn't that be Cecilia's role? I answered. The truth is, comandante Juan said, that Cecilia will have no interest in this.

He was like a suitor showing up at his beloved's door with a bouquet of dead fetid flowers. I don't know why I even put myself through this, he said. You did it for Nicolás, I said, as much as for Cecilia. Coño, I wish I could believe that, he said. You have to tell her, I said, you have to give her a choice. I paused. To mourn for her own son, if that's what she wants. It's not, he responded. What she will want is for him to be alive and healthy and serving arroz con pollo and boliche at the paladar like you.

I'll have to tell her, he said.

He took off his military cap, held it with both hands in front of him.

Or not.

Ostensibly, we could just let her go on thinking that her son was another of the disappeared, out of sight, unavailable, the onslaught of his illness slowing, as if he were traveling to some distant galaxy and no longer had to submit to the laws of this maldita city.

That night, Cecilia took it upon herself to set up the whole paladar. When Juan and I walked back in after our long cigarette break, the first customers were already seated at my station. She handed me the orders she had taken, and refused

to look me in the eye the rest of the night, barking out instructions and reprimands. I took too long to first greet the guests.
I wasn't reciting the menu right, leaving out ingredients. I was
letting food get cold on the hot line.

By the time of her last harangue, I wanted to grab her by
the shoulders and make her look me in the eyes and scream,
Your son is dead, muchacha! But I left it to comandante Juan,
who before our meal after the dinner service grabbed me by
the collar and pressed me to my seat, helping Cecilia serve the
food like he had never done before. Inocente St. Louis ate as
usual behind the hot line, but he must have already known
because he never took his eyes off Cecilia.

We went through most of the dishes and half of the dessert,
a rich coconut pie that Inocente St. Louis often made when
Cecilia could procure enough eggs and cream. Comandante
Juan barely touched his food. Maybe he was waiting for me
to say something, or maybe he just wanted me there because
he was afraid that there would be no grief at all.

At about midnight, the usual apagón made the house go
dark and the ceiling fans stopped whirring, but Cecilia had
already lit the oil lamps. Finally, after she had served us our
coffees and kissed Inocente St. Louis goodbye on the cheek,
assuring him that she would finish up with the cleaning, she
motioned for both of us to follow her into the house. We
passed through the darkened parlor, Cecilia leading the way
with the lamp to the writer's study, a room that I had only
gone into before to help Renato carry out books. Cecilia
moved toward the center of the room, and it was only then
that I noticed that a pair of the bare bookcases was missing
from the far end of the room, the moldy wall and termite-
eaten posts visible. Cecilia signaled with the lamp and pulled
away a bedsheet from something in the middle of the room.
Comandante Juan and I took a step back. Don't be frightened,

she said. It's empty. She knocked on the lid to prove it—a hollow double beat that sounded like the first notes of a *bomba*. She brought the lamp closer so we could admire the simple craft quality of the piece. The artisanship top-class. A mahogany coffin fit for the cadaver of a prince. Will he fit into it? Cecilia asked. Because of the length of the bookcase pieces, the inner compartment was perhaps more than a few centimeters shy of Nicolás's height. A lo mejor you can place him sideways, curled up as if he were sleeping, she said. She passed the lamp around the perimeter of the box. I don't want anyone to see his body, except for the person that places him in here. Comandante Juan had taken another step back, his body pressed to the far wall, listening to the instructions he had thought would have been impossible to get from the mother. I don't want to see it, either.

How did you know? I asked.

The ladies of the Comité knew where comandante Juan was going before he even knew the night of the helicopter. Nothing gets by them.

So you don't want to see the boy? comandante Juan asked, the disappointment evident in the bruised gentleness of his voice. The body? The body I sought out for you, I thought he was going to add, but he didn't. It's better if I don't, Cecilia said. There is a spot in Colón, she said. A spot beside Pascual's parents. A very pretty spot under a stone statue of the archangel Gabriel. That's where I want you to put him. Us. We'll all do it. We don't have to tell Renato. It's not good for him to see such things. Not now. Cecilia looked around the room at the other empty bookcases, perhaps making calculations for a second coffin when the time came. She straightened, handed me the lamp, spread the sheet again over the coffin and left us in the room, on the way out pausing by comandante Juan, still pressed against the wall, and passed a hand over his grizzled cheek. Comandante Juan wept, for Cecilia I thought, for the lukewarm quality of their love, for the son.

Later, I sat on the bottom step of the stone stairway and watched her finish cleaning up that night, huddled over the sink, scrubbing pots and pans that Inocente St. Louis had left for her, waiting for the burden of everything to force her to drop the heavy pans and lay her prostate by the running faucet until the sink overflowed. It would then be easier to go to her, to hold her. But Cecilia finished her task, and on the way past me on the stairs offered a similar gesture to the one that had broken comandante Juan's stoic façade.

That's why I never told you the exact date, I said to Renato on the roof of the pueblaire, knowing he was awake by how he shifted his head on my shoulder. Because I would never have stood for you hating your mother on the day we buried him. For every exertion of will that Renato spent forgiving his brother, for every indulgence granted for the transgressions committed against him, there was a diametrical buildup of venom collected for his mother. So the hatred of the mother was something that I sensed every first Friday of the month, from his obscene nickname for her, to his refusal to allow her to visit him or to go see her on Calle Obispo during his furloughs. But had he seen her lay her oldest son to rest, had he watched the calculated manner that she accomplished the task, setting aside no more than an hour in the middle of the morning, in between her produce shopping and the almuerzo hour at the paladar, drawing a map with a black *x* for comandante Juan and me to meet her at the exact spot in Cemeterio Colón, arranging for the sealed coffin to arrive at exactly the moment she did, bending down to kiss it on a corner before the undertakers slid it into the pulleys, murmuring that both Nicolás and Pascual would have laughed at the irony of it all, that the son had taken the spot of the father, had Renato watched his mother as the coffin descended into the tomb, so erect and tearless that she may as well have been one of the hundreds of stone statues in the camposanto, except for her posture, which was not one of adoration, or contemplation, or lamentation, but a rigid sufferance that was betrayed only by the fidgety tapping of her right sandal heel and by the putting on and taking off of her sunglasses, not because it was clear she was about to tear up, but because she could not decide what to do with her hands, clearly not willing to reach them out to comandante Juan or me by her side. Had her younger son been there, he would not have stood for it like we did, for her mulish lack of mourning.

I was angry at her. But she didn't seem to notice. Once the grave was sealed, she finally reached out and took me by the arm.

I don't want him finding out. It's not your place to meddle in this. ¿Entiendes? Not that I don't think of you as family, but that you don't know, you don't know enough to get involved in this. If that poor soul behind us, if Juan wants to go the sidatorio and tell him, then that's his business. But I don't want any of this to come from your lips. ¿Entiendes? If you do it, I'll consider it a betrayal. She kissed me on the shoulder.

I could have diffused her threat at that very moment, could have made clear to her that the only reason we were putting Nicolás to rest was because it was Renato who had alerted me to his death, that keeping him from this burial was tantamount to disowning him, to opening up a chasm between mother and son that would never again be bridged, that, mira, if there is any betrayal here, it was her betrayal of him. But when she reached for me and kissed me again, this time on the cheek, I realized that anything I told her were things I had already told myself on countless occasions, that we were bonded by our delusions—hers that somehow her youngest son would escape the fate of her elder one, even if it meant severing all ties from him, a sacrifice that she was almost too willing to make, and mine that I could at some point be forgiven for my sins of omission, or at least that Renato would one day recognize how I had failed him, thus acknowledging our intimacy.

It would not be long before both of these illusions shattered, though on that early Christmas morning when Renato snuggled beside me, I thought for a moment back to those two kisses on the cemetery path, and that perhaps there was time yet, that I was leaving one to save the other, even if it meant risking that conformity that had been ingrained in me through long years of revolutionary schooling. I had thought, pues in hindsight, to find some semblance of a family in that house, something more substantial than bedridden Abuela Puebla and her officious brood, and in some ways I did, all of them taking me on in their own way, Nicolás as a lover; Renato as a friend, as an acolyte, and maybe a fellow rebel; comandante Juan as a mock acolyte; Cecilia, Cecilia . . . I don't know, as a surrogate son, an employee, a shadow that could have in some other life been a lover, or maybe more importantly as someone whom she had the power to save, if only I would have let her. I became most a son in that I didn't let her. In the end, we would both betray one another, me by fleeing, her by imagining she could begin her life again, without me, without her sons. I would see her twice more after that Christmas morning, but the formality with which she handled both meetings, the brusqueness with which they were cut off, the first time by comandante Juan chasing me out, the second by Cecilia disappearing almost as soon as she saw me, stamped the kisses on the cemetery path on the morning of Nicolás's burial with a severe finality.

FESTIVAL OF WATER

They seemed less like rebels about to unleash their bloody violence on the dictator and more a troupe of harmless and nomadic vagabonds—houseless, aimless—an army of the unarmed.

Renato had fallen asleep on top of me. At the time, I thought we had been left to our privacy, ignored by the others milling about us. But after having spent a few days in the pueblaire, I realized that the same four or five young men always surrounding Renato had been there that night, in their customary outfit, the camiseta and torn jeans, the gaunt look that could either be the consequence of a prolonged illness or an itinerant jejune youth. They hovered around Renato like satellites, sometimes drifting too far away to be able to prevent any sudden assault, other times huddling so close to him you'd think he was a marked político. When Steffen returned to sit beside me, putting his fingers under Renato's chin and tilting his head up to confirm he had truly dozed off, exposing his neck for a mere moment, the five muchachos suddenly found reason to circle in, pretending drunkenness, grabbing Steffen under the armpits, coiling themselves to him and pulling him away in a festive mêlée, allowing him to approach us again only when it was clear that he, too, had been deemed welcome and harmless.

Renato slept through it all.

As Christmas morning rose over the city, a covering of twisted tangerine rind clouds, folks began to disappear into their shacks and down into buildings where they squatted in rooms that had at least two or three walls left. Someone, one of the bodyguard muchachos, pointed to Renato's shack and Steffen and I shuffled him into his windowless hovel. I couldn't help thinking about the room where Nicolás had died, the light seeping in through the cracks in the wooden slats giving the room the air of an ill-constructed poor-man's mausoleum. Renato plopped on the bare sackcloth mattress and Steffen and I pushed aside some of the stacks and lay on the tar floor, our heads on either edge of the mattress. The sun must have risen above the roofs of the city and pierced the tangerine clouds, for the room suddenly felt lit from within, and Renato's soft snores lulled me to sleep.

When I awoke, the door of Renato's shack was thrown open, and he sat on his bed cross-legged, receiving visitors. He noted I was awake but otherwise ignored me, focused on each guest that came and kneeled by the mattress and asked how he felt, sometimes offering a gift, a book, sacks of nonperishable foods or small coins, which went into an earthen jar. Two of the muchachos had made their way into the tiny space and leaned against opposite corners of the shack, their eyes downcast but vigilant. I imagined that my presence was not required and I made to get up, but Renato stopped me with a hand on my shoulder. After every visitor, Renato would go through whatever they had brought and pass it over to the muchachos.

All those that came to visit were permanent dwellers of the pueblaire, Renato explained, all dark-skinned like me, women with children or older men, in stark contrast to Renato's banda, who but for a few exceptions were white and young men. At the end of the reception line came my helpful friend from the night before, this time attired for the occasion in a guayabera, linen trousers, and leather sandals. He did not crouch down by Renato like the others, but offered Renato as much adulation and cheer. It was clear the men talked often by the way they grabbed each other by the shoulder, leaned in, and spoke into each other's ears. When he left, Renato stood up and walked out into the light, trailed by his muchachos.

Why all the gifts, the money? I asked.

So we have something when we go. So we're not starving and left without nothing, he responded offhandedly. There is much already in storage in one of these buildings.

The muchachos nodded.

But that's not what I really need, Renato added, turning back to me and letting the muchachos pass by him. What I really need is you. He paused, put his face as close to mine as he could without grazing me. You, and maybe your German friend, and many others to come with us, mejor dicho, to not just come, to join with us. It's nothing without you, without everyone, vaya.

To do what? Why did you come here?

He took in a gulp of air as if thickening his blood to make some confession, but then signaled for me to come out with him. They all come in the morning before their community hours, he said. I can't leave them waiting. You have to ask that question of yourself.

Another group of people waited for Renato outside, Steffen among them, who either had been thrown out of the hovel by the muchachos or had awoken early and gone out exploring on his own. I hesitated before going out, not sure what role I had been meant to play in this new day, not sure which one

I wanted. For the rest of that morning, I decided to do two things, one, to listen, to let me decide why I needed to stay here, and the other, if I did stay, as I imagined Steffen would— simply because this had become the ultimate adventure experience, a real tropical insurrection, either that or because he was still under Arcadio's directive—to get a message out to Cecilia somehow, who might be expecting me back in the paladar that night for Christmas dinner, even if I had missed all my other shifts of the month. I don't know why I thought about her then.

Were these shacks atop the rotted abandoned buildings the new Sierra Maestra?

Who else belonged to the group?

What factions?

How much did the State know?

Was there to be an aggressive offensive, or would they, like Fidel in the mountains, wait to tire the patience of the dictator?

Steffen asked Renato one question after another that first morning after the visitors had departed, nothing that Renato denied or confirmed, but simply answered with vague utterances and evasions.

At one point, something did seem to break in his inscrutable demeanor—when Steffen began to praise la Revolución, in the terms of any overinformed but naive European, its gains in education and health care, literacy rate, and life expectancy, and just in case Renato wasn't tempted by such fat baits, la Revolución's noble stand against the rapacious nature at its essence of northern yanqui late capitalism. As Steffen continued with his litany of statistics, a favorite revolutionary tactic for almost half a century, he finally got the response that he had been aiming for. He knew how to play the ignorant idealist European to a T, the kind of *Salonkommunist* that probably comprised half if not more of his extended family in Bonn or Hamburg, or wherever he was really from.

Renato jumped up close enough to him that the German was forced to take two long strides backward, and his butt grazed the waist-high parapet of stacked cinderblocks, the space directly beyond it opening up to the chasm below, Renato suddenly so close that he was either going to send him over the parapet or kiss him. Steffen's hands gripped one of the wobbly cinderblocks on top, and after a few moments where they now both seemed in peril—for surely if Steffen tipped backward, he would clutch Renato by the waist and they would both go—Renato took Steffen's right wrist, leaned toward me with his hand outstretched, and let me pull them both back.

Renato seemed pleased with the success of his stand, although he must have known that he was being baited. The incident made Steffen go quiet, but not so much from fear, but because, he told me, he had been convinced enough to stay, that Renato's mock threat not only implied that he was at least somewhat as ideological as his brother, as fervently counterrevolutionary, but more importantly, that it was clear that he had use for us.

We must be staying, he said.

I'm not going anywhere, I assured him, surprised at how brusque and definitive I sounded.

I wasn't sure why I needed to rely on Steffen, except that I knew that as a professional tourist, a peripatetic thrill-seeker, he had traveled much of the world perfecting the art and practices of guesthood, skills that would be in demand during our early days in the pueblo in the air. I, on the other hand, on my first journey ever from home had arrived in the capital hoping to become one of the citizens of its vibrant nucleic life. No such thing existed. There was a destabilizing centrifugal force that pushed life (any life except for those that belonged to the Party or foreigners) to the perimeters. Now, in the pueblaire, we had reached its outermost ring, and were perhaps on the verge of disengaging, deorbiting.

That made it feel more real than maybe even Steffen had use for. This place, these people, was why I had left home, to become what Abuela Puebla had once been and long since abandoned, a true revolutionary, not the paper version we had been taught to become in school, with our neatly ironed pionero hankies tied around our necks.

Bertila had first posited this vision of the disintegrating capital for me, so when I saw her that Christmas morning, it felt like a confirmation of my newly adopted mindset. I did not expect her hurtful snub. I had expected her to be more heartily welcoming after the incitement she had proffered during our meeting outside the cathedral. She lumbered past the German and me, glancing once at us, her vibrant yellow eyes sunken now. They rested on my face for a moment and then on Steffen and passed over us, devoid of any sign of surprise or bonhomie. As usual of late, she was wrapped in her countless dark mantles—even though the hot breezes bouncing off the zinc and tin used for the shacks had become insufferable by early morning—and accompanied by the tall gaunt Inocente St. Louis, who did not so much as look at us. They bore gifts more extravagant than all the others who had come to visit Renato: headgear woven from pigeon feathers, colorful crystal bottles, and a silver-lined wooden chest—a pair of ragged magi.

I went to the parapet where Renato and Steffen had had their confrontation, looked down the circuitous iron whirl-pool skeletons of exposed balconies and structural beams, went to the opposite side of the roof, looked down again, the children playing ball in the treeless, sun-punished streets small as flies flitting over a bone. Steffen surmised that Bertila and the chef must have thought it prudent to ignore us at first, at least until they were sure that we had won the good graces of Renato's group.

He came up with a set of strategies of how to do just that, to win them over, rehearsing them on me tirelessly as he had played out his doubting questions on Renato. Foremost, we would prove our commitment to the cause by simply staying, being present for when we were summoned, never wandering too far away from Renato. Presence was always they key in these things. We needed to make it seem as if we were every-where that anything important occurred.

The cause? What cause? How do you know there is a cause? I interrupted him. You still think this is a game. That we're some allegory to use in stories you make up in your journals for the Directorate.

Look, you must, he stammered, yes, it took me a while to truly understand the nature of things, and I am not from here, but neither was Che. You must know I can become com-mitted.

Not if you can hitch to the airport and get on a plane any-time you want.

He walked away and stood precariously, looking at the edge of the rooftop where a piece of the wrought-iron parapet had been ripped off, twisted and bent outward like a design on the bow of a ship.

These moments, he said calmly, belong to the commu-nity of the world and not just to those in the nation. This is important to know. These things don't just stay on their own. They're bigger than that.

Is that what your textbooks say about the revolutions across the ocean, the ones that have always gone so wrong in your continent?

All revolutions go wrong, you must know. Maybe we need to prove ourselves to each other and not just to them.

I approached him, put a hand on his shoulder. I wanted to stop the pissing contest about who could be more committed.

Como carajo does she get up here? I mused, my eyes still on Renato's locked door, Bertila and the fire-eating chef still conferring with Renato within.

Steffen looked at me, inquisitive at first—and then, finally comprehending the gist of the question, a look of consternation came over him, as if the mystery of Bertila's climb and descent needed to be solved before anything else, lest it prove the entire enterprise a sham, this war camp hundreds of feet in the air no more than a mass hallucination.

The chef must carry her.

Carry her? Pick her up and throw her over his shoulder and bear her entire mass up those flimsy rotted stairs?

Maybe he must not, Steffen said. He sat down, lowered his head, and wrapped his arms around them. He proffered other theories: Bertila helicoptered into the pueblaire, borne on a bier, laid out like a corpse, by dozens of boys, or rising on her own powers like the Virgen María, or that maldita Mary Poppins. Or, as he had explained to me before, Bertila was not really Bertila, not all the time, but only meant to resemble her as played by a boy in makeup and drag, or there were two of her, one for below and one for above, or maybe more, one for the cathedral, one for each of the banda's hideouts, all in constant communication, wired under all those mantles, so that as one disappeared another one could take her place.

Could that have been true of Renato and his brother, I thought more seriously as Steffen went on. Was there more than one of them, several versions that they had devised to confront the funhouse-mirror tartuffery of their childhoods as heirs apparent of Pascual's revolutionary convictions and the counterrevolutionary derelicts they could not help becoming.

While we were in the middle of this—I don't know how much time had passed—the door to Renato's shack opened and Bertila and Inocente St. Louis shuffled out. This time, they stood watching us before they moved on. I nodded and smiled at Inocente St. Louis. Now, he had turned into someone else, he approached us warmly, said he was glad to see we had finally made it, carajo. He even embraced me briefly and the fever of his body lingered on me long after he had let go. I was afraid to look into Bertila's face, either because it might confirm Steffen's chiflado notion that she was too often nothing more than a made-up boy or because I could not bear to see myself in the stained-glass saffron of her eyes.

Moments later, the entire pueblaire underwent a full mobilization, as if preparing for an invasion. Renato came out of his shack and told us to follow him. He had somehow overheard our conversation—which meant that Bertila herself must have heard—and he told Steffen that he had a great imagination and perhaps would have been of much use to the Directorate after all. It needed visionaries like him to replace all of the ones Fidel had murdered. We followed. After every crossing outward from the center, Renato patiently waited for us, bemused, his hands on his hips, as we doddered through the crossing planks.

Eventually, we made it to the open roof near the spot where we had ascended the night before, a plaza area full of barrels and tubs. Renato seemed at home with the crowd of people there, mingling among them, leaping on barrels from which I suspected he might start to proselytize, but instead leaned down and helped me onto the stack. He whistled for us to follow him up, then vaulted from barrel to barrel to a far edge of the roof. We rolled the empty barrels to the precipice as if they were full of boiling oil to throw on invading armies at the castle walls.

Soon, the three of us hung suspended atop an iron cage that began to descend to the street below. The people on the rooftop cheered. Renato warned that the lower the cage went the more it swung from side to side, sometimes knocking against the façade of the building. A shaky contraption but one that could hold twenty Bertilas, I figured, glancing at Steffen. The cage didn't just swing, it rocked back and forth like a ship tossed in a tempest, Renato whooping as the helm master.

It's easier on the way up, Renato shouted after we had crash-landed. Only the stacked empty barrels all around us prevented us from being thrown off or smashed into each other. The added weight helps, Renato added.

We spent the rest of the afternoon that Christmas going up and down with Renato, filling the wooden casks with water from the State trucks that Renato said arrived at noon every Friday. Most residents in the outskirts of the capital had no running water. Water remained the only thing cubanos could not do without for long (and perhaps sex). The pueblaire had a fund with which to bribe the officials from the Ministry of Public Utilities every Friday. But others in and around Cerro had to make do with the five-gallon ration per person, to drink, bathe, and cook, imagínate. If this is happening in the capital, Renato said pointedly to Steffen, think about the rest of the Island. There is your glory.

I wanted to add something to prove to Renato that I agreed, that he could win my political heart, but nothing came to me. Or maybe he already knew that he had it, that I agreed with him intellectually and psychologically but may have lacked the cojones to put such disaffection into action.

Both he and Nicolás often told me that I lacked the heroic

gene. Not my fault, a twist of fate, and not that such a lineage is holy, plenty of those with the gene end up as megalomaniacal tyrants or as absent fathers. Maybe I was lucky, even if determined to prove them wrong.

That night, Renato announced, as every Friday night, there would be the festival of water, the bathtubs filled, a ritual bathing.

We must bathe too, the German said, embracing me awkwardly from behind and sniffing at the back of my ear. You stink. I nodded, thinking about the way that Renato had helped me wash on my first day at Calle Obispo.

As the entire community drank the fresh water, some lacking containers, by the handfuls, Renato led us away again, this time to a spot not far from the cage elevator, where one of the largest and most ornate shacks that we had seen sat. It was sturdier than the rest, the walls made of solid boards and painted in such a way, with such a variety of tiny colors that it appeared luminous in the harsh light, floating in place. As Renato walked us to it, the colors seemed to break up and from very close something recognizable emerged. The signs we had been seeing in the streets of Havana, the tiny painted *sacrificios* in all their variant colors covered the shack.

Bertila's shack, he said. Go ahead, knock. She wants to see you. The fire-eater chef stepped out, squeezing past the half-closed door and embraced me, again welcoming us in an effusive manner as if to make up for the initial snub that morning. Has your . . . compadre . . . found you a place to sleep yet? he asked Renato. Not waiting for a response, he took me by the hand and led me to a smaller shack a few paces away, the door opened, the bed neatly made. We would be neighbors. I gave him one of the canteens and he thanked me, drinking in gulps, letting the fresh water splash over his newly grayish beard, which made him look older, less a danger. Did he still perform in the streets? I asked, curious if his life had been wholly subsumed into this new world and concerned about the dangers his new beard may present with his art. He grabbed another canteen and walked back to the front of the prismatic shack.

Always, always performing, he muttered, and I thought I saw a thread of black smoke emit from one of his nostrils.

Bertila came out—free of her mantles, in a flowing white dress, her wiry hair loose, barefoot, a glazed expression, all which made her seem like a santera mounted by her orisha. Niño, she said to me, when did you arrive?—as if she hadn't even seen us before. Her demeanor had changed. She fingered my tight curls and gave out a disappointing grunt. This was the real one if there were more than one of her. I could tell by her sacramental smell. She grabbed my head, leaned me over, and kissed the top. Her hands splattered with paint, as kaleidoscopic a replica as the colorful coat of paint on her shack. She watched Steffen examining the tiny graffiti on the walls like an archeologist, an artist at an opening watching a befuddled critic.

Who else could we have learned it from? Renato explained somewhere in the background of this scene. The first time since we had arrived when he was not center stage.

Without her, we would be without a mark, a formless movement. Because of her, the State is now aware, frightened. Cowering because of a little color! He snorted and then fell into a fit of giggles at the last phrase.

It made me think that he had wanted to sound postapocalyptic, like his brother. For a moment he had, his jade eyes glittering, his words racing to some point just beyond the end of the sentences, as Nicolás's sentences often raced toward some unfinished paragraph and off the tablet of his mind.

But he quickly caught himself, subverted his performance

with the broad comedy of his final sentence. He couldn't help himself. He wasn't Nicolás. Maybe he had found that out soon after he went to the sidatorio. Yet, when he spoke of the inchoate movement he now clearly led, his voice grew more roguish, became sandier, like his brother's also, which claro he knew only I and maybe Inocente St. Louis would have caught. When the fit of giggles passed, he looked at me and sighed deeply.

She will teach you if you want. He looked at Bertila for approval, then gesturing in miniscule as if holding a tiny brush between his pinched fingers. She smiled and nodded. One art, he said in an almost dismissive tone.

But not today, viejo, Inocente St. Louis interrupted. The ceremony of the waters is tonight.

Each second I spent in the pueblaire pulled me a step away from my first life in the capital, every hour I stayed here with Renato became a concrete slab in a gargantuan wall that separated me from those months on Calle Obispo. Did you love her? Renato asked me bluntly as we headed back to the roof with the wide plaza. It's as if he wanted me to not just dissociate from the time in Calle Obispo but from any protracted emotions that were still tugging me from there.

I loved all of you, I think, I said.

Not very convincing, he said. Commit yourself to us, he added. It doesn't have to be love. You have to do it for you. Allow yourself to become something greater than that proper pionerito that your grandmother raised, a devotee of a dead idea. Nothing worse than a dead idea whored out a hundred times by others. Live, hermanito. That's all I want for you. He paused, left space for the spoken words to breathe. It's all Nicolás ever wanted for me, that's when he respected me most, when I fought hardest against my conformist nature.

With Steffen, it was different. He was far more interested

than I was in the larger workings of Renato's gang, in whatever danger it was courting by biting at the heels of the State
like some rabid rodent. If his father had sent him to educate
him about humane socialism, the experience with Arcadio
seemed to have the opposite effect. But whatever he did, he
did it with the immutable knowledge that he could at any
moment renounce his actions and step away from them, that
the State no more wanted to get into the business of unleashing
its revanchist justice on Steffen than it did with any tourist.
That would be political and economic suicide.

Renato let me go and went into one of the shacks, took a
washbasin and put it on his head as a helmet, humor surely
meant to offset the gravity of what he had told me, but it
revealed more than perhaps he meant to, for the thing sat
snug on his head, and with a strap it could have easily been
mistaken for a helmet in the jarring early afternoon light. See
if you can find a lance and shield and you are all set, I said.
Only if you'll be my Sancho, he responded.

When Steffen caught up to me, the nature of the graffiti
symbol still nagged at him. They don't say what it stands for,
Steffen said. They must do it, but they don't say what it rep-
resents.

Like when we fuck, you mean, maybe, I laughed.

He considered this a bit too seriously.

It's a word. It stands for what it means, I said.

But that's so dependent on context, on how the message is
delivered.

I improvised. It's a mark of a tiny victory, a gnawing away
at the framework of the State, a little termite trail bringing the
mansion to its knees.

That's not enough, he responded, not close enough. There
must be something else.

Would that help you commit, whatever else? Steffen, I

suspected, could no more be committed to this cause than he had been committed to his hackneyed sleuthing for Arcadio. He wasn't one of those who lived in the mansion or one who'd been cast out—more like some annoying relative that overstayed his welcome. What did the half-assed socialists of Europe know about the sacrifices and generosities of true socialism, any Fidelista worth his salt would admonish him.

I decided to challenge him. Where did that leave us? How else were we to become legitimate members of Renato's troupe if not by the same ritual that I had witnessed in the henhouse? How else to prove our loyalty? Was Steffen ready for that?

Steffen responded that I was being dramatic, too cubano. Everything is a battle-for-the-soul crisis for you people.

Can you blame us? I said.

We would become part of the troupe, he explained, by simply participating in the more common rituals of the community, the Friday water festivals, the sharing of meals, nightly chats with Renato and any other community leaders. This made sense because Renato began to depend on us for getting a feel for how the group was perceived from the outside, keeping us at a distance so he could make use of our dissociated viewpoint. But Steffen was right. Clearly, there were things we weren't being told yet, things beyond the political éclat of the graffiti. When and if we were deigned worthy of such knowledge, then and only then we would be able to decide if we truly belonged. No doubt Steffen was right, whatever it might be, it had much more to do with other more dangerous tasks than painting with little brushes.

None of this was spoken aloud, claro. Little was spoken of Renato's mission, how much of the mantle he had inherited from his brother and how much he improvised moment to moment. Outwardly, he welcomed us into the innermost recesses of his world as if we were his most trusted conspirators.

When he saw us wade into the water festival early that eve-ning—shuffling, meek, fully clothed—he approached and theatrically began to free us of our garments with the same ease with which he had walked into the bathroom the day I arrived at the house on Calle Obispo. He was wet, gleaming with droplets in the torchlight, his dark tattoos like shadows shifting just beneath the surface of his being. His face did not betray how emaciated he had grown again, not just muscle that had wasted away at the bone, but blood too that had trickled in its coursing, the veins like brittle ribbons of bluish sand, in contrast to his sex, plump and pendent, the only part of him where the blood seemed to be fulfilling its duty.

He guided us into the middle of the exuberant crowd, an area with an impressive network of filled plastic pools and porcelain tubs and makeshift bucket showers. From some-where, Renato procured a rough-hewn bar of soap and washed our backs, our chests, our bellies, our legs, our feet, our faces, our crotches with the precise, disinterested focus of a watchmaker. When he was finished, he poured water from a small cup on each region he had washed, which only did about half the job.

So he took me by the hand and led me to one of the filled porcelain tubs that had been specially reserved for rinsing. Steffen followed close behind. This tub was deeper and wider than all the others—a rich man's tub—and its legs were the iron talons of a falcon. It seemed to grip onto the soft tar of the roof. We waited for others to finish rinsing, but when they saw Renato, they interrupted themselves and quickly stepped out. I climbed into the tub and didn't expect Renato to follow me in.

The other bathers grew interested and scrutinized us. Renato put a hard hand on one of my shoulders and forced me to my knees so the dead cloudy water rose to my belly button. He knelt beside me, and without even glancing at me, put one hand on the back of my head and the other on my chest. He shoved my torso back until my whole body plunged under. I kept my eyes closed and resisted the natural urge to fight what he was doing. I remained submerged until the hand on the back of my head lifted it out of the water.

He smiled. I baptize you in the name of Jesus Christ, he said in a somber tone that almost belied the joke, born today and the greatest revolutionary anti-imperialist that ever lived.

The surrounding bathers, naked and rinsed all, clapped and ballyhooed.

Steffen stood there, expecting somehow that he was next to be baptized, but Renato took another bar of soap, broke it in two, and gave us each a half.

Vayan, now you do it, he said with the tone of an evangelist. Just the soap.

Steffen and I nodded, not quite wanting to understand our mission, and went to the place where many entered the festival, leaving the clothes in bundles at the shore of the makeshift lake of tubs and pools. We saw how easily pairs were formed, a hand reached out, a wave, and after the initial hesitancy, trust. There was no pattern to the couplings. Sometimes old with old or young with young or men with men or men with women or women with each other. I eventually chose some decrepit vieja, only because she stumbled on the edge of the lake and grabbed my forearm for balance. I took care to follow Renato's command, performing the task with as much care and devotion as he had, the woman's osseous flesh soon loosening under the pressure of my soapy hands. It was as if I were cracking thousands of jelly-filled pebbles inside her. I guided her to a rinsing pool.

After we had fulfilled our duty, Steffen caught up with me. He had washed a virile husband who showed up at the shores of the lake with his wife and what seemed like a parade of daughters or mistresses. Steffen took great care in fulfilling his task as, also, in washing the titan more as a servant than as a would-be lover, scrubbing the great hairy legs, the callused feet, kneading his fingers into the tight curly hair, and even when it came to cleansing the genitalia, improbably delicate and boyish for such a puncheon of a man.

Renato approached and made it obvious that he had been watching us all the time, scrutinizing. He led us to the bespectacled dark-skinned man with the paunch, the only one who seemed to engage with Renato without any sense of adulation. His nakedness seemed more fitting to him than the outfit he had been wearing that morning, but again that stalwart cheerfulness in the face of a misunderstanding world was what reigned over his demeanor. Ay, los huevos, he said when he saw us, waving us toward him and bidding us to join the group. Renato formally introduced us to Luis Luis, otherwise known as Guichi the Mayor.

Like many who now lived on the purlieus of the society, Renato began, Luis Luis had once been a formidable presence in the experiment of la Revolución. Guichi had been only three on the brilliant January morning when Fidel rode on his tank into the capital and remembered the images only in flowing swaths that would often disappear in the whirlwind of his memory and then flutter to the forefront. The river of shadows created by the milling crowds on the sun-bleached cobblestones, the faces of the jubilant barbudos floating by, the massive trunks of the tanks that he had thought were somehow a strange new kind of elephant. But one memory that never wavered far from the forefront of his waking days, that lingered most prominently, was the feel of the long-fingered hand of el comandante-en-jefe when he stepped down from his tank and reached out to the child being lifted in the air to pat him on the head and caress his cheek. It was the softest hand the boy had ever felt. Renato leaned toward me and caressed my face with his fingers wrinkled by the water festival. It made the touch of anyone else feel scabrous for years afterward to the boy. By the time he was old enough to go to school, he had made up his mind that he would feel that hand again on his cheek, that he would so excel as a pionero that el comandante-en-jefe would summon him personally to congratulate him, to touch him again.

Oye, ya coño, Guichi the Mayor said, now you are making it seem dirty. He laughed and pretended to chat with some of the other bathers, but with an ear to what was being said about his past forgotten.

This was a dream that the boy would soon see fulfilled, but in the most disappointing manner. One afternoon, el comandante-en-jefe did show up at his school. He was of late leading tours of foreign journalists, showing off the recently built schools, hastily raised structures consisting of a series of cinderblock buildings set around a giant courtyard, the walls coated with murals of revolutionary heroes spouting dictums in comic book bubbles. The students lined up in the sunny courtyard for the benefit of the photographers and eventually el comandante-en-jefe showed up. Those were the days when he still wore his olive uniform everywhere, sometimes with a beret, but it was not hard to pick him out from the group of other similarly clad barbudos. He strode Moses-like through the parting ocean of periodistas. Little Luis Luis already looked and acted like an intellectual at age seven, Renato said with a snort, not a mischievous hair on his head, and he waited patiently in file for el comandante to turn his gaze on him and recognize him, the child whose sullen demeanor had so caught his attention on the day he rode into La Habana. But though el comandante, for the benefit of the press, turned and posed several questions to the students, whose answers they had rehearsed for several weeks, el comandante never called on him, never even looked at him, in fact, kept his eyes focused on some spot above the children's heads, as if in his mind he saw the bright future so clearly and eagerly that they had already sprouted into full-grown revolucionarios. It was the last time that the boy would see el comandante that close for over twenty years. For years afterward, Luis Luis attended speeches in the Plaza de la Revolución, and in rallies at sugar mills and in muddy cane fields in the provinces, at the dedications of new monuments or welcoming ceremonies for foreign dignitaries, el comandante always a small but looming figure in the distance, his magnified reedy voice like the echoes of creatures in a cave. Guichi excelled as a pionero and later as member of the Communist Youth League, then at el Instituto Preuniversitario Vocacional de Ciencias Exactas Vladimir Ilich Lenin and at the university (where he studied literature and economics), and later on the lower rungs of the revolutionary bureaucracy, quickly becoming enmeshed in the sticky web of the new government. Ese mismo allí, Renato laughed and pointed to the paunchy, naked, bespectacled Mayor, a man who, even naked, seemed as autarkic and sovereign as an unnamed animal. He became an aide to a high-ranking member of the National Assembly, a stern comandante who had been one of the most vicious judges in Che's infamous tribunals, a short-haired stout woman whose emasculating harangues to Batista's henchmen before she sentenced them to death earned her a nickname that would later be used by even her grandchildren, Our Lady of the Eunuchs. Guichi soon became trusted enough to be her primary speechwriter. When Fidel heard how the assemblywoman's speeches, from one session to the next, changed from bitter sermons against the enemy of the Cuban people, tirades razor-sharp and dangerous as the leaves of unburned sugar cane stalks, to loftier orations, their vision on the achievements of the future and not the assaults of the past, their tone comprehensive and paradoxical as the Sermon on the Mount, he ordered that her new speechwriter be brought to him. Because the devil well knows a scrotumcrunching, driedcunt vieja could not have come up with such visionary beauty on her own. Besides, the Assembly needed her the old way, with her vengeful realism to temper the schoolgirl stargazing of most of her young male counterparts.

Which at that time included Pascual Zúñiga, the most disastrous dreamer of them all, Renato said as an aside to me. Pero colorín colorado con eso.

Bueno, the young speechwriter was now in demand by the biggest bocón in the history of the Island. But the planned meeting never took place. Instead, he was taken to a dilapidated rooming house in Vedado, an old mansion whose marble front had been stripped to its brick core and subdivided into dormitories for foreign students at the university, mostly Russians then. Guichi got a room on the top floor, its solitary window (it was half a room) covered by the branches of gigantic níspero. He could pick the nectary fruit from his writing desk. He was given lined paper and a stack of pencils, three erasers, six fresh shaving navajitas to sharpen his pencils, and an antique Underwood that he used for last drafts. The speeches that were delivered every Monday to a pair of barbudos (when they dropped off the topic for the following week) and slipped into a briefcase with a miniscule silver lock, were often covered with dark stains from the juice of the nísperos on the base of Guichi's palm. Guichi continued going to rallies and ceremonies, had a battery-operated radio perennially tuned to the channel where he could hear the speeches. His words were often recited back to him, but not in the form he had written them. It was as if he were a playwright at the service of a petulant child actor, that's what Guichi later told Renato, for he would hear the beginning of his own thoughts and sentences, elegant uplifting clauses that nevertheless waged their lives on what followed, but that in the mouth of el comandante-en-jefe only seemed like so much other nonsense, Guichi's poetry corrupted by hatred for the Northern monsters, or made quotidian by a battalion of numbers and statistics. In his room, picking at nísperos from his lone window, listening to the speeches over the radio, he began to imagine the process that followed his níspero-stained manuscript once it left his lonely room. First of all, there had to be hundreds, if not thousands like him all over the Island, each secluded in his own little cell (or her own, Guichi thought, for he could often trace a feminine genesis to certain turns of phrases, like the rags of a summer linen dress), kept apart from each other, unwittingly constructing el comandante's endless orations.

After all the Monday speeches were collected, each in their separate locked briefcase, they were likely brought together in some out-of-the-way room in the Palace of the Revolution, or in the unfurnished living room of whatever hacienda el comandante-en-jefe was currently residing in, separated by topics to prepare for the difficult task, the culling of the finest phrases from each one, then rearranging them so that, at the least, it sounded as if it made sense to the ear—which is all it had to do, for they would never be printed anywhere (by his first two decades in power it was calculated that el comandante had given so many speeches that if the words were strung together they would shoot out from the center of the capital halfway to Mars).

After less than a year, Guichi's every move outside of his cell was monitored by government agents, difficult to detect, for Guichi grew to believe that even the sinewy-flanked, hardy-thighed muchachas that he brought back to his room were government agents, paid to watch him, to make sure that he did not leave. He tested them: to see what kind of devotion they had for la Revolución, how far they would degenerate themselves for the cause, beginning with positions, their legs and arms becoming tools not just of support but of balance and adornment—solidly on the termite-eaten floor or pointed toward the cracked plaster moldings on the sagging ceiling and the stained walls—in service of the versatile torso, bent back, crouched, fetal, splayed, supplicant, skyward, air-bound—there were moments when he wasn't quite sure how, but they levitated.

So he knew. None failed. Not once, coño. Not one muchachona betrayed la Revolución. And so he knew. He was being watched, he himself one of the agents of his own surveillance through the twisted labyrinths of his perversions, for often in the pell-mell of torsos, arms, and legs, he would find his vision suddenly detaching from the furious endeavors of the two creatures in the room, the glaze of the eyes like flattened raindrops rising to the ceiling, growing hazy, watching, too. And so he knew. They had made him into his own watcher, and he noticed little self-accusations sneaking into his speeches that he would later hear repeated almost word for word by el comandante-en-jefe, the longest stretches of uncut narrative that he had heard in months. Things of which he had accused himself. The greatest betrayal.

One morning, his own eyes now perennially on him, a shifting pair of tobacco-smoke disks on the ceiling, he abandoned the triangular room. The disks and all the rest of his followers trailed him like iron shavings after a magnetized ingot. He could have ended it right there, could have led all of them to where they assumed he was going, to where any desperate fucked cubano eventually goes, the sea, ill-equipped with an inner-tube balsa floja and chancletas as fins. And they would have followed him, not like rats after the piper, not entranced so, but because eventually all of them would have taken to the sea anyway, even the pair of ghostly eyes, and all they had to be given was un poquito de embullo, a little push. But something, maybe his boyhood fear not of the sea but of roads near the shore (as a child he had almost drowned after a particularly covetous wave reached over the Malecón wall and snatched him from in between the fourth and fifth squares of a hopscotch grid), maybe a deep-rooted habanerismo that forbid him from wandering too far from the heart of the capital, much less to other lands, maybe the idea that he could fool his followers, put one over on the maldito pendencieros, algo, algo made him head inland south of Vedado toward the purlieus of the greater city. The air cities then had not yet risen to the skies, la gente not yet evacuated tenements where floors would soon rot through, because hurricane-torn windows had never been replaced and tropical rainstorms ripped through the dwellings as if they were straw huts, because multiple holes in the pigeon-shit-covered roofs slowly opened up and cascaded their way down floor by floor, so that in the end it seemed as if bowling ball–sized meteors had one night rained down on the entire barrio.

Guichi shacked in an empty room on one of the lower floors, the buildings disintegrating from the top down like ant colonies. His seguidores, the acrobatic muchachas, the other students who had lived in the beehive Vedado mansion with him, the shadow of his own eyes, took up the rooms around him. It felt as if the only thing that he had left behind were the words, phrases, and butchered sentences he had lent to el comandante-en-jefe, illegible now, a palimpsest strip in the ribbon of the old typewriter. At any moment, he expected the stalkers from the Directorate to tighten their perimeter around him, or for them to disappear altogether, the Directorate agents to just grab him, not even ask for his carnet o nada, just grab him and take him back to some other mansion, some other rooftop corner, sit him in front of another old rickety clack typewriter and continue his work for la Revolución, his labor of words.

But no one ever came.

Renato stopped. Guichi was still chatting with the elders; he had long ago forgotten about us, looking nothing like the desperate imprisoned character of his own story, except when he glanced at us once over the rim of his gold wire glasses, and for a moment, in the pointed focus, I could see the younger version of the man, I could imagine him looking at the blank piece of State-approved typing paper or whatever else he worked on later. Porque (Renato continued) in those early days in the pueblaire he quickly ran out of the meager weekly paper supply that he had taken with him and he had to make do with whatever material was suitable, anything that was thin enough to roll through the drum of his typewriter and dry and absorbent enough to soak up the quickly exhausting ink from his ribbon. He tried dried palm fronds, shaved tree bark, but finally settled on making his own. He visited the sewer lines in the Malecón to gather discarded clumps of used toilet paper coming from the nearby hotels where he knew that Soviet dignitaries stayed, gathered them by the bagful and meticulously dried the bundles on the parapets of roofs, letting the sunlight bleach their microbes and their streaks. When they were just the right texture, the outside crusty and the inside still moist, like a baked merenguito, he used an old marble rolling pin to spread them into odd-shaped sheets, aberrant mottled pieces that would bleach again in the sun, this time hung on the laundry lines with tiny clothespins used for lingerie, then he would layer seven or eight of these muslin-thin sheets and press them down with flattened aluminum sheets torn from discarded refrigerators, weighed down by bricks that had dislodged themselves from the rusted skeletons of the buildings. As he worked on making his paper, he composed sentences in his head, repeating one after the other as he went, each period forcing him to go back to the beginning to follow through the text sentence by sentence (sometimes editing) until he arrived full speed at the precipice of the last period. When there was no more room in his head, that would be the end of a story or a chapter—for he reasoned that he had been fabricating stories in his speeches anyway, why not go all the way with it—and he would need to wait until he had a decent stack of his layered sheets and then cut them with precision surgical blades stolen from the clinic where one of his muchachonas worked as a night cleaning woman. They had stayed with him, most of them, slowly closed their circle around him and instead of smothering him as he had feared, returned as their old selves, resuming their erotic games, although now it was they who gave the orders and Guichi who complied. Many of them became his first wives, others joined with each other, and adopted many of his children, for it seemed Guichi was as busy at producing them as he was at cranking out his homemade paper, at inventing new inks in which to soak his threadbare typewriter ribbon: the dried flowers of the hibiscus picked from park gardens, discarded coffee grinds, the inner hulls of crushed walnuts, clay dirt mixed with egg yolks, but finally settled on the longer-lasting stain produced by crushed beets, which gave his manuscripts a vampiric air and made the key of his typewriter keys look complicit in murder.

The word itself seemed to dispirit Renato the storyteller. He stopped, looked around, and mumbled that there wasn't much else to the story, to which Steffen replied that he had only waded into the river of the tale, that there seemed to be a long stretch from where he had left off, with a secluded horny writer, persevering with his crimson manuscripts, using whatever little means available to pursue his craft to this, the seeming jefe of an entire village in the sky, half the kids his own. And to put it bluntly, vaya, one who was putting all at risk now by harboring traitors to the State.

Sí, Renato agreed, looking around as if for Guichi's help to make official his own place in the pueblaire. But the Mayor had vanished, the other bathers, elders mostly, now sitting with their heads bowed, pondering the varied wisdom that he had imparted on them.

Renato walked toward his bundle of clothes, signaled for us to do the same. He slipped into his jeans, camiseta, and sandals in one full motion—an old skin. I had almost forgotten that we were all nude and the effort to put on our clothes now seemed greater than the hesitancy to take them off when we had first arrived at the festival. A handful of children remained, splashing about in the receding waters, and some viejitas, not watching the children but in a sort of comatose daze, shuffling from parapet to parapet. Renato gathered their garments and tried to hand them to the peripatetic viejitas. He let the children run naked.

Eventually, he said, continuing Guichi's story, it became unsafe to live in the buildings. An entire plaster of Paris ceiling crashed down on the bed Guichi and two of his wives slept in one night. It was as if the hand of God had punched them when it came down, though covered in the gray white mud, they continued to fuck—ever so slowly due to the insufferable weight of their new hide, which eventually began to dry again, paralyzing them before they could fully satisfy each other. Wresting free from the prison of his carapace, Guichi went up to the roof to work on the homemade sheets of paper he dried there, washed himself in an afternoon agauacero, and built the first shack on the roof with aluminum and tin sheets ripped off useless appliances, wood from doorframes, and cabinets and rusty nails he pulled off studs in the upper floors. This was the shack that would be later used to house the guest of honor, the shack where Bertila now roomed. The town grew from that center, not policed, its own entity apart from la Revolución but forbidden from disrupting the glorious socio-political experiment of the Island.

Which was fine with Guichi.

He had finally wrested himself free from the shadow of what he now considered his traitorous art, which had served only the criminals in power. He was everything in the pueblaire, master builder, husband to many, father to many more, and eventually unacknowledged legislator, though he purposefully made his system of laws as pliant as la Revolución's was rigid, so that he became the de facto leader, which left him little time for his burgeoning writing career. Stories and poems lingered in fragments beside the homicidal typewriter, now stored in a tiny rainproof shack. It is an old story; it has happened to many a promising writer (this was now Renato quoting Guichi): life intrudes.

The life of the town had its own ceremony, maybe more holy than writing for Guichi. But also the cause of creating a world separate from the revolution. How does the State retaliate? And what does that do to Guichi's conception of what his work should be, free from the ceremony of living?

How did you come to know him? Or was it your brother? Steffen asked. I too remained unclear about which of the brothers had found this place first or whether Nicolás had thought of it as a refuge when he died here.

I knew about it through him, Renato said, not mentioning his brother's name. Then he considered something for a

moment before offering something more specific. I had been
here before.

The children once again approached, surrounding Renato
but ignoring us. He shooed them away and continued. After
he and his group had fled the sidatorio, this loose confedera-
tion of ex-patients had passed the time by sleeping with each
other. There was a list, I said, by your bedside . . . with names.
The old man showed me. I had forgotten his real name, the
one called El Alacrán. Renato acknowledged the existence
of the list, but he said that it was not his, that it was the
old man—Laguna was his surname—who kept the list. It
kept him entertained. It was accurate, up to a point, Renato
admitted. A body grows alone after a while, he said, as if
apologizing for the endless first Fridays that he had teased me.
But it was meaningless. Many on the list did flee the sidatorio.
Some didn't. Many were too ill to flee, or already dead.

They slept in parks, snuggled into the wide shoulders of
ceibas to avoid la fiana, who sometimes amused themselves
by firing blanks into the canopies. Their ventures camping
in the trees eventually led them to deserted rooftops because
that's what Renato knew best from his brother, although he
didn't quite remember how to get there. They traveled at night
and slept during the day. They found the pueblaire almost
by chance after wandering in circles for weeks, going too far
south. One dusk they were getting ready to abandon camp
atop some other deserted building south of the pueblaire. In
the haze created by the falling light it seemed a mirage—a
floating elfin city on a cloud of fire. The following day they
followed their instincts toward the base of the mirage city. It
was farther away than they had imagined. When they climbed
to a roof the following night, it seemed as if they had made
no progress at all, as if the city had traveled with them, just
out of their reach. Each night afterward, Renato realized that

the floating city spread a bit wider than the night before, that what he had previously thought from his few visits there with Nicolás was a collection of shacks on a single rooftop, was in fact a massive compound spread out over the area of an entire barrio, dozens of blocks squared. The vision grew larger and more substantial, until they were close enough that they could make out the flimsy materials of the abodes, the inhabitants there, skittering from one roof to the other on magically suspended planks.

Once they had arrived at the base, they found themselves unable to ascend, afraid, fearing that the vision they'd had might have been some nocturnal mirage. They lingered below, went hungry, thirsty, their lips chapped, their tongues grimy—attenuated, not daring to ascend. After three days of circumspection, they prepared to move on, to look for some sustenance in the more tourist-traveled areas and return emboldened. But as they were leaving the lair they had created on the first floor of one of the buildings, they felt the foundation shake and heard the rumble of the walls. They were sure that the army had taken the handful of tanks it owned, remnants from the Soviet era, and had come barreling into the abandoned neighborhood, crushing anything that got in their way.

What they saw when they ran out was a sight more breathtaking than the ancient tanks: a threesome of trucks with gleaming blanquísimo tanks and tires as big as a man, following one upon the other and then veering in different paths to the base of the roof city. A lonely miniscule Cuban flag flew atop each cabin. There were no license plates, heightening the feeling that the monumental ghostly trucks had come from somewhere where nothing, not even such colossal things had an identity. By the time the men had walked to the back of the truck, and adjusted their hoses to the outtake valve, there was a block-long line of people waiting, all carrying buckets or small barrels. The line soon grew into a swarm, people descending from the sides of the building like bichos, their buckets slung with straps over their shoulders.

The man orchestrating the procession, bespectacled, lighter-skinned, paunchier, guiding people off the wall and encouraging them up the worn stairways of the entrance, noticed the group of boys watching, recognized Renato, handed them each a full bucket, and wedged them into the ascending line. Guichi found shacks or upper floor aeries for each of them, either vacant or emptied of occupants who moved in with others. They were never forced to sleep exposed to the elements again.

No questions asked, no need unmet.

Questions about what? Steffen asked in English.

Vaya, sabes, who were we? What were we doing here? These phrases in English also, the first time I had heard Renato speak English since our drunken night at the Hotel Habana Libre. His accent was thicker, his phrasing hacked, but he went on, the change in language allowing him to continue the conversation that Steffen was intent on starting without others snooping. A good sign. It's not that he didn't want to talk about it, it was that he didn't know how. We could have been, pues come se dice, State observers, como se dice, cronistas like you. He snickered the accusation at Steffen.

I doubt you would be confused for a chronicler, Steffen responded.

Right. Renato turned toward me, a playfully ignorant look on his face.

What were we doing? Renato repeated the question with an ironic lilt, looking directly at me. He switched back to Spanish. We were proving our mettle. Same thing you're doing now. He turned and looked out over the ravaged barrio. Not to me or to anyone here. To yourselves. See if you have that thing in you to help us overthrow this maldito government while the whole world watches.

How? I asked, returning to English, finally getting into the conversation, thinking back to my last meeting with Nicolás, where he was as maniacal and unhinged as Renato was now logical and discerning. With what? Where are your . . . your arms?

Arms, hermano? ¿Los brazos? He put out his arms in front of him, palms outward. He smiled lewdly, signaling for me to come to him. By the time I reached him, he had lowered one of his arms and reached the other one out to me. I took it by the wrist. He gestured for me to look down. On the crook of the elbow there was a new tattoo, almost imperceptible from anywhere but up close. He lifted his arm closer to my eyes so I could read the word, an impossibly neat script that could have fit on the wing of a baby moth.

Arms, hermano? Arms like weapons?—We don't need them. There are over three hundred of us. We are our own weapons.

V

Now, of course, was the time, while darkness drained into the bottom, for him to make his peace. Between the stirrup and the ground there wasn't time: you couldn't break in a moment the habit of thought: habit held you closely while you died.

Graham Greene
Brighton Rock

ARMS

Renato lied. They had weapons.

I knew about them by the time we saw the Pope that first morning in his protected bubble racing down La Avenida de Independencia behind the State motorcade. In the rush past us, he seemed not ancient but beautifully preserved, Steffen said. Like those perfect butterflies pinned in glass boxes in el Museo de Historia Natural. Crowds chanted, Se ve, se siente, el papa está presente. It would be the only time we would see him in the capital as a group. By the time he was seen again in public in La Habana, a mere four days later, under the shadow of the iron Che in the Plaza of the Revolution, our group would have grown to three times its size, caught the attention of an intrepid Miami journalist, achieved renown far beyond the shores of the Island, and been mostly extinguished. But the morning of the Pope's arrival, Steffen and I were convinced that this would be as far as the cause went.

Renato's boys, outcasts all, willingly separated themselves from everything, we reasoned. They would not commit to any mission. In some ways, their illness had served them well, I thought. It had liberated them. Perhaps saved them. For the moment. From the moment. By leaving the sidatorio, they had stopped treating the disease, refusing any kind of medication. In that month in the pueblaire after Christmas, the chisme was that the new antiviral drugs were actually a government plan to do away with those infected with the virus. Poison.

In the weeks before the Pope arrived, the first of the boys had died in the pueblaire, suffering intolerable chills and wrapped in countless bedsheets inside a sun-punished shack. Many others from that original group escaped that fate for years to come. I still see them now sometimes in the streets of the old city, the decade passed, an endless season of hurricanes for some, their bodies assaulted, their flesh battered and sunken into the cavities of the body, their skin ashen and corrugated, their gait a shuffle. Yet, many of them seem to have only passed a balmy spell, a profane lassitude in their movements the only sign that time has trodden on. I watch from a distance, afraid that they would entrap me in their nightmares as Nicolás had any time I dared to get too close to the wildfires that fueled him. I had thought that I would witness each of their deaths, that I would see their bodies ceremoniously burned in makeshift pyres down on the streets below like the first boy had been on the afternoon before the Pope's visit.

Later, I had wanted to burn with them.

Renato announced our departure from the pueblaire on the morning before we saw the papal motorcade. The planning for it had been going on almost from the moment they had arrived at the pueblaire, but, because Steffen and I had yet to be fully trusted, and given that we had made it our mission to lose ourselves in the daily life there, things were easily kept from us until the very last moment. Guichi the Mayor and his band of wives and children taught us how to contribute to the daily life, the purchasing of food from itinerant vendors—both black market farmers and European relief agencies—the cooking, the disinfecting of the central latrine, which drained into a makeshift wooden gutter down the side.

Not long after this visit, Renato came and pulled us from our domestic chores one afternoon. We were to visit with the Mayor. We had never been in the aerie the Mayor called home with two of his wives and a few dozen of his children. It made up two or three of the top floors in one of the buildings that had not been as thoroughly disemboweled as the others. Except for the missing exterior walls, the hard, briny breeze whipping in from the bay, and the makeshift rope ladders drooping off the precipice to connect floors, the place could have been mistaken for some bourgeoise penthouse in the capital in films about the time before the revolution. Once-fine mahogany furniture tarnished and rotted by the humidity and the elements decorated every room, with four-poster beds in the spaces farthest from the openings to the sky shielded by mosquito nets. Stacked parapets of cinderblocks must have been to prevent Guichi's dozens of children and hundreds of cats from stepping off into oblivion in the middle of the night. Guichi said the furniture had come to him a long time ago when he had still been a writer for the Party, abandoned at the embassies and hotels by the fleeing imperialists.

He gave us rum to share from a flask in one of the inner rooms not exposed to the elements and only accessible by crawling through a rabbit hole on the rotted floor of the upper area. The windowless room had been purposefully sealed off, mortared with broken bricks and cracked cinderblocks so that even as the western sun lit the rest of the penthouse in fiery colors this place remained completely dark once the wooden cover was replaced over the rabbit hole.

Guichi lit a lantern. He lit a cigarette from it and offered us each one. He asked Steffen if he had a permit to drive on the Island, to which he responded that Arcadio had secured him a temporary one that was still valid. Guichi picked his teeth and signaled to Renato that this was good. He needed Steffen to drive one of the máquinas in their possession, an old VW van some Finnish hippies had given Bertila in exchange for lodging, to carry supplies for the group.

Supplies? I asked, although no one had been talking to me.

Food, a little rum, water. Guichi tapped one of the crates we sat on, the types of crates that we used to transport supplies from down below. He passed the flask around once more. Not a problem, right? It's better if it's a Yuma at the wheel. Less suspicious.

Steffen nodded.

Also money to bribe anyone we have to. Security will be tight. Better done by a Yuma.

Why would they care about food and water? And rum? I looked at Renato, but he had kept his eyes lowered throughout.

After a long silence, he took my forearm and said, They'll care about everything. The world is watching. You'll be with me. The rest of us. In the government truck-transports.

What else is in the crates? I wanted to ask. But Guichi stood and made clear the meeting had ended just as brusquely as it had started.

Steffen was elated coming out of the rabbit hole. Did he have a real sense of what he had just agreed to do?

He did not want to go back to our tasks. He was too exuberant with his new promotion. I immediately regretted not going back to our old duties because I had struck up a new kind of friendship with Inocente St. Louis that had never been possible in the paladar, where he dwelt only among the infernal airs around the stoves and broilers that no one else could survive more than a moment. Whereas here, a week after he had arrived, Guichi had put him in charge of coordinating the ration deliveries with the Ministry of Economy and Planning, of bartering for other necessities with the black market farmers that stopped here first on their way to the city, of stretching it all out to make it last the week. Now all this seemed unimportant, or at best a tepid prelude to something of much more significance.

We wandered to Bertila's kaleidoscopic shack as if looking for some secret that had been withheld from us in the dark room with the crates. Other mini shacks had risen around it, many already half covered with pointillist coats that shimmered in the dry season heat. A group of young men, half-naked, covered in paint, some perched on step stools, others crouching near the base, worked on one specific shack with tiny brushes and a makeshift palette that held thimble-fuls of colors. The artists worked with a psalmist's intensity, their thumbs and index fingers pincering tiny sable brushes, sweat dripping off their noses, their eyes like those of croco-diles, periscoped on the task at hand.

It was unsettling just to watch them, each of their smallest gestures measured and weighty, confident in the way of the broad movements of grand orators. After they finished one piece, they dipped into a different set of thimbles in the palette with their wispy brushes and moved onto the next and the next, their heads slightly shifting. They practiced their insur-gent art as if our lives depended on it.

Bertila saw us and approached, holding up her mantles with both hands. Do you remember what I told you that afternoon we walked the Prado? Sí, I remembered. The counting game, counting people, counting ghosts.

This is how we even the score. She was casual, modest even. This is how we stand up and be counted. She turned. This is the cavalry, she said, facing the painted shacks and the squinting, paint-splattered muchachos. They continued working, not taking notice of us.

She handed us each a palette with fresh thimblefuls of black paint. The head of the brushes were gossamery, some of them no more than a few hairs thick—the paint held to them by some magnetic force when dipped. At first, we did nothing but practice the word, to make it legible in such a cramped space. We either made the letters so large that they seemed obscenely illegible or so small that they flooded into each other. Bertila instructed that we use only the very tip of the brush. She held our fingers and showed us. By the end of the day, she assured both of us that we had the drawing talent of hoofed creatures, the vision of intestinal tapeworms. She was right, unlike the other shacks, iridescent in the dusk, ours seemed pelted with the paint, a thing abused.

Jesting, I opened the small door on one side and realized that these tiny abodes were more than just practice canvases for the graffiti artists. Sealed crates were stacked snugly inside, larger than the ones in the room of Guichi's penthouse and covered with thick plastic tarps to protect them from the leaky tin roofs. I ducked under the miniature doorway and stepped inside when no one was looking—the artists grown too myopic with their work. I tried to pry open one of the crates, but they were all nailed shut tight. I picked one up at one end and could barely lift it on my own. I heard the rattle of metal.

Now, I felt suddenly nervous. Steffen had been the only one to see me go in, but Bertila might now have come back wandering back on her rounds. I pulled the door slightly ajar and felt a hard tug from the other side, startling me. Steffen had offered a hand before anyone noticed my absence.

They're not telling us everything, I said.

They are, he responded, you're just not listening.

There are weapons or material for weapons in there.

Probably, Steffen said. And I'm not the only one that must be driving a separate vehicle, estoy seguro.

Just a few days later, Renato made his announcement. The group would move on. To Santa Clara and the Pope's first Mass. Steffen and I spent that morning concocting stratagems with how we could communicate with each other in case something happened to one of us. None of them made sense. We might as well have been talking about sending messages to each other by pigeons. Soon enough, Renato appeared in front of our shack with a sackcloth bag and told us to throw our belongings in. It would be marked with our name and carried in the máquina driven by Steffen. The van would travel at night, safer, ahead of the group, so Guichi was already summoning Steffen to get things ready. The rest of us would leave the following morning, hopping into the many flatbed camiones transferring pilgrims under the State's aegis. I imagined two things, an endless convoy of trucks packed with the pious, the desperate, and the plain curious, or its converse, a handful of trucks, half-filled, not many interested in doing one iota more than had been commanded by the State, to attend the Masses in the hometowns and to show respect. The reality of the pilgrimage was somewhere in between my imaginings, not a convoy, but many pilgrims traveled from place to place, most of them originating from the capital, more than half, young foreigners.

I almost missed the entire trip.

On the afternoon that the preparations to move started, I abandoned the pueblaire. I managed to catch Steffen briefly before I left to tell him that I would meet up with the group the following dawn at la Plaza de la Revolución, and with him in Santa Clara. I repeated my concerns about his involvement and exposure as a driver of whatever cargo the crates contained. Steffen dismissed this, but feared that he would lose me again, he said. He added that without me all of it would be meaningless. All along, I thought then, his stay had been one of some anthropologist in a foreign land, an unethical anthropologist, at that, who became involved in the rituals of the natives, who wanted to experience some kind of atavistic passion but lacked the wherewithal to summon it. He actively cared about me (even if just in a bungled sexual manner), about Renato, about Bertila, about all the citizens of the pueblaire. But that wasn't the same thing as becoming one of us, which might have been why he accepted the driving task. It tethered him to the danger the others faced. He made me promise I was not going to turn traitor, as if he had the authority or the history to demand such a promise from me.

The thing he didn't know involved Fidel's talent at making traitors of us all, double agents, and triple, quadruple, quintuple agents, until we had no idea exactly which side we were on, and it didn't really matter because there was always one side anyways, and we were never really on it.

It's the woman then you must see? he asked. But why?

I'll be back, I said, trying to convince myself more than anything.

She'll convince you that you must stay behind.

Even if Cecilia wanted me to stay, if she did not feel betrayed by my summer departure, she would be more interested in my keeping watch over Renato. That card I could play forever, although my own interest had gone beyond that. I wanted to commit myself to him the way no one else in the family had, like no one else in his life had, the way he had committed himself to his brother. Cecilia might have already been aware that she had lost him inalterably, may have even hired the carpenter to begin work on his coffin from the remnants of the writer's fancy bookcases, but I was sure that she would want me, as part of the family, to remain with him. She had been the first to concoct this fantasy, the first to call both Nicolás and Renato my brothers, and she would be the one who would hold on to the illusion of it until the very end, even when I would return to her months later for the last time, after the cataclysm in the abandoned train station in Santiago, after my sequestration, and she let me in, served me coffee, and proceeded to walk out on her own life, leaving me with the vestiges of it, the vanished husband, the lost sons, the stolen house.

But that afternoon, the day before we left on our pilgrimage, I thought would be the last time I would set foot inside the house on Calle Obispo. Comandante Juan let me in through the side gate. He had come back from his hideout during the bombings. They were already awaiting the first guests of the night. He shook my hand and stood so stiffly that I thought he was going to give me a military salute, but he simply let me pass. Not much had changed inside, a few more tables wedged against the henhouse. A new cook dawdled in the kitchen, a dwarfish boy, the grandson of one of the viejas in the neighborhood Comité, I learned.

Cecilia came down the stairs, smoothing her hair. It was her habit to go up to her room and smoke three straight cigarettes before every shift and then rinse her mouth with rosewater. When she saw me, she untied her apron, threw it at me, and headed back up the stairs to look for another one. Ay niño, I'm glad you showed up finally, she said with her back to me. The nonchalance in her voice stunned me. As if I were an old chunk of butter that she had misplaced in the fridge and suddenly found. I had no choice but to get to work. By the time she returned, I was already waiting on the first guests of the night. By seven, every seat had filled up; if I wanted to talk to Cecilia it would not happen until after the shift. A few times, Cecilia took me by the shoulder and leaned over to say something—I thought to ask about my absence, but she merely noted some point of service. Once, when I took a break by a corner of the henhouse, to wipe some sweat from my face and gulp down a glass of water, she slid by and said, You're zombied. Pajeao completamente. She was right, I was beyond rusty, not quite sure if the paladar had suddenly grown busier after the slow summer or if I had simply forgotten how to do this.

When we sat down to dinner after the service, we ate in silence until the new chef finished preparing the dishes and sat down with us. He had not addressed me the nightlong except to recite the ingredients in every dish he gave me in a singsong voice that could have made rat poison sound appetizing. He introduced himself, Manuel Ernesto, had heard a lot about me, he said, not all good, vaya. He signaled for everyone to eat as he sat. Comandante Juan poured rum.

I found Renato, I said after gulping a second shot.

Comandante Juan took a long swig and looked at Cecilia. We know, he said, somewhat unsure. We had pretended for the few hours of the dinner shift that time had not passed, that the troublesome long summer of the bombs had not come upon us, that I was still a member of Cecilia's family. Manuel made a gesture to leave the table but Cecilia put a hand on his forearm. It's all out in the open, she said as if explaining a simple math problem. Rafael was here, but now he is with my other son, the living one. She turned to me, told me that they had known almost since the day I had returned to the capital that I would go searching for him.

You found him. So good.

I nodded but had the feeling that any story that I might come up with they could already guess from what comandante Juan had found out through his minions in the Directorate. So I gave them the ending. I told them we were leaving in the morning for Santa Clara, following the Pope. He's found God, comandante Juan chortled, and threw a napkin down on the table like a challenge.

Manuel giggled with a mouth full of food. It's the thing

these days. Even Cara de Coco seems to have found the Almighty. My grandmother has set up rosary sessions with the other old ladies of the Comité.

I am not following the old man. It's Renato. Renato and his group.

Trouble, Manuel stated as if parroting his grandmother.

I said I didn't know. There might be. Likely. That's how these things go.

So now you have some death wish, too? Cecilia whistled with frustration.

My long silence irked her.

I came to say goodbye.

Cecilia pushed away from the table, swallowed another shot of rum, and wiped her mouth with the back of her hand. She threw her napkin at me. Goodbye, she said. As she headed for the sink, Manuel mentioned that it was his turn to wash the pots and dishes, but he continued to eat with great gusto, reaching for Cecilia's unfinished plate. When she refused to rejoin us, comandante Juan took me out to Calle Obispo to smoke.

He said that I couldn't blame her, lighting a cigarillo for me. She thought that with me it would be different.

What would be?

You . . . you were like a gift to her, everything she'd never had in this house. She thought you of all of them would be loyal. Vaya, no seas bobo, viejo, she knew about you and Nicolás right away. There was nothing that boy did that escaped her, guessed what he was up to with you perhaps before you even did. And she knew about the German, too, that he was no more than an overly curious student or man of bisnes or whatever mierda he said he was. He paused. Knew *everything,* he stressed, but never mentioning the night in the henhouse aloud.

I told comandante Juan the story of Steffen's involvement

with Arcadio, with the Directorate, but he seemed unfazed. Claro, claro, he said. It's the newest thing, recruiting the young foreigners to do the dirty surveillance work on insurgents. Great access. Downside, of course. Impossible to enforce loyalty. Or the truth.

He took a drag of his cigarillo, stared at me as if he were waiting for a response. Never had he admitted aloud to me that he had any power within the juggernaut of the State.

He finished his cigarillo, lit two other ones, and waited until I had finished mine to approach me, hand me the second one, and throw his arm around my shoulder. His voice grew gravelly, splintered. You'll never set foot in that house again. Vaya, it's good you said your goodbyes. I tried to pry loose from him, but he put a claw hold on my shoulder that made me drop the cigarillo and wince. He reached out with his foot and stomped out the cigarillo, the smoke from his own blinding me. He let go, pushed me against the wall, and put his cigarillo in my mouth, which sent me into a spasm of coughing. Comandante Juan laughed heartily. He grabbed me again, but this time in a fatherly way, patting me softly on the back. He apologized. It's for her, he said. He wasn't sure how much more she could take of her sons, if she could survive another death. If it happens, it was better that she didn't know. Let her think that he's off wandering the Island, tilting at the windmills of the State, but alive. She would suffer, claro, but there would be no final proof of her ultimate failure. He had heard that Pascual had returned to the Island. What the fuck do you make of that?

I shook my head, the dull pain in my shoulder refraining me from telling him that I had heard the rumors, too.

Masquerading as a pilgrim, Pascual will be following the Pope, the comandante said. In search of what, who knows? It's possible that he had not heard about his oldest son's death until recently. Because try as they might they could not locate him when . . . when the boy died. And now what? He returns broken with tardy grief. It cannot be good.

I wasn't sure what to believe about this. Was it a way to just get rid of me? To finally keep Cecilia all to himself? I asked him if he had told Cecilia, and he gave me a confounded look. Had I not learned anything in my time at Calle Obispo? Why would he tell her such a thing? He was telling me so that I knew. Likely Renato knew, perhaps Renato had even contacted Pascual.

You don't know what you're getting into, he said. Renato and his little group.

They're not doing anything. Not yet. They're living on abandoned rooftops in Cerro.

That's not what the Directorate thinks.

I explained that the German submitted fiction not intelligence to the Directorate.

Yes, yes, the truth is a wily mistress. Do you want to know what they think is happening with these hombrecitos that escaped from the sidatorios?

They didn't escape. They were let go.

They were let go for a reason. Easier that way to do what they wanted to do with them in the first place.

Comandante Juan motioned me to follow him. He lit another pair of cigarillos and apologized for my shoulder. We walked east toward Centro Habana and then south, away from the Malecón. The comandante seemed to have mapped out this route before. The closer we worked our way into the central city, the easier it became to find them, the small signs that just a few weeks before Steffen and I had seen sporadically were now everywhere. He led me to an alleyway where many of the crumbling brick walls were covered with the colorful signs of the sacrificio cult, as comandante Juan called them, crawling up the sides of buildings like ivy.

This will be here on the walls long after the government

has extinguished the group—mementos, he said, touching the painted walls with the tips of two fingers as if to ascertain its political voltage.

We came out onto a plaza crowded with late-night tourists leaving bars and on the way to the clubs. It felt good to see the city alive again. Like coming upon a terminally ill relative that has miraculously regained his health.

We sat at a table and ordered cafecitos. The comandante sipped and smoked watching the young tourists and grunting indiscriminately at both the males and females. After the coffees, he ordered a carafe of rum, which we sipped straight, saying nothing. When he peeled his eyes away from the asses of the tourists, he spoke emphatically. When they extinguish, they are not picky. If you're some innocent bug caught along the stampede of cockroaches. He stomped his foot hard. Don't think you can escape because you've done nothing.

At some point, I imagined, he must have had this exact conversation with Renato, and with Nicolás before him, releasing them from their duties to their mother. Now you can't say you didn't know. Cecilia could also be made to pay for your stupidity, as could I. Comandante Juan stopped, clearly reconsidering how he wanted to phrase things. Look, I'm no ignoramus. Every good nation needs its good share of insurrectionists to keep things honest. Every revolution. Every wholesome home, even. But this house has provided more than its share. He pointed to the graffitied walls. Esto es el colmo. No one should be asked to tolerate this, to have to pay an awful price for such a petty crime. Which is exactly what will happen. But think about what else they might be punishing. He took another shot of rum. Think. That's how it works. On both sides. That is why you will not set foot inside the house on Calle Obispo again. I made that business for her. I didn't let her sons destroy it, and I won't let you.

Did she know? I asked. Did she know that I had watched when Nicolás injected his brother?

Comandante Juan attempted a belly laugh, but the gesture sputtered halfway, and the effect of the slight trembling of the cheeks made it seem as if he were about to succumb to an epileptic fit. When a smile finally burst through the tremors, it had no vigor—cowed, yellowy, false. She knew something had happened that night, the comandante said, knew I was not to blame. Lack of true courage, maybe, but she blamed herself for that also, and him, comandante Juan, blamed him too, for not ridding the family of Nicolás sooner.

How did you know? I asked.

What don't I know? he said. Nicolás was not going to perish without leaving—leaving something. His voice trailed off. In some ways, he said, you should consider yourself lucky. Comandante Juan thought that I would have been the chosen one. But I must have failed some test along the way, a test, he said, that I seemed hell-bent on passing anyway with this tardy obsession.

Murder, now that would be the justification for the extermination. Murder of the innocent pilgrims coming to see the Pope, whether it was really happening or not, and he had his doubts. But it didn't matter.

I wanted to tell him about the crates but I resisted the urge out of fear for Renato.

These people never need much when it comes to justification. Just a whiff of the crime. He spoke of them, the Directorate, the whole Party intelligence arm, as if he weren't one of them.

He stood up, took out his useless, rusty pistol and pressed it to my cheek, leaving the cool metal there long enough so I could replay in my head the whole of his lecture.

Listen to your doubts, that's why you're here now, he said, stood, and walked away.

I finished the carafe on my own and headed south toward the pueblaire, hitching a ride in a máquina with a group of young Canadians on the way to a club.

It was almost two when I arrived at the pueblaire—goodbyes ending, the Mayor addressing the group, a battalion going off to war, Renato standing beside him with his arm on the Mayor's shoulders. Renato looked at me with a pity that made me want to strike him. The Mayor bemoaned the dozing hordes of the capital, those masses that had been conditioned only to survive, whose nobler instincts they had long ago abandoned, and who would die unremembered, buried in unmarked graves, mocked the fact that they would never be able to tell their children and their children's children that they were here on this rooftop on this historic night, when a handful of the chosen few set forth to change the course of the Island's sad serpentine history again. There was time yet, there was time to set things on their proper course. He paused to look up briefly at the incandescent torch-lights of the pueblaire, people from other rooftops on casks and atop the shacks watching. The Mayor raised his voice in increments as the speech hit its stride. It only took but a small atmospheric shift, a slight change in the water temperature to alter the track of the deadly storm of history passing over the oceans of time. He was glad to be counted as one among them, if only as a provider. Renato and some of his group, Bertila whom I now spotted, raised a protest to this last bit. They had all been much more than that, Renato shouted, raising his fist to the cheer of the villagers. History will be changed, the Mayor rang out in conclusion. Maybe not tonight. Maybe not tomorrow. But it will be changed. With that, he turned and embraced Renato like I had never seen him embraced by his mother or his brother, like I had never done it myself. Steffen was nowhere in the crowd, likely already waiting for Guichi in Bertila's old van.

Then the move was on, the lights dispersing and scampering earthward from the sides of the building and from within. Many years later, I imagined the flaming pueblaire, not from the fires that rained down on it from the heavens later, but from the flames that lit it from within that night, like an ancient man spontaneously combusting, a twisted frame with a wick buried in his fatty gut.

PHANTOM FLAMES

They could have only invited us to come along to participate, Steffen warned me when I found him during the first Mass in Santa Clara. Otherwise our presence here was meaningless.

Was I ready for that? he asked me.

Participate in what? Painting little cartoons on the street? That can't be it.

It's much more than that, he said. They're planning something in Santiago.

The Autopista Nacional, the motorway that runs east–west through the southern side of the Island, proved a more direct route to Santa Clara than the central highway on the north. By dawn, our flatbed truck passed north of the Zapata swamp and I imagined the legendary creatures that existed there, some like the Zapata rail, native to only this broad peninsula, almost extinct and rarely seen by man, secluded in many ways from the rest of us and from the stormy history Guichi had railed on about. We passed through cleared cane fields north of the southern port city of Cienfuegos, the nearby sugar mills, and even in the distance, the shadow of an abandoned nuclear reactor. By the time we entered the province of Villa

Clara, the sun was high in the sky and the flatbed began to feel more like a cattle cart. The ill effects of the rum from the night before took over. There were a few from Renato's group on the truck (though Renato had jumped on another one at the last minute). We huddled together, near the center, holding onto the makeshift railings. In many ways we were indistinguishable from the rest of the tourists, young, shabbily dressed, mostly unwashed. There were groups of older churchladies that had brought chairs and secured them to the railings with rope, then bound themselves onto the chair Houdini-style. We in our group conducted ourselves with the understanding that many on the bus were undercover agents from the Directorate—foreigners, natives, and viejas, all possibilities. Renato had warned us to remain silent, to say nothing about who we were to strangers.

My own mission was twofold, to find Renato and stay as close to him as possible and to ferret out his true motivations— he had been fully committed to other causes before from the time he was a dutiful pionero and just as expediently abandoned them. After the conversation with Juan, I also wanted to find Pascual—this mythic hero–cum–deserter–cum–returned-prodigal-penitent. For that, I had to figure out from Renato what he looked like. If this was to come to a peaceful end, if there was even a possibility of that, I could not lose Renato again.

As planned, our group did not reconvene immediately when we dismounted the trucks, lest we attract the attention of agents in civilian clothes that now became a little more obvious from their perches in the bleachers, side by side with la fiana, who for the first time in my life appeared without their weapons slung over their shoulders, in respect to the pontiff. Throughout our journey, however, I remained sure that there were others armed nearby and out of sight, por si acaso the Pope were to incite counterrevolutionary activity as they said he had done in Poland years before. For most in the crowd of the first Mass—which did seem to grow to at least half of the hundred thousand that was reported later, spilling out of the modern Estadio Sandino, home most of the year to the beisbol Villa Clara Naranjas—the Mass was an exercise in the cryptic rituals and chants that they did not understand. The pontiff's sermon on the duties and responsibilities of family and the State's relation to it sounded like one of Fidel's speeches but inverting the hierarchy between the communal and the personal—that is, vaguely familiar, like hearing the Lider's sermons underwater or while hanging upside down like a bat.

Before we had separated into smaller groups in Havana, Renato had given each of us a blackwood rosary to hang around our necks. I fingered mine as I tried to maneuver toward the altar. I found Steffen behind the main section of seats, cross-legged on the outer infield amidst a dark swarm of priests and nuns. He made room for me beside him, looked around to make sure it was all right. He was the only one wearing the blackwood rosary in this area, although I could see others close by and many others scattered in the open-attendance field.

There were other drivers for other vans, most of them heading directly for Santiago. Guichi had continued on his way there. The group, the blackwood rosaries, the graffiti, the ceremony with the needles—all distractions, Steffen said.

I told him that I wanted to ride with him from now on. I needed to see what he was transporting.

He deduced that he was likely no more than a decoy. That he could be carrying empty crates for all he knew. Or filled with rocks—to throw the Directorate off. He suspected that other vans had taken back roads along the edges of the Zapata swamp and down the southern coast toward Santiago.

After the Mass, we were to mingle with either the curious townspeople or the devout—anyone not wearing the blackwood rosary, now all around us, many with binoculars and mini telescopes focused on the throne upon the altar. Our first rendezvous would be Parque Vidal in the center of town. From there, we would move to our campground in a finca east of the Che memorial on the outskirts of town. Aside from that, Steffen didn't know anything else. The pilgrimage trucks would leave for the second Mass in Camagüey early the next morning.

Who owns the finca?

Steffen shrugged. No one had told him. Maybe one of the conspirators. But unimportant, he said. This whole thing was no more than a charade. He seemed offended by this. That we had just been trusted with the decoy part of the mission. But I wasn't sure he was right if Renato was still with us.

It's bigger than him, Steffen said.

When the sermon started, he casually asked to borrow one of the binoculars from one of the nuns. They were plastic, church-yellow, and light as a toy, but powerful—when he handed it to me, I could see the milky spittle in John Paul II's wizened lips as he spoke. With a finger, Steffen shifted my field of vision to an area on the far-right side of the altar, almost behind it. I focused in on the telltale blackwood rosaries, a whole group, some that I had never seen at the pueblaire, older, perhaps even locals. The group's growing, Steffen whispered. He then shifted the binoculars farther to the right, the bleachers by the outfield, not as packed with people. On the highest row, in the far corner, Renato sat alone, his elbows on his knees, focused on every movement below, seemingly incognizant of the pair of revolutionary guards standing a few meters to the right of him.

Steffen took the glasses and pretended to watch the inert old sermonizer for a while. When Fidel spoke at rallies, no one used binoculars—I doubt if they were allowed—but it didn't matter. Everyone had every single one of his mannerisms memorized in cadence with his voice and the subject matter of the oratory. The masses at his speeches could have as well been blind and we'd still see him. We knew him carnally by memory, as one knows an old lover. We switched back and forth with the borrowed binoculars, until Steffen had pointed out everyone we knew from the group we could find, spread out all over the stadium. I tried to keep track of Renato, but eventually the exasperated nun demanded her binoculars back.

I asked Steffen about Pascual, but he said he had heard nothing about that from Guichi or anyone else in the group. But he'd seen others I might be interested in. He called out to Dinnya, the little Russian sex dervish, wearing a blackwood rosary like the rest of us, behind the first-base dugout, standing and waving his arms around as if he were at a roquero concert. When had he appeared?

He had been driving one of the other máquinas loaded up with something. When he pulled up alongside the road on the way, Steffen realized that he wasn't the only foreigner tasked as a driver. There were others, it was not just Dinnya. The foreign students, we would find out soon enough, comprised a large part of our group.

We made our way back toward the bleachers, trying to meet up with Renato, but about halfway there, a murmur seemed to spread among the masses. It passed like a whitecap through the crowd. A group of merchants, the whispered rumor said, had gathered at Parque Vidal, the main town square, hawking everything from freshly shot quail and live chickens to homemade toothpaste and rum and hemp paper—but no sooner had the rumor reached one end of the crowd, many already shuffling toward the exits, than another rumor took shape somewhere near the altar, that no, the plaza was desolate, even the pigeons had made their way to the other side of town and the Che monument where the merchants had moved in fear. It was impossible that there were envoys coming back and forth confirming or denying each rumor—the disinformation had to be coming from inside—so like much Cuban gossip, the more tangled and illogical you made the story, the more likely it was to latch unto some semblance of the truth. So throughout the service, the imaginary merchants circled and encroached on the town like a stealthy conquering army.

By the time the service was over, a third of the stadium had left in chase of the roving black market even as the fiana tried to stop the clearing. Seemingly satisfied with having stirred the proper havoc, Renato returned to his original spot in the upper bleachers.

The Pope mounted his bubble, circled the crowd once, and disappeared, followed by his pedestrian retinue. The Pope could not have been absent from the horizon for more than a few minutes when the yellow-and-white banners began to come down. We later confirmed that they were taken overnight from Santa Clara to Camagüey to Santiago and then back to Havana. There was a shortage of cloth, and you could dress a battalion of altar boys with the material from these banners. Many pioneritos shifted in threadbare shorts to make the old pontiff feel welcome, Renato joked later on the trip. The same happened at Parque Vidal later, when it was clear that the Pope's entourage had left the parish for his flight to Havana, they stripped the welcome banners off the old colonial buildings and replaced them with the usual Cuban flags and placards of revolutionary slogans.

Before that happened, we noticed two odd-looking con-
traptions—spidery hoses protruding from a central globe,
insane-asylum white, or papist white for the occasion—
making their way along the base of the wall and reaching up
with their tentacles, blasting spots on the wall with sprays of
water. Paint chipped off, and the wet burnished clay of the
exposed brick surfaced in scab-like lesions on the façades of
the ancient buildings. When we got close enough, we noticed
that there were two soldiers sitting inside the bubble of one of
the machines, like in the belly of a tank, one clearly driving,
his eyes set forward, the other directing the tentacles, looking
up at the walls. Their attention elsewhere, we were easily
able to sneak around the back of the contraption in a wide
circle to observe its movements up close. But just as we were
about to get a look at what the thing was doing to the walls
and why, it spun around like a robotic ballerina, the glass dome
lifted and the tentacle man had a semiautomatic aimed at us.

We were disrupting revolutionary business, he said, gesturing with his weapon for us to scram. Not a good time to
do that, the driver joked, could get someone shot. What did
we want? Steffen pulled out his German passport. Stupid,
because it forced me to pull out my Cuban carnet, which I did
lifting my rosary at the same time.

The Pope, I said.

The viejito's gone, adios, the tentacle man laughed, back to
la Revolución, muchachos.

What are you doing? Steffen dared.

Cleaning, the driver said. There are little pest birds that have
been shitting on the walls. He looked at me. The tentacle man
waved his rifle again. From far away it was impossible to see
what their targets were, arbitrary spots on the wall, but from
the looks on Renato's and Bertila's faces when they joined us,
we could guess. We had only been in town a handful of hours

and the group was already leaving its marks, under the papal banners, so that it seemed that they had been there longer than that very day. Now I knew for sure that all the rumors about wandering vendors had been somehow generated from the lonely corner spot on the top of the bleachers, to better sneak his boys out with hungry members of the crowd. Or was it for something else? Was this a dress rehearsal on how to get the crowd riled up as a distraction?

The following morning the same walls that were now being cleansed would be covered with the sacrificio graffiti again, on top of the bleached scabs on the wall, the word encircled by flames, but the white tanks would have moved on to Camagüey. Only but for a lagging reporter from the *Miami Herald,* who I am convinced Renato had purposefully gotten so drunk that night so that he missed his ride, would the phenomenon become known to the entire world, what he called in a style fueled by nothing more than the hangover poisons of jarfuls of aguardiente a plague of colorful locust shells, phantom flames that threatened a coming conflagration, proclaiming perhaps one of the greatest youth threats to the Castro regime in its forty-year history, a clear sign to the rest of the world that all is not as well as the government would want to make the pontiff believe from its well-behaved crowd at the first Mass.

His byline was Otto Torres, but he asked us to call him Ototó, which made him sound like some orisha. A real cubano-americano, vaya. We didn't see a lot of them in those days. He wore a white linen guayabera, khaki pants, and shiny white Yuma sneakers with the swoosh. This was only his third time in the country. He had been born in a military base in Albuquerque, New Mexico, and looked more American than a yanqui comic book character, dirty blond hair, pale skin that tanned surprisingly well, and eyes, I would notice, that changed color throughout the day, a hazy gray in the morning, pellucid green right before the siesta hour, and a milky blue before the sun went down. When he approached us, he said he had noticed us in the lull before the Pope left the Mass for the airport.

Who are you? he said in perfect Spanish, but with that leeched Miami accent. We smiled at his nickname, the name of a god perhaps, but also likely an appellation for an engorged vagina in some parts of the Island. We told him he should make it his byline. He said he'd think about it. But the ribbing belied the seriousness of his task in the country. He wanted something more than some drab feature story about communists going all Christian overnight, which no one bought anyway. I think from the moment he saw us, he picked us out for what we were, a band of dangerous malcontents that hadn't come for the spectacle, or on a religious pilgrimage, or because the State had forced us. When Renato saw me chatting with him under a tamarind tree, he came and sat by us, put his arm around my shoulder and listened.

Hola, I said to Renato. I had not talked to him since before I had left for Cecilia's. He had not, and would not in the future, inquire as to what had happened there, although Steffen told me he knew that's where I had gone from the moment he noticed me missing. Sigue, sigue, he said, making a gesture toward the reporter. This is Ototó, I said. Renato kept a serious expression. He reached out his hand to Ototó, and repeated that we should continue, not mind him, even as he scooted closer on the bench, put his hand on my thigh. Ototó repeated the first questions he had asked me, and then read the answers I had given from his notebook. We were a group of young Catholics, an organization banned on the Island until two or three months before the Pope's visit, technically, we could still go to church and celebrate Mass, none of them had been officially closed, but many of them had been torn down, condemned as abandoned structures, or expropriated for more useful purposes.

These are not all lies, Renato proffered when Ototó had finished. He removed his rosary and slipped it over Ototó's neck, took another one from a pocket, and donned the new one. These conditions, they exist. He jabbed Ototó's open notebook. But it's not who we are. Tell him the truth, he commanded me, sin miedo. It was as if he was challenging me to tell the reporter who I wanted to be. Ototó straightened. He looked at me and then at his notebook and let out a sigh. But then he flipped to a new page, and put his pen to it, waiting.

We're not Catholics, I said. The pen did not move. Renato's eyes were closed, his chin lifted now. He whispered, Tell him, that's what he wants to write about. I don't know where I began—it might have been the night in the henhouse, because as soon as I said something, Ototó began to jot down words in his notebook, and it was not until he had run out of paper and had to run to his máquina to get another notepad that I stopped.

When we were alone, Renato encouraged me again to tell him the truth. It would be good for the outside world to know. That's what we needed.

I'm not sure I know the whole truth, I dared respond.

None of us do.

When Ototó returned, I told him about Nicolás, about his death, his burial, about Cecilia, about comandante Juan, about my visits to the sidatorio, about the Russian, about Oliver who was now Steffen, about the pueblaire, about Guichi, about our exodus in the pilgrimage trucks. I had not mentioned Renato directly at all. I don't know why, and he remained still beside me. I told Ototó about the graffiti, about the curse we were about to unleash on the shaky revolutionary framework.

I told him about the injected ones, and he said he had read about it in the yanqui newspaper story.

¿Y usted? Ototó turned to Renato in Spanish, using the awkward formal address, as if he were questioning a head of state. You are El Líder? Renato smiled. El Líder was being pampered in the Palace of the Revolution, he said, his gray beard trimmed, his bloody hands manicured before his audience with the Pope. It was a ready-made quote, and Ototó underlined it after he wrote it. He waited for more, but Renato did not offer anything else for now. He kissed me on the cheek before he walked away. He turned. Stay with us, he promised Ototó, and you'll have more story than by following the viejito back and forth to Havana after every Mass.

The group had begun to move on to the encampment for the night. Ototó protested that he had to cover the audience of the Pope with Fidel in Havana, but that he would meet up with us on the way back. I told him that if he left, Renato would not talk to him again. I opened his notebook, put his pen in position. This time I remember going back over the details of the night in the henhouse, Nicolás's awkwardness, Renato's tragic docility, my own inexplicable inertia.

Then Ototó began to pepper me with so many questions, even as I put the words together myself it seemed that the story had suddenly become a feature on me. Is that what you're doing here? Some sort of redemption, o algo así? Trying to save the younger brother? Or trying to become one with him, pues? Some great rebel hero yourself? All of us are obsessed with that, no?

Us, who? I asked.

Us cubanos, he said somewhat ridiculously.

Unlike the young leader, though, Ototó scoffed, I did not seem like I had much of the counterrevolutionary or counter-anything in me. *Dale,* no offense. Among his string of questions, a few jumped out: When had it happened to me? Had I submitted to it just as willingly? Were we all acting out some collective death wish? When I replied aloud that some of us weren't infected, Ototó clicked his tongue in irritation, convinced I had begun to lie again. He looked at me as he might on a senile old uncle whose delusions he indulged so as not to upset into a deeper bout of dementia. Then I saw a part of him, the eyes grayish now and broken up into sharp crystals, wanting to breach some frontier for the first time.

What about the violence this past summer? he asked, keeping the query as general as possible so that I could wander freely across my own frontier.

Cubans knew better than to talk about the events of the long summer of the bombs with foreigners, much less a journalist, but the Visit had gulled us into a false sense of security. I tried to explain some of this to Ototó, and he continued taking notes furiously but soon afterward walked off, not really pressing me for an answer to the original question. I thought he had made his choice. But when he made it back to the group before we had left for the encampment, he would explain to us that he had gone to phone in his first story on our group from his hotel room. I would later learn it appeared on the *Miami Herald*'s brand-new website that very night, and on the back page of the special coverage section of the Pope's visit the following morning. It was not the volatile type of piece of the days that followed, but one that raised the question of certain groups following the Pope trying to get attention to modes of civil disobedience that would certainly not be endorsed by the Church or any human rights groups. Ototó's editor had asked him to confirm that the groups were native born and not some MacGuffin set up by the folks in Miami. When he returned, he told me this and asked me directly if we were receiving money from Miami or Spain.

We had no money, I laughed, but also told him about Pascual Zúñiga, the fallen hero father in exile, and Ototó promised to have the paper run a check on him—although he seemed taken aback that I knew the name, which made it clear that he did also.

He said he would stay with us and then moved to try to talk to others, getting information for the follow-up story. Before we walked to the encampment, Renato led us to a small hill to the north, one of many spots in the city where time froze to celebrate el Che's final victory, the derailment of a government munitions train on December 28, 1958. The original bulldozer used to block the path of the train sat on a concrete plinth, looking more functional than most vehicles on the road in these parts of the provinces. With the train itself, the central piece of the memorial, the violence of what must have been the original crash had been sublimated, the effect now aesthetic, the wooden tracks not mangled but shooting heavenward like spears. The monument evoked an effect as disturbingly sterile as the original crash must have been gut-wrenching. Renato asked the journalist what he knew about this moment in Cuban history—but before Ototó could respond, he told the tale. The derailment had split the Island in two, government troops east of Santa Clara lay down their arms and fled west. Che then assumed his role as mythical revolutionary, all because of that night in this town. The foreigner, the great hero.

No revolución, no matter how just, is guaranteed success. And this was one of the most just, Renato added dramatically. For a while. He went in and climbed on one of the train cars. I saw a few uniformed revolutionary police watching from a distance on the side of the hill, but they remained still, smoking their cigarettes, pretending to look elsewhere. Unaware, Ototó continued taking notes. The policemen looked on unfazed, chatting with each other now. Tonight, Renato finished, we'll camp in a field near the monument of the tyrant's flunkey's mausoleum. Maybe break in and pull out the bones, crush them, and use the holy dust as camouflage. The boys in the group cheered, but this time even Ototó looked up and waited for someone to interrupt Renato. Little remained perhaps as sacred in Cuba as the handless bones of the revolutionary hero—no insult against a dead compadre considered higher treason than an assault on Che. Renato put on a show for the journalist, but he also wanted to taunt the uniformed men into responding. It was not yet their time, I realized.

It began to drizzle, and we moved on. Steffen ran up to Ototó and me. He had reconnected with Dinnya, who greeted me effusively walking alongside, then he greeted Ototó. I introduced the reporter, and he quickly grew interested in Steffen, interviewing him in English on the way. I nodded at Dinnya, as if we had met once at some formal occasion and not fucked in the wilderness.

At the encampment, Inocente St. Louis had dug a pit, fired coals, lined it with banana leaves to protect the fire from the rain, and roasted a pair of buried pigs, donated by the Church he said, but I knew they had come in one of the trucks, black market goodies. As he waited for the meal to be ready, he doused his face with a bucketful of water, pulled out his torches, lit them from the embers in the bonfire pit, and performed for those gathered there, spinning the fires so that they became burning wheels that in a moment turned into single long flames following on the tails of each other heavenward before separating again and spiraling downward. The first extinguished in his mouth as Inocente St. Louis leaned back and swallowed it, then the others. I could smell the singeing of some of the coarse hairs of his wet beard. Impossibly, the fire seemed to remain alive in his mouth because after swallowing the last flame, he relit each of the torches with his breath and continued his performance. Ototó, for once, stopped scribbling, his mouth agape.

Don't they eat fires in el exilio? Renato asked, slapping him on the shoulder. Sometimes that's all we have to eat here.

Many who were staying in the hotels in the city for the night came to join the twilight feast, younger Europeans and South Americans, some Canadians. The longer they lingered in the perennial drizzle, the higher that mud rose up their bright, crisp clothes and rendered them indistinguishable from us. A group of drummers had formed a circle near an abandoned barn. Others joined in, transforming the finquero's farming tools and supplies into makeshift drums, gigantic maracas, claves, and güiros. From somewhere, a barrel of rum appeared, and the crowd grew larger—bonfires dotted the campsite, and other musical conjuntos took shape. I drank with them, let the Miami reporter get his information from others, thinking that perhaps later he would be able to cue me in on anything he had found out—though if he were to uncover anything of real importance, he would have to shake off Steffen, who now served as his erstwhile host, formally introducing Ototó to others. I should have warned Ototó—he better hide under Bertila's musty mantles, let her guide him to his story from there. But I didn't see her anywhere.

I would have hardly recognized Ototó when I saw him again after dark a few hours later if I had not noticed the black notebook rolled up into his back pocket. He had shed his button-down guayabera and expensive Yuma sneakers and adopted the uniform of the tribe: dusty leather sandals, grimy camiseta, and pionero hanky tied around his head like a pirate—even some patchy down on his chin and jaw muscle that I must not have noticed before. He sat by Renato around the central bonfire in deep conversation. It was late, past midnight. Steffen, Dinnya, and I had retreated from the festivities into one of the makeshift tents, rusted pipe tubing and rigged plastic canvases borrowed from Guichi, the young Russian a spur biting at the haunches of our drained desires. We joined the semi-public sex spectacle that became so increasingly evident throughout the night. With the Russian, Steffen and I became the lovers we could not be to each other alone—within the confines of the shoddily erected tent, the only article that we did not shed, the blackwood rosaries. When we were finished the first time, Dinnya left in only a pair of briefs and an inch-thick layer of mud and procured two canteens full of rum, which we sipped while we waited to revive, wordless, lying separately in the mud, waiting, growing drunker not so much with the rum, but with the possibility of the night outside of the cheap plastic canvas.

Tonight, we join or no, Dinnya said. He tapped the inside of his forearm. He did not smirk as usual, which produced an ironing effect on his words. I let the comment pass because of his drunkenness and the lingering euphoria of the sex. But Steffen drew a deep breath, grimaced as if he had just been asked to eat dog flesh. Dinnya scoffed. He put on his clothes and moved out. Steffen's reaction made it feel not as if he were complicit with the authorities but as if he knew that he couldn't commit himself to such mass lunacy like some of the other foreigners.

We followed the Russian out so we wouldn't have to talk about it.

We moved toward the roasting pit. At the edge of the bonfire, the journalist was disguised like some ragged king among his troops. Dinnya rejoined us and filled new rum canteens. Steffen procured platefuls of dinner and we sat and watched, others gathering around the central bonfire as the smaller ones burned out. Some, very drunk, tried to replicate the feats of Inocente St. Louis and burned their faces. In the distance, the glow of the illuminated memorial to Che seemed like a distant galaxy, casting light that no longer existed at its source. This was all part of the act—I wondered how long it would take the reporter to figure it out—the fire-eating, the injected ones, the civil disobedience, the foreign students, maybe even me.

I thought I saw Bertila wrapped in her mantles, but it was a pair of naked boys, huddled together by the roasting pit, sharing a ragged blanket. Inocente St. Louis had devotedly set up a bed of palm fronds all around the pit for folks to sit and eat. He seemed somewhat at a loss now without Bertila by his side, hesitant with others, his mountainous presence diminished, as if the empty spaces beside him presented a threat. Maybe that's why he kept performing his fire-eating tricks that night—not just to keep the group amused but as if to mock the empty spaces surrounding him.

As he performed with the fires one more time, the journalist and Renato disappeared. They're doing what everybody else has been doing, Steffen announced. He's irresistible that one, no? I wasn't sure which one he was talking about. He passed the canteen to me, pulled off his camiseta, and circled the fire, getting closer and closer and closer with each go-around, so that his pale skin grew covered in darkening cardinal patches.

Others joined him—and the more the group grew, the tighter their synchronicity, guided by some instinct of which they were wholly unaware—methodically shedding articles of clothing, though from the mud it was hard to tell who was still wearing what. At one point, an arm reached out—it must have been Steffen's, but I couldn't tell—and pulled me into the fray. It held me by the wrist for a moment, two, until I had gathered momentum, found my spot in the orbiting mass, and then let go, abandoned my body to the energy of the whole. My arms and legs fell into a natural rhythm—suddenly treading air—as if some current had hurled me into a kneading whirlpool.

By the time I saw Renato clearly, my skin felt clean and smooth and new. I did not notice my own nakedness until I noticed the nakedness of others. It was different than in the pueblaire water ritual, nudity soon forgotten. Here, it seemed the beginning of something, requisite and sacramental. The fire still raged, but the persistent drizzle that had been falling daylong now intensified into a hard rain, long and straight as house nails—whatever pockets of caked mud remained on our bodies washed off—the sky at war with our ceremonial fire. Renato appeared to emerge out of it, a hand reaching out for me in a pleading gesture that nevertheless conveyed dominance.

Where was the reporter? I thought, somehow sensing there could be no logic in anything I tried to figure out at the moment. I'd been transposed from one side of the stage to the other. Ototó had his story now—I wanted to think *this* was it. I let Renato's hand fall on my shoulder, and incomprehensively it seemed to provide a cover from the pelting rain—or had the downpour suddenly stopped? What Renato began to perform with me became quickly reflected in other groups scattered around us. I kept my eyes on the wiggling figures beyond the fire's exhalations, feeling like that doleful figure trapped inside a mirror—move arm outward, turn it, palm heavenward, stretch it out as if serving some miniscule precious stone nestled in between the love- and lifelines of the palm, wait, the rain dwindling, innocuous, a dribbling showerhead.

Renato was much more adept than his brother had been, using his teeth, his elbow pinned against his ribs, his other hand quickly knotting a tourniquet around his arm, then mine.

The rest of it clinical, ordinary. Actions that Nicolás had cow-
ered and hesitated over were performed by his brother with
the dexterity of an experienced butcher going at a chicken.

Renato had my wrist—but for the first time, I saw him
hesitate. I thought he was looking into my eyes, seeking per-
mission, something I was not able either to give or deny—I
owed him that at least, I thought. His call. Just like it had
been mine not to act. But Renato looked beyond me, past my
shoulders, guessing at what distraction lay beyond the halo
of the fire. He grabbed my arm and then pushed me away,
ripping the tourniquet off my arm in one tug without even
undoing the knot, the syringe still held aloft in the other
hand, loaded still, his hand still on the trigger, but some safety
had been set off, not in the mechanism itself, but in Renato's
hand—the syringe now seemed small, harmless, disposable.

Someone's looking for you, hermano, he said in a mocking
singsong, a three-note melody he had stolen from his brother,
signaling behind me.

I did not turn or move away. I felt his arm wrapped around
my belly, pulling me away—but that would have been impossible, he was backing away two meters across from me. The
laughter, now singed with ridicule, beyond the fire from which
he had appeared, and which was also his.

In the shadows on the other side of the fire, I realized that
Ototó had been the one to grab me, violated his professional
code and become a participant, his disguise of no use to him
in the shadows, his squarish muscular frame unmistakable.
He led me toward a taller figure, much taller, the torso slightly
curved forward, the neck bent downward so that it seemed
an effort to look up at us. Ototó, behind me, held me by the
shoulders, but the closer I came to the other figure the more
I resisted, pushed back. I heard Renato laughing from some
other planet and told myself that it was only a hallucination,

a trick of the eye, the mind, all the senses—the rum, the crazy sex, the two days without sleep. But there he was, as the glow of the fire finally let me see his face, his hair longer and threaded with silver strands, the face wrinkled but only in a way that seemed to defeat time after a long struggle, not submit to it, his eyes risen from the craggy caverns of the last days of his illness, his body whole, thin still, but not ravaged, disguised as priest, with the white collar and everything.

He's confused, the figure said with a sympathetic tone I had never heard him use before. And then addressing me with the formal *usted*, I'm not who you think. He smiled—his teeth yellowed, an upper one on the right rotted and brown. Is this the great indignity? I thought. We get our flesh back but rotted, disfigured, made ancient.

This is the one, Ototó said in his Miami Spanish.

The little maricón better not have harmed him, the figure said in perfect English. The voice, also, was like Nicolás's in tone now, but grainier, this phantom receiving a bad transmission from the soul that had once been my novio. Wrap him up, coño, he's in shock. Ototó pulled a dirty blanket from somewhere, maybe tugged it from the naked boys. The phantom stood on tiptoes and glanced toward the fire. He got another one, Ototó said. We should have done something. Done what, estúpido? With an infected needle in his hand. At least we got this one. We didn't get him; he let him go. It was because of me, the phantom said, slapping his chest. He took my face in one hand and squeezed it. It's okay, it's okay, machito. Out of harm's way. For now, Ototó said. They chit-chatted back and forth, finally deciding on taking me to the phantom's tent, where they built a small fire. They washed my body with damp cloths, clumsily put borrowed clothes on me, and forced me to eat cold rice and black beans.

What? Have you all gone on a fast as well? the phantom

asked me. If one thing doesn't get you, the other one will. He chuckled. ¿Qué es esto? The new revolution of skeletons and zombies?

Ototó pulled out his notebook.

Mira, the phantom said, switching back and forth between Spanish and English, many things have been said about me. I don't want you to get scared. In some versions I am the grieving, repentant father returning for his dead and dying sons. In others, I am still in the employ of the State, for whose sake I abandoned family to live my life abroad as an agent, Madrid, London, Miami. Graham Greene himself couldn't have invented such garbage. He put a hand on my knee. Me llamo Pascual. You must know lots of other versions of me. He pointed back toward the central fire. That's not a revolution, optimism, life out there, that's just a culture of death. And it's going to get worse. I won't allow that.

That's why I brought this one from Miami. The best investigative journalist south of the *New York Times*. He has put many a tainted político behind bars in el exilio. Not that we are expecting that here.

Does Cecilia know you're here?

He seemed surprised by the question, hesitated before answering. Juan knows, so there must have been some pillow talk, he finally responded with a smile too bitter by several doses. He has taken care well what I left him, except for my sons . . . except for my sons.

It was not comandante Juan's fault, I said in a surprisingly defensive tone. Whatever charge you left him, the only one he took seriously was the protection of your wife. And why would you leave your sons to anyone, de todas formas?

He ignored the question. Protection . . . sí, que bien. All right, protection.

As far as I know, I said, Cecilia has still not slept with him.

You don't know much, niño, do you? Pascual passed a hand through his long, straggly hair. That and so many of his other gestures had been passed down to his older son that it was like watching an actor made up for the second act of a play years later, a tragicomedy about failed promises. Was that why Cecilia had so readily abandoned her older son? Had she seen it from the other side of the mirror, too? Had she pushed Pascual out of the country, demanded that he not return, so that he would not leave his sons with the awful farcical inheritance of revolutionary responsibility? A doomed mission, she must have recognized from the start. Only she had failed to see that such a weed had a colossal root system.

I was throwing my thoughts at the father, out of order, a chaotic desire for some semblance of concrete knowledge. If la Revolución had succeeded in subjugating its people, it had best done it in this fashion, in its willful confluence of appearance with reality, so that one both defined and distorted the other. Bertila had been right. We were a nation of ghosts, the world moving past us, leaving us trapped in some pocket of the last century, stranded, a curiosity at the international carnival. I turned to the reporter. This is different. Write that in your stories. People think that they are living in some State-generated dream. Only that like in all dreams, it takes a life of its own, and the State's dream becomes the collective pesadilla of hundreds of thousands. Write that.

That's not what he's here for, Pascual interrupted. He's here for you. For these young souls throwing their lives away.

By what? By telling the entire world. That's what we want. You threw yours away, I said. Your life.

Okay, okay, the reporter intervened. We're not here for recriminations. I have to leave you two, and I don't want either of you getting involved. I likely spent whatever trust I had built up with that intervention back there.

It was a favor to my wife, cabrón. I owed her that much, Pascual shouted to me apropos of nothing, and then turned to Ototó. And you owe me. I've handed you the story of the end of the century. And it's not even begun yet, I'll kill the end of it yet. You can write that.

Ototó nodded politely, clearly not understanding the last part, and left us.

These gusanos, he said, they think they can save anything. Maybe it's good to let them keep believing that. Someone has to. But this one is over his head already. I thought he had more grit in him.

They had met when Ototó worked a feature story on exiles that had risen in the Communist Party and eventually abandoned the Island. Not a small bunch, vaya, from the armed forces, to the arts and the universities, to the core of the People's National Assembly, even a character that claimed to have once been Fidel's personal masseuse. Naturally all these former Fidelistas railed against the system that they had been instrumental in constructing, Pascual included. But that was not the aim of the piece—the aim was to try to get at the exact moment when each of the former comuñangas decided that they had had enough. At what point exactly did Cuba's sublime socio-political experiment become all fucked up for them? And this became the question that stumped most of them. All of them to the person could remember the exact date and time of day when they had become enamored of la Revolución, thunderstruck by the bearded Cupid in fatigues. But as for the letdown, many of them came up with different events, some that had left them disillusioned at first, and others later, already knowing that one day they would leave, but few could pinpoint that exact moment in time when their conception of the socialist experiment shifted from one extreme to the other. Otto Torres concluded in his feature that maybe it was the wear of even the most honorable and boulder-sized utopian convictions from a life that did nothing but fail to live up to itself, until the boulder was no more than a pebble that could be skipped across the Florida Straits.

It was very poetic, Pascual said. Pero la cosa es, when he interviewed me, I *had* given him my epiphany moment. Vaya, I didn't think he really believed me after interviewing all the other exiles. There was no such thing, they all asserted. Falling out of love is a process that you could endlessly lie to yourself about, so you can extend the timeline forever. The opposite of falling in love, in which there is no lying, the body and the mind don't allow it. Maybe even el viejito had fallen out of love, the article stated somewhere, but could not imagine abandoning his ailing beloved, the Island itself. Understandable to a degree, Otto Torres wrote, which infuriated not only most of the readers in Miami, but also the old Fidelistas who had granted him interviews. But Ototó never writes a single thing that he does not believe to be the truth, which can sometimes get you in trouble in Miami. The truth there has to be coated in the rancid nostalgia of forty-year-old compost heaps.

That's why I thought he had some cojones. Why I brought him along.

But that was it. That was the moment that he had described for Otto Torres. One evening coming late from his office at the National Assembly, he came upon his youngest boy on the patio, diligently doing his reading and writing. He was a child but could already parrot everything that Pascual heard every day at the capitol, about la lucha and el honor and el sacrificio as if he thought such shit on his own. Except it was worse, because the child actually believed what he said. Pascual sat down and helped Renato with his homework until the boy could not keep his eyes open. Then he took him and carried him up the stairs pretending that his son was still a toddler, the boy's head resting on his shoulders. On the way up he decided—he would not let his own life happen to his boy. Not that he was disillusioned himself, not with his role in la Revolución. But the legacy that they were supposed to pass on to future generations was one of prosperous equality, no matter the gender or race—pero en vez de eso, they had created a labyrinthine fidelocracy, como le dicen por ahí, where only those slavishly loyal benefit. His younger child would have grown into a stalwart member of the Party if not for his decision to leave, so he decided to flee, to lead by example, thinking his sons would follow, and eventually his wife.

So why return to this shit show now? Or was that all bullshit, too? Like the stories he had made up about political imprisonment. Who are you?

He had not returned for his wife, he responded, ignoring my question, although he still loved her—but whether I knew it or not, she was more comandante Juan's now than anyone's—not for his dead son, although he had grieved, moved from Spain to Miami when he heard, a letter from comandante Juan dated the day after the burial in the mahogany coffin—and not for his youngest son, not exactly.

He'll remember me, Pascual said, standing up and stepping out of his shoes, undoing the priest's collar, and removing his shirt, his pants, his underwear. His pale unmuddied body, the tiny hairy breasts womanish, the incongruous protrusion of the belly just above the crotch, his shrunken sex cowering under a thick briar of pubes, the long skeletal legs and feet made it seem as if his ravished flesh was another apt disguise that he had donned for the occasion. He made a gesture with both of his hands down the length of his body. This is what exile does to a man, muchacho. Rots you from the inside. Stay here. I am glad my family did. The inferno that's yours is preferable to the inferno invented by others. Some poet wrote that, no? He walked away from me toward the fire, the mud rising up the stilts of his legs as if by osmosis.

It did not take long for him to find his son among the youths still flitting around the flames. He did not reach out and embrace him or attempt to say anything, but stood there, as some of the dancing boys began to gather around.

He reached out his arm.

Renato at first hesitated, either because the moment for the ritual had passed, or because he recognized the floating torso—but then the boys began to whoop, throwing up their arms and calling for one more. Someone handed Renato a pair of cloth bands and syringe. The figure of his father bent toward him, his extended hand now almost touching Renato's chest, the arm turned upward, docile. When Renato reached out and took it by the wrist, Pascual's torso jerked backward as if stung and almost threw the two figures into the mud. But Renato dug in and held on, tying the tourniquets without ever letting go—on his father's arm, on his. He drew blood from the arm that held on to Pascual, the syringe filling up in an instant, and he plunged it into Pascual's arm without even searching out a vein, a stab that sent a surge of pain through the tall figure, which momentarily straightened and then dropped to the mud, the syringe still in its arm.

FAVOR FIRE

Ototó's most read and reprinted story on the *Miami Herald* website would not be phoned in until after the night of the fire in Santiago. But by the morning of the second Mass in Camagüey—in the belly of the crocodile-shaped Island—Ototó had already sent in a pair stories—working on a third—that appeared in both the Spanish and English language versions of the *Herald,* and the series had instantly attracted a large readership. His editor had told him to forget about his original assignment on Pope detail. By that afternoon, he told us, news websites around the world had begun to syndicate the pieces.

The articles portrayed a large subset of attendees at the first Mass as those marked by the State as desvinculados, translated in the article as outcasts or undesirables, engaging in inventive, dangerous, and suicidal forms of civil disobedience while the authorities did their best to ignore them, hoping the rest of the world would, as well. No names of the numerous sources for the articles had been printed to not endanger the nihilistic young protesters, who claimed to ride the cusp of a new revolution for the new millennium. Ototó mentioned the graffiti only in passing in the second article, referring to it as perhaps signs or heralds of more aggressive subversion to come to embarrass the State and its ruling Party while the eyes of the world were upon it—in the end, making the connection that not even Renato had dared to make with many in the group, including me, to the violence of the recent long summer of the bombs.

After this, it seemed that the only way to keep from getting rounded up by the increasing presence of undercover agents of the Directorate, more than I had ever thought possible but easily spotted by the fat in their cheeks, the healthy resplendence of skin, and their revenant stares, was to remain within watching distance of the reporter. The last thing the government wanted was stories of arrests during the Pope's visit. Responding to the "foreign little stories," *Granma* reported in its special coverage of the Pope's visit that very morning, that although, "like those in Cuba," international reporters were free to write whatever they wanted, certain stories sent from the Island seemed more in the vein of the fantastical tales of the yanqui horror writer Edgar Allan Poe. The sturdy Cuban populace did not need to resort to such base expressions of discontent. There was no discontent, moreover. All Grand Guignol fiction created by the cruel propagandists of the Miami and Washington Mafias.

At the Mass in Cienfuegos that afternoon, even the pontiff seemed to make an elusive reference to Ototó's articles in his homily, quipping that the freedom of the individual need not be acquired through random acts of violence or harm to the innocent but rather through the collective and peaceful force of charity, that those in despair should not fall to the easy temptation of vengeance, that instead, it was Christian charity, for those less fortunate, for those who have failed to accept the light, and sí, sí, hasta for our oppressors, that it was only such charity that opened up the soul to the possibility of true liberty.

It's easy to talk that way, Pascual said, doing a drooling imitation of the Parkinson's-stricken pontiff, when you can hop a plane in two days and leave.

Pascual was dressed in his crisp priest's outfit again, somehow free of mud, and told anyone who asked that we were a youth group from his congregation of Nuestra Señora de Guadalupe in Pinar del Río. No one seemed to notice or care that there were so few pious females in the congregation from el monte.

Everyone had been so drunk the night before that the lofty sentiments coming from the altar seemed unattainable at the moment. I had been one of the last to rouse out of our muddy beds and wash in a nearby stream, so I had never seen Steffen leave with the other drivers. Most of us had to trudge to the Autopista Nacional to hitch a ride on the trucks carting the pious to the next Mass. We arrived late, just as the ceremonies started, so we all got grouped together far from the stage in the purlieus of the crowd. Steffen, Dinnya, the group of drivers and their companions quickly found us. Ototó approached with them, and I became curious about what he had found out during his side trip. Perhaps they had been using him to avoid any confrontation with the authorities. He said he wanted to talk to me but wanted to interview some of those in the congregation outside of our group for his current piece.

Renato grew nervous that all of us had been bunched together and led a large troupe to the opposite side of the field where they dispersed further, and I lost sight of them until they all circled back during the Communion service to leave early. Most headed for the trucks, but I followed Ototó who now seemed to have formed a bond with Steffen and Dinnya as they separated from us to return to their máquinas. They all ignored me at first as I walked alongside, but eventually Steffen turned to me, insisting it was too dangerous for me to go with them. The agents from the Directorate, he pronounced assuredly, were keeping much closer tabs on the Cuban nationals. They would just stop the máquinas and grab me. I would give them an excuse to seize the "cargo." I should stay with Renato and his father. Go, before you lose them, he said as he tried to shake me.

I grabbed his forearm and held him as the others hurried to wherever they had hidden their cacharros from the goons of the Directorate, Ototó with his notepad out as always. The man was devoted, if anything. Steffen tried to pull away, but I wouldn't let him, and he quickly got annoyed.

I'm not the one you should be bothering with this. You know the position I'm in is not any different than yours.

Oh, now you have a position?

Look, go with him. He said he must let you know tonight. Before we arrive. He looked around, itchy to try to get away again, but now also clearly eager to get something out. Anyone can leave if they want to. Anyone. Before—

What have they told you? Who?

I have to go. He looked. The others had stopped, turned, and were waiting for him, still fervently discussing whatever they had been talking about before I caught up with them.

Almost everyone knows now, Steffen conceded, but Renato, he must tell you himself. That's what he wants. He has to hear from your own lips with his own ears. To make sure. He paused. I'm not sure I am, but we're all in now. We must be.

Has someone threatened you?

Steffen shook his head, grabbed my face with both hands and gave me a long kiss, rubbed the cross on my blackwood rosary, and then rubbed the one on his—as if that could fix things.

I'll see you in Santiago, he said. You'll be another person then. He ran to catch up with the others, who all turned to speak to him, but he turned from them and waved at me before they all disappeared into a nearby alleyway off the main street.

As I made my way back to our gathering spot on the Autopista Nacional, through the old colonial town that now seemed to have forgotten about its holy visitor and gone back to the daily business of resolviendo, I hoped that they had all left without me. Not that I would not follow the group to Santiago, but that I would make it there on my own. But as soon as I came within sight of the group, still huddled on the shoulder of the road, waiting for the trucks, Renato spotted me and dashed toward me. ¡Hermano, te me pierdes! He guided me to a specific spot up ahead where some of the trucks with new pilgrims had begun to pull up.

Some of them won't make it, he said, indicating to the back of the line where I'd been heading. I thought he meant something else, at first. Most of the ones with the blackwood rosaries had bunched up front. Pascual had taken the helm again, it appeared, and loudly negotiated with the driver about just how many could mount on his flatbed. Renato walked up to his father and tried to interject something, but the driver ignored him, concerned with negotiating only with the man in the priest's outfit. Finally, Pascual waved for a horde from our group to climb up. Renato grabbed me. He made sure I remained close by on the crowded flatbed but barely said anything for the first few hours. It would be a long ride to the southeast coast of the Island, and no one was in the mood for the trip.

As night fell, it grew cool and drizzly, and we huddled in small groups on the rumbling flatbed to keep warm and relatively dry. The truck rose through the hilly terrain into the heart of the easternmost province, making no stops, so some of the men leaned dangerously across the railing to relieve themselves. Others tried to distance themselves to avoid the splashes. At one point near dawn, Renato scooted through the flatbed to check on those in our group. He brought back a thermos of cold coffee and a chunk of cheese, which he bit into and handed to me. He wrapped one arm around me and signaled with a fist to the dozing figure of the priest, whom I didn't realize had mounted the first truck with us, letting others negotiate for themselves. When Pascual looked up, Renato beckoned him over. The father crawled over, lay beside his son, curled up, and promptly dozed off again, gently snoring. Renato pulled one of the blankets from the others and placed it over his father.

He whispered in my ear that if I wanted to return to the capital, things could be arranged—circumstances might call for greater sacrifices in Santiago. The State would be ready— it did not take such embarrassments lightly, not underneath the watchful eye of the world. Was I sure I wanted to stay?

I nodded. He was about to get up and go sit with others, have the same talk with them before we arrived, I imagined, but I held him.

Explain to me what all this is. Por favor, just explain it to me, I pleaded. I meant everything, from the cryptic graffiti, to the willful infection of each other, to whatever was going to happen in Santiago, for what? He could not possibly believe all the bobería that had been coming out of his brother's mouth during his last days. Renato listened, said nothing, waited for me to go on. Did you believe it? I asked. You're not doing this for him, are you? You've never been the type, conversant with ghosts like your brother was.

Never been the poetic type like you, either, he said.

What about your father? Your own father? Was all this necessary to get what you want? I told him I was with him, wherever this went. I just wanted to understand. I couldn't abandon him because I had nowhere else to go, even here, near my home province. Nowhere else I wanted to go, mejor dicho. Not anymore. He huddled closer to me, an arm draped around me again.

The rush of air from the rumbling truck blew his hair into his face, and I could not read his expression, though I had purposefully turned my body to face him.

You know I wasn't forced into anything, he said. It's what I wanted that night in the henhouse. I had asked him to do it while we were out drinking that night. It saved me from the military service without having to beg Juan for the favor he had pulled for Nicolás. You're lucky you've never been rounded up for that. No one has been forced to do anything. And I wouldn't do it to you. Not the other night by the fire. Not now. Not if it's not what you want.

He added that I had it wrong, anyway. The ritual is just a symbol, like all rituals.

A symbol? I said. You're really infected. No jodas. So is your own father now. You're dying, or you will be soon. I looked over at Pascual, now hidden completely under the blanket.

Santiago will be a turning point.

What's going to happen? I asked.

Fidel will fight back there. He's not going to let this subversion get to the Mass in the capital. This is our only chance. But he's got a big problem, the world is watching, and he doesn't have as much control so far out in the provinces.

He also keeps tabs, I added, for when the world turns its eyes away.

Renato smiled and nodded. It's true, he muttered.

But what's going to happen? How do you need me?

There's an abandoned depot in the harbor with an underground printing press run by a professor from the University of Oriente. You'll go there first to pick up papers. You'll be with our hallowed priest helping to cause a distraction and a little havoc at the Mass, passing out the printed articles of the gusanito Ototó. We'll take care of the rest. You'll be safe, Pascual will make sure.

I don't want to be safe, I said.

Renato chuckled, clapped my thigh. Don't worry then, you'll likely be arrested, roughed up. These people don't like shows in their little ceremonies. This is crucial, dangerous, actually. I don't know if the priest will be able to save you this time.

Where will you be? The others?

Pascual stirred, poked his head out, and seemed to open his eyes and look at us, but soon he was snoring again. Renato put a gentle hand on the old man's head, kept his eyes on him, and when he spoke again it was in a loud stage whisper, as if he thought that Pascual was now listening but wanted him to hear anyway.

It was me who failed you, a propósito, he said. I should have grabbed you from that bathtub that first day and thrown you bare-assed into Calle Obispo. Let you find your own way. That's what any decent person would have done, saved you from the misery of the tragic Zúñigas. He patted the old man's head now. But I was lonely, supongo. He waved away the thought with one hand. Any other way to look at it is . . . I don't know, perverse. Fuck you with your drama. I told you it was a voluntary thing. It was me who failed you. He paused. I'm sorry I made fun of you when your time came. I was very drunk. The thing with Pascual? he added, as if averting any more questions. Then interrupted himself. No, no, no, don't worry about him. He'll bury all of us. That's always been more than clear. He's the kind of survivor none of us are. That's its own kind of heroism? No?

It was too late to continue the discussion about tactics, he reasoned. You don't argue with a general about his battle plan as he crosses the frontier, do you? he asked. I had my marching orders. He shifted to speaking about how he had tried to save me from all of this, how he thought about throwing us out of the pueblaire, hoping that the German could somehow arrange to get me out, build me a candy house in the Black Forest. But Bertila commanded him not to. Nothing else was ever going to happen. The bit by the fire pit was a show for the reporter, he confessed. It gave the old man a chance to be a hero for once in his life. Or some shit like that, all a performance.

But now you're with me, he said. Así es, *dale*. This is the real thing. That's all I want. But you can't become something you're not. It took me a long time to learn that with Nicolás. Maybe I still haven't fully learned it, yet. He laughed in the same singsong tone that he had laughed at me by the fire, but this time the derision directed inward.

What about Steffen?

He has his own task. We all have one. Don't worry.

We're like steer trotting into a slaughterhouse. Is that *your* task? The voice came from under the blanket, muffled but animate. Pascual poked his head out. With his scruffy beard, his sunken eyes, his lank greasy locks, and his priest's outfit covered with the ragged cloth, he looked somehow as committed to his own purpose as his son.

Renato looked down and smiled. Buenos días, your eminence, he said. Do you always feign sleep to eavesdrop? Is that something you perfected as a spy in el exilio? He passed the thermos and the remaining cheese to his father. Pascual sat up and took them both. We're riding into the center of hell, he said. Someone else stirred beside him and looked up at Renato, and in a moment all the boys around us had awakened, as if a trumpet had blown. The eyes floated into various positions in the background, keeping a modest distance.

Renato snickered at the sudden direct interest, a forced nervous reaction. The possibility of such an outcome as Pascual predicted had been baldly suggested in what he said to me, but he clearly had not said it aloud to the many others, whatever their assigned roles in the day. Renato made it a point not to seem annoyed at his father's summation of events-to-come by ignoring it.

But Pascual did not let up. He scooted closer and said that indeed it was the sacred duty of an honorable soldier to question suicidal orders from a superior. I had been right to do it. And that indeed Renato was not my brother. What kind of a brother would do what he has done to me?

If he was really a brother, you would not be here, he said.

Renato grabbed the thermos back and took a long gulp. He wiped his lips with the back of his hand, and I saw him take a deep breath, but before it was all in, he began to exhale, evenly and methodically, speaking in an eerie monotone.

We give the reporter something more to continue to write about. We bring to life the story he put out for the world. Our only asset is our lives, if they have to be used as weapons, then let them be used.

When Pascual responded, his voice now sounded as if Nicolás had possessed the father with all of the older son's bitterness. A real rigamarole at the high altar, entonces? Like we're all old-fashioned Aztecs or something? Even as he mocked it, I believed in it and wanted to have the heart to participate in such a delusion with Renato.

Renato put a hand on my thigh. He caressed it, as if he pitied my doubt, my lack of apocalyptic conviction. There was no returning to the capital after a certain point, he announced loudly, and others awoke, the cat's eyes in the dawn grayness doubling, tripling. Those who wanted to return now, he said, could do so as soon as we arrived. There was an avioneta waiting there that Pascual had rented for just this purpose. It's what he had privately offered me but now he extended the offer to the others. Those who stayed would do all that was called for to throw the government into a state of *shock* (the word in English).

He looked at me, at the constellation of eyes that never lowered and knew the avioneta was not necessary. Neither of us could imagine that hours later I would be on it, en route to the capital.

It was almost as if Renato had known in advance the theme of the Pope's homily during the Mass celebrated in la Plaza de la Revolución in Santiago that day, the altar partially obscuring the stark monument to the revolutionary whose mother, according to the opening of the homily, knelt before a crucifix and prayed that her son would commit wholly and without reservation to the freedom of Cuba. The pontiff called for freedom and social justice. The weapon?—individual faith. It was, Pascual said, a call for rebellion, directed at the masses.

Because everyone got thoroughly frisked before entering the barricaded quadrangle in the plaza, Pascual and a handful of others from our group that had been tasked with handing out leaflets at the Mass remained a few blocks distant, outside of the perimeter of the checkpoints. The feeble voice of the pontiff amplified by giant speakers in the plaza reached well beyond us, its echoes lapping toward the bay. If there is anything the State knew how to do well, it involved the broadcasting of tedious homilies.

Copied off some Internet site—translated, typewritten, and hastily mimeographed so that it was almost illegible—the material on the leaflets was not only dangerous because of its content—the translated text of Ototó's three articles on the *Miami Herald*'s new website—but because of the source, access to the Internet was illegal. We had spread out to distribute the leaflets to as many in the still incoming congregation as possible, which left us vulnerable when the agents of the Directorate figured out what was going on.

When we had arrived in Santiago early that morning, we scrambled straight to the abandoned railway depot where most of the group had gathered. On the shores of the bay, the abandoned wharfs surrounding it had been part of one of the busiest ports in the Island before the Soviet collapse, but product had long stopped moving through during the período especial.

The large Y-shaped harbor made the half-deserted port in Havana look like a beehive. But there was a vanquished beauty to its deteriorating piers and its shuttered wooden depot. We walked on a narrow alameda bordered by single, red-tiled houses on the north side. No sign at all of the bustle in the narrow streets of the center of the city, no fiana, no graffiti. When we reached a long narrow building with shuttered wooden doors every ten or so meters, Pascual paused—he approached each door and examined its perimeter, passed his palm over the surface as if feeling for heat or any sign of life on the other side of the peeling green paint, then moved onto the next one, looking around to make sure no one watched us, his son now trailing behind him as if he had given up his epaulets for the coming battle. There were some workers away in the distance, unloading something from one of the few working piers, but otherwise only the water and the green hills across the bay looked on. Pascual finally settled on a door. He glanced at his son, who nodded. Pascual knocked a beat of three soft taps, pause, and three more percussive knocks. There was the bustle of movement and low voices on the other side. Renato scooted next to his father and traced a half-circle with his index finger around the hole where the old lock used to be, a crescent graffito in a slightly darker shade of green—*sacrificio*. He pressed it harder with his index finger as if he were flattening an insect until it smudged, and the colors tinted his finger. A rusty chain slipped out of the lock hole, and the door pushed open, as if on its own.

After passing through the doorway—a sudden blindness came on, but quickly lifted, for from the inside it became clear how dilapidated the wooden walls and doors were, streams of mottled light pouring in from all directions like water into a sinking boat, half-lit figures moving in and out of the shadows, a maelstrom of floating body parts. The sudden relief from the shadeless morning heat soon took on another dimension as well, for the warmth inside the cavernous building exerted a humid pressure on the skin, the collective breath of all those souls inside slowly condensing. A final sensation took hold, one that endured and even intensified the longer I lingered in there, the rank caged animal scent.

Renato must have noticed also, because he immediately became jittery at the sight of everyone so defenselessly packed together in one place. He separated himself from us. He seemed intent on gathering a group together and getting out. I wondered if there were other meeting places. There was a thrum in the room, undulating whispers like the shudder of locust wings.

It's too dangerous to all sit in one place like this, Pascual confirmed Renato's misgivings. He looked toward his son. He didn't trust Renato with this, he told me. He's a boy. He has no idea what he's up against. He went to find the printer, and I quickly lost him in the throng.

As my eyes adjusted to the broken light inside the abandoned depot, I spotted Bertila and Inocente St. Louis at one end of the long narrow building, a pair of cauldrons over low fires beneath them. Inocente St. Louis lit his finger with one of the fires and ate the little flames to keep a small group around him entertained. At times, he breathed out what was left of the flames and his hot breath dissipated in the fractured morning seeping in. Bertila stood beside him with a stern expression, her hands folded in front of her, not amused at all like the others by the antics—a resigned chaperone at a quinceañera feast.

Her demeanor immediately changed when I approached, although she must have seen all of us come in through the door no more than a few meters away. She beckoned me closer, grabbed my face with both her meaty hands, and kissed me on the brow, keeping ahold of me with an affection she had not expressed since before our walk on the Prado. She had shed her usual outfit and wore an oversized gray worker's coverall underneath an apron of thick cloth. Her many mantles missing, she looked less herself, leaner, less burdened and tethered to the ground beneath her feet. Inocente St. Louis wore a similar apron, but unlike when he worked in the infernal heat of the kitchen of the paladar, in his long-sleeved chef's jacket, now he wore nothing underneath the apron but a pair of ragged denim shorts.

Something had changed in Bertila. She seemed to know much more about what was to come than she had at the pueblaire, which only made sense a little later when I realized she was one of the architects of the day, perhaps of the long summer, also. She held onto my wrist as if there were an urgent secret that she needed to pass on to me if only she could get me away from the others. I was more than anything excited by this energy and the possibility that it could reignite our old antic friendship.

Inocente St. Louis tapped me on the back. I was afraid that

he would set my shirt on fire and turned quickly. He knew I wouldn't back out, he articulated, chuckling and whistling. He knew that I always wanted to be here with them. This is where I belonged. He embraced me from behind while Bertila kept ahold of my wrist and I became enveloped in the heat of the sweltering womb between them.

They offered me a bowl of the rich goat stew simmering in the cauldrons, and I realized by the jolt of hunger that struck me how long it had been since I had eaten a hot meal. I devoured two bowlfuls and would have had one or two more had Bertila not grabbed me by the arm again and pulled me away.

There was a false wall that hid a smaller room behind it. The short waist-high opening to it was covered by a door that had been unhinged from somewhere else. Inocente St. Louis hefted it to one side, and I ducked and went in first, not expecting Bertila to scurry in behind me so nimbly on all fours. She stood and brushed her apron free of dirt and led me to the other side of the room where what looked like an older child in similar work gear cranked a mimeograph machine with Pascual, who watched intently beside him, in his hand one of the copies that had come spitting out of the machine.

When Pascual saw me, he called me over, handing me the sheet of paper. The boy working the machine stopped the cranking and walked over to me. He had the face of a dried and rotted níspero, spotted and sunken with shiny black eyes like níspero seeds that seemed to be pilfering energy from the paltry residues of fat within the cavern of his skull. He was of such diminutive stature that I only recognized he was the printer and professor by imagining him standing on a soapbox when he lectured behind a lectern at the university. Yet, he projected an air of confidence from the unlikely eloquent if reedy voice, his enunciations precise, the syllables so finely chiseled that anything he uttered could easily be taken for the truth.

He said that he had done much more dangerous things in this life than print this gossip for us. And that I would be called upon soon to do much more dangerous things than distributing paper at a Mass—so to not be afraid of this.

There is a rare window of opportunity here, a gift, he proffered. It's as if the government has shut down its inquisitional offices for a spell, like abusive parents who are on their best behavior while visiting others. For the first time in his life, the child can mouth off to the parent without fear of immediate retribution and harm. Even strike out at the parent. He paused and gestured for me to peruse his handiwork on the sheet. He was enormously proud of his translation and thought he had properly captured the gusano journalist's deliriously myopic optimism about the impact of social disobedience.

He glanced at Pascual as if to beg pardon for his unflinching evaluation of the articles, and perhaps at once, of us. Pascual grunted at him to finish the work with the copies. Pascual seemed as desperate to abandon this place as his son had been. The elfish printer kept cranking the machine at the same languid pace. He complained that the letters would get smudged if he went too fast. Is that what Pascual wanted, some purple blots to start the uprising?

I began to read the leaflet that Pascual had handed me then remembered that Bertila was at the other end of the hidden room. She had not moved, and I got the feeling that she had kept her eyes fixed on me the entire time. She stood with her back to a small workstation that I had not noticed when I crawled in. I recognized the wooden crates from the pueblaire stacked to one side of the station. Most of them had been plied open and emptied. A small generator to one side powered a single bulb from directly above the working surface scattered with loose wires, half-filled beakers and flasks, tin cans full of nails, and small rocks.

The thick apron now seemed something other than a costume for playing chef by the cauldrons. There had been more important work at hand. That's why she had come ahead to Santiago. This is what her work must have involved before she had been expelled from the university faculty. This dealing with chemicals. I went to the worktable to examine it closer, but she moved for the first time and intercepted me. The look on my face likely belied any questions I did not dare ask aloud.

There are things that you don't need to know, not yet, she said. You just need to do what you need to do, with him. She pulled me away from the worktable toward Pascual. As I glanced back over my shoulder, I saw Inocente St. Louis crawl into the room and begin to attend to something at the table. I was absurdly afraid that the heat of his breath would detonate whatever pyrotechnic substances were kept there. I was confused about why Bertila had brought me back here if she didn't want me involved.

Pascual finally gathered all the sheets from the printer and led me out of the room. Shoved me out with a hand on the small of my back. He didn't let me say goodbye to anyone. He gathered a few others and hurried out of the depot. When we were climbing the escalinata—the famed stair street that led down to the railway and the bay—back into the city, I finally caught up with him.

What are they doing in there? What are they making? I knew the answer. Pascual hurried forward, leaving the small group of others behind. He didn't seem in the mood for chatting, but I pressed.

What was on that table? Will there be more?

He walked on, handed me half of the packet of mimeographed sheets.

More what, comemierda? He stopped and grabbed me by the shirt and pulled me toward him. The others saw him and stopped a few meters behind. A few passersby looked but must have thought that it was nothing more than a priest disciplining an ill-behaved youth.

You stay with me, Pascual muttered, his spittle spraying on my cheeks. You stay with me, listen to me, and stop asking questions. You saw what you saw. You've known what you know longer than you have wanted to admit it to yourself. Everybody around you has known. Why do you think I'm back here? Because I couldn't wait to come back to this bayú, this demented cockfight? He let go of me and continued up the long escalinata. The others began to walk again and passed me as if they didn't know me.

I wanted to be with Renato, with Nicolás again on that beach in Cojímar, and not with the ghost of their father disguised as a monsignor. I wanted to be with Renato not because I wanted to save him as I had made everyone else believe but because I wanted not to be saved with him. I didn't want this protection that he thought I needed. This phantom niñera trying to keep me at bay from whatever dangers had been summoned. I had stopped in the middle of the stairs and began walking back down to the harbor to find Renato, to go with him wherever he was going. By the time Pascual noticed, he had reached the top of the escalinata, and he sent his muchachos running back down to get me.

They made to grab me, but I snapped my arm away and walked ahead of them up to Pascual. He had taken a seat on the top step and put his hand out for the leaflets he had given me when I reached him.

I walked past him. Let's go do this.

My son gave you a choice, carajo, he said when he caught up with me. Déjate de pendejadas. You don't have to be here. But you can't just go wandering around. It's too risky, not for just you, for everyone, Y mira, maybe it's better if I . . . I can still—

I'm not going anywhere. I'll stay with you, I promised.

It didn't take long for us to reach the flow of worshippers still streaming into the square even though the services had started. Pascual had the others spread out to distribute the leaflets but always kept me within sight even as I lost track of him a few times. He barely glanced at those to whom he reached out a sheet, muttering, Noticias importante. Most of the people grabbed the flyers, perhaps thinking that it had something to do with the service, a way to follow the Mass for those untutored in such rituals. Almost no one stopped to read it, so we were able to continue to pass it out without disruption until we were almost out of copies, getting closer and closer to the checkpoints for the entrance.

It took a while, but there was a palpable change in the murmur of the crowd once the contents of the leaflets became evident to those that first read it on the way in and passed on the knowledge to others. It seemed the focus pulled away from the altar in the distance and the worshippers became more interested in their own lives than the heavenly one con-cocted by the old pontiff and his cronies up on stage with their conjuring of bread into flesh and wine into blood. The startled movement by the uniformed fiana and undercover agents of the Directorate to confiscate the sheets began soon after. They milled through the crowd, ripping them out of the hands of worshippers. A rustle of protest passed through the huge congregation, the largest of the three Masses so far, and the pontiff paused in his homily, and only continued when one of the priests behind him whispered something in his ear, so it must have spread to the very edge of the makeshift altar. Pascual grew concerned that eventually the buzz would settle on us like a pack of angry wasps, as many had already pointed to the source of the forbidden literature back beyond the entrance where we stood.

But just as he assured me the roundup had begun, a large group of Directorate goons moved quickly past us, and soon we began hearing from the sibilant whispers of the throng that a series of small bombs had gone off in and around the city. One near the center of the city. One in the fortress at the entrance of the harbor. One at the airport on the southern bayshore. If anyone heard them it was only the specter of the explosions as conjured by el chisme passing from one member of the congregation to the other. We had seen this at the first Mass, the word passed down and made reality in the harried unsettlement of the worshippers. The pontiff continued his homily, ignorant of the simmering panic that had taken control of the faithful. Many worshippers had begun collecting their things—blankets that they had spread out, coolers full of water to keep the midday heat at bay, plastic binoculars, missals with hymns, folding chairs—hurrying to return to the safety of home and away from the rumors of new bombs. Otra vez, they said, otra vez. ¡No que va!

But those in charge—the agents from the Directorate more than uniformed fiana—moved to keep the crowd in place, to stifle the burgeoning rumors of new violence. Pascual watched closely. He muttered, more dismayed than surprised, that the agents seemed to make up about a tenth of the crowd. Some even dressed as nuns or clergy like him.

Nothing had happened.

Stay in place.

No, no, nada de eso es verdad.

Tranquilo.

The uniforms pulled their rifles from their slings and held them with both hands at their chest, lined hip to hip at the exits.

Pascual gathered as many from our group as he could find and ordered us to move out, to scatter, to separate if necessary. He removed his blackwood rosary and ripped mine from my neck, the beads flying everywhere. By the time we got moving, the phalanx of uniformed fiana had widened and trapped us within its circle. Others wearing the blackwood rosaries had been stopped, rounded up, and loaded into detainment vans.

A plainclothes agent grabbed hold of Pascual with a hand on his chest. Where are you going, Father? Mass is not over. El papa sigue hablando su mierdita. Ven.

He ordered us to follow him, confidently walking ahead. I thought of running, but Pascual, who immediately read my perturbed expression, jutted his chin toward a group of army soldiers that had arrived as reinforcement. We were not herded to a van as some of the others, so that was some relief.

We followed the plainclothes agent to the lobby of a newly refurbished movie theater across the street from the plaza, the terrazzo floors gleaming. There, we saw others from our group, sans wooden rosaries, which were all piled on a desk where a woman in uniform was checking everyone's ID and copying any pertinent details. After identification, they were separated into another area, inside the theater itself.

We don't want to go in there, Pascual whispered. Stay with me. When the plainclothes agent demanded that we get in line with the others and get our identification cards ready, Pascual pulled out a European Union passport, protesting in an exaggerated Castilian accent that he was a citizen of Spain, feigning outrage. On the truck he had shown me a perfectly forged Cuban ID card, or maybe it was the carnet that he had used before, or one the government had given him to provide cover for his work as a foreign agent. I had never seen his Spanish papers.

The man examined the passport closely, put it up to the

light, leafed through the pages, and grunted that Pascual was free to go.

Pascual tried to grab me before the plainclothes agent could see that he was taking me, but the man stopped him with an extended arm. ¿Qué haces? he said, pulling me away from Pascual. He wanted my identification and asked to see Pascual's again. Pascual moved quickly toward me and held my wrist as I was about to produce my carnet, an almost involuntary reaction of mine after years of having to do it without question anytime we were asked. He's my son, he told the man, left it in the hotel in the excitement over seeing the Pope. The plainclothes agent looked at Pascual's collar.

¿Y eso? the man said.

Before I heard the calling, vaya, Pascual explained.

Hmm. ¿Dónde viven? he asked.

Barcelona. I hissed the "c."

Ah, comiéndose el jamón de Franco.

Franco had been dead for twenty years. Even I knew that.

¿Qué edad tienes?

Diecinueve, I stressed, the hissing this time a little too pronounced. The plainclothes agent nodded.

Por favor, caballero . . . we have to meet our group, Pascual said, giving the name of some hotel.

The man handed the passport back to Pascual. We won't let the Pope know about your son, padre, he chuckled. Make sure el muchacho carries his carnet—o perdón, mejor digo—his passport next time. Your *son*, maricón. Pascual let that insinuation pass and took me.

We moved down Calle Heredia and by luck found a máquina that pulled over for us after Pascual waved his EU passport and a wad of yanqui money. We drove through the heart of the city toward the bay. The graffiti must have appeared on the walls of some buildings because we saw the cleaning machines out, but they had been abandoned and looked like faulty spacecrafts discarded on some distant planet.

I smelled smoke and burning. For the first time since he had joined us, Pascual seemed nervous, uncertain, jittery, though he was trying hard to hide it. He paid little attention to the tumult in the streets, now even more heavily patrolled by la fiana and the military than it had been when we were taken from the Mass. Pascual gave direct commands to the driver about what streets to take, which to avoid. The driver too became restless, and I was sure we would be arrested again soon.

I needed to get back to Renato. I should not have allowed Pascual to separate him from me in the first place. We have to find him, I said, tempted to just exit the máquina and do it on my own.

We'll find them. All of them. Then go.

What happened?

I knew he knew. We could see the cloud of black smoke rising from one of the sections Pascual had ordered the driver to avoid.

Something, he said. Something.

He now ordered the driver to turn back. Go the other way. We were getting too close. He said the name of the hotel that he had told the plainclothes agent. Pascual seemed to know the city well. Or anywhere near the water, he added. The driver protested and said he could take us to the hotel. He wasn't afraid of those pendejos. They had nothing better to do than harass people. Yo me hago el guillao. I'll take you wherever you want, padre. But he said the last word in such a mocking tone that I thought he was going to drive us straight to the Intendente, the police station near the famous escalinata on Calle Pico. Pascual insisted on a street near the water, which was just a few blocks away. He massaged the driver's shoulders as if to soothe both of their nerves, and a minute later we stood at the entrance to the hotel Pascual had named originally and waited for the máquina to drive away.

People were coming into the hotel quickly, many carrying missals from the service. The homes in the nearby streets had been shut, the colorful shutters drawn closed, as if a ciclón approached. I began to walk the other way, toward the harbor, but Pascual made me turn and head south, away from the melee in the center of the city. I resisted. I told him I needed to see Renato. I wasn't leaving the city without him.

Go that way, or we'll be rounded up again. Ven.

We blended in with those herded away from the site of the fire. Sirens wailed behind us now. When we had walked far enough south and the throng of people had begun to thin out, finding other routes to their hotel rooms or homes, Pascual and I turned toward the water. Many were saying that it had just been a fire, the rumor of bombs unfounded, alarmist gossip. Pascual said nothing. He kept his head low and looked for an entrance into the harbor away from all the commotion on the north end. We walked through a break in a chain-link fence well south of the depot, moving closer to the water to avoid detection, most of the commotion contained by the perimeter of the city streets above.

The billows of inky smoke, coming directly from the center of the city high up in the hills had thickened and begun to spread above the cloudless sky like a witch's curse. Pascual kept me close, at once remaining a few steps behind me and trying to guide me with a hand on the small of my back, but he avoided talking or telling me what he knew about all this. He apologized once for putting me in this situation. For bringing you back here, he said. This is the last place in the city we want to be. I told him that I was the one who had chosen this. I needed to find his son. We sidled back to the depot, using the trees in the nearby alameda and abandoned oil tanks to keep from being spotted from the streets above the escalinata. A confident determination had possessed Pascual now, as when he had casually offered the back of his arm to his son for the sacrificio, the unquivering assurance of a man with nothing to lose.

Yet, there was something perhaps that he still possessed and did not yet mean to lose. I realized it the moment that the chain slipped from the hole in the door and we were let back into the depot. There was only one reason he had returned here and only one reason why he had brought me.

He asked several times for his son then grabbed me. We crawled into the back room. Renato sat on the floor alone, his head lowered, his long hair matted and smudged with blood and soot on his face. His expression reminded me of the lost vacant eyes the last time I had seen his brother. His arms and naked torso were scattered with an archipelago of rosy lesions, already ulcerated, as if he had been sprayed with liquid fire. I imagined the tattooed winged figure on his belly scorched and singed, defeated as he was.

Something had happened, he explained to his father in a thread-thin voice.

Happened? Pascual responded, his expression cryptic, a shuttered window. Were there casualties?

The question seemed to have shoved up against Renato, and he leaned away from it as if it stung the burns on his arms and naked torso.

He nodded. His whole body slumped, a limpness that suggested he did not have the bones in him to ever move from that spot again.

Pascual asked for a number. Of casualties, he clarified, but his son simply kept on nodding deliberately, slowly, and with a dogged purpose as if he had to remember how to perform each miniscule movement of the gesture.

We need to get out, Pascual said. But when he took a step toward Renato, his son flinched. He seemed to regain some strength—not to move, not so much as that, but to push the voice out of his lungs, which I imagined had been scourged and blistered as badly as his upper body.

It wasn't supposed to go off, he said. Not this one.

Then silence. Pascual again shuffled toward him, but Renato continued as soon as his father moved, and his flicker of a voice made Pascual stop in mid-motion, as if to continue would snuff it out forever.

He had taken an armed group to occupy the colonial City Hall during the celebration of the Mass. As planned. Hold it until after the Mass had ended. Get the foreign press to cover it. Ototó had come with them but had remained back, hidden in the shadows of the cathedral across the square. He had contacted other journalists, who also gathered there. They had easily made it past a few harried administrators and the two dozing guards at the municipal building and occupied the place. But not long after they had cleared the upstairs floor of any remaining workers, one of the explosive devices that they had brought with them had detonated accidentally. Torn to pieces the giant Dominican as if his massive bulk were the gossamer wings of a moth to a bonfire or as if he just all of a sudden became all the fire that he had ever swallowed.

The blaze engulfed him, Renato said in an eerie monotone. From the shape of him it was clear that he himself had not been far from the explosion. Those that could had fled, but the damage had been done. The plan to hold the building in which Fidel had given his first victory speech for the world press to see was foiled.

Everything caught fire, Renato said. It consumed the whole floor. We couldn't save the ones that didn't scatter out. That was the bomb that wasn't supposed to go off, he added as if he were trying to explain some peccadillo. He asked if the others at the airport and the fort had detonated. Is that why it took them so long to get to the square? He didn't think they would make it out. But they did. Those that could.

He stopped talking long enough that his father took the opportunity and quickly approached him. He smoothed the hair from his face and scrutinized his body for any other wounds than those we could see. It seemed as if Pascual was going to sit by him and hold him in his arms, console him, tend to his wounds, but the momentary coddling suddenly turned to urgent concern. He helped Renato to his feet, ordered him to go out with me. The long way through the harbor like we had come, he instructed me. It wasn't safe in here. We needed to go. He gestured at me to start going out, but Renato seemed unable to move. I wondered where his ubiquitous group of bodyguards had gone, if they too had perished in the fire, but we had no time for that. Pascual pushed us along toward the exit, although I saw how cautious he was not to put his hands on his son for fear of exacerbating the pain of his burns. But Renato's back appeared free of injury. He must have been facing the conflagration.

When we were at the door, and they began to pull away the chains, Pascual seemed to quickly rethink the situation. Wait, wait, he said. He scattered away from us, and his son, eager not to appear despondent about the situation in front of the others, went after him calmly. The others there looked at me with envious eyes, the sad look of mastiffs waiting to be fed. They wanted to come with us, but a large group would be too conspicuous. When they returned a few minutes later, Pascual was half-naked again as he had been the night in Camagüey, wearing only his underwear, his saggy breasts exposed. Renato was in the process of buttoning up Pascual's black shirt, the white collar undone, the thick fabric clearly sticking to his burns although he seemed anesthetized from the shock of what he had witnessed. I saw the butt of a pistol tucked into the crotch of the black pants, an antique small thing that reminded me of comandante Juan's useless weapon in its smelly holster. Renato wiped some of the blood and soot from his face and pressed three fingers to my cheek. Then he wiped fresh blood coming from a gash on his brow and smudged it on my shirt. You came from the scene of the accident if anybody asks, Pascual said. You are here for the Mass and were touring the cathedral square when the bomb went off. Renato smeared some more blood on me, on my face, neck, and arms. He seemed to have regained his volition.

Pascual thought twice about it and refused to let us out the main door from where we had come in. Renato and I followed him to a far corner of the depot where he loosened a few of the rotting planks low on the wall so we could crawl out. They might be watching the entrance, Pascual warned us.

They? I asked, but he did not respond.

When we were outside, Renato grabbed one of the planks and took it, carrying it over his shoulders like a rifle. As we scuttled away, crouching and looking out for the fiana, I clearly heard something I had missed before, how the old depot structure hummed with the huddled masses still inside, how poor a hiding place it was even in this deserted part of the port. It throbbed and glared with the life inside, I'm not sure how, but it was as if the rotted wooden slats of the walls had been splashed with a fresh coat of pastel paint just like the hotels near the cathedral packed with Yuma. Pascual had made sure that he put his son in charge of getting me out of there. We quickly moved south, staying as close to the water as when Pascual and I had come in.

Renato said he felt like jumping in the waters to cool his burns. Then he asked me if I had seen Steffen at all inside the depot. I told him I'd barely had time to look at any face if I'd wanted to. Why? Had Steffen been with them at the City Hall accident?

Renato shook his head. His legs must have been injured also because he limped and after a while began to use the long plank as a staff, leaning on it to walk.

We gave the German the easy target, he explained. The airport by the bay.

My look of consternation must have betrayed my fear for what might have happened to Steffen. No harm, Renato said, to him or anybody else. There was no one at those places because of the Mass. Not even security.

Where is he then?

Hopefully somewhere with the people up there—Renato gestured to the city up on the hill—and not stupid enough to have returned like us. Maybe we'll find him.

When we had moved far enough south, we crossed the waterside carretera and began to climb the hill toward the bayside streets. Renato stopped me and pointed south where two thin plumes of gray smoke rose from the far shores as seemingly harmless as the chimneys of sugar mills. It was something, he said, even if the occupation of the City Hall had failed.

We took one of the side streets. I followed Renato, unsure of where we could go to hide and wait for the others to quit the depot in small groups. I was sure that this was what Pascual had in mind. They wouldn't hurt anyone with him in there. The mass of people evacuating from the center of the city had grown much smaller, and more of the city natives became evident, the doors to their darkened homes now slightly ajar, eyes peeking out at passersby and monitoring the roving fiana and army soldiers. Some were brave enough to be sitting on kitchen chairs out on the narrow sidewalks, playing dominoes or cooling themselves with paper fans, some higher up in the tenements, visible through the rusty iron grilles of the balconies, heads and half torsos suspended out of the windows of airless cells, the bisected souls of some grisly torture chamber. I expected more of the fear I had seen during the summer in the capital, when we shut ourselves in from the calculated and careful violence of the vacant bombs. But now that I was on the other side, I wondered if these others too had unwittingly joined in like I had, simply biding their time until someone came to take them away.

Renato, meanwhile, seemed intent on circling back to a spot where we could see the depot from the hillside. He grabbed my wrist now and led me. A few soldiers looked at us—must have thought about stopping us but hesitated because of Renato's outfit despite the tattoos on the young priest's arm (what did they know about the savage witchery of this religion?)—but their attention seemed now focused on the port below. By the time we had turned onto Calle Bartolomé Masó at the top of the escalinata, a view of the bay and the dark shadows of the mountains across like the humps of lounging prehistoric beasts, something must have already started down below, because as soon as I was about to get a look, Renato became concerned, grabbed my arm again, and pulled me away.

He backed through the open door of what seemed like an abandoned courtyard. He let go of my arm, turned me around, and pushed me hard with both hands to the chest into a crevice under a cantilevering balcony—out of sight of the blind and shuttered broken windows overlooking the courtyard—into a spot where a brick wall had collapsed and the thing hung precariously suspended above us, a place where rats might confer before a night of foraging. He threw me up against a wall and kissed me, pressed his body into mine so that the framework of our rib cages seemed suddenly interlocked. I fell back and he tumbled on top. He spoke with his chapped lips pressed to mine, not wanting to abandon what he had begun, a fecal smoky stink hissing through his clenched teeth that we had become accustomed to since our trip from the capital—our last good washing at the festival of the waters in the pueblaire—and that as the days passed bound us to each other, the more it intensified the easier it became to identify each other, seek each other out across the hordes at the Masses, sense each other in the entrails of the city. That's how they had done it all along, I thought, half on my back now, my shoulder blades pressed against the gouges in the crumbling brick wall—why they had been so successful at their graffiti campaign on our trip, signaling to each other through the austere and lonely radar of their stink. There had been no assaults, no flagitious sexual terrorism, as was claimed in Ototó's articles. Who among even the most despondent and deviant Yuma would approach us for sex, with our rank breaths and body stink binding us together? Teeth scraping now more than kissing, Renato snarled, Remember me. Remember me. And then: That's all I want. And then, softer: That's how you save yourself. That's your liberty. We scurried deeper into the crevice, as if the wall had been crumbling in a fearful asymmetry under the balcony expressly for this purpose, for lovers shrinking into repose, until we were in a recess that was no more than the size of a pen for traveling animals, a crypt, just enough room for the shift of a limb, a turn of the head, our bodies concomitant, like a pair of puppets with strings entwined, negotiating the space to the calculus of our needs, our clothes slithering off us, shoved by our feet and gathering with the cold metal of his gun and debris and loose rock and the rubbish of other lovers that had preceded us into the opening. Our own private apagón.

They say that a man whose bleached bones are strewn in the rain somewhere has suffered the ultimate indignity. But what of the opposite? What if we were to become *too much of this life*? What if we were to become all flesh for a moment, the mind severed from its capacity to sit in judgment and control, even of the smallest gesture of an erect pinky or a curling toe? I think that's what Nicolás had wanted to do with me from the moment he met me—for me to reach that state, and what Renato had not shown any interest in with me until this last trip. Now he had become more than his brother, more than I had ever allowed Nicolás to be. His hands ripped away from the invisible cords that were holding our limbs together. They set on exploring my body like possessed centipedes. They sunk into the mesh of my solar plexus then froze, as if paralyzed but about to birth a whole brood of other insects, which scattered down my belly and into my groin. Renato pinned my skull into a nook, held it there with the weight of his own head. I felt the skin in the back of my head tear, something ooze, our bodies curled tightly upon one another and having mastered the low narrow confines of the chamber to such a degree that we needed only this little space, this far-off corner of a suddenly miniscule universe. His fingers went into me first and then I felt the absurdly cold metal of the thick hoop at the end of his pinga. A pause, but not a requisition, not a solicitation for approval, but a pause so that I would know, headless and boneless, there as I was, all flesh and nerves. The insect sunk its legs deeper into the mesh in my belly and Renato went in. My brow ground against the worn cement of the ceiling of our catacomb, his face pressed to my neck—my back got traction on the rubble and pushed back, shoddily at first, out of sync, but the hand that had seized the bundle of nerves in my belly relaxed and tightened its pressure to teach me how, relaxed and tightened, a dance, so that it was from there now that my body would respond. A pain shot through me, but was just as quickly manipulated into something else—something más sabroso—by the hand buried in my gut, now guiding my every sensation, my every movement, so that as we shifted from position to position, I had more feeling for the sound of the skin of his back rasping against the craggy ceiling of our ensconcing as he rose and fell in ripples and whitecaps over me, more feeling for the shadows of other critters doomed in that urban cave with us, rustling about, hugging the walls to avoid us, more feeling for the clamor of passersby on the escalinata about something, something ghastly, as we grew louder and louder and the smell of panic—like a miasma of old urine almost—seeped in so that Renato could not even finish what he had started, and when he pulled out and let go of the bundle of nerves that he had gathered in my belly, I saw him back out of the hole like a crab, reach for his pants, but then think better of it, wearing only his sandals and carrying the plank he had ripped from the side of the depot in front of him like a scabbard. By the time I had regained a sense of my bones and bungled into my jeans, he was beyond the crowd, on the bottom steps of the escalinata heading for the harbor, for the fire that rose at the knees of the shadowy mountains like an offering, a votive.

The crowd gathered on the top steps for a better view, giving me the impression that they were an audience at a grand street performance, silent, reflective.

The next day, the local issue of *Granma* would report that since the old long-abandoned depot sat distant from other buildings, with no concern of spread, the fire department had waited until it burned to the ground—so after breaking through the initial mass of spectators, it was easy to run after the figure of Renato. By the time I caught up with him, I could clearly see what we had done to each other, his back lacerated and sparkling with jewels of fresh blood, cool and crystalline. He stood no more than twenty meters from the burning depot building, naked, still for a moment, and not even the infernal drafts enveloping us and pulling us in could touch the calculated coolness of his thoughts. I could not see his expression, but I read it in the position of his body, the absurd splintery sword raised. I was much closer to him than he was to the doomed structure, but he was as unreachable as a small bird perched on a nearby branch. When he dashed forward, his arms opened, the scabbard held high, swinging it and closing his arms over his head only right before he crashed into one of the doors that stood alone in a conflagration of flames high as a monument. No sound, the impact pillowed by the rising blaze. If Renato called out something to me, to the world he was abandoning, to the souls trapped inside, his voice never reached me.

VI

I realized then that a man who had lived only one day could easily live for a hundred years in a prison.

Albert Camus
The Stranger

HERE

I am like Fidel now—here but unseen. The guests at Calle Obispo come and go as if the house is tended to by a half-creature, something not fully existent—they address me not with disdain but with the miffed curiosity of a child that has come upon a talking cricket. Sometimes, when out gathering provisions for the guests, I see Bertila and Inocente St. Louis milling about the cathedral plaza, going inside lighting candles, saying their rosaries, and exiting through the chapel. Only when I get too close, or when the tall companion ignores me too obviously, or when by chance they turn and head in an unexpected direction do I realize it is not them, that the man is not tall enough, that what I thought were the woman's layer of mantles is her actual flesh, that they walk too fast or too slow, that they are too young, though never too old. The old are hidden away in this city, drooling on the breezy patios. They don't mill about. There are few of them anymore. El Líder wanders the hallways of some top-secret hospital in his Adidas track suits, sending missives out to his people as if from some other dimension. When they let him speak, the reedy voice is not his, the jumbled philippics inside-out versions of his hit oldies. My generation, not even in our thirties yet, has become useless to the future of this Island. They should have separate homes for us now that the sidatorios have mostly closed, now that the illness is no more an inconvenience than the lack of paper to wipe our asses (it is easier to get the medication for one than tissue for the other). But it would be difficult to pick us out, because we don't roam the streets of the capital in packs as before, but have rather become solitary creatures, loitering in the parks and alleyways at night, asleep on rooftop shacks or the high thick roots of banyans. We are less noticeable than the tiny graffiti marks of the last decade. Perhaps the last time we mattered was in the weeks right after the fire. They arrested me at the Plaza de la Revolución on the day of the Pope's last Mass in the capital. An odd arrest for someone so inconsequential. Two men in civilian clothes, serious expressions and acne-scarred cheeks, looking like ne'er-do-well brothers from a yanqui Mob film, put their hands under my armpits and picked me up from the curb in the middle of the Mass. They led me quietly to a private máquina that drove east to a dark holding cell in a handsome villa from where I could hear the ocean. I asked once who they were. One of them, the driver, responded that I should let them ask the questions. They kept me in a windowless room in the basement with a cot and gave me clothes that seemed to have been left behind by some gusano in the fifties, linen trousers and silk guayaberas the color of Impressionist fruit. Three times a day they brought me meals and let me use a bathroom with a tall narrow window from where I could see a sliver of the sea. I had burns on my cheeks, my arms, my shoulders, my thighs—and for the first few days a nurse came into the room to tend to them, applying lotions and wrapping gauze around the worst ones on my shoulders. Once a week, we took a stroll three times around the perimeter of the property. It was the only time that the two guards appeared at the same time. I asked for a cigarette, which one of them lit carefully as if I would jump back from the fire in terror. I asked for reading material and after a few days, they brought me translations of English mystery novels that Spanish tourists had left behind at a nearby resort. At night— I only knew the passing of the hours from my visits to the bathroom—I tried to listen for the sounds of others like me in the house, scurrying barefoot in their own rooms. Weeks passed. Like during the summer of the bombs, I learned to communicate without words. When I was finished with my meals I pushed the plate aside, when I wanted a third cigarette I would motion with two fingers pressed to my lips, and when I felt like taking an extra minute in the shower, I would let out a salacious grunt to keep them from bursting through the door. We had sunk beneath the need for language. When I encountered it in the books, it seemed odd to me that these marks on the page could lead to any kind of sound, so I began to read aloud to not let me forget how to do it. I read aloud daylong and required extra water and extra trips to the bathroom, and the brothers happily obliged. But they soon deemed it wise to stop bringing me books, perhaps to stall the onset of madness. So I picked separate passages from books that I had already read and wove them together into different stories, one with no end and no beginning, all middle, all turmoil, a lawless world where characters change identities in the middle of a scene and murdered bodies reappear to wreak vengeance on meaning. They began to remove the books they had brought me, and I sunk into almost complete silence again, muttering only passages that I could recall from memory, mingling these with phrases from Chekhov and Martí that I remembered from school. I grew afraid for my sanity. There had to be a reason for this half-detainment, this notquite prison. I tried to raise the issue again with the brothers, haltingly, because although my voice itself was in decent shape from the reciting, I had forgotten how daunting it could be to look someone in the eye and address him. When will I be questioned? I asked in between cigarettes. The brother whose turn it was to care for me that day looked up from the business of lighting my other cigarette. He gazed at me with a disappointment that lit up the tip of the cigarette as he drew in breath. He smoked the cigarette himself, and I was not offered one for an entire week for my impertinence. From then on, my silence became complete—eating, shitting, napping, bathing twice a week surrounded by it. I lost track of long-time, but I fought hard to maintain my sense of short-time. I counted seconds. Still, sometimes when I went into the bathroom, I expected it to be the middle of the night and the sun glittered on my little sliver of ocean and cast an oblong Dutch yellow streak on the immaculate claw-footed bathtub. Once my cigarette privileges had been returned, the brothers became more generous with the portions of food, even allowing my reading privileges again as long as I did not do it aloud. They confessed there was nothing they could do but keep me there until new orders came. Before my release a few weeks after that, I had begun to pity them for the burden of caring for me. The night I was let go, they shuffled me into the same private máquina that had brought me there and dropped me off at the front entrance of the house on Calle Obispo. I did not know what time it was or what season of the year, so I had little choice but to knock on the mesquite door, if but to reorient myself to whatever life was left for me in the capital. After the third knock, the door opened slowly—Cecilia in a threadbare nightgown, her arms wrapped around her upper body. She stepped aside and let me in, then hurried to the patio kitchen to brew some cafecito. She was in a bit of a rush, she said, not even looking me in the eye, dealing with me at an angle as if I were an image from a crooked projector. Her loose hair fell like a gray mantilla on her face. Her body seemed to be repelled by mine, maintaining the distance of wary prey. It was all right, she had been awake, she announced. Sleep found her only in rare instances those days, she offered, often during the middle of the day as she was performing her necessities or while serving the Yuma. They still came, but not like before. The Spanish hotels had grown more sophisticated with their restaurants with each new venue. She still served the few that showed up, like a sleepwalker. Pero vaya, when she beckoned sleep at night, olvídate, it was like catching fish with your hands. She put the two cups on the table and motioned for me to sit. She apologized. For what? For the last months, she said. It had been comandante Juan's idea, as a way to keep me safe from the roundups. It was more difficult to bribe the right folks once someone was deep inside. I hope they didn't harm you. I shook my head and spread my arms. I was fine, healthy as a Nochebuena pig, ready for the roast pit. She chuckled— at my crumpled viejito's outfit, not at my comment, she explained. I had not realized I had never been given my old clothes back, that I looked like I should be chucking bread-crumbs to the pigeons from a bench in the Prado. The brothers, it turned out, were comandante Juan's nephews, cousins really, high up in the Air Force, whose officers those days with as little as a handful of grounded MiGs, lived in a perennial state of vacation. We sat in silence. ¿Y Pascual? she asked. Did he ever come see you? After Renato had thrown his shoulder against the miraculously suspended door of the blazing old depot, I dashed toward it, my body telling me that there was a chance I could follow him in through the parting of the flames, that the falling door momentarily opened up a space for me, too—not to grab him and pull him out, to follow him in. But by the time I had gotten close enough the curtain had sealed, and the gust of flames eagerly closing the void threw me back on my ass. It wasn't until some kids watching the fire from afar ran screaming toward me that I realized that my hair and my jeans were on fire. I rolled on a patch of nearby dirt and might have suffered a more serious fate had the kids not jumped on me to snuff the flames out. I thought I was being taken to the hospital and did not recognize, after I had been wrapped in blankets and treated, that I was alone with Pascual, in a máquina first and then in a plane on the way back to the capital. I wanted to ask him who had made it out? But I could not muster the air to speak. He gave me coffee mugs of tepid rum to ease the pain of my burns, and when we arrived at José Martí Airport under the cover of night, I could hardly walk. We slept in a hotel room near the Plaza de la Revolución—the face of the lit Christ, imitating the iron sculpture of el Che, visible from our window. He gave me a cool bath, patted me dry, and made me lie naked and faceup on the stripped bed while he applied salve to my burns. He kept a vigil over my drunken sleep, he told me the next morning. Whenever I had tried to turn over onto my belly, he flipped me back. The following morning, he reapplied the ointment that the medic had given him, dressed me in loose linen garments, chancletas, and a wide-brimmed campesino hat and dropped me off at the Mass in the plaza, under one of the makeshifts tents packed with Peruvian nuns. I asked no questions, could not utter a single word, still in shock at what I had seen and felt. He told me he would return in a few minutes to get me. He never once mentioned the death of his son, or the fire, or the many others who surely must have perished there. I wandered away from the tent, although one of the Peruvian nuns noticed the burns on my face and tried to prevent me from going out in the sun. I sat on the curb, the old pontiff's metered rant as if timed to the flickers of hazy sunlight slowly reigniting the burns on my face and shoulders. By now, I had guessed I was waiting for another—for someone—to approach, to be taken, I told Cecilia. The cousins knew about my burns, they were careful not to touch me anywhere on my body but under the armpits. We drove to the villa on the outskirts of the city in probably the only máquina in all of Havana with a working air conditioner. I realized as I told her the story that I had no idea what details she had been told about Renato. Although by the way she filled any momentary gaps in our conversation with small talk about the paladar, with chisme about the old ladies of el Comité, with details of comandante Juan's diminishing health (one of his lungs had collapsed during the middle of service one night), I could sense that she would not allow me to tell her any more than what she already knew. Her very insistence on avoiding the conversation made clear that she knew that I had been there, that I had witnessed one of her sons die this second death, and eventually she would run out of small talk, out of questions about my cellar room, about the small acts of kindness of comandante Juan's nephews, and she would have to ask me to tell her what I had seen, what I had done, like in the old days when I would reveal to her piecemeal my Fridays with her son. She had enjoyed this because in some sense she could control it, keep the version of her wayward son's life nearby. She soon left me under the avocado tree to go make her rounds with the bolsa marketers, she informed me. I offered to help, but she said that these days she could fit everything she brought back in a small handbag. She dressed hurriedly and left, a light touch on my shoulder as farewell. I did not dare move from under the avocado tree for more than an hour, sipping on the dregs of the mucky cafecito and sensing the air grow still on the patio, the breeze that generally made the rounds through the subdivision of patios—carrying the insidious whispers of the nosy viejas into the amused ears of diners—gone. Total silence except for the chatter of passersby on Calle Obispo, nothing changed in these three months, the two topics always on the agenda, sexual hustles and the acquisition of provisions for another day of survival, the two often intermingled, interchangeable, a dickering that played off the cubano's greatest strength (his sexual presence) and his greatest weakness in el período the sacrificio (a material dearth so ubiquitous that it must have made us seem saintly to the world, all of our joys and sins filtered through our lack, rendering them even more exotic, like diaphanous orchids clinging from the branches of a barren tangerine). This degrading prattle lent me the rashness to stand up from the table and seek refuge in the rooms upstairs. All doors were open, bedsheets tousled, as if an entire family had rushed out in a hurry that very hour. This is how she slept now, from mattress to mattress to mattress, a trail of cigarette butts. Before leaving, Cecilia had offhandedly asked me to move back in, concerned about the Ministry of the Interior evicting her and giving the house to a larger family. It was true. All those unused rooms were as counter-revolutionary an act as many of the things her sons had done. She made a dismissive gesture with her hand. She had caught herself off guard by bringing her sons up, so she left without saying any more. Before I stood up and went upstairs, I thought I heard her return, a long sigh coming from within the darkened parlor, the writer's old study. I thought, she's right, unless comandante Juan can work a miracle, Cecilia would be put out just like the writer's widow had been, a family with proper revolutionary credentials given access to the house that was palatial by Havana standards. A rare occurrence these days, indeed, not to see such a large space subdivided into apartments for smaller families, or the elderly, or young singles, or students. Over the next ten years, in my nocturnal wanderings, my feeble attempts to escape the burden of the house on Calle Obispo, I would sleep in many houses that were no larger than Nicolás's old bedroom, often shared by three or four, coordinating their sleeping hours so they fell on opposite ends of the day. I entered each of the rooms upstairs, unlatched the shutters, and threw open the windows. A dusky, nicotine fog lingered in each room, a thick placental haze of Cecilia's nights of puffing on twice-smoked cigarettes. Why had I gone into those rooms? Was such a simple act a sign that I was willing to stay? Or did I have a choice? Was there a pair of fiana waiting for me outside the mesquite door if I made the wrong decision? Maybe that had been the long sigh, one of the bored policemen, waiting for my inevitable attempt to escape my fate in this house. I waited for the rooms to air out and then did something odder. I went to the linen closet in the hallway and found clean sheets and blankets to put on each of the beds, even Renato's old mattress on the floor. It was as if I were doing anything to disturb whatever comfort and routine Cecilia found at night wandering from room to room. I leaned out a balcony and stole a glance at the front door below—no one there. I surveyed the area more fully. No one even glanced up, though I am sure the passersby must have gotten a whiff of the insomniac fog. If I hopped down to the street below, I could say goodbye to the house on Calle Obispo forever. Whatever troubles came my way after that would be of my own making. But as I contemplated the leap, I heard fumbling steps on the stone stairs. I called out, then heard the steps descending. I called out for Cecilia specifically, although I knew it could not be her, since I had been watching the street below. ¿Comandante Juan? The tall figure with his back to me stood by the kitchen stove on the side of the patio, wrapped in a bedsheet and wearing a colorful scarf on his skull. For a moment, I thought of Inocente St. Louis, my first of many sightings of his wandering ghost in the coming years, the only time that he appeared at the place where I had known him best, the cook's line. The figure fumbled with a match at the gas stove and then bucked backward when it lit in a pale blue gust. Afraid of fire. It could not be him. The coffeepot tipped off the stove and the man got down on his knees collecting the parts, disappearing under the counter. When he rose, he faced me, his hands sticky with coffee grounds. I had grown so used to him in a priest's collar that without it he looked diminished, bereft. Underneath the sheet, which spread open now as he tried to hold all parts of the scattered coffeepot pressed against his belly, he wore only a pair of long pajama bottoms and a thin gold crucifix around his neck, part of the priest's disguise that he had never bothered to discard. She won't be back for a few days, he said, as he began to put the pot together. Went to visit family in Pinar del Río. She asked me to move back in, I said. Impossible, muchacho, he responded. You must leave. It's not for her to say, anymore. He repeated that I could not stay in such a harsh tone that I half-expected him to pull out comandante Juan's rusty pistol and walk me out the door. But he fumbled with the reassembled cafetera and gestured for me to sit, rustling through the cabinets for something to offer me to eat, settling on stale crackers and hard cheese. Not much of an inventory, he sighed. I don't understand how anybody could pay for food in this mierdero lugar. It was worth it once, I said with a note of pride. Best cheap food in the old city. Me lo creo, he chuckled, that old cabroncito Juan could probably squeeze flour out of a Martí statue. It would have been impossible without him, coño, I thought. Whatever price Cecilia did or did not pay, comandante Juan had made our lives possible. There was no arguing that. The only question for me was what sort of arrangement he had made with the husband and father before Pascual had disappeared. When I asked that question aloud, Pascual responded. Do you know where she hides the coffee? Under the upturned pot . . . with the rum, I said. Ah, the rum, even better. He set the cafetera aside and poured two glasses of rum, grabbed the plate of cheese and crackers from the table and motioned for me to follow him, stumbling on the train of his sheet so that I had to hold him up. He was as light as Nicolás had been on the eve of his death, but Pascual quickly recovered and pulled away from me, leading the way to the writer's studio. The bookcases had all been taken apart and refashioned into practical, almost-sleek furnishings. A plain board for a mattress, underneath which I noticed the shape of what must have been Renato's coffin as a base, a boxy night table and an elfish doorless armoire with shelves. A priest's outfit hung from a hook on the wall, though it couldn't be the one he had given Renato. Couldn't be, I assured myself. The window out to Calle Obispo had been exposed, but the panes were covered with dark paint and the only light in the room came from a small flashlight suspended from the ceiling by an almost invisible fishing line. When Pascual sat on his bed, directly under it, the room took on the atmosphere of a torture chamber. No place to sit, so I stood, my back to the wall in the half-shadows. Pascual reached for the glass of rum and ate the cheese and crackers all by himself. He did not prompt me or look up at me. He was either going to force me to initiate everything or let me go as ignorant as I had arrived about what had happened in Santiago. I sipped the rum to work up some courage. You tried to save him, I said—a statement. You used me to try to save him. You must have known, then. Beforehand. It wasn't a question, so he did not reply, but continued to gnaw on the edges of the hard cheese, breaking off pieces with his

canines and laying them affectedly on the crackers. I had given
this a lot of thought during my captivity, after the burns had
healed (remarkably—for the pain they caused me—with only
the shadow of scars) there had been little else to dwell upon
but the identity of the brothers and what had really happened
at the end of our journey. Y claro, I knew what the official
story would be the moment I saw the fire, what would be
printed in *Granma* during the following days. After a while,
you didn't have to read the government paper to know what
was in there. Every single adult citizen could have been a staff
writer. The gas stoves used for cooking the stews, the dilapidated wooden structure, the trove of chemicals used for the
bombs, the countless doors locked from the outside, the trapped
mob confused by the darkness. A recipe for tragedy. The
counterrevolutionaries misguided and befuddled right up to
the moment of their ill-fated demise set off the fire themselves,
locked themselves in the infernal oven of their own making.
That would have been the official script. Suicide, self-destruc-
tion, the fate of all wicked. Journalism as revolutionary
parable, that's all *Granma* ever is—even with El Líder in his
hospice seclusion these days, his voice like the sound of a
cracked flute rising from a tomb. There are parables yet
unlearned. But the fire had been too perfect a setup. Pascual
had known the soldiers were coming when he hurried us out.
When he gave his son his disguise. He knew about the tear gas
canisters often used to break up protests. In the basement of
the villa, I thought about how easily Pascual had finagled my
release in the lobby of the movie theater. There had been no
reason to let me, a raggedy Cuban national, go. Thinking
back, I had noticed that some that had been in the movie theater later showed up at the abandoned railway depot. What
directive coming from where guided us all there? Rounded up
and then released. Under whose authority? If they had really

been looking for the source of the three bombs, they would have kept everyone in custody until at least the following morning, after the pontiff had boarded a flight to Havana for his last Mass the following day. Which is what they did with Steffen. I thought of that later, I did. You're right, Pascual said. Some had been let go so they could go die. Maybe the fire had been set from the outside, not from the inside as *Granma* said in its story. Hard to tell. He went back to his cheese and crackers. The fire had consumed the structure quickly, feeding on the dried-out skeleton of the building. Ototó had written that it seemed as if the fire had encroached from the four separate corners inward, as if the flames had crawled in from the bay and surrounded the building like ceremonious sentries. Pascual rummaged in one of the makeshift drawers for a copy of Ototó's final story from Cuba. The kid likes being poetic, he said. Who knows? Ototó had not even bothered to go to Havana, and when he returned to Miami he had been put on another story a day later. This is what Pascual said he could not understand about the Western media. One day, they're captivated by a story of dissent and freedom seekers, the following day when the dissenters are eliminated there's little follow-up interest. They don't really care about liberty or the means to achieve it. Westerners had either no knack for the concept of revolution, which is nothing but a series of continuous rebellions against the State, Pascual expounded, or had such a sophisticated take on it, that they could not understand the small failures and sacrifices as part of the process, the other world's own kind of inchoate democracy, too often, unfortunately, choking on its umbilical cord. As the American democracy itself almost had, Pascual chuckled too violently and broke into a coughing fit only eased by a generous chug of rum. Whatever the case, the fact was that three months after Renato's group was obliterated, there was no memory of it, within the Island or outside of it. But Pascual took comfort in the fact that it had kept the revolutionary process alive, that his sons had been truer to the principles of the barbudos in the Sierra than the bureaucrats and sycophants that ran the government these days, than he himself ever was. Heroes in the true sense, he whispered resignedly. See that's where they mattered. Mis niños. His puny chest swelled. Revolution for Pascual was an infinite series of eruptions against the State, one feeding off the other, one degenerating and the next profiting from the spoils. There was no such thing as triumph, he said, the very concept of triumph was counterrevolutionary. What we Cubans had was the opposite: the defeat or the betrayal of one rebellion after another, that had been our history. But you came back to disrupt it? I said. To save Renato? Pascual thought on this more measuredly this time, bits of cracker on his chapped lips. I wish I had that power, he mumbled. If that had been my mission, vaya, I failed miserably. On both counts. Why are you here? I didn't come here of my own choosing, I replied in a louder voice than I had intended. Better where you were than the alternative. But sit, stay—your Cecilia won't be returning for a while, if you want to know the truth—went to visit family como te dije. Might as well get used to dealing with me if you're really going to stay. You're free to leave, claro. No one will pick you up this time. Juan has made sure. On your own, coño. Thank you, I said. He made a dismissive gesture. Then a nettling silence. Pascual finished his crackers, took a pill from a vial by the bed, chugged it down with the rum, his hands trembling, and then as if I weren't in the room, pushed the sheets aside and snuggled underneath them in a fetal position, his back to me. The chills, he said. It's worse when the weather is hot like this. The house is yours, then. At some point, we need to go out in search of food. Maybe I'll gather up some strength after a nap. That's what we'll do. Within minutes, he was snoring softly. I felt the weight of my body sink back against the wall and my legs slowly give underneath me. I would have to wait for any answers. I could have left then, risk my future in a city where I had already heard from the cousins things were worse than before the Pope had arrived, or stay here and watch and care for Pascual until Cecilia returned, a day or two at most, I thought confidently— I had never heard of any family in the westernmost province she could still casually visit. I rested my forehead on my knees and when I awoke it was dark, the dark of apagones—the batteries in the hanging flashlight must have died. Luckily, my nocturnal vision had been sharpened by the three months of nights in my prison, so soon I could make out the shadow of Pascual on the bed, in much the same position as when he had turned away from me. Instinctually, I climbed toward him, fearing that his lack of movement signaled something more drastic. He was clammy, sweat soaked through the sheets and stained the wood-board mattress. The source of smell that I had noticed when I stepped in the room was coming as much from the fetid sheets as from Pascual himself. I shook him to make sure that he was at least sensate, and he grunted and pushed my hand feebly away. How could Cecilia have allowed him to sink into such squalor? I could imagine a scenario where Pascual had snuck back into the house and kept to the lower floor while Cecilia, ignorant of his presence, remained ensconced in her smoke-filled rooms upstairs, missing each other as they carried on with their necessities like some characters in a farce. This would have been just for both of them, feckless spirits in their own purloined home. The truth I learned from Pascual later proved more mundane. Cecilia had welcomed him back into the house, although it was he who insisted on sleeping downstairs. At first, simply throwing

bundles of sheets over the closed coffin and using it as a makeshift cot, objecting when Cecilia brought in the carpenters to
dismantle the rest of the bookshelves and fashion the bedroom set, something that they had not even had when they
were first married. She had cared for him meticulously during
the first few weeks after his return, bathing him and shaving
him when Pascual could barely muster the enthusiasm to do
his necessities, feeding him three and four small meals a day,
changing the bedsheets every third day as if he were staying at
one of the Yuma hotels on the Malecón. It was a way to
grieve, Pascual admitted to me later. He had purposefully
grown feeble so that she would be able to care for him like she
had not cared for her sons. But soon, the body caught up with
his pretense—he grew to need her. Y bueno, there were other
reasons for his frailty too, things he couldn't tell her. Then she
abandoned him, one morning not coming down from the
rooms upstairs. The truth was that the paladar had not been
open for business ever since he had returned, and Pascual was
not sure how Cecilia subsisted, because he never saw her come
out of the rooms, and whatever meager stock remained in the
kitchen he soon went through, taking afterward to wandering
the streets of Vedado at night, milling about the tourist restaurants for handouts, leftovers wrapped in tinfoil or half-finished
bottles of Spanish wine that certain waiters would save for
him in exchange for the crisp yanqui ten-dollar bills that he
gave them every Friday. He had survived in this manner for
the better part of the last six weeks, but he could not do it
much longer on his own, he could barely make it out the door
now without the aid of his cane—perhaps why Cecilia had
waited for me. Had she abandoned him earlier, it would have
been to his death. The house—it's your reward for watching
over her dying husband, till the Ministry comes, por los
menos, Pascual said. With a stack of bills from a series of rolls

that he kept in a mason jar, I bought a rickshaw attached to a rusty bike from one of the street boys and used it to pull Pascual around during our late-night forays into the Yuma spots in Vedado and Miramar. A full-scale market set up late every night in parked bicycle carts and toy trollies all along the streets leading to the Malecón, with more plentiful and varied merchandise than could be found anywhere else on the Island, particularly these days. Each night, Pascual explained, they set up on a different street and paid watchers to keep their eyes out for the marauding fiana, ready to toss blankets over the goods pilfered from the hotels and restaurants and vanish into the alleyways and side streets. A sight to watch, a whole street lined with toiletries and produce and even small appliances, at the sound of a birdcall from the watchers, disappear as if swallowed into the bowels of the city. Before venturing into the roving market, we usually stopped for dinner, often our only full meal of the day. Pascual's waiters catered to him as if he were a European statesman or a Canadian millionaire. In the darkened after-hours dining rooms, the waiters lit the stubs of candles and turned tablecloths inside out and reused them. They reheated the leftovers tableside with fuel canisters, so there was little time for us to be alone. They circled Pascual as he timed their revolutions, and the delivery of each course, handing out folded ten-dollar bills. After we had made a ritual of these outings, Pascual began to speak, and not until he had three or four drinks, better when there was rum and not just the dregs of wine or warm beer. He opened up about the past, at first addressing pointed questions to himself (accusations) and pondering the replies (justifications) as he picked his teeth or swirled whatever liquor was available in a tumbler—Sí, sí, I did leave them. I had no choice; once you start falling out of favor with the Party, the first to suffer is your family—¿vez?—so they know, begin to

ask for things, information on neighbors who might be ped-
dling illegal goods, o peor, what they really want, denunciations
on who chatters or scribbles counterrevolutionary mierda.
That's the prize, la Revolución could not exist without the
malcontents, without its chivatos. What had he done to
deserve all this? Pascual whistled a boozy sigh. My time had
simply run out, or I had moved too fast up the ranks, he said.
Who knows? But they found other uses for me. I was as good
a canary as I was everything else, my tragic flaw—and what a
feeble flaw, no?—I excelled in the gossip gutter, genes that I,
no doubt here, passed on to my eldest, though it was he whom
I was afraid I would one day betray, so I left, rather than that.
I accepted some international mission, anything to avoid
what I knew I would do. Betray my own. And Nicolás knew
it. He sensed it, and he had begun to hate me. Pascual leaned
in so as not to let the waiters hear, for what he was about to say
made him suspect in the underground night town that we now
existed. I stayed on the government payroll. I sought asylum as
a discontent, but I began to work the gutters of the diaspora, in
Madrid first, then London, then Miami and New Jersey,
reporting back, cutting out newspaper clippings, transcribing
radio programs, joining exile organizations, so steeped in the
life that there were days and nights, entire weeks, I truly
believed I was one of them, even as I mailed my monthly
reports to the Cuban consulate on Lexington Avenue in Man-
hattan. Can one not play a role so long that one's true essence
dissolves into it? Pascual mused, leaning into the stripped
bones of our meal. And weren't they roles in the end—the
ardent revolutionary, the bureaucrat político, the informer,
the international spy. The grieving father, I interjected. He
nodded, smirked, the objective of his story—was it not?—a
way to pique my interest, to get me to start asking questions,
so that the brumous silence that had thickened the air inside

Calle Obispo would dissipate. Who knew how much of it was true? Even as he continued opening up late nights, we maintained our collusion of silence during the day, not necessarily avoiding each other, but lounging on the patio, sipping watery coffee, seated at tables diagonally across, as far apart as we could get from each other. If we had been lucky enough to find pomegranates in the night market, he would sit all morning picking every seed from the pale white rind, when he was finished, his hands incarnadine as a murderer's. Other mornings, he would read whatever books Renato had left back in his room. At times, Pascual looked up, his reading glasses almost sliding off the end of his nose, and recited from the book, but not the text, rather something that was scribbled in the margin, and he would have me guess whether it was the thoughts of the dead writer or Renato's. When I grew tired of reading, I snuck into the henhouse and napped on the hammock still strung out there. I yearned for the disturbing hammock dreams, the too-solid fleshiness of their fury melting at the instant I awoke. I couldn't remember if they had been about what had happened in that henhouse, or about the metamorphosed ghosts of the skeletal chickens, or of the stories that Pascual would tell me at night. He had written a best seller in el exilio. A renowned author, he said. Except that he hadn't written it—not really, but culled pieces from other Cuban prison memoirs—Arenas, Valladares, and the rest—the same catalogue of atrocities from a world familiar to almost a third of the native population. There is a statistic you will never see the State release with its infant mortality rates and education advances, he said, almost a third of the population has at some point been held in prison for crimes against la Revolución. To those who attended the packed readings in Barcelona and Miami and New York, Pascual presented as a certain type of cubano archetype, the repentant comunista that had been tortured and humiliated in so many ways, abided in so many airless dungeons, that he had to be treated as someone who had emerged from another world altogether, like a heretic bishop returned from the Inquisition or a treasonous apparatchik from Stalin's death camps. No better cover. There was no better cover, he giggled too delightedly. His reports grew thick. He continued his tale of how he had risen in the ranks of the diaspora, the reports he filed back full, perforce, of intrigues and cabals that only a pulp novelist could conceive. Not that they couldn't be true. But many of them were tales from another time. By the late eighties, the exile community had degenerated to a state of ultimate resignation. The Pope's visit in the near future offered some teensy hope, Pascual said. But just as he had guessed, things became even more repressive afterward. Still the embers of the old rage burned, especially in Miami. But enough about the gusanos, he said one night at dinner. I had to live that world for too long. If you want to know the essence of the purgatorial condition, this hankering for a bygone time while dreamily concocting some delusional future one, then live among them. Pero vaya, I don't recommend it. He bared his teeth and hissed during one of the dinners when he had been previously lively, telling stories without inciting me to ask questions, interacting with the waiters, freer with his yanqui bills. Other nights, he had no more energy than on the first day I found him at the house on Calle Obispo. I had to bring him the food to the cab of the rickshaw and cover him with blankets when we prowled for the medianoche market. Some days he left the house early in the morning and would be gone for two or three days. When he returned, he handed me a bundle of bills from the jar and locked himself up in his room, coming out only to drink coffee and rum and feed on whatever reheated victuals I had procured, which he took back on a tray into his room. When I asked him where he had gone, he said only that he needed treatments. I would only know he was ready to venture out in the rickshaw again when he rejoined me during our afternoon ritual in the patio, reading and napping, sidestepping each other, shifting from table to table like the last knights left on a chessboard. Without exchanging words about it, he then appeared in the cab of the rickshaw near midnight. After he had disappeared for the third time, I prologued questions about his treatments by telling him about my last meeting with Nicolás, how the sudden suspension of his medications seemed to have done something to his brain, his theretofore ratlike survival instinct suddenly transformed into a kind of Cuban gasconade that is almost always the shortest road to martyrdom. What are you saying, Pascual asked, that they put something in their medication that the body can't do without afterward? This seemed to disturb him as much if not more than my memory of his son's last days. So you *are* seeking treatment from State doctors? Good. It was the first time I quizzed him so directly, and he deflected while baiting me. It's not what you think, he said. But you don't deny it? You are seeking treatment from State doctors? Have you seroconverted? Is that what it is? This is good, this is good. They have new drugs. Pascual replied that he was glad that we were having this conversation, and that he was touched by my concern, but he did not answer the question. He motioned for the waiters to clear our empty plates and bring some more rum, palmed some more bills to them and then tightened a rubber band around the bundle and threw it at me. Have you noticed that our jar at home just seems to replenish itself? I nodded. I had figured, I said, that there was another place where he had more dollars stashed that he didn't want me to have access to. He laughed. What did I think, that he came into the country wrapped in

American presidents? He was making his dollars from the State. That was all he was going to say for now. Still on the payroll? I asked, thinking that the only person he could be spying on these days was his housemate. It's not what you think, he repeated. When the time comes I'll tell you. Vaya, it's better if you don't know for now. But it will answer a lot of your questions. He paused, took a long sip of his rum. He couldn't look at me suddenly. He slid his chair back away from the table and faced it to the side. In the shadows, his profile was his older son's but cast in a more pensive and grief-stricken pose. Catching what must have been an affectionate expression on my face, he said, The government had nothing to do with the fire. They were going to go in, sure, they had found the depot, maybe they even shot a few tear gas canisters, but those things don't start a fire. You're just covering up for your old bosses, I said angrily, pushing the table into him and walking away. It took awhile, but he caught up to me, and I could not watch him huff and stumble for long. He mounted the rickshaw. Está bien, maybe I don't know any more than you do, he said. Then why are you asking me if you don't want to hear the truth? I took us farther into the noise of the roving market, ignoring him. The merchants had camped out more toward the southeastern end of Vedado, on an alleyway close to Necropolis Colón. From farther away by the Malecón, la fiana whistled their own signals to throw off buyers, but it was easy to distinguish their tyro efforts from the real thing. Because we were so far inland, and because he had not been to the market in over three weeks, Pascual dismounted from the rickshaw and I followed alongside as he wandered through the wooden stalls on wheels. After I had turned away from him, he had shut up about Renato, about the fire, about blame. His revelations had made me think the worst things about him and his current involvement with the government that he had tried to exculpate as if he were a *Granma* scribbler. I let him wander, grateful for the separation. Most of the merchants were either very young or accompanied by the very young, probably for the same reason, to help in the event of a getaway. I was thinking how good I would be at the task, watching the merchandise, the throng of buyers crowding each stall with their fistfuls of dollars, when I heard a commotion behind me, a merchant bursting through the crowd calling my name. Fearing the worst—that Pascual had already betrayed me, that his cryptic revelation that night had been a sucker punch to throw me off balance—I leaned on the pedals and began to ride away hard, but a hand reached out and grabbed me by the shoulder. I slapped it away and got back on the seat, but then a pair of arms wrapped around my waist and other smaller arms around my legs, all to a chorus of shouts and carcajadas. They had to wrestle me down to the ground before I stopped struggling, a band of kids pinning my limbs, and standing open-legged above me a grinning Guichi the Mayor. He commanded his brood to let go of me and reached out a hand. Coño, I wouldn't have bet that you spoke the bird language, he said, wrapping his arms around me. I heard . . . I heard, he whispered in my ear, what happened. Didn't know who survived. At first, it stung that *he* had survived all this, while others, my others, had not. He pulled me away from the rickshaw toward his stall—leaving two of the children to stand guard by my vehicle— where he sold perhaps the only luxury item in the whole market, the same kind of writing paper he had learned to make in the pueblaire from scraps of discarded flyers, newspapers, tissues, and toilet paper fashioned into fibrous elegant milky sheets. Amazingly, folks were willing to pay a steep price for each set of ten sheets, for letters to write or secrets to spill. In a few years, as the world just beyond the purlieus of the Island inevitably flooded in with the growing tourism, the State's primary concern would be communication through computers and strict control of access to the Internet and e-mails, but about that time, perhaps the greatest spiritual need on the Island was a blank piece of paper. The substantial profits from his nightly sales went to purchase more wood and tin for the rebuilding of large parts of the pueblaire city, Guichi told me. Though he was not sure it was worth it, after what had happened. The fires had started on the week after the Pope had left. Every other night a different section would catch on fire and about the time the last hovel in the section collapsed the army helicopters swooped in, dumping barrels full of water, ruining anything that might have been spared by the fire. For over a month, the pattern continued, so regularly that eventually they learned to predict rather successfully which area would catch on fire next and evacuate it beforehand, even set up open barrels to catch some of the water that eventually poured down from the night sky. Retribution, Guichi said, offering some of his elegant sheets for examination. By the third or fourth time it happened, they prepared, they waited outside near midnight when the fires usually broke out, and from the silent skies fell what looked like spittle from the sun, sulfur orange elf flames that were not so many to be a spectacle but enough that they couldn't put all of them out before things started catching on fire. Pebbles dipped in paraffin oil or something. El maldito diablo could only guess where they were getting such precious fuel. Weather balloons gliding unseen above—there was no other way it could be done, Guichi said. There was no way to defend against it except by evacuation. And then just like that, after half of the commune had been destroyed, the assaults from the heavens stopped. Whatever the sentence, it had been fastidiously meted, and when pueblairians were sure that it had been served, more than ten days after the last fire, they began to scavenge for wood, tin sheets, and other scraps to rebuild. You should come visit now, coño, Guichi said, who knows when they'll decide to punish us again.

I rejected his invitation. Too dangerous for those there. I remained persona non grata, I explained. He told me that a few from our group who had straggled behind on the way to Santiago had found their way back to the pueblaire and found permanent residence there. At first, Guichi had imagined that they were the reason for the State's retaliation, and it said a lot about the heart of the aerie's denizens that even then there was no urge to cast them out. And that was the end of it, Guichi said, holding on to me by the shoulder, because I was pulling away, only half-listening to him, worried that my rickshaw was going to disappear, and I would have to carry Pascual back to Calle Obispo on my shoulders. Or so I thought, he added hurriedly, knowing I was getting away from him. I thought I had seen the end of it by now, that I would never see the likes of you again. Then before I escaped his grip—as I looked over the crowd to see Pascual squaring off to fight Guichi's brood with his cane as an épée, poking them in the legs and the bellies to their great delight, so that more swarmed around the rickshaw—Guichi said that he had known he would never see Renato come back. That had been the plan all along. A suicide no less foolhardy than Martí's ride into battle against the Spaniards. I dashed off, pulled Pascual from Guichi's kids. Who was that man? he asked on the ride home. Why was he so important that you risked losing our only mode of transportation? Do you know what it was like trying to get around the capital late at night without it? Who was that man? Someone your son knew, I said, knowing right away that the question would soon appear again in another guise. It's best to separate yourself from that part of your past, if you want a word of unvarnished advice, Pascual muttered, not even asking which son. But even as I maneuvered the dark unlit inner streets of Vedado leading to the capitol and the old city, I knew that I would find a way to return to the pueblaire. About a month later, Pascual disappeared again. Before leaving, he warned me that he was not sure how much longer he could sustain his negocios with the State, a lo mejor two or three more trips, that soon we were going to have to find a way to bring in our own money, and he couldn't cook, and he had heard that I was a dervish on the floor as a waiter but not good for much else, so a new version of the paladar was out of the question. Besides, such things were too conspicuous when they did well—everyone in the capital knew about them. Too much exposure. They'll come for the house. Did he need me to take him somewhere now, since it was no longer a secret what he was doing? Taken care of, he said, as he stepped out onto Calle Obispo. A máquina picked him up. Say hello to the compañeros, I said. It did not take much genius to figure out what to do about our situation. I had been sleeping in a nest of soiled sheets on the floor besides Pascual for weeks, the rooms upstairs, except for my initial airing out, just as Cecilia had left them—a ritual in this family of which I had now become a participant, to leave the rooms undisturbed when someone abandoned the house on Calle Obispo, as Cecilia had done first with her husband and then with each of her sons. Before Pascual returned from his last dealings with the State, I had come up with a plan for our future. I would put the house itself to use. That would be substantially less exposure than a paladar. It took me almost three days to clear the upstairs rooms of everything but the beds, mattresses, dressers, and armoires, cleaning with a watered-down bleach solution and lye soap hawked from the old ladies of el Comité, using whatever scrap wood was left from the writer's library to prop up Renato's mattress off the floor, and the few tattered volumes left to set in little piles by the beds, a feeble attempt at a lived-in warmth, but it was all I had. It took me countless washes to scrub the stink of old nicotine off the sheets and bedcovers, a few trips to the roving midnight mercado to find enough lightbulbs, and muslin for new curtains. I thought of paint, but I might as well have wanted to sprinkle the walls of the rooms with resplendent moondust, I could probably find that sooner. When I had finished, I cleared all the rusty tables and chairs from the brick patio and stored them in the henhouse, along with the clothes and other junk from the rooms. We were ready for our first guests—a true native experience at a quarter of the price guests would pay at the Spanish and Canadian hotels. I even toyed with a few names, and none fit better than Casa Cecilia. It was my gift to Pascual, I thought then, what I would leave him as recompense for saving me from the fate of so many of the other terroristas. Before he returned, I wanted to have a plan in place to escape the house on Calle Obispo forever. I went to Cerro to see Guichi. The only traces of the fire and flood from the heavens were the houses and sections that had suffered peripheral damage but had not been destroyed, the shadows of flames licking at the wooden clapboards of walls, the corrugated metal roofs bent in with the falling force of the waters that followed. Otherwise, the new shacks looked no different than the old, same scrap material cobbled together like an intricate puzzle, a small miracle of physics, equipoised, inscrutable, like the stillness of a dancer between notes. The only way to tell the old from the new abodes was by the tiny sacrificio graffiti missing from the recently built ones. But it wasn't the rebuilding that Guichi wanted to show off— although I could see it was a matter of stubborn pride to him, that it could be done, that the juggernaut State had still not found the way with which to crack his will to *resolver*, to redeem what had been lost or not yet found. We crossed several plank bridges moving to the inner core of the pueblaire, where Guichi and his extended family resided down in one of the open apartments below. After the fires, many—even from his own family—had abandoned the community, deeming it safer to live in the outer parks of the city, nesting in trees, or inside abandoned buildings much closer to the old colonial barrio. The surest way to land in jail for vagrancy, Guichi said. The smaller the group squatting somewhere, the easier it was for la fiana to justify acting. He mentioned all this as a prelude to an invitation. There was room, many empty shacks. I could even stay with him and his family until I chose my own place of residence in the compound. I didn't come to ask you for a place to live, I said. I know, he responded, but it would have been rude not to offer it to you again. The offer remains open as long as I am in charge here. Were you in charge here during the summer? I asked. I've been in charge here going on two decades. That's not what I meant, I said. He remained silent for a while and let me work up the gumption to ask the next question. He knew what it was, and perhaps he had invited me to visit so that I would have the liberty to ask it. The bombs in the summer? I paused. They came from here, I said, answering my own question. His blank expression did not ruffle. It seemed that not a muscle in his body twitched, an unnatural rigor mortis, my recriminations met with such disarming stillness. I could answer my own questions because I already knew, like Pascual had made clear to me during our argument on the escalinata in Santiago. Anything I didn't know was because I hadn't wanted to know—maybe from the very moment that Nicolás had picked me up on the beach in Cojímar. I asked Guichi when Renato had become involved? Why? What was the endgame to the absurdist bombing campaign aimed at only killing pigeons? Why the charade with the injection rituals, the sacrificial infections, the graffiti? Vaya, every movement has its formulary, no? Guichi said. You're right, though. Those were just the symbols. The infections were his brother's idea—picked up when he became a sidatorioca. He thought that by committedly unleashing an Old Testament plague across the entire Island he could topple the old revolutionary guard. Fantasies. But Renato bought into it, at first. Tried hard to convince his brother, who resisted, to initiate him. In the end, it would have proven Nicolás a charlatan if he was not willing to bring his own brother in, so he relented. It brought Renato directly into the hornet's nest of undesirables in the sidatorio, right where he had wanted to be. I was there the night Nicolás infected his brother, I confessed. I know, Guichi said. We had lots of empty hours to chat when he first arrived. That's why Renato could never really let go of you after that. It was as if you too had been initiated that night. He wanted badly for a cause to believe in after his apostasy from la Revolución. He wanted others to believe, also. But all those things are from a century that's already past. What things? I said. Causes, he said, untarnished and pristine revolutions. They never existed in the first place. Liberty. The world has left us behind with all that. It's now one rowdy global family, and we don't even have a seat at the table. When did you return? Why? I asked, needing him to give me more solid information. I lost heart, he said. I knew where I was needed. Or you knew the whole thing was doomed, as Pascual did, I said. Guichi did not respond to this. Instead, he stood and took me back outside to the houses in the aeries. Maybe there was something else for me to do. It's not like we too didn't pay, he said as we climbed the air bridges away from the center. We reached a new subdivision where a crew of boys threw a ball from one edge of the roof to the other, testing how far they could push the other to the very edge of the precipice. They were half-naked, as was the custom up here, desperate notes to their movements. They mostly kept to themselves, Guichi said, though they had not seemed frightened when they arrived in groups of six to a dozen, hours apart (almost sixty of them altogether) calling Guichi on his pledge to take in those that had survived the trip after the Pope, a pledge I had never heard him make, but he insisted. That's exactly the language I used when I made my promise before we left, he said. It was as if I were speaking to Martí's suicidal white horse, you're right. Many of them arrived during the nights of the first fires, but still they weren't frightened. Only later would Guichi think that they behaved like creatures that had been pardoned for something and have suddenly become hidebound with the alleged offense, cowering, keeping to each other. He encouraged them to help build, play games, even one as dangerous as the one they played now, anything so that they would not think that they could rebuild their movement. One night there had been a scuffle, or a game that got out of control and ended up with one of the newly arrived boys getting badly stabbed in the abdomen, leaving them no choice but to rush to the makeshift State clinic set up on the outskirts of Cerro. The boy survived and returned to the pueblaire. Guichi pointed him out among the boys to me, easy to pick out, the only one among them whose movements were skittish, scurrying in semicircles near the center of the roof and never giving serious chase to the rubber ball. The bigger surprise was that when he came back his carnet was clean, no defining mark of the infection. At first, Guichi took this to be an oversight, for they would have certainly done blood tests, and he had seen the ritual performed in the pueblaire. But according to his carnet, and therefore to the State, the boy remained negative for the virus. Guichi knew that there would be no official investigation of the stabbing. The State didn't conduct such official business in these parts. It didn't want to become enmeshed in things it couldn't control. We've always policed ourselves, Guichi said. The boy who had done the stabbing, another newcomer, was sentenced with extra community service. But Guichi grew curious; he made up excuses for some of the other newly arrived boys to visit the clinic for checkups, fearing an outbreak of hepatitis he told them, sending longtime residents along with them to disguise the purpose. No one came back with a mark on his carnet. It couldn't have been a coincidence. Listen for yourself. Guichi shouted out for the stabbed boy, who seemed more than glad for an excuse to leave the dangerous game (more than once, one of the boys had caught the ball on the very frontier of the roof and tilted over like a toppling tyrant statue just to adroitly shift his feet at the last minute and regain his balance).

By the look in his eyes I could tell that he recognized me. Guichi addressed him with leading questions like the good lawyer he would have been, and the gist of the boy's story soon became known, that he along with others had been picked out of the group and convinced to hitch rides back to Havana. From before even the first Mass in Santa Clara. Not hard to convince them. Twenty-dollar yanqui bills, folded into tiny squares, were offered to each one who took the offer, five dollars for anyone else that they could convince to join them. Impossible, I said aloud. Why hadn't I seen any of this? No one had approached me. The boy made a dismissive gesture with his mouth. The priest was incredibly careful how he did it, while others were busy trying to get a word in with the reporter or out painting the graffiti. He asked first if we had been injected and then told us to bring him others who were still clean. He? Who? The gaunt priest, the boy said. Guichi gave me an inquisitive look. Coins are round so they roll. That's what the priest said as he handed out money, except that the refrán didn't quite fit since his money was in little squares. But what a curita, his pockets were full of the little squares. Y vaya, he said, it wasn't hard to convince others to join them on the way back to Havana. They pooled all their dollars together and went to Playas del Este for a few weeks first, stayed there till they had spent the last dollar on rum and Canadian ham at the dollar stores. Then they took Guichi up on his promise. Y ya, not much else to the story. The boy said after they heard what had happened while at Playas del Este they realized that the priest had probably saved their lives. I didn't have to tell Guichi who the priest was. He told me that Pascual had presented himself to Renato long before the night in Santa Clara, before Renato and his group had even reached the pueblaire, and more than once visited him there, long nights where son would accept father into his shack and they would not emerge until the following dawn, the awkward cordial embrace at the door evidence that whatever they were in the process of negotiating was still not settled but open to further consideration. Truth is, Guichi said, again offering his invitation for me to come live at the pueblaire, that I fear for your safety in the company of that man. He was as entrenched in the inner workings of the State as he had always been. I told him probably not so entrenched anymore. Anyway, Guichi said, Renato had known that, that his father had never really disengaged himself from the State, and perhaps because of that never gave in to his advances. One day they embraced outside of Renato's shack and Pascual never returned. For you, who is not his flesh and blood, Guichi said, bueno, what could I expect from a man that let his own son—Guichi could not finish the sentence. La verdad es that he had been so concerned with this that when he had heard from other vendors at the roving market that I visited regularly with the unrepentant comecandela in tow, he had figured out a way to procure a spot to sell his luxury paper just to catch me. Come live with us. Their city-state would outlive the larger State, he promised. There was a future here that was truer to the ideals of la Revolución than anything the country had seen since Fidel first strode into the capital. When he asked me about my own health status, I told him I didn't know. I didn't want to know. I was fine, I asserted. Maybe I was less a survivor than Guichi gave me credit for, because I never considered his offer, although I thanked him for his concern, telling myself that if Pascual had plans for me in some State dungeon, then maybe that should be my fate. Yet, the idea of continuing in the role of his manservant suddenly seemed repugnant. Something would change. I might be back soon, begging for a place to live, I told Guichi, a devoted citizen of his intrepid city in the air that will one day see the arrival of the modern conquistadores from the New World. A place would be there for me, Guichi promised. I returned to Calle Obispo. Pascual did not return for over a week, longer than he had ever stayed away. At first, I thought that he had gone the way of Cecilia, and I set out to investigate with the waiters in the hotels in Vedado how to get the word out about the new *penzione* on Calle Obispo. Our first reservation was due in on the afternoon that Pascual walked through the mesquite door shuffling as if someone had spent the entire time he had been away spanking the soles of his feet, looking more haggard than ever. Life on this Island is a fucking dream, he said. I can't imagine whatever made me want to leave it. I had to help him up the stone stairs to show him the refurbished rooms upstairs, fresh Poinciana branches plucked from a tree in Plaza de Armas in a vase in the room that would be occupied. He commended me on my capitalist spirit and told me, as he passed by his marriage bed, that what had most surprised him about Cecilia was how well she had survived without him, making a life as if she had never needed him in it in the first place. In fact, not taking this house into account—which had been his bane, forced him to pay off debts to so many in the Ministry of the Interior that he may as well have given up his firstborn, which he *had* in a sense, no?—it could be said that he never once gave his wife a single thing of material value, not even a wedding ring, since such things were deemed bourgeois. ¿Qué cosa, no? he said. What a provider! I let him sleep away his melancholy as he usually did after his appointments with the State and tended to our guests on my own, even opening up the kitchen and offering them a traditional breakfast of eggs and revoltillo, from produce procured in the roving market. It would pay off in the future—soon the three rooms were more often filled than not, Pascual a ghostly presence in the writer's study, and me in the hammock inside the henhouse. The more time that passed, the more absurd that Guichi's notion of Pascual as a dangerous active State agent seemed, for since we did not have time for our lengthy after-hour dinners, he grew despondent in his isolation, letting a spotty gray beard grow and only bathing in the upstairs bathroom when I forced him, while the guests were out touring the city or on day excursions to the nearby playas, doing it myself when I had to, using as little water as possible, saving the rest of the monthly ration for the guests, fishing out Nicolás's clothes from the bags in the henhouse and tying the pants around Pascual's waist with a rope, for he had continued to lose weight. If he was ill, why did he not check himself into a facility and seek treatment? I asked him. There was nothing wrong with him, the doctors had said so during his last visit. Sorpresa! The virus had somehow refused to set up shop in his body. It happened with some people. A natural immunity. One in ten thousand? Or maybe it was just the other stupid kind of luck. But once he had reported that he had been injected with infected blood and they failed to find any evidence of the virus in his body, test after test, they had offered him the opportunity to help la Revolución in its newest cause, finding a vaccine, Fidel's last grand quixotic quest, perhaps as grandiose as the rest of them. Did I remember his fucking with genetics to create the perfect steer? Pascual asked. Was I even alive then? Or the French quality wine from grapes grown in the hills of the east coast provinces? Todo, todito, the whole thing has been a long office of sheer madness. But who was to say, what if in the end that's what this maldita Revolución will be remembered for? A cure for the modern plague. What a finale, no? Whatever they were doing to him he didn't want to know. So many needles went in and out of his arms, so many instruments probing his every orifice, so many pills before and after that each time he was released he felt as if someone had been playing volleyball with his organs. But true to his character to the end, for that he had to give himself credit, a loyal servant. Did you know that they meant to set the depot on fire? I asked. Pascual nodded. There was little resistance left in him. I imagined that they had taken that with their probing as well. I tried to save him, he said, I tried to save him by asking him to save you. That's why I took you there. So he would take you out and avoid the mass execution that he had orchestrated for the others. He wanted something grand, something unforgettable. I didn't become aware of the details until that very last minute, but I knew, he said. I brought you there to save him. To force him out. Because I knew that— But you were willing to sacrifice all those others? I asked. He hunched his shoulders, a gesture not of repudiation but of powerlessness. Renato had convinced them too well. He had convinced himself. When he looked up at me, I wanted to read the milk-iness in his eyes as regret, or at least a scrupulous admission of error, that the time to have saved his son had passed him, that he should have warned anyone he could about what had been planned inside that railway station. How many fools had his son convinced to abandon this world with him? It was my only living son, he said. God himself did as much with the innocent firstborn of Bethlehem. Then I thought how I had been one of those fools, how I would have followed him through that gate of fire if my body had let me. You would have been willing to sacrifice me if it came to it? I asked Pas-cual. The cataract fog in his eyes was that of a beast of burden, a thing that has given the pith of his being to the service of something to which it cannot participate in now but as an interloper. There was no need to answer my question. I told him I knew about those he had paid to leave. I am not in the mood to be sainted, he said. The Pope had come and gone, anyway, and only he had the power for that. He went into his room and fished out the clean bill of health from the State, placed it on the table under the avocado tree and slapped it for emphasis, but reading it over and looking at him was a quick lesson in the swiftness of mortal treachery, whatever the paper said about how his body was and should be doing well, every perfidious cell in him had turned against such purpose, his statuesque frame now crackling and wheezing and curved upon itself, as if all its energy were being sucked inward toward some unreachable core, leaving the outer reaches undernourished and decaying. Soon, that unmistakable redo-lence of tooth rot came upon him, and as much as I rubbed him with soap and doused him with his son's pilfered Euro-pean perfumes, I could not hide it. I had begged him to leave. He was a citizen of the world, with a passport that could take him almost anywhere, which he continually tucked under the band of whatever pants he was wearing. Even if he wanted to die, carajo, surely there were better places to do it than here. So when he did disappear from the study one afternoon, I searched all over for his passport and was glad to find it nowhere. I gave him three months to send word from the outside world, with a picture of how his body had regenerated itself, squelched the revolution within. Two weeks later I heard the news. For the first time since I had known him, comandante Juan knocked before entering the house on Calle Obispo, on the mesquite door first, he said, which I must not have heard, and then on the side gate. There were guests milling about what I now called the garden, since I had planted hibiscus and birds of paradise and dahlias, little by little, with profits earned, so comandante Juan asked if we could speak inside, in the study preferably. In spite of the somber tone, I realized that perhaps he was the single one out of all of us who had not been transformed by the previous two years. He was sunburnished, inky spots on his brow and arms, which made me guess he was out with Cecilia in Pinar del Río, toiling as a campesino. But his obscene cheer and optimism were untarnished. He hugged me and congratulated me on how well I had done with the house, congratulated himself for guessing from the moment he saw me about my industrious nature. Then he looked down, let his gaze hover over the corner of Renato's mahogany coffin, and asked if he could have it with a pleading seriousness that made it seem as if he were asking me for something that I myself had struggled for and obtained and not some relic belonging to another. I must have registered some shock on my face, because he immediately explained that Cecilia was fine, that she was taking well to life in the country. She was, he said, like those sorts of giant flying cucarachas that are indestructible and can adapt to any environment. He had received a telegram, he went on, from someone in the Directorate a few days ago about Pascual. The Cuban coast guard found his body in a dinghy floating just beyond the national waters with a group of six others, younger men who had survived. They had run out of fuel on the way to Florida and the current had pushed them back toward the tip of the Island, off the rocky coast of Pinar del Río, almost, comandante Juan said, as if Cecilia were summoning him back. Pascual had died of thirst and heatstroke, a European passport tucked in his waistband. ¡Qué cosa! Comandante Juan tapped the tiny mahogany coffin and repeated his request. He had procured a spot in Cemeterio Colón not far from where his son and parents were buried. For over half a year he had been trying to get whatever traces of Renato's ashes existed from the State but was told that they would not be released until a thorough investigation of the fire was completed. At this, comandante Juan could not resist a snort. They would have to relent at some point, and there would be space for an urn in his father's crypt, he would make sure. Only proper. If I erred, comandante Juan said, guiding me to help him carry the coffin out, it's that in trying to protect Cecilia from their madness, I alienated her from her own sons. Pero mira, she couldn't have survived and saved them at the same time. Not here, not in our world. ¿Entiendes, no? If it wasn't for me, he said, they would have *all* perished. There was a violence in all of them that would have squashed the flying cucaracha. I couldn't let that happen. As we loaded the coffin into the trunk of one of his private máquinas, I asked him when they would be returning, that I could be out that very night, but that there were guests lined up for the following three weeks. Comandante Juan took out a notepad and pencil stub from the glove compartment, scribbled down something, and handed me the note. She doesn't want to set foot in this house again, he said. It is yours until the Ministry comes knocking, which won't be long now, so make plans. The note had a time and date. I watched Pascual's burial from a distance, half-hidden by a giant statue of St. Lazarus of the Wounds, not sure if comandante Juan and the two State ministers knew I was there as they officiously watched the mahogany coffin lowered into the crypt, remaining in place until the marble slab was secure atop. I decided to honor all the reservations at Casa Cecilia, and would, week by week book new ones and honor those, and so on, at times feeling that I was the last pawn left on the board of some preposterous chess match and was only waiting for a merciful hand to pull me out and start the game over with a whole new set of pieces. In the intervening years, I have lived from reservation to reservation, guest to guest, with the profits from each busy season making needed renovations to the house, buying new linen curtains for the rooms, new mattresses and furniture, all from deals in the roving market, once three years ago even procuring paint through the connections of a New York artist turned film director who was shooting in the capital. At about the same time, I began to receive colorful boxes full of dark chocolate bonbons and licorice and marzipan, the German postage surrounded by stamps of Cuban woodpeckers. I put the sweets out in the garden for my guests, keeping the notes together in the midget mahogany dresser in my room. Promises to return. Unless the Ministry finds some nobler revolutionary purpose for the house on Calle Obispo . . .

I'll be here.

ACKNOWLEDGMENTS

I could not be more grateful that this novel will be ushered into the world under the stewardship of Juliet Grames and Mark Doten—the Don Shula and Dan Marino of the New York publishing world. From my very first inspiring lunch about this work with Juliet eons ago to the last revealing conversation about the art of storytelling with Mark, they have been nothing but a blessing. My agent, Jesseca Salky, is another angel, a persistent and bold winged creature, whose sharp eye for both the art and the business of literature is unmatched.

The team at Soho Press has been nothing but superb in the care of and dedication to the process, from the meticulous concern for the inflection, the comma, and the word of Rachel Kowal and her team—NaNá Stoelzle and Conrad Burnham; to the captivating artistry of Dana Li; to the dedication and unflinching hunt for readers of Erica Loberg. Other readers such as Rachel Altemose, Robin Desser, and Alexis Gargagliano were also invaluable in their critiques of earlier drafts. Tom and Elaine Colchie, also priceless readers, but thank you most for your dedication to me, my family, and your devotion to art and literature—one of the reasons that people like me get up in the morning. Lorayne and Michael Carbon—may everyone who falls hard be lucky enough to find two such guardian angels. My brother in teaching and literature, Joshua Henkin, to you I owe too much to mention here, but thank you for your trust and guidance, and for letting me participate in the finest writing program in the country. My students, my-scribblers-in-arms: the world would be a lesser place without your dogged pursuit of beauty and meaning.

To my big, beautiful family and friends, without the love you provide beyond my limited imaginings or desert, nothing is really possible. And to those still suffering from the crimes of autocracies and dictatorships all over the globe, may you always find the courage to resist and to imagine new worlds.